The Wreck

The Wreck

The Wreck

Rabindranath Tagore

RUPA
PUBLICATIONS INDIA

First Published 2003
Fifth Impression 2011

Published by
Rupa Publications India Pvt. Ltd.
7/16, Ansari Road, Daryaganj,
New Delhi 110 002

Sales Centres:

Allahabad Bengaluru Chennai
Hyderabad Jaipur Kathmandu
Kolkata Mumbai

Typeset copyright © Rupa & Co. 2003

Typeset by
Mindways Design
1410 Chiranjiv Tower
43 Nehru Place
New Delhi 110 019

Printed in India by
Gopsons Papers Ltd.
A-14 Sector 60
Noida 201 301

Contents

THE WRECK

Chapter 1

*N*o one doubted for a moment that Ramesh would pass his law-examination. The Goddess of Learning, who presides over universities, had always showered petals on him from her golden lotus and had rained on him medals, and scholarships to boot.

Ramesh was supposed to be going home after the examination, but he seemed to be in no particular hurry to pack his trunk. His father had written bidding him return home at once. He had replied that he would come as soon as the results of the examination were announced.

Jogendra, son of Annada Babu, was Ramesh's fellow-student and lived next door to him. Annada Babu belonged to the Brahmo Samaj and his daughter Hemnalini had recently sat for the First Arts examination. Ramesh was a constant visitor at their house. He appeared regularly at tea-time, but tea was apparently not the only attraction as he was to be found there at other hours also.

Hemnalini used to walk up and down on the roof drying her hair after her bath and reading as she walked. Ramesh, likewise, used to sit, book in hand, by the stair-turret on the roof of his lodgings engaged in solitary study. Such a place is certainly suitable for quiet reading, but there were considerable distractions also, as a little reflection will show.

So far there had been no talk of marriage on either side. There was some reason for Annada Babu's failure to raise the subject; a young friend of his had gone to England to read for the bar and the old gentleman had his eye on this youth as a possible son-in-law.

A lively discussion was in progress at the tea-table one afternoon. Young Akshay was not very successful in passing examinations, but he was not a whit behind more scholarly youths in his thirst for tea and for other harmless indulgences; so he too made frequent appearances at Hemnalini's tea-table. He once argued that the masculine intellect is like a sword and that even without a keen edge its weight makes it a formidable weapon, while woman's wit is like a penknife — sharpen it as you will it is capable of no serious task, and so on.

Hemnalini was ready to submit in silence to Akshay's preposterous contention, but her brother Jogendra likewise advanced arguments in depreciation of feminine intelligence. This brought Ramesh into the fray; he roused himself from his torpor and began to chant the praises of womankind.

In the ardour of his feminism Ramesh had finished two extra cups of tea when the bearer brought in a letter addressed to him in his father's handwriting. Glancing through it he was constrained to accept defeat while the argument was still at its height and he rose hastily to go. There was a chorus of protest, and he had to explain that his father had just arrived from home.

"Ask Ramesh Babu's father to come in," said Hemnalini to Jogendra, "we can offer him a cup of tea."

"Please don't trouble," Ramesh interposed hastily," I had better join him at once."

Akshay rejoiced inwardly. "The old gentleman might object to taking anything here," he observed, in allusion to the fact that Annada Babu was a Brahmo and Ramesh's father an orthodox Hindu.

Braja Mohan Babu, Ramesh's father, greeted his son with the remark, "You must come home with me by the morning train to-morrow."

Ramesh scratched his head. "Is there any special urgency?" he asked.

"Nothing in particular," said Braja Mohan.

Ramesh looked inquiringly at his father, wondering why in these circumstances he was in such a hurry, but Braja Mohan did not think it necessary to satisfy his son's curiosity.

In the evening, when his father had gone out to visit his Calcutta friends, Ramesh sat down to write him a letter; but after he had written the traditional form of address to an honoured parent, "To thy revered lotus foot," his pen refused its task, although he told himself repeatedly that he was bound to Hemnalini by an unspoken vow and that it would be wrong to conceal this tacit engagement any longer from his father. He composed various drafts in various styles, but finally he tore them all up.

Braja Mohan went peacefully to sleep after supper. Ramesh ascended to the roof and prowled disconsolately up and down like some spirit of night with his eyes fixed on his neighbour's house. At nine o'clock Akshay made his belated exit, and at half-past nine the street door was locked. At ten the light in Annada Babu's sitting-room went out, and by half-past ten the whole house was buried in slumber.

Ramesh had to leave Calcutta early on the following morning. Braja Mohan Babu took care to give him no opportunity of missing the train.

Chapter 2

$\mathcal{W}$hen Ramesh reached home he found that a bride had been chosen for him and that a day had been fixed for his marriage. In his youth Braja Mohan had fallen upon evil days, and he owed his subsequent prosperity to a pleader named Ishan, a friend of his boyhood. Ishan died before his time, and it was then discovered that he had left nothing but debts. His widow and her one child — a girl — suddenly found themselves destitute. This daughter, now of marriageable age, was the bride whom Braja Mohan had chosen for Ramesh. Some of the youth's well-wishers had protested, pointing out that according to report the girl was not good-looking. To such criticisms Braja Mohan had but one reply. "I fail to see the point," he would say. "You may judge a flower or a butterfly by its looks, but not a human being. If the girl turns out as good a wife as her mother was, Ramesh may consider himself lucky."

Ramesh's heart sank when he heard the gossips discuss his forthcoming marriage, and he took to wandering aimlessly about, trying to devise some means of escape, but none seemed feasible. At last he plucked up courage to say to his father, "Father, I really can't marry this girl, I'm bound by a promise to someone else."

Braja Mohan. "You don't say so! Has there been a regular betrothal?"

Ramesh. "No, not exactly, but—"

Braha Mohan. "Have you spoken to the girl's people? Is it all settled."

Ramesh. "I haven't actually spoken about it, but—"

Braja Mohan. "Oh, you haven't? Well, as you've said nothing so far you may as well keep quiet a little longer."

After a short pause Ramesh shot his last bolt. "I should be doing her a wrong if I married any other girl."

"You would be doing a still greater wrong," retorted Braja Mohan, "if you refused to marry the bride whom I have chosen for you."

Ramesh could say no more; there was just a chance he thought, that some accident might still prevent the marriage.

According to the astrologers, the whole of the year following the date fixed for the wedding was inauspicious, and it occurred to Ramesh that once that fateful day were over he would gain a whole year's respite.

The bride lived in a distant place only accessible by river. Even by the shortest route, taking advantage of creeks that linked up the larger channels, it was a three or four days' journey. Braja Mohan left an ample margin for accident, and his party set off on a day, officially announced as auspicious, a full week before the date fixed for the wedding. The wind was favourable all the way and it took them less than three days to reach Simulghata, so that there were still four days to elapse before the ceremony. The old gentleman had another reason for wishing to be in good time. The bride's mother was very badly off and it had long been his desire that she should leave her home and migrate to his village, where he could support her in comfort and so discharge the debt that he owed to the friend of his youth. So long as there was no tie of relationship delicacy forbade him to approach the lady with such a proposal, but now in view of the forthcoming marriage he had sought for, and obtained, her consent. Her family being reduced to this one daughter, she readily fell in with the suggestion that she should fill a mother's place beside her motherless son-in-law. She clinched the matter by saying, "Let the gossips talk if they like, my place is with my daughter and her husband."

So Braja Mohan spent the intervening days before the wedding in preparations for transferring the lady's household effects to her new home. As he desired her to accompany the wedding party on its return journey he had brought some of his womenfolk with him to render her assistance.

The wedding duly took place, but Ramesh refused to recite the sacred formula correctly, closed his eyes when the time arrived for the "auspicious look" (the privileged moment when bridegroom and bride see each other for the first time), wore a hang-dog expression, and kept his mouth shut during the jesting in the bridal chamber, lay throughout the night with his back turned to the girl, and left the room as early as possible in the morning.

After all the ceremonies were over the party set out, the women in one boat, the older men in another, the bridegroom and younger men in a third; the musicians who had played at the wedding were accommodated in a fourth boat and beguiled the time by striking up various ditties and random snatches of music.

It was unbearably hot all day. The sky was cloudless but a dull haze lay over the horizon. The trees on the bank had a strange livid aspect and not a leaf stirred. The rowers were bathed in sweat. While the sun was still above the horizon the boatmen announced to Braja Mohan: "We'll have to tie the boats up now, sir; there's no place where we can moor for miles ahead."

But Braja Mohan wanted to get the journey over as quickly as possible.

"We can't stop here," he said, "there's a moon for the first half of the night; we'll go on to Baluhata and tie up there. I'll make it worth your while."

The men rowed on accordingly. On one side were sandbanks shimmering in the heat, on the other a high crumbling bank. The moon rose through the haze, but it shone with a lurid glare like the eye of a drunken man. The sky was still cloudless, when suddenly, without warning, the stillness was broken by a hoarse rumble as of thunder. Looking back the travellers saw a column of broken branches and twigs, wisps of grass and straw and clouds of dust and sand, raised as it were by some vast broom and sweeping down on them.

There were frantic cries of "Steady! steady! Hold on! Hold on! Mercy! Help!"

What happened next will never be known.

A whirlwind, following as usual a narrow path of destruction, descended on the boats, uprooting and overturning everything that lay in its track; and in a moment the hapless flotilla was blotted out of existence.

Chapter 3

$\mathcal{T}$he haze cleared and bright moonlight covered the great expanse of sand with a dazzling white garment such as our widows wear. On the river not a boat, not a ripple even, was to be seen, and peace, like the unbroken calm that death bestows on a tortured sufferer, overspread stream and shore.

When Ramesh regained consciousness he found himself lying on the margin of a sandy island. Some time elapsed before he could remember what had happened, then the whole catastrophe came back to him like a fevered dream, and he sprang to his feet. His first impulse was to discover what had befallen his father and his friends. He gazed around, but nowhere was there sign of mortal man. He started off along the water's edge searching in vain. The snow-white island lay like a child in arms, between two branches of the great Padma river—a tributary of the Ganges. Ramesh traversed one side of the island and had just begun to search the other when he espied something that looked like a red garment. He quickened his pace and found, lying as if lifeless on the sand, a young girl clad in the crimson dress of a bride.

Ramesh had learned how to bring back to life the apparently drowned. For a long time he persevered in his efforts to restore respiration by drawing the girl's arms above her head, then pressing them against her sides, till at last she drew breath and her eyes opened.

Ramesh was completely exhausted by this time and for the next few minutes he was unable to command enough breath even to question the girl. Nor had she, it seemed, fully regained consciousness, for hardly had she opened her eyes than she wearily closed them again. Ramesh found, however, on examination, that her breathing was unimpeded. For a long time he sat gazing at her in the pale moonlight. It was a strange environment for their first real meeting, this deserted spot between land and water, as it were between life and death.

Who had said that Susila was not good-looking? The moonlight flooded the landscape with a glorious effulgence, and the overarching sky seemed illimitably vast, yet all Nature's magnificence was in Ramesh's eyes but a setting for one little sleeper's face.

Everything else was forgotten. "I am glad now," reflected Ramesh, "that I did not look at her in the bustle and turmoil of the wedding. I should never have had a chance to see her as I see her now. By bringing her back to life I have made her mine much more effectually than by repeating the prescribed formulas of the marriage rite. By reciting the formulas I should merely have made her mine in the sight of men, whereas now I have taken her as the special gift of a kindly Providence!

The girl recovered consciousness and sat up. She pulled her disordered clothing round her and drew the veil over her head.

"Do you know at all what happened to the others in your boat?" asked Ramesh.

She shook her head without a word.

"Would you mind being left alone for a few minutes while I go and search for them?" Ramesh went on. The girl did not answer, but her shrinking body said plainer than words, "Don't leave me alone here!"

Ramesh understood her mute appeal. He stood up and gazed round him, but there was no sign of life on the glistening waste of sand. He called to each of his friends by name, shouting at the top of his voice, but there was no response.

Finding his efforts fruitless Ramesh sat down again. The girl's face was now buried in her hands and she was trying to keep back the tears, but her bosom was rising and falling. Some instinct told him that mere words of consolation would be useless, and he sat close up to her and stroked her bowed head and neck very gently. She could no longer restrain her tears and her grief burst forth in a torrent of inarticulate utterance. Tears flowed from Ramesh's eyes in sympathy.

By the time they had cried their hearts out the moon had set. Through the darkness the dreary waste showed like a baleful dream and the white wilderness of sand was ghost-like in the gloom. Here and there the river glistened in the faint starlight like the dark glossy scales of some huge snake.

Ramesh took the girl's hands — tender little hands chilled by fear — in his own and drew her gently towards him. She offered no resistance, fear having deprived her of all instincts except the desire for human companionship. In the unplumbed darkness she found the refuge that she longed for on the palpitating warmth of Ramesh's breast. It was no time for bashfulness and she nestled confidently into the embrace of his enfolding arms.

The morning star set, and over the grey expanse of the river the eastern sky grew pale, then reddened. Ramesh lay in a deep sleep on the sand, while the young bride lay buried in slumber beside him with her head pillowed on his arm. The morning sun fell lightly on their eyes, and both started up out of sleep. For a moment they stared around them in amazement, then suddenly they realised that they were cast-aways and that home was a long way off.

Chapter 4

$\mathcal{I}$t was not long before the river was flecked with the white sails of fishing-boats. Ramesh hailed one of these crafts and with the fishermen's help engaged a large rowing-boat for the journey home. Before starting he gave the police instructions to search for his luckless companions.

When the boat reached the village landing-place Ramesh learned that the police had recovered the bodies of his father and mother-in-law and of several of his kin; a few of the boatmen might have survived, but everyone else had been given up for lost.

Ramesh's old grandmother had been left at home. She greeted the advent of her grandson and his bride with loud lamentation, and there was weeping in all the households which had been represented in the wedding party. No conches were blown and none of the wonted cries of welcome hailed the bride on her arrival. No one offered to entertain her; in fact people shunned the very sight of her.

Ramesh had decided to leave the place with his wife as soon as the funeral ceremonies were over, but he could not stir until he had put his father's affairs in order. The bereaved ladies of his family had besought him to let them go on pilgrimage, and for this, too, arrangements had to be made.

In his hours of respite from this sad business he was not wholly unmindful of the claims of love. His bride was not the mere child that report had described — indeed the village women taunted her with being beyond the conventional age for marriage — but when it came to making love the youthful B.A. could find no help in his books. Sober reason insisted that it was neither possible nor even right that he should undertake such a task. And yet, curiously enough, though his book-learning helped him not a whit, he felt strangely drawn towards the little maid and even his erudite mind could not resist her charm.

He saw her in imagination as his future helpmate. Visions of her in various aspects, as his girl-bride, his adored mistress, and the chaste mother of his children, swam before his dreamy eyes. As a painter enthrones in his heart the perfect picture, and a poet the perfect poem, of his imagination, and then lavishes all his devotion on it, so Ramesh enshrined this slip of a girl in his fancy as his heart's delight and the bringer of joy and prosperity to his home.

Chapter 5

*I*t took Ramesh nearly three months to settle his father's affairs and to make all preparations for the old ladies' pilgrimage. A few of the neighbours had begun to make advances to the young bride. The loose knot of affection that bound her to Ramesh tightened gradually as the days passed.

The young couple formed a habit of spreading mats on the roof and spending their evenings under the open sky. Ramesh now allowed himself familiarities; he would pounce on the girl from behind, press his hands over her eyes, and draw her head on to his breast. When she fell asleep early in the evening before supper he would startle her into wakefulness and earn himself a scolding. One evening he playfully seized her coiled hair, shook it, and remarked:

"Susila, I don't like the way your hair is done to-day."

The girl sat up. "Look here, why do you all persist in calling me Susila?" she asked. Ramesh stared at her in astonishment, at a loss to know what she meant by this question. "Changing my name won't change my luck," she went on. "I've been unlucky since I was a child and I'll be unlucky all my life."

Ramesh's heart gave a throb of dismay and the colour left his face. The conviction was suddenly forced upon him that there had been a terrible mistake somewhere.

"Why do you say you've been unlucky all your life?" he asked.

"My father died before I was born, and I wasn't six months old when my mother died too. I had a very bad time in my uncle's house. Then all of a sudden I heard that you had turned up from somewhere and taken a fancy to me. We were married two days later, and you know what happened after that!"

Ramesh fell back helplessly on his pillow. The moon had risen, but there seemed to be no lustre in its rays. He dreaded to put another question, and he tried to thrust aside what he had heard as a dream, a delusion. A warm south wind began softly to stir like the sigh of an awakening sleeper, a wakeful cuckoo was chanting forth its monotonous notes in the moonlight. From the boats moored at the neighbouring landing-place the boatmen's song rose in the air. Finding Ramesh apparently oblivious of her existence the girl nudged him gently. "Sleeping?" she queried.

"No," said Ramesh, but he gave no further response, and she quietly dropped off to sleep. Ramesh sat up and gazed at her, but there was no indication on her forehead of the secret that Fate had written there. How was it possible that so dreadful a destiny could be masked by such loveliness?

Chapter 6

Ramesh knew now that the girl was not his wedded wife, but it was no easy matter to discover whose wife she was. Once he asked her artfully, "What did you think when you first saw me at our wedding?"

"I didn't see you," she answered; "I never looked up all the time."

Ramesh. "Didn't you even hear my name?"

The Girl. "I only heard of you for the first time on the day before we were married; my aunt was in such a hurry to get me off her hands that she never even told me your name."

Ramesh. "By the way, I was told you could read and write; let me see if you can spell your name." And he gave her a sheet of paper and a pencil.

"As if I couldn't spell my own name!" she cried contemptuously. "As it happens, it's quite an easy one," and she wrote "Srimati Kamala Debi," in large letters.

Ramesh. "Now write your uncle's name."

Kamala wrote "Srijukta Tarini Charan Chattopadhyay."

"Did I make any mistake?" she asked.

"No," said Ramesh. "Now just write me the name of your village."

She wrote "Dhobapukur."

By such expedients Ramesh gradually amassed a number of facts about the girl's former life, but when all was done he was as far off as ever from the main object of his inquiries.

Ramesh now set himself to think out a future plan of action. Her husband had in all probability been drowned. Even if he could find out where the husband's people lived and send Kamala to them it was very doubtful if they would receive her, and it would not be fair to her to send her back to her uncle's house. What sort of reception would she have from society if it were known that she had been living all this time with another man as his wife? Where could she find sanctuary? Even if her husband were alive was it likely that he would wish or dare to take her back? Whatever Ramesh did with her he would be casting her adrift on a chartless sea. He could not keep her with him on any footing except that of a wife, and he could not hand her over to anyone else; and yet he and she could not live together as man and wife. Ramesh had hastily to smudge out the charming picture of this girl as his future companion in life though he had painted it in such glowing tints while love mixed the colours!

A continued stay in his own village would be intolerable, but in the teeming population of Calcutta he would be a mere noteless unit, and there he might discover some solution. He carried Kamala off to Calcutta accordingly and took lodgings at a considerable distance from his former abode.

Kamala found the experience intensely exciting. They had no sooner settled into their quarters on the day of their arrival than she ensconced herself in the window-seat. The unceasing stream of humanity was a spectacle inspiring her with a curiosity that nothing could satisfy. They had a solitary maid-servant to whom the Calcutta streets were no novelty, and she looked on the girl's wonder as sheer madness.

"What on earth is there to gape at? Aren't you going to have your bath? It's quite late," she cried peevishly.

This woman was to work during the daytime and go home in the evening, it being impossible to find a servant who would stay for the night.

"I can't sleep any longer with Kamala," thought Ramesh, "but how's the child going to spend the nights alone in a strange place?"

The servant went away after supper. Ramesh showed Kamala where she was to sleep, and said, "You go to bed now; I'll come later when I've finished reading."

He opened a book and pretended to read. Kamala was tired and soon fell asleep.

This served for the first night. On the following night, too, Ramesh contrived to send Kamala to bed alone. The day had been very hot. Ramesh spread a coverlet on the balcony outside the bedroom and settled down there for the night. He lay for a long time meditating and fanning himself, but at last towards midnight he fell asleep.

At two or three in the morning he half awoke and realised that he was not alone, someone was fanning him gently. Still not fully awake he drew the girl towards him and murmured drowsily, "Go to sleep, Susila, you mustn't fan me." Fear of the dark made Kamala nestle into the fold of Ramesh's arm, where she went peacefully to sleep.

Ramesh awoke early and started up in consternation. Kamala was still asleep and her right arm was round his neck. With alluring confidence she had exercised her authority over him and was using his breast as a pillow. His eyes filled with tears as he gazed at the sleeping girl. How could he rudely tear asunder the sift noose of the trusting child's arms? He remembered now that she had stolen to his side in the middle of the night to fan him.

With a deep sigh he gently released himself from her clinging arms and arose.

After much anxious thought he decided as a temporary solution of the problem to send Kamala to a girls' boarding school, and he broached the matter to her accordingly.

"Would you like to have some lessons, Kamala?"

She looked up at him with an expression that said plainer than words, "What *can* you mean?"

Ramesh discoursed at length on the benefits of education and the pleasure to be derived from study, but he might have saved his breath, for all that Kamala said was:

"All right, you teach me."

"You'll have to go to school," said Ramesh.

"To school!" exclaimed Kamala; "a big girl like me!"

Ramesh smiled at Kamala's pretensions to maturity. "Girls much older than you go to school," he told her.

Kamala had nothing more to say, and one day she drove to the school with Ramesh. It was a huge place and there seemed to be no limit to the number of girls, older or younger than Kamala.

Ramesh consigned her to the headmistress's care and was on the point of leaving when Kamala made a move as though to accompany him.

"Where are you off to?" he said. "You'll have to stay here."

"Aren't you staying here?" asked Kamala in a tremulous voice.

"I can't," said Ramesh.

"Then I can't stay either," said Kamala, seizing him by the hand. "Take me away with you."

"Don't be silly, Kamala," said Ramesh, releasing his hand.

The rebuke reduced Kamala to speechlessness; she stood as if spellbound and her face seemed to shrink away and contract. Sore at heart Ramesh hastened off, but hurry as he might he could not forget the look on that lovely helpless little frightened face.

Chapter 7

*R*amesh now intended to start practising as a pleader at the Alipore Courts in Calcutta, but he seemed to have completely lost energy. He lacked the necessary determination to set to work with a settled purpose and to overcome all the obstacles that beset the budding lawyer's path. He contracted the habit of going for purposeless walks across the Hourah bridge or round College Square, and he was contemplating a trip to the north-west when he received a letter from Annada Babu. The old gentleman had written:

I saw in the *Gazette* that you had passed, but I was sorry not to hear this from you personally. It is a long time since we heard from, or of, you. You must allay your old friend's anxiety by letting us know how you are and when you are coming to Calcutta.

It would not be out of place to mention here that the youth in England on whom Annada Babu had cast his eyes as a possible son-in-law had been called to the bar, had returned to India, and was already engaged to a young lady of means.

Ramesh doubted greatly whether after all that had occurred it would be right for him to renew his acquaintance with Hemnalini on the old footing. For the present, at all events, he could not reveal to anyone the nature of his connection with Kamala, for that would involve exposing the innocent girl to social ignominy. And yet, if he were to resume his former relations with Hemnalini he would have to make a clean breast of it.

In any case he could not, without being uncivil, delay answering Annada Babu's letter; so he wrote:

Please forgive me for not calling on you; I have been prevented from doing so by circumstances over which I have no control.

But he did not give his new address.

The day after he had posted his reply he donned the traditional headgear of the pleader and set out to make his first appearance at the Alipore Court.

One day he had walked part of the way back from the Courts and was on the point of hiring a cab to take him home, when he heard a well-known voice exclaim: "Dad, there's Ramesh Babu!" "Stop, driver, stop," cried a man's voice, and a carriage drew up close to where Ramesh was standing. Annada Babu and his daughter were returning from a picnic at the Alipore Zoo, hence this unexpected meeting.

No sooner had Ramesh set eyes on Hemnalini in the carriage — Hemnalini with her sweet serene face, her dress and her hair arranged in the distinctive style so familiar to him, the plain bangles and the gold bracelets cut in facets on her wrists — than a wave of emotion surged up in his breast and choked his utterance.

"So it's Ramesh!" exclaimed Annada Babu. "What luck meeting you like this in the street! You've stopped writing to us nowadays, or if you do write you don't give your address. Where are you off to now? Doing anything in particular?"

"No, just coming back from Court," said Ramesh.

"Come along then and have tea with us."

Ramesh's heart was full, and there was no room in it for hesitation. He took his seat in the carriage, and overcoming his diffidence by a tremendous effort asked Hemnalini how she was.

"Why didn't you let me know that you had passed?" she inquired, instead of answering his question.

Ramesh could not think of any reply, so he merely remarked, "I saw that you had passed too."

Hemnalini laughed. "Oh, well, you didn't forget us altogether, that's always something!"

"Where are you putting up now?" asked Annada Babu.

"In Darjjipara," said Ramesh.

"Why, your old lodgings in Kalutola were all right," remarked the old gentleman.

Hemnalini looked at Ramesh, intensely curious to see what his answer would be. Ramesh did not fail to notice her glance, and he was conscious of the reproach in it.

"Yes, I've decided to go back to them!" he blurted out. Ramesh was fully aware that Hemnalini had sat in judgement on him and had mentally found him guilty of a serious crime in changing his domicile. The thought caused him acute distress and he could not immediately think out a line of defence. However, cross-examining counsel was silent for the moment, and Hemnalini ostentatiously kept her eyes fixed on the road outside.

When the silence became unbearable Ramesh volunteered the statement:

"A relation of mine lives near Hedua and I took quarters in Darjjipara in order to keep in touch with him."

This was not an absolute lie, but it sounded a pitifully inadequate explanation; as if Kalutola were not near enough to Hedua to enable him to make occasional inquiries after a distant relation!

Hemnalini kept her gaze fixed on the road, and poor Ramesh racked his brains for another remark. Once only he asked, "What's the news of Jogen?"

But it was Annada Babu who replied. "He failed in his law-exam. And has gone up-country for a change of air."

When the carriage reached its destination the familiar rooms and furniture casts their spell over Ramesh. He heaved a sigh in which relief and regret were oddly blended, and sat down without a word.

"It was business, I suppose, that kept you so long at home?" remarked Annada Babu suddenly.

"My father died—" began Ramesh.

"You don't say so! Dear me! Dear me! How did it happen?"

"He was coming home up the Padma in a boat. A storm came on suddenly, the boat was swamped and he was drowned."

As the sudden onrush of a high wind drives the cloudbanks before it and clears the sky, so the announcement of this misfortune swept away the misunderstanding between Ramesh and Hemnalini.

Hemnalini thought regretfully: "I did Ramesh Babu a wrong. He was distracted by sorrow at his father's loss and by all the worries it entailed. He may be still grieving over it. We held him guilty, never stopping to inquire whether he might not have had family troubles or other preoccupations," and she became very attentive to the fatherless youth.

Ramesh had little appetite and Hemnalini pressed him to eat.

"You're not at all well," she said, "you must look after your health." Then she turned to Annada Babu. "Dad, Ramesh Babu must have supper with us here to-night."

"Certainly," said the old gentleman.

At this point Akshay arrived on the scene. For some time he had had no rival at Annada Babu's tea-table, and Ramesh's unexpected appearance was a disagreeable shock to him. However, he pulled himself together and exclaimed cheerfully:

"What's this? You here, Ramesh Babu! I say, you know, you had completely forgotten our existence."

Ramesh only smiled feebly, and Akshay went on: "When I saw the way your father marched you off I felt certain he'd keep you under arrest till he had you married. Did you manage to escape that fate after all?"

A glance of indignation from Hemnalini stopped Akshay's mouth.

"Ramesh has lost his father, Akshay," said Annada Babu.

Ramesh bent his head to hide his sudden pallor. Indignant with Akshay for flicking him on the raw, Hemnalini hastened to intervene. "I've never shown you my new album, Ramesh Babu," she said, and bringing the album she placed it on the table in front of Ramesh and began to discuss the photographs with him. She found an opportunity to remark in an undertone: "I suppose you're living all alone at your new lodgings, Ramesh Babu?"

"Yes," replied Ramesh, "quite alone."

"Well, you must come back to the old place next door as soon as you can."

"Yes, I'll move in next Monday whatever happens."

"You see, I'll want you to help me now and then with the philosophy for the B.A." she added ingenuously.

Ramesh was delighted at the prospect.

Chapter 8

*R*amesh was not long in returning to his former lodgings. Of the misunderstanding that had clouded his relations with Hemnalini, not a trace remained. He was treated like a son of the house, shared in the family jokes, and was never absent on any festive occasion.

Long spells of close study had given Hemnalini a fragile appearance and one would almost expect her slender form to snap before a strong breeze. She had been reserved and silent, and her friends hesitated to address her for fear she should take offence.

A few days produced an astonishing change in her appearance and manner. A delicate flush took the place of pallor in her cheeks and at every word her eyes danced with merriment. There was a time when she had considered it frivolous or even a crime to pay much attention to dress. What induced her now to change her ideas on this subject will never be divulged, for she took no one into her confidence.

Ramesh on his part had been scarcely less serious and conscientious. Mind and body alike seemed weighed down by a sense of his responsibilities. The stars course freely in their orbits but the astronomer's observatory with all its instruments must needs be firmly fixed on stable foundations. Even so Ramesh had remained rooted to his books and their philosophy amid the giddy whirl of the world's life. Now, however, a new and unprecedented liveliness lightened up his sombre demeanour. He still had difficulty in finding a retort to sallies, but he could mark his appreciation by an honest guffaw. If his hair was still innocent of pomade, at least he was never shabby in his dress. Both mentally and physically he seemed brisker and more responsive.

Chapter 9

*C*alcutta is singularly lacking in all the stage-properties that poets provide as the correct environment for young lovers. The groves of blossoming *asok* and *bakul* trees, the canopied foliage of the *madabhi*, and the song of the tawny-throated cuckoo are conspicuous by their absence; and yet Love the magician does not retire discomfited from the arid unlovely modern city. Who can follow the youngest and oldest of the gods on all his courses as he darts in and out with his bow through the thronging traffic, dodging the steel-armoured trams, and evading the eye of the red-turbaned policeman?

Ramesh and Hemnalini dwelt in apartments, let off from houses in Kalutola opposite a shoe-maker's, next door to a grocer's, and yet the course of their love ran as smoothly as if they dwelt in romantic bowers. The circumstance that their rendezvous was Annada Babu's shabby little table with tea-stains on the cloth and not a lotus-studded lake did not trouble Ramesh. No swain of legend caressed his mistress's tame fawn with more ardent affection than Ramesh displayed when he tickled the throat of Hemnalini's favourite cat; and when pussy arched his back and roused himself to perform his toilet, he seemed to the infatuated youth the most beautiful creature that ever licked fur.

At the time when all her thoughts were concentrated on the examination Hemnalini had neglected her sewing, so for some ·time past she had been taking lessons in needlework from a friend. Ramesh regarded sewing as a wholly unnecessary pursuit unworthy of serious notice. He and Hemnalini could meet on the common ground of literature, but where needlework was concerned he had to retire into the background.

"Why are you so keen on sewing nowadays?" he would exclaim a little pettishly. "It's all right for people who have nothing better to do." Whereat Hemnalini would merely smile and thread her needle.

Akshay once remarked sarcastically: "Ramesh Babu despises everything that is of any use in the world. His Worship may be a great philosopher and poet but mere depreciation won't carry him far."

This aroused Ramesh and he girt up his loins for an argument.

Hemnalini, however, interposed. "Ramesh Babu, why must you always have a retort? There's enough useless talk in the world as it is." And she bent down to count her stitches and once more plied her needle carefully through the silk.

One morning when Ramesh entered his study he found on his table a blotting-book in a silk binding with flowers embroidered on the cover. In one corner was an "R" and in another a lotus worked in gold thread. Ramesh was not long in doubt concerning the donor's identity or the instinct that had prompted the gift, and his heart beat fast. All his contempt for needlework vanished in an instant and he was prepared to stand forth as its champion against all comers. As he clasped the blotting-book to his breast, even

Akshay would have found him ready to acknowledge his error.

He opened the book, put a sheet of paper in it, and wrote:

> If I were a poet I should send you a copy of my verses, but as it is I cannot make any return. The power to bestow has been denied me, but there is such a thing as the power to receive. What this unexpected gift means to me is a secret between the Omniscient and myself. The gift itself can be seen and handled, but my gratitude is an intangible thing for which you must take my word. Everlastingly in your debt.
>
> Ramesh.

Hemnalini duly received this letter, yet neither she nor Ramesh alluded to it.

The rainy season was at hand. The rains reserve their chief benefits for the countryside and they are not an unmixed blessing to town-dwellers. All efforts are concentrated on keeping out the wet, and to this end householders close their windows and patch up their roofs, wayfarers raise their umbrellas and tramcars their screens, yet in no time all are wallowing in damp and mud. River, mountain, forest, and field hail the downpour with shouts of welcome as a friend. In their natural environment we see the rains in their true magnificence, and there is no jarring note in the festivities when heaven and earth unite their voices to greet the advent of the rain-clouds.

Young lovers are like the mountains. The constant downpour only accentuated Annada Babu's indigestion, but it could not damp the spirits of Ramesh and Hemnalini. As often as not the rain prevented Ramesh from attending Court. Day after day it came down so heavily that Hemnalini would exclaim anxiously, "Ramesh Babu, how will you get home in weather like this?"

"It's really nothing," Ramesh would reply shame-facedly; "I'll manage somehow or other."

"What's the use of getting wet and taking cold?" Hemnalini would urge, "better stay and have a meal with us."

Ramesh was not nervous about his health. His friends and relations had never noticed in him any tendency to take cold easily, still on rainy days he submitted with surprising readiness to Hemnalini's dictates, and it was considered sinful rashness on his part to walk even the few yards to his lodgings. When the sky looked more threatening than usual Ramesh was invited to Hemnalini's room to partake of a breakfast of kedgeree, or a supper of fried dainties, according to the time of day. The anxiety that was felt about his lungs evidently did not extend to his digestion.

And so the young people spent day after day wrapped up in their emotions. What the outcome would be was a question that Ramesh never faced; but Annada Babu did face it, and his friends and relations found it an absorbing topic. Ramesh's worldly wisdom was not equal to his erudition, and his infatuation made his outlook on mundane matters cloudier than ever. Annada Babu was always scanning his face expectantly, but he found no response there.

Chapter 10

*A*kshay's voice was of mediocre quality, but when he sang and accompanied himself on the violin only a very severe critic would refuse him an encore. Annada Babu had no great fondness for music. He never admitted this, but he had certain methods of self-defence which he employed when he thought that the music-lovers had had it their own way long enough.

If anyone asked Akshay for an encore, Annada Babu would interpose:

"You really mustn't; why should you persecute the poor fellow just because he can sing?"

Akshay would reply indulgently: "That's all right, Annada Babu, don't you worry. The only question is, who is the persecutor and who the persecuted?"

Then the first speaker would exclaim, "We'll decide that after you've favoured us again."

One afternoon the sky was heavily overcast. Night was approaching and still there was no pause in the rain. Akshay had been storm-stayed and Hemnalini proposed that he should sing, and began to tune the harmonium (one of the small portable kind that we use in Bengal).

Akshay tuned his violin and broke into a Hindustani ballad:

Báyu bahin purbainá
Nida náhin bin sainá.

The language of the song was unfamiliar to its hearers, but it mattered little that the words were unintelligible for when emotions are at a high pitch the merest hint suffices. The general drift was clear — rain-clouds were dripping, peacocks were calling, and a lover was pining for his mistress.

Akshay was trying to utter his unspoken thoughts through the medium of the ballad, but it gave expression to the emotions of two other persons present. Two hearts beat in unison, immersing themselves in the waves of melody. Nothing now seemed common or unclean and the whole world swam in a rosy mist. It was as though all the passion that had ever throbbed in human hearts were gathered up and showered on these two lovers, and that it now pulsated within them in all its super-abundance of bliss and anguish, longing and distress.

There was no pause either in the rain or in the singing. Hemnalini had only to say, "Don't stop, Akshay Babu, give us another song," and he burst out, nothing loth, into another ballad. This time the melody was like dark banked-up masses of clouds with lightning darting through them, but in this too lay ambushed the yearning of a human heart.

It was late when Akshay went home that night. As Ramesh took his leave he gazed for one moment at Hemnalini as though through a mist of song. Hemnalini met his eye with a dazed glance, for the glamour of the melody had also fallen on her.

There had only been a momentary break in the rain and as Ramesh went home it came pouring down again.

He could not sleep that night. Hemnalini likewise sat for
a long time in the darkness listening in a reverie to the
continual patter of the raindrops. The refrain,

> *Báyu bahin purbainá*
> *Nida náhin bin sainá,*

haunted her also.

Next morning Ramesh said to himself:
"Heigh ho! If only I could sing. I shouldn't mind
exchanging any other accomplishment for it," but he knew
that no training in the world could ever make him a vocalist.
However, he could learn to play some instrument at least.
He remembered how on one occasion when he found
himself alone at Annada Babu's he had drawn the bow
once across the strings of the violin; but that one stroke had
been enough! The Muse had scolded him so severely as to
convince him that to condemn himself to the cult of the
violin would be far too harsh a sentence. So he moderated
his ambitions and bought a harmonium. He took the
instrument into his room, shut the door, and began to
finger it very gingerly. He did not take long to discover that
the harmonium is a less exacting instrument than the violin.

On his next appearance in Annada Babu's house
Hemnalini greeted him with the remark, "We heard
someone playing a harmonium in your rooms yesterday!"

Ramesh had supposed that by keeping his door shut
he could escape detection, but someone's hearing was
good enough to catch sounds that came through his closed
door. A little shamefacedly Ramesh had to confess.

"It's no good shutting yourself in and making hopeless
attempts to learn by yourself," said Hemnalini. "Much
better come and practise here. I know a little about it, so
I'll be able to give you some help."

"I'm so clumsy," said Ramesh, "it'll be very trying for you."

"I'll be able to teach you all I know," said Hemnalini, "even if you are awkward."

It soon became apparent that in describing himself as clumsy Ramesh had not erred on the side of modesty. Even with such an instructress to help him it was difficult to drive any conception of music into his skull. You have seen a man who cannot swim fall into a pond and strike out madly with his arms and legs. This will give you some idea of Ramesh's floundering, though in his case the water was only knee-deep. He had no notion where each finger ought to go; he struck a false note in every bar without wincing; harmony and discord were alike to him and he violated all the rules with sublime unconsciousness. Did Hemnalini cry out; "What are you doing, that's all wrong!" he would hasten to correct his first mistake by making another. But our serious-minded, persevering Ramesh was not one to take his hand from the plough. As a steam-roller pursues its leisurely course oblivious of what it crushes and grinds beneath it, so Ramesh rolled, irresistible and unobservant, over the keys of his unfortunate harmonium.

Hemnalini laughed at his mistakes and he laughed at them himself. His exceptional capacity for doing the wrong thing appealed to Hemnalini's sense of the ludicrous. Love has the power to derive pleasure from mistakes, discords, and incapacity. A mother's love overflows at the false steps of the child whom she is teaching to walk, and Ramesh's extraordinary lack of any aptitude for music was a secret delight to Hemnalini.

Ramesh said once or twice: "It's all very well your laughing at me like this, but didn't you make mistakes yourself when you were learning to play?"

"Certainly I did," said Hemnalini, "but honestly, Ramesh Babu, nothing to compare with the mistakes you make!"

Nothing daunted Ramesh, and he merely laughed and started again from the beginning. Annada Babu was, as has been already remarked, no judge of music, but now and then he would assume a portentous expression, prick up his ears, and enunciate, — "Say what you like, Ramesh is becoming quite an adept."

Hemnalini. "Adept at discords."

Annada Babu. "No, no, he has improved a lot since I first heard him. You may be sure if Ramesh sticks to it he'll be no bad performer in time. There's only one thing and that's constant practice. Once you learn the notes the rest is straightforward."

There was no contradicting a pronouncement like this. When the old gentleman laid down the law his family had to listen in respectful silence.

Chapter 11

The "Puja" holidays in Bengal correspond to the English Christmas. For ten days or so all work is suspended and families are reunited.

Almost every autumn Annada Babu and Hemnalini took advantage of the cheap tickets issued at the holiday season and went for a change to Jubbulpore. They stayed with Annada Babu's sister's husband, who was in Government service there, and Annada Babu regarded this annual cutting as a tonic to his digestion.

It was now the beginning of September, the holidays were not far off, and preparations for the journey kept Annada Babu busy. Hemnalini's absence would interrupt the harmonium lessons, so Ramesh tried to make the most of the time left to him. One day in the course of conversation Hemnalini remarked: "Ramesh Babu, I think you would be better for a change of air. It would do you good to get away from Calcutta even for a short time. What do you say, dad?"

Annada Babu considered the suggestion appropriate. Ramesh had suffered a bereavement and a change of air would cure his depression.

"Certainly," he said, "a few days' change of air is an excellent thing. Do you know, Ramesh, I've noticed that—

whether one goes up-country or anywhere else—it's only for a few days that one gets any benefit. For the first week or so one's appetite improves and one eats heartily, but after that there's no difference, the old feeling of oppression in the stomach returns, heartburn comes on, and whatever one eats——"

Hemnalini. "Ramesh Babu, have you seen the Nerbudda?"

Ramesh. "No, I've never been there."

Hemnalini. "You ought to see it. Shouldn't he, dad?"

Annada Babu. "Well, look here, why shouldn't Ramesh come with us? He'll have a change of air and see the Marble Rocks too."

This two-fold tonic being considered an essential item in Ramesh's cure he did not quarrel with the prescription.

His whole being seemed to float on air that day. To calm the tumult of his heart he shut his door and turned to his harmonium, but his soul soared above pedantic accuracy and his fingers danced insanely over the keys in a riot of harmony and discord. The prospect of an early separation from Hemnalini had plunged him into the depths of depression. Now in the exuberance of his joy he flung to the winds all his painfully-acquired knowledge.

He was interrupted by a knock at the door and a voice crying. "In Heaven's name, stop, Ramesh Babu! What *are* you doing?"

Ramesh turned red with confusion and opened the door. Akshay stepped in, remarking: "Ramesh Babu, aren't you making yourself liable to be hauled up in your own Court by indulging in this secret vice of yours?"

Ramesh laughed: "I plead guilty."

"There's something I want to talk to you about, Ramesh Babu, if you won't mind," went on Akshay.

Wondering what was coming, Ramesh waited in silence for Akshay to begin.

Akshay. "You must know by this time that Hemnalini's welfare is not a matter of indifference to me?"

Ramesh said neither "yes" nor "no," but waited for the next remark.

Akshay. "As a friend of Annada Babu I have the right to ask what your intentions are with regard to Hemnalini."

Ramesh resented both the words and the tone, but he had neither the inclination nor the ability to make a sharp retort. He answered quietly: "Is there anything that leads you to suppose that I have any evil intentions?"

Akshay. "Look here, you belong to a Hindu family and your father was a Hindu. It was because he was afraid of your marrying into a Brahmo family that he took you home to have you married there — that I know." — Akshay had good reason to know, for it was he who had dropped a hint to the old gentleman. For a few moments Ramesh was unable to look Akshay in the face.

"Do you think," resumed Akshay, "your father's sudden death has left you free to do what you like? When his wish ——"

"Look here, Akshay Babu," interrupted Ramesh, whose patience was at an end, "if there's any other subject on which you're entitled to give me advice, you can give it and I'll listen to you, but my relations with my father are no concern of yours."

"Very well," said Akshay, "we'll leave that part out; but what I want to know is this — Do you intend to marry Hemnalini and are you in a position to do so?"

These successive thrusts were too much even for Ramesh's placid temper.

"Look here, Akshay Babu," he said, "you may be a friend of Annada Babu, but you and I have never been so intimate as to entitle you to talk like this. Be so good as to drop the subject."

Akshay. "If my dropping the subject meant that the whole question dropped and that you could go·on indefinitely enjoying life thoroughly without regard to consequences, then there would be nothing to say; but society isn't merely a happy hunting-ground for people like you who never worry about consequences. You may have the highest motives and may be quite indifferent to what the world says about you; but you might try to understand that you're liable to be called to account for playing fast and loose with a girl in Hemnalini's position. There are those who will demand an explanation from you, and if it's your intention to bring into public disrepute people whom you respect, you're going the right way about it."

Ramesh. "I'm much obliged to you for your advice. I shall decide in good time how I ought to proceed and shall abide by my decision. Have no anxiety on that score. We needn't discuss this further."

Akshay. "I'm delighted to hear that, Ramesh Babu. It's a great relief to me to know that after all you're going to make up your mind, and that you intend to stick to your resolution. You might have decided this a little sooner. However, I have no desire to discuss it further with you. Forgive me for interrupting your musical studies. Please resume them; I shan't intrude on you any longer," and Akshay hurried away.

Ramesh, however, had no inclination for more music, discordant or otherwise.

He lay on his mattress with his hands clasped behind his head while the hours slipped by. Suddenly the clock struck five and he rose hastily. Heaven only knows what decision he had reached, but that it was his immediate duty to proceed to his neighbour's house and drink two cups of tea admitted of no doubt.

"Are you ill, Ramesh Babu?" exclaimed Hemnalini when she saw him.

"There's nothing much the matter with me," replied Ramesh.

"It's only your digestion that's out of order," put in Annada Babu, "just biliousness. You try one of the pills that I take——"

Hemnalini smiled and interposed: "Now, dad, you want all your friends to take those pills, but I've never seen anyone the better for them."

Annada. "No one has been the worse for them, anyway. I've found by experiment that no other pill that I've ever taken has done me so much good."

Hemnalini. "Whenever you start taking a new kind of pill you find it the most marvellous panacea for the first few days."

Annada. "You people won't believe what I say. All right, just ask Akshay if he has benefited by my treatment or not."

Hemnalini dropped the subject, fearing that Akshay might be called in to corroborate. The witness, however, appeared at that moment to give his testimony unsolicited and the first remark that he addressed to Annada Babu was:

"You'll have to give me another of those pills; they have done me a power of good. I feel extraordinarily fit to-day."

Annada Babu brought a glance of triumph to bear on his daughter.

Chapter 12

$\mathscr{A}$nnada Babu was too hospitably inclined to let Akshay depart as soon as he had taken the pill, and Akshay on his part showed no disposition to hurry away. He kept glancing disapprovingly at Ramesh out of the corner of his eye. Ramesh was not particularly observant, but he could not fail to notice Akshay's disapproving looks and they disturbed his equanimity.

Hemnalini had been gloating over the prospect of the trip to Jubbulpore, the time for which was now fast approaching, and she had decided to take the opportunity of Ramesh's next visit to discuss with him her plans for the holidays; they were to prepare in consultation a list of books to take with them for reading in their hours of leisure. It had accordingly been arranged that Ramesh should make his call an early one, for if he delayed his arrival till tea-time Akshay or some chance visitor might drop in and spoil their *tête-à-tête*.

But as it happened Ramesh had been later than usual in arriving, and when he had come he wore a preoccupied air. Hemnalini spirits were correspondingly damped. She found an opportunity to remark to him in an undertone, "You were very late to-day, weren't you?"

Ramesh's mind appeared to be elsewhere.

"Yes, I'm afraid I was," he replied after a moment's pause.

Now Hemnalini had made a special point of being ready in good time. She had dressed her hair and changed her clothes early in the afternoon and had then sat down to wait with her eyes on the clock.

For a long time she had consoled herself with the thought that Ramesh's watch might be slow and that he would turn up at any minute. When that theory became untenable she had settled down into the window-seat with her needlework, controlling her impatience as best she could. On the top of it all, Ramesh, when he did arrive, wore an abstracted air and made no attempt to explain his tardiness. He appeared to have completely forgotten his promise to come early.

The tea-hour was a trying ordeal to Hemnalini that day. When it was at last over she made a special effort to pierce Ramesh's abstraction. On a table set against the wall some books were laid out and she lifted these and made as if to take them out of the room. Her movement aroused Ramesh from his stupor, and he was at her side in an instant. "Where are you taking them to?" he asked. "Wasn't it to-day we were going to choose the books to take with us?"

Hemnalini's lips were quivering and it was with difficulty that she restrained the tears that welled up in her eyes.

"Never mind," she said in a tremulous voice, "we can't do it now." She hurried upstairs and flung the books on the floor of her bedroom.

Her flight deepened Ramesh's despondency.

"You don't seem to be very well to-day, Ramesh Babu," remarked Akshay, laughing in his sleeve.

Ramesh muttered something that no one could catch. Annada Babu, however, had pricked up his ears at Akshay's allusion to Ramesh's state of health.

"That's just what I said myself when I saw him," he remarked.

"People like Ramesh Babu," Akshay went on with his tongue in his cheek, "consider it *infra dig.* to devote any attention to their health. They live in the regions of the intellect and if they suffer from indigestion they think it vulgar to investigate the cause."

Annada Babu commenced laboriously to demonstrate that good digestion is as essential to a philosopher as to anyone else. Ramesh sat between the two, enduring tortures in silence.

"My advice to you, Ramesh Babu," concluded Akshay, "is to take one of Annada Babu's pills and to go to bed early."

"I have something to say to Annada Babu," retorted Ramesh, "and I'm waiting for an opportunity."

Akshay rose from his chair.

"Well hang it all, you might have told me that a little sooner. Ramesh Babu sits on a thing for hours and then flings it at one's head when it's too late." And he took leave of his host.

Gazing fixedly at the toes of his boots Ramesh began:

"Annada Babu, I feel extremely fortunate to have been given the run of your house and in being treated like one of the family; I can't tell you how much it has meant to me."

"That's all right," replied Annada Babu. "You're our Jogen's friend, and it's quite natural that we should treat you as though you were his brother."

Ramesh had, as it were, stood up to dance, yet was at a loss for the next step.

To smooth the way for him Annada Babu went on, "In fact, it's we who are lucky in having a lad of your stamp as a son of the house, Ramesh."

But even that did not give Ramesh a lead.

"You see," Annada Babu continued, "the gossips have begun to couple your name with Hemnalini's. When a girl reaches the marriageable age, they say, she ought to be very careful in her choice of companions. I tell them, "I've absolute trust in Ramesh; he's not a man who would ever let us down.' "

Ramesh. "Annada Babu, you know all about me; if you think me a suitable husband for Hemnalini, then— — "

Annada. "Say no more. The fact is, my own mind was practically made up; it was only because you were still in mourning that I made no definite proposal. Now there's no point in putting it off any longer, lad. People are talking and we want to stop that sort of thing as soon as possible. Don't you agree?"

Ramesh. "Just as you think. Your daughter, of course, has the first say in the matter."

Annada. "Quite true; but I fancy I know what her decision would be. Anyhow we'll talk it over to-morrow morning and make definite arrangements."

Ramesh. "I'm afraid I've kept you up very late. I had better leave you now."

Annada. "Just a minute. I think, you know, it would be as well to have the wedding before we go to Jubbulpore."

Ramesh. "That's quite soon now."

Annada. "Yes, only ten days. You could be married next Sunday; that would leave us two or three days in which to prepare for the journey. You see, Ramesh, it isn't that I want to hurry you, but I have to think of my health."

Ramesh assented to this. He gulped down one of Annada Babu's pills and departed.

Chapter 13

Kamala's school would be breaking up at an early date, but Ramesh had arranged with the headmistress that she should remain there during the holidays.

On the morning after his talk with Annada Babu he rose early and went for a constitutional, choosing one of the unfrequented roads on the Maidan—Calcutta's chief open space. He decided to tell Hemnalini all about Kamala before he married her. Later on he would explain her true situation to Kamala. Thus all possibilities of misunderstanding would be removed. Kamala would find a friend in Hemnalini and would readily agree to make her home with the young couple. There might be gossip if they lived among their own people, so he resolved to migrate to Hazaribagh and practise his profession there.

On returning from his walk Ramesh looked in at Annada Babu's and happened to encounter Hemnalini on the stairs. In ordinary circumstances such a meeting would have been the signal for a friendly conversation, but this time Hemnalini blushed—a ghost of a smile like the first glimmering of dawn illumined her countenance—and hurried away with downcast eyes.

Ramesh returned to his rooms and began to thump out on the harmonium the tune that Hemnalini had taught him, — but one cannot play the same tune all day, so by-and-by he turned to a book of poetry; but no poetry, he felt, could rise to the heights that his love had scaled.

Hemnalini too went about that morning treading on air. By midday her housework was finished and she shut herself into her room and sat down to her sewing. Her tranquil features glowed with supreme happiness and the consciousness that she had found her destiny in life seemed to pervade her whole being.

It was some time before the usual tea-hour when Ramesh flung aside his poetry-book and his harmonium and hurried across to Annada Babu's. On ordinary occasions Hemnalini was always prompt in putting in an appearance, but on this afternoon he found the room empty, nor was there anyone in the sitting-room upstairs. Hemnalini was still in her own chamber. Annada Babu appeared at his usual hour and established himself at the tea-table, while Ramesh kept glancing nervously at the door.

A step sounded, but it was only Akshay. He greeted Ramesh with the utmost friendliness, "Hullo, Ramesh Babu, I've just been to your rooms." Ramesh looked a shade uneasy when he heard this.

Akshay laughed and went on. "Nothing to be afraid of, Ramesh Babu; my intentions were perfectly peaceful. It's only right that your friends should congratulate you on the good news; and that was the object of my call."

This speech drew Annada Babu's attention to Hemnalini's absence. He called to her, but there was no response, so he went upstairs in person to fetch her. "What's this, Hem?" he cried. "Still at your sewing? Tea's ready and Ramesh and Akshay are here."

"Please have my tea sent up here, dad," said Hemnalini with a faint flush, "I really must finish my sewing."

"Now that's so like you, Hem. Once you're keen on a thing you forget everything else. When you were working hard for your exam. you'd never lift your nose from your book. Now you're so taken up with your sewing you'll do nothing else. No, no, it'll never do. Come along, you must come down and have your tea," and he had practically to drag his daughter downstairs. She made straight for the tea-tray and became apparently so absorbed in pouring out tea that she could not lift her eyes to greet either of the guests.

"What are you doing, Hem?" exclaimed Annada Babu. "Why are you giving me sugar? You know I never take it."

Akshay began to snigger. "She can't restrain her generosity to-day. She'll be distributing sweets to everyone!"

Ramesh could not bear to hear Akshay sharpening his wit at Hemnalini's expense and he instantly resolved that once they were married they would cut Akshay out of the list of their acquaintances....

A few days later the same party was assembled round the tea-table when Akshay remarked, "Ramesh Babu, you had better change your name at once." Akshay's attempts to be humorous merely intensified Ramesh's dislike of him.

"Why should I?" he asked.

"Here you are," said Akshay, opening a newspaper. "A student of the name of Ramesh induced another student to personate him at an exam. and so succeeded in passing, but he was caught in the end."

Hemnalini knew that Ramesh never had a retort ready on his tongue, so whenever Akshay dealt one of his thrusts she took on herself the task of administering a counter-thrust. This was an occasion that called for her intervention. Suppressing her real indignation she remarked pleasantly, "For the matter of that the jails must be full of Akshays."

"Hearken to her!" cried Akshay. "I try to administer a friendly warning and you take offence; I'll have to tell the whole story. You know my little sister Sarat who goes to the girls' high school? She came home yesterday evening and announced, 'Do you know, your Ramesh Babu's wife is at our school.' I said, 'Silly kid! Do you think ours is the only Ramesh Babu in the world?' 'Whoever he is,' said Sara, 'he's very unkind to his wife. Almost all the girls are going home for the holidays and he has arranged for his wife to board at school. Poor thing, she's crying her eyes out.' Then I said to myself, 'This won't do at all; other people may make the same mistake as Sarat.' "

Annada Babu burst out laughing. "Akshay, you're perfectly mad! Why should our Ramesh change his name because some Ramesh or other has left his wife crying at school?" But Ramesh suddenly turned pale and left the room.

"What's the matter, Ramesh Babu?" cried Akshay. "Where are you off to? Have I offended you? You surely don't think that I suspect you," and he hurried out after Ramesh.

"What on earth is it all about?" exclaimed Annada Babu. To his astonishment Hemnalini burst into tears. "What's this, Hem? What are you crying about?"

"It's too bad of Akshay Babu, daddy!" she sobbed out; "why does he insult a guest in our house like that?"

"Akshay was only joking; why take it so much to heart?"

"I can't stand that sort of joke," and Hemnalini fled upstairs.

Since his return to Calcutta Ramesh had left no stone unturned to trace Kamala's husband. With great difficulty he had found out where Dhobapukur was and had written to Kamala's uncle Tarini Charan.

The reply came on the day after the incident just described. Tarini Charan wrote to say that he had heard nothing of his niece's husband Nalinaksha since the catastrophe. Nalinaksha had been a doctor practising at Rangpur. Tarini Charan had made inquiries there, but no one had heard anything more of him, nor did he know where Nalinaksha's native place was.

Ramesh now definitely banished from his mind the idea that Kamala's husband could still be alive.

The same post brought him a number of other letters. Several of his acquaintances had heard of his forthcoming marriage and had written to congratulate him. Some of them demanded a dinner from him and others rallied him playfully for keeping them in the dark so long. While he was reading these letters one of Annada Babu's servants came in with a note for him and his heart beat fast when he recognised the handwriting. It was from Hemnalini. "She could not help suspecting me," thought Ramesh, "after what Akshay said, and now to reassure herself she has written me this letter."

He opened the letter. It was very short. "Akshay Babu was horribly rude to you yesterday," she had written. "Why did you not come round this morning? I was expecting you. Why should you worry about what Akshay Babu said? You know I never pay any attention to his foolishness. You must come round early to-day. I am not going to do any sewing." Ramesh read between these few lines the pain that Hemnalini's gentle sympathetic heart had suffered, and tears came to his eyes. Since the evening before she had longed passionately to pour balm on his wound, and this craving had remained unabated with her throughout the night and the morning until, unable to restrain it any longer, she had given it expression in this note. He saw it all clearly.

He had felt since the preceding evening that he must reveal to Hemnalini his true situation at once, but yesterday's incident had made his task harder. Not only would he present the appearance of a criminal caught in the act and trying to exonerate himself, but the disclosure would seem to be a triumph for Akshay, and that was too humiliating to contemplate.

He reflected that Akshay must suppose that Kamala's husband was some one else of the name of Ramesh, for otherwise he would not have remained quiet so long, confining himself to covert allusions, but would have proclaimed his discovery on the housetops. All these considerations led Ramesh to seek some means of staving off trouble for the present instead of taking the straight course.

At this point the post brought him another letter. Ramesh opened it and found that it was from the headmistress of the girls' school. She wrote to say that Kamala had taken so terribly to heart the prospect of being kept at school during the holidays that the management must decline to be responsible for her; school would break up on Saturday, and Ramesh must be prepared to receive her at home that day.

Kamala was to come home on Saturday and his wedding was tot ake place on Sunday!

"Ramesh Babu, you really must forgive me!" It was Akshay who broke in upon him at this crisis in his affairs. "If I had thought that you would take offence at such an everyday piece of foolery I should have kept quiet. People resent a joke if there's some truth in it, but in this case there was no foundation at all, so I don't know why you lost your temper in company. Annada Babu has been scolding me ever since and Hemnalini won't speak to me. I went to see them this morning and she walked out of the room. Why are you all so offended with me?"

"I am not at liberty to tell you at present. I must ask you to excuse me now; I'm rather busy."

"Oh! preparations for the wedding! The bandsmen want something in advance, I suppose, and you don't want to waste time here. Well, I shan't keep you any longer. Good-bye."

Ramesh hastened to Annada Babu's as soon as Akshay's back was turned. Hemnalini had anticipated an early visit and was waiting expectantly in the sitting-room; her sewing lay on the table folded up in a scarf and she had the harmonium beside her. She was looking forward to some of the usual music, it is true, but there is another kind of music that only the soul can hear, and this she had anticipated also.

A faint smile played on her lips as Ramesh entered the room, but it vanished in an instant when he merely asked, "Where's your father?"

"In his room. Why, do you want him for anything? He'll be coming down soon for tea."

Ramesh. "I must see him at once: it's something very urgent."

Hemnalini. "Very well; you'll find him in his room."

Exit Ramesh.

Something urgent, was it? Everything must yield place to it! Even Love must wait at the door till his turn came! The bright autumn day seemed to sigh as the golden doors of its storehouse of delight swung to. Hemnalini drew her chair away from the harmonium and sat down to sew at the table, but as she plied the stitches an invisible needle worked its way into her heart. Ramesh's important business seemed to take some time; and Love went a-begging.

Chapter 14

*W*hen Ramesh entered Annada Babu's room he found the master of the house dozing in a chair with a newspaper over his face. At Ramesh's cough he awoke with a start and holding out the paper, called his visitor's attention to the heavy death-roll caused by a cholera epidemic in the city.

Ramesh, however, went directly to the point.

"I want you to put the wedding off for a few days," he said, "I have some very important business."

This surprising announcement drove the Calcutta death-rate out of Annada Babu's head. He stared at Ramesh.

"What do you mean, Ramesh? The invitations are all out."

"You could write to-day and say it has been put off till Sunday after next."

"You take my breath away, Ramesh! It isn't like a case in Court, you know; you can't apply for adjournments and get them just when it happens to suit your convenience. What is this important business of yours?"

Ramesh. "It's very urgent. I can't put it off."

Annada Babu collapsed into his chair like a tree felled by a hurricane.

Annada. "We can't put it off. That's a fine idea of yours, a most excellent notion! Well, do what you like. I leave it to you to explain matters to the people whom we've invited. If anyone asks me I'll say, 'I know nothing about it. The bridegroom knows his own business and he'll be able to tell you when it'll suit him to be married.' "

Ramesh kept his eyes fixed on the ground. "Have you told Hemnalini about it?" Annada Babu went on.

Ramesh. "No she knows nothing about it yet."

Annada. "She must know at once. It's her marriage as well as yours."

Ramesh. "I thought I had better tell you first."

"Hem! Hem!" called Annada Babu. Hemnalini came in. "Yes, dad?"

Annada. "Ramesh says he has some pressing business; he hasn't time to be married at present."

Hemnalini turned pale and her eyes sought Ramesh's face. A criminal caught red-handed could not have looked guiltier.

He had not anticipated that the news would be communicated to Hemnalini in this blunt fashion and his own feelings told him what a rude shock the unceremonious announcement must be to her; but an arrow once discharged never returns and Ramesh knew that this arrow had pierced Hemnalini to the heart.

There was no way now of softening down the brutal truth, for the facts were unalterable — the marriage must be postponed, Ramesh had some urgent business, and he would not divulge what that business was. What gloss could he add?

"Well, it's your own look-out," said Annada Babu, turning to Hemnalini. "You two must decide what is to be done."

"I know nothing about it, dad." Hemnalini raised her eyes with a glance that was like a wan shaft from the dying sun falling on a storm-cloud and left the room.

Annada Babu took up his paper and pretended to read, but actually he was thinking hard. Ramesh sat still for a minute or two, then rose suddenly and went out.

Entering the large sitting-room he found Hemnalini standing at the window silently gazing at the street outside. Along every thoroughfare and alley poured a stream of humanity like a river in flood, every face bright with anticipation of the coming holidays.

Ramesh hesitated to take his stand beside her and he paused on the threshold with his eyes on her motionless figure. Framed in the mellow autumn sunshine of the open window it made a picture that was to remain indelibly fixed in his memory. Every detail—the soft curve of her cheek, the elaborate braiding of her hair, the delicate wisps about her neck and the glint of the golden necklace beneath them, the graceful sweep of her garment off the left shoulder—made its lasting impression on his sick brain.

Slowly he approached her. She took no notice of her lover, but gazed the more intently at the panorama of the streets. His voice trembled as he broke the silence. "I must beg something of you."

Hemnalini felt the pain that throbbed in his utterance and she turned towards him.

"Do not lose faith in me!" he cried; "tell me that you will never distrust me. I call Heaven to witness that I will never cease to deserve your trust." It was the first time that he had used the "thou" of close intimacy in addressing Hemnalini.

Not another word could he utter, and a film of tears gathered over his eyes.

Hemnalini looked up pityingly, and gazed steadfastly into his face; then suddenly she melted, and the tears rolled down her cheeks. And so, as the lovers stood side by side in the seclusion of that window-bay, their eyes met. Though not a word was spoken, a blissful peace descended on them both, and in the rapture that it brought in its train they tasted heaven.

With a deep sigh of relief Ramesh broke the stillness. "Do you know why I suggested postponing our marriage for a week?" he asked. Hemnalini shook her head. She did not want to know.

"I'll tell you the whole story after we're married," said Ramesh. The allusion to their marriage brought a faint blush to the girl's cheek.

Early in the afternoon, when Hemnalini had been making her preparations for Ramesh's visit, she had light-heartedly looked forward to much animated talk, confidential discussion of future plans, and lightly-sketched miniatures of the happiness that was to be theirs. She could never have imagined that in the space of a few minutes they would exchange vows of constancy, that tears would be shed, that instead of conversing they would merely stand side by side, and she could not have conceived what full and complete peace of mind and implicit trust would be the sequel.

"You must go to my father at once," said Hemnalini; 'he's quite vexed."

Ramesh went off cheerfully, ready to bare his breast to any stab that the world might choose to inflict on him.

Chapter 15

*A*nnada Babu looked up anxiously as Ramesh re-entered the room.

"If you give me the list of guests," said Ramesh, "I'll write to them all to-day about the change of date."

"Then you're determined to put it off?"

"Yes, there's nothing else for it."

"Well, look here, lad," said Annada Babu, "remember I wash my hands of this. You must make all the arrangements yourself; I decline to make myself a laughing-stock. If you choose to make the business of marriage a sort of children's game, then a man of my age can have nothing to do with it. Here's your list of guests. I've spent a good deal of money already, and much of it will be wasted. I can't afford to throw away money like that."

Ramesh declared himself quite ready to bear all expenses and to make all arrangements.

He made as if to rise, when Annada Babu went on. "Have you decided where to practise after you're married, Ramesh? Not in Calcutta, I suppose?"

"No, I want to find some suitable place up-country."

Annada Babu. "Up-country? That's a sound idea. Etawah isn't a bad place at all. The climate suits one's digestion very well. I spent a month there once and I found I could eat twice as much as I can here. You see, lad, she's my only daughter, and we should never be happy apart. That's why I want you to choose a healthy place."

Ramesh having offended him, Annada Babu took the opportunity to press certain of his own somewhat exacting demands. In his present frame of mind Ramesh would have readily agreed to migrate to Cherra Punji or the Garo Hills, or any such mist-drenched mountain-top, if Annada Babu had suggested it instead of Etawah.

"Very good," he said, "I'll join the Etawah bar," and he departed after undertaking to countermand the invitations.

No sooner had he gone than Akshay appeared and learned from Annada Babu that Ramesh had postponed his wedding for a week.

Akshay. "Really? He can't do that! Why, it's to be the day after to-morrow."

Annada. "He shouldn't be able to do it. Ordinary people don't do that sort of thing; but with you modern young men anything is possible!"

Akshay assumed an air of portentous gravity, and his mind began to work rapidly. At length he went on:

"When you think you've found a good husband for Hemnalini you shut your eyes to all possibilities. Everything should be ascertained about the man a daughter is to be entrusted to for life. No caution can be dispensed with, even if he be an angel from Heaven."

Annada. "If a lad like Ramesh has to be suspected, then no one in the world can be trusted."

Akshay. "Has he given you any reason for the postponement?"

"No, he gave us no reason," said Annada Babu, rubbing his head. "When I asked him he said he had important business."

Akshay turned away to hide a smirk. "He has given his reason to your daughter, I suppose?"

Annada. "I suppose he has."

Akshay. "Wouldn't it be as well to have her in and make sure?"

"It would," and Annada Babu shouted for Hemnalini. When she came in and saw who was present she took up a position behind her father where Akshay could not see her face.

"Has Ramesh given you any reason for putting off the wedding?" asked Annada Babu.

"No," and Hemnalini shook her head.

Annada Babu. "Didn't you ask him?"

Hemnalini. "I did not."

Annada Babu. "What an extraordinary thing! You're just a pair! He comes in and says, 'I haven't time to be married yet,' and you say, 'All right, we'll be married some other day,' and then you drop the subject."

Akshay now ranged himself on Hemnalini's side. "After all," he said, "when a person clearly indicates that he doesn't want to give his reasons one can hardly question him further. If it had been anything that he could divulge, Ramesh would have told you of his own accord."

Hemnalini flushed angrily. "I don't want to hear third parties' opinions on the subject. Personally, I am quite satisfied with things as they are," and she hurried out of the room.

Akshay turned green, but he forced a smile. "That's the way of the world—try to do a friend a service and a scolding is your reward. It only illustrates what a priceless thing true friendship is. I consider it my duty as a friend to express my suspicions of Ramesh, however much you dislike me and revile me for so doing. I can't rest easy when I see any trouble threatening you. It's a weakness of mine,

I must admit. However, Jogendra will be here to-morrow. If after he has heard the whole story he has no anxiety on his sister's account, then I won't say another word."

Annada Babu fully realised that this was the psychological moment for asking Akshay what Ramesh's conduct really meant; but he who probes a mystery may let loose a whirlwind, and the old gentleman was constitutionally averse to such an operation.

He vented his feelings on his visitor. "You're too suspicious, Akshay! When you have no proof why should you——"

Akshay had remarkable power of self-control, but successive rebuffs had at last worn out his patience. "Look here, Annada Babu," he burst out, "you're imputing all sorts of vile motives to me! You insinuate that I bear a grudge against your future son-in-law and that I'm suspecting an innocent man. I'm not clever enough to teach ladies philosophy, and I can't boast of any ability to discuss poetry with them; I'm quite an ordinary sort of fellow; but I've always been fond of and devoted to you and your family. Though I can't vie with Ramesh Babu in any other respect, I pride myself on never having had anything to conceal from you. I am capable of displaying rags to you and begging for a copper, but not of burgling your house. You'll know to-morrow what I mean."

Chapter 16

*N*ight had fallen before all the letters were despatched. Ramesh retired to rest, but he could not sleep. His thoughts flowed in two currents, one clear and one turbid, like the confluence of the Ganges and the Jumna. The two streams mingled and disturbed his rest. For some time he tossed from side to side, then suddenly he threw off his coverings and got up.

He crossed to the window and looked out. The houses on one side of the lane were in deep shadow, while those on the other side stood out sharply outlined in the bright moonlight. Ramesh stood wrapped in silent thought. Casting off the trammels of his material environment with all its strife and uncertainty, his innermost being seemed to float away into the boundless cosmos where all is eternal, peaceful, and universal.

In a vision he saw birth and death, toil and rest, beginning and ending, for ever issuing, to the ineffable rhythm of super-terrestrial music, on to the stage of the finite from the silent and illimitable behind the scenes; and from that infinite in which there is neither light nor darkness Ramesh beheld the twin loves of man and woman emerge into the starlight of this world.

Slowly Ramesh climbed to the roof. His eyes turned to Annada Babu's house. Not a sound disturbed the stillness. The moonlight and the shadows had woven a pattern on the wall of the house, under the eaves, in the interstices of the doors and windows, and on the roughcast of the roof. How marvellous it was! There in that unpretentious house, in the heart of the teeming city, dwelt a wondrous being in the modest guise of a girl-student.

The metropolis swarmed with people like Ramesh— pleaders, graduates, foreigners, natives. Why should he be singled out for a special mark of divine favour denied to the rest? Why should it have been he and none other who had stood at the window with this girl by his side in the mellow autumn sunlight and beheld in a vision all creation floating on an illimitable sea of joyful mystery? What a miracle it was! A miracle that had transformed his innermost soul, that had transformed the world about him!

He paced up and down the roof till the night was far advanced. The setting moon was hidden behind the opposite house, and the darkness of night settled over the earth while the firmament still glowed with the farewell embrace of her light.

Ramesh's weary limbs shivered with cold, and a sudden fear leapt upon him and held his heart in its grip. On the morrow he would have to face battle again in life's arena. No line of care scored the face of the heavens, no restless activity ruffled the serenity of the moonlight; the stillness of the night was unbroken, and the whole universe with its countless stars in everlasting motion was nonetheless steeped in everlasting repose; only in man's restless strife is there no pause. Alike in prosperity and in adversity human life is an unceasing struggle against odds.

On the one hand the eternal peace of the Infinite, on the other the eternal conflict of the world! How can the two exist side by side? Obsessed as he was with his own difficulties, Ramesh paused to speculate on this insoluble problem.

A vision of Love in the everlasting and boundless tranquillity of the womb of creation had just been granted to him. Now he beheld Love in contact with the world trampled and tossed about in the press of life. Which was the true vision and which was illusion?

Chapter 17

*J*ogendra returned from up-country by the morning train next day. It was Saturday, and Sunday was to be Hemnalini's wedding-day; yet as he approached the house he observed none of the signs of festivity that he had anticipated. No festoons of *debdar* leaves hung on the verandah. In fact there was nothing to distinguish the house from its dingy and unlovely neighbours.

He dreaded to hear a tale of sudden sickness, but as he hurried indoors there was no sign of anything untoward. A meal was ready for him, and Annada Babu sat at the table reading the newspaper with a half-finished cup of tea before him.

"Is Hem all right?" exclaimed Jogendra as he entered the room.

Annada Babu. "She's quite well."

Jogendra. "What about the wedding?"

Annada Babu. "It's to be the Sunday after next."

Jogendra. "Why was it put off?"

Annada Babu. "You had better ask your friend. Ramesh merely told us that he had some urgent business and that the wedding couldn't take place on Sunday."

Jogendra inwardly cursed his father's supineness. "When I'm not here you people make an awful muddle of everything, dad," he said. "What important business could he have? He's his own master. He has no relations that count. If he has got into a mess over some business matter I don't see what there was to hinder him from telling you all about it. Why did you let it rest at that?"

"After all, he hasn't run away! You have better go and ask him yourself."

Jogendra swallowed a cup of tea and dashed off. "Hold on, Jogen," called Annada Babu after him; "what are you in such a hurry about? You've had nothing to eat," but Jogendra was out of earshot. He rushed into the next house and stamped upstairs, calling, "Ramesh! Ramesh!" but there was no sign of Ramesh, though he looked for him in the bedroom, the sitting-room, on the roof, and on the ground floor. After hunting high and low he found the bearer and asked him where his master was. "He went out early," was the reply.

"When will he be back?"

The bearer informed him that Ramesh had taken a supply of clothes with him and had said that he might not be back for four or five days; but where he had gone the man did not know.

Jogendra wore a preoccupied air as he resumed his seat at the breakfast-table.

"Well, what luck?" asked Annada Babu.

"What can one expect?" replied his son testily. "Here's a man who is about to marry your daughter, and you take no interest in his actions and his movements; and that though he lives next door!"

"Why, he was there only last night!" said Annada Babu.

"You didn't know that he was going anywhere," exclaimed Jogendra, "and his bearer doesn't know where he has gone. There's something very fishy about it. I don't like the look of things at all, dad. Why do you take it so coolly?"

In the face of this tirade Annada Babu was obliged to grapple with the situation.

"What's the meaning of it all, then?" he asked, assuming the expression of gravity that the occasion seemed to demand.

Ramesh had really been let off very easily by Annada Babu on the previous night, but the lad was too ignorant of affairs to realise this. He supposed that in stating that he had something important to do he had said all that was necessary, and he had gone about his immediate business in the belief that this explanation gave him full liberty of action.

Jogendra. "Where's Hemnalini?"

Annada Babu. "She had her tea earlier than usual this morning and then went upstairs."

"Poor girl!" exclaimed Jogendra. "I suppose she's thoroughly ashamed of Ramesh's extraordinary conduct, and that's why she doesn't want to face me," and he went upstairs to comfort his sister in her shame and distress. Hemnalini was alone in the large sitting-room. When she heard Jogendra's step she hurriedly picked up a book and made a pretence of reading it. She laid the book down as he entered and greeted him cheerfully:

"Hullo, when did you come in? You're not looking as well as you should be."

"How could I be?" cried Jogendra as he flung himself into a chair. "I've heard all about it, Hem. However, don't you worry; it's only because I wasn't here that such a thing happened. I'll put things right again! By the way, Hem, did Ramesh not give you any reasons?"

Hemnalini found herself in a dilemma. She chafed at the suspicious attitude shared by Akshay and Jogendra, and she was reluctant to admit to Jogendra that Ramesh had given her no reason for postponing the wedding. On the other hand she refused to tell a downright lie.

"He was prepared to tell me, but I didn't think it necessary," she answered.

"Pure pride," thought Jogendra; "characteristic!" Aloud he said, "All right, don't be afraid; I'll make him disclose his reasons this very day."

"But I haven't been afraid," said Hemnalini, aimlessly turning over the pages of the book in her lap, "and I don't want you to pester him for his reasons."

"Pride again!" thought Jogendra. "All right," he said, "you need have no anxiety on that score," and he made as if to depart.

Hemnalini rose from her chair. "Now mind, you're not to say anything to him about this. You others may think what you like, but I don't suspect him at all."

It struck Jogendra that this hardly sounded like pride. His affection and compassion for his sister gained the upper hand and he smiled inwardly as he reflected: "These learned ladies have no knowledge of the world; she knows a lot that she has learned from books; but when an occasion for suspicion arises she is as innocent as a babe!" Then Jogendra contrasted her simple trust with the other's duplicity. His heart hardened against Ramesh, and his determination to force him to state his "reasons" became stronger than ever. Once more he rose as if to go out, but Hemnalini was too quick and caught him by the arm.

"Promise not to breathe a word of this to Ramesh," she said.

"I'll see," replied Jogendra.

"There's no 'seeing' about it. Promise me before you go. I assure you that there's nothing for you to worry about. Just do this one little thing for me."

Hemnalini's insistence convinced Jogendra that Ramesh had given her a full explanation. Still it did not follow that the explanation was a true one; it would have been no very difficult task to deceive her with some cock-and-bull story, so he said: "Look here, Hem, it's not a question of distrusting anyone; but when a girl is going to be married her guardians have duties. He may have given you some explanation that you're keeping to yourself, but that isn't enough; he has still to explain matters to us. To tell the truth, Hem, at present it's more our concern than yours to hear his explanation. Once you're married we shan't have much more say," and Jogendra hurried off.

Of the veil with which lovers seek to shroud their ways not a shred remained! The bond between Ramesh and Hemnalini — a bond which in their fond hopes would grow more intimate with the passage of time till it created for the two a world apart — had become a target for the missiles of unsympathetic outsiders.

The onset of the storm so agitated Hemnalini that she shrank even from the sight of her friends and relations. After Jogendra's departure she sank into a chair and spent the rest of the day in the seclusion of her room.

As Jogendra left the house he met Akshay, who greeted him with: "Hullo, Jogen, you've turned up! Have you heard about it? What do you think of it all?"

Jogendra. "I've thought a lot about it; I don't propose to go on talking it over and making useless conjectures. It's no time for sitting round the tea-table, splitting psychological hairs."

Akshay. "Splitting hairs isn't much in my line, as you know, any more than psychology or philosophy or poetry. I'm a man of action — that's what I came to tell you."

"All right, I'm for action," said the impetuous Jogendra. "Can you tell me where Ramesh has gone?"

"I can."

"Where?"

"Shan't tell you yet," said Akshay. "I'll confront you with him at three this afternoon."

"Why can't you tell me what it's all about?" cried Jogendra; "you're all so devilish secretive. I go off for a few days' holiday, and as soon as my back's turned fearful mysteries spring up on every hand. Come, Akshay, no more concealment! Out with it, man!"

Akshay. "I'm glad to hear you talk like that. It's through not concealing things that I've got into hot water. Your sister won't look at me, your father scolds me for having a suspicious nature, and Ramesh Babu doesn't exactly jump for joy when we meet. Now you're the only one left, and I'm afraid of you. You're not a man for subtle argument. Downright action is more in your line. I'm a miserable specimen physically and I couldn't stand up to you!"

Jogendra. "Look here, Akshay, I don't like all this crooked work. I know you have something to tell me. Why do you keep it back and haggle over it? Tell me the truth now; out with it!"

Akshay. "All right, I'll tell you the whole story from the start; most of it will be new to you."

Chapter 18

The lease of Ramesh's lodgings in Darjjipara had not yet expired, but it had never occurred to him to set about subletting them. For some months past he had been living in a world in which financial considerations carried no weight. Kamala, however, must have a roof over her head when she left school. At daybreak, accordingly, he repaired to his lodgings, had the rooms swept, provided the necessary mats and coverlets, and re-stocked the empty larder.

Some hours intervened between the completion of these preparations and Kamala's arrival. Ramesh spent the time reclining on a wooden bench wondering what the future had in store for him. He had never visited Etawah, but one north-western landscape is very like another and he had no difficulty in picturing his future home — a bungalow on the outskirts of the town, fronting a broad tree-lined highway; across the road a wide expanse of ploughland dotted about with wells and with the raised platforms on which watchers sit to scare birds and beasts from the ripening crops; the unceasing wail of the Persian wheels, as the patient oxen toiled all day raising water to irrigate the fields; an occasional *ekka* dashing along the road raising clouds of dust, the jingle of its harness disturbing the stillness of the baked air. He was appalled at the prospect of the listless afternoons that Hemnalini would spend in the solitude of the bungalow — barred and shuttered against the burning heat — pining for home. Only if she was to have Kamala always at her side could he condemn his wife to such an environment.

Ramesh had decided to tell Kamala nothing till after the marriage. Then Hemnalini would watch for her opportunity and taking Kamala to her heart would unfold her real life's history to her with loving tenderness — as painlessly as possible would unravel the meshes of the intricate net in which Fate had wound her. And thus, far away from home, cut off from all their acquaintance, Kamala would drop into her place in their little household without shock or strain.

The silence of the noonday had fallen upon the lane. Workers had departed for the scene of their labours, and leisured folk were preparing for their siesta. The coolness of the coming winter seemed already to temper the heat, and the air was pervaded with the enlivening prospect of the approaching holidays. There was nothing to distract Ramesh in his delineation of the happiness that was to be his, and he laid on the colours with no sparing hand.

His dreams were interrupted by the noise of wheels; a large vehicle had driven up to his door and stopped there. Ramesh knew it to be the school omnibus bringing Kamala, and his pulse quickened. How was he to receive Kamala? What subjects of conversation had they in common? What would be her attitude to him? These were disturbing questions, and he could not face the prospect with equanimity. His two servants were waiting downstairs. They were the first to appear, dragging along Kamala's trunk, which they deposited in the verandah. Kamala followed them as far as the doorway and halted there.

"Come in, Kamala," said Ramesh. Overcoming a momentary impulse of hesitation Kamala entered the room. Ramesh had planned to leave her at school during the holidays, and his apparent neglect had cost her many tears. This recollection combined with their long separation to produce in her a sense of estrangement. So Kamala after her entrance refused to look at Ramesh and kept her eyes fixed on the open door.

Kamala's appearance was a surprise to him; he seemed to be contemplating a total stranger. In these few months there had been an astounding change in her. She had developed like a young plant. Gone was the bloom of health that had glowed about the unformed limbs of the rustic maid. Her face had lost its youthful roundness, and the features had become more pronounced and had gained distinction. The dark sleekness of her cheeks had given place to a delicate pallor, and her gait and movement were free and unconstrained.

After her entry she stood erect with head half-averted in front of the open window, and the light of the autumn afternoon fell on her face. Her head was bare, her braided tresses, tied with a red ribbon, hung down her back, and her merino robe of a saffron tint was fastened tightly round her half-developed body.

Ramesh gazed at her for some moments in silence.

Kamala's beauty had been only a vague memory to him during the past few months. Now with its added lustre it startled him profoundly and found him unprepared to resist her charm.

"Sit down, Kamala," he bade her. Kamala sat down without a word.

"How's school?" he went on.

"All right," she answered curtly.

Ramesh was racking his brains for something else to say when an idea occurred to him.

"I don't suppose," he said, "you have had anything to eat for some time. There's food ready for you here. Shall I tell them to bring it in?"

"No, thank you," said Kamala. "I had something before I started."

"Won't you eat anything at all?" asked Ramesh; "there's fruit if you don't care for sweets—apples, pomegranates, custard-apples."

But Kamala merely shook her head.

Ramesh again gazed at the girl's face. She was looking at the pictures in her English Reader, with her head slightly bent forward. A beautiful face is llike a diviner's rod, it draws out any beauty that lurks in its surroundings. The mellow sunlight seemed in that instant to become a sentiment being; the autumn day appeared to take form and shape. As the sun rules its planets, so this girl drew sky, air, light, and everything about her into her orbit, while she herself sat unconscious and silent, looking at pictures in a lesson-book.

Ramesh hurried out and fetched a plateful of apples, pears, and pomegranates.

"You don't seem to want anything, Kamala," he said, "but I'm hungry and I can't hold out any longer." Kamala smiled, and the light of that unexpected smile dissipated the fog that had come between them. Ramesh took a knife and began to slice an apple, but he was quite devoid of any kind of dexterity. His avid haste and his clumsy attempts to cut the fruit were too much for Kamala, and she burst out laughing.

Her unrestrained merriment delighted Ramesh. "I suppose you're laughing because I'm no good at cutting apples," he said. "All right, just show me how you can do it."

"I could if I had a chopper," said Kamala. "I can't do it with a knife."

"I suppose you think we haven't got a chopper here," said Ramesh, and calling a servant asked if there was one. "Oh yes, sir, we brought along everything that was needed for the kitchen last night," was the answer. "Clean it thoroughly and bring it in," commanded Ramesh.

When the chopper arrived Kamala took off her shoes, opened the blade, sat down, and deftly peeled the apple; then she began to cut it into slices. Ramesh sat down in front of her and caught the slices on a plate. "You'll have to eat some too," he said.

"No, thank you," said Kamala.

"Then I shan't have any."

Kamala looked up at him. "All right; you have some first, and then I'll have some."

"Look here, you won't back out, will you?" said Ramesh.

"No, honestly, I won't back out," replied Kamala, shaking her head emphatically.

Satisfied with this assurance Ramesh took a piece of the fruit from the plate and put it in his mouth.

In that instant he saw something that arrested his jaws. Jogendra and Akshay were standing opposite him outside the door.

Akshay was the first to speak. "I beg your pardon, Ramesh Babu. I thought we should find you alone. Jogen, we shouldn't have dropped in on him like this without warning. Come along, we'll go and wait downstairs."

Kamala had let the chopper fall and leapt to her feet. The two men blocked the exit from the room. Jogendra moved slightly to one side and left the way clear; he did not, however, take his eyes from Kamala's face, but stared fixedly at her. Kamala fled in confusion into an adjoining room.

Chapter 19

"*R*amesh, who is that girl?" demanded Jogendra.

"A relation of mine," answered Ramesh.

"What's the relationship?" asked Jogendra; "she's not one of your elders, and I presume the tie has not been created by affection. You've told me about all your relatives, yet I never heard anything about this one."

"Steady on, Jogen," broke in Akshay. "Surely there are things that a man likes to keep secret even from his friends."

"Well, Ramesh," said Jogendra, "is this such a great secret then?"

Ramesh turned red. "Yes, it is a secret," he said. "I should prefer not to discuss this girl with you."

"But unfortunately," retorted Jogendra, "I particularly want to discuss her with you. If you hadn't been engaged to Hemnalini there would be no need to investigate the ramifications of your family tree; you might have kept your own secrets."

"This much I can say," said Ramesh; "there is no one in the world with whom I have formed such a connection as would be a bar to my marrying Hemnalini with a clear conscience."

Jogendra. "There may be no bar from your point of view, but there may be one from the standpoint of

Hemnalini's relations. I'll merely ask you this much — whether you're related to her or not, why do you keep her hidden away here?"

Ramesh. "If I tell you my reason the secret will be out. Can't you take my word for it without asking for reasons?"

Jogendra. "Is this girl's name Kamala or not?"

Ramesh. "It is."

Jogendra. "Have you or have you not passed her off as your wife?"

Ramesh. "I have."

Jogendra. "Do you expect me to believe you then? You want to tell us she isn't your wife. You've told everyone else that she is. You don't set a very good example of veracity."

Akshay. "You mean, it's hardly the sort of instance that one would use in a college lecture on truthfulness. But after all, my dear Jogen, it may be necessary in practice to tell two different stories to two different sets of people when the circumstances are exceptional. The probabilities are that one or other of the stories is correct. Perhaps what Ramesh Babu told you is true after all."

Ramesh. "I'm not going to tell you people anything at all. I only say this much, that I am doing Hemnalini no wrong in marrying her. I have a very good reason for refusing to discuss Kamala's affairs with you. It would be wrong for me to do so, however suspicious you may think my conduct. If it were only a question of my own happiness and reputation I should keep nothing from you. But I decline to say anything, when by doing so I may jeopardise another's future."

Jogendra. "Have you told Hemnalini everything?"

Ramesh. "No, I'll tell her after we're married. If she likes, I'll tell her even now."

Jogendra. "Well, may I put a few questions to Kamala about this?"

Ramesh. "Most certainly not! If you consider me guilty you can pass on me whatever sentence you think fit. Kamala is perfectly innocent, and I will not expose her to your cross-examination."

Jogendra. "It's quite unnecessary to question anybody at all. I've found out all that there is to know. You have given me sufficient proof. I tell you most distinctly that if you set foot in our house again you will have to submit to insult."

Ramesh turned pale, but said nothing. Jogendra went on. "I've something more to say. You're not to write to Hemnalini or hold the slightest communication with her — openly or in secret. If you write to her I'll publish abroad the secret that you wish to keep with the proofs that I have. If anyone asks us now why your engagement to Hemnalini has been broken off I'll say it was because I refused my consent to the marriage; I shan't give the true reason. But if you're not careful the whole story will come out. You may wonder why I show such restraint in the face of your heartless behaviour. Do not think I have the least sympathy for you; it is only because this matter affects my sister Hemnalini that I have let you off so lightly. My last word to you is never to give the least indication, by speech or behaviour, that you ever had any acquaintance with Hemnalini. It's no good exacting any promise from you; I can't expect sincerity from you after such deceit. But if you have any shame, any fear of exposure left, then you won't disregard this warning, deliberately or otherwise."

Akshay. "Really, Jogen, really! Aren't you sorry for Ramesh Babu at all? Look how quietly he takes it! We'd better go now. Never mind, Ramesh Babu, we're off now."

Jogendra and Akshay went out, leaving Ramesh too stunned to move. When his numbed senses began to recover from the shock his first impulse was to go for a brisk walk

and review the situation in the open air, but he remembered
that he could not leave Kamala alone in a strange place.

He went into the next room and found the girl sitting
by the window overlooking the street, holding one of the
slats of the venetians open. At Ramesh's footfall she closed
the slat and turned her head; Ramesh squatted on the
floor.

"Who were these men?" asked Kamala; "they came to
our school this morning."

"Went to your school, did they?" exclaimed Ramesh.

"Yes," said Kamala. "What were they saying to you?"

"They asked me what relation you were to me."

Kamala had never sat at the feet of a mother-in-law
and learned on what occasions to display the bashfulness
becoming in a young wife. Still, her own instincts made
her blush at Ramesh's words.

"I told them," he went on, "that there was no
relationship between us."

Kamala regarded this kind of pleasantry as extremely
bad taste. She turned away angrily exclaiming, "Don't be
silly!"

Ramesh wondered if he could possibly tell Kamala the
whole truth.

Suddenly she started up with the exclamation, "Look
out, there's a crow gone off with your fruit!" She hurried
into the other room, scared away the crow, and came back
with the plate of fruit. "Aren't you going to have some?"
she asked, setting the plate down in front of him.

Ramesh's appetite had gone, but he was touched by this
little attention. "Won't you have any, Kamala?" he asked.

"You have some first," she replied, in the role of the
wife who may not eat till her husband's hunger is satisfied.
It was the merest trifle, but Ramesh's nerves were on edge
and the innocent girl's delusion brought him to the verge

of tears. Speech failed him, but he controlled himself and began to eat. When he had finished he remarked, "We must be off home to-night, Kamala."

At this announcement Kamala's face fell. "I don't want to go there," she said.

Ramesh. "Would you like to stay at school?"

Kamala. "No, don't send me back to school; the girls there only ask me questions about you, and they make me shy."

Ramesh. "What do you tell them?"

Kamala. "I don't tell them anything. They used to ask me why you wanted to leave me at school for the holidays. I—" Kamala could not finish the sentence. The recollection reopened the wound in her heart.

Ramesh. "Why didn't you tell them that I'm nobody to you?"

Kamala glanced impatiently at him out of the corner of her eye. "Don't be silly!" she repeated.

"What on earth am I to do?" Ramesh asked himself. His secret was like a worm in his vitals trying to gnaw its way out, and the process was painful. His mind was distraught with tormenting questions. What had Jogendra told Hemnalini by this time? How had Hemnalini taken the news? How could he explain the true state of affairs to her? How could he bear eternal separation from Hemnalini? But he was too distraught to think out the answers to them.

This much he knew, that his relations to Kamala had become a topic of absorbing interest to his friends and his enemies in Calcutta. His false step in describing Kamala as his wife would inflate the rumours that were already current. Not another day could he remain in the place with her.

His abstraction did not escape Kamala's notice, and she glanced up at him.

"What are you worrying about?" she asked. "If you want to go and live at home, I'll come too."

That the girl should subordinate her own wishes to his was a fresh stab to Ramesh. Again he wondered what course he should pursue. He relapsed into absent-mindedness, gazing intently at Kamala without responding to her last remark. Kamala felt that the occasion demanded seriousness. "I say, you weren't annoyed because I didn't want to stay on at school for the holidays, were you?" she asked. "Tell me the truth, now!"

"To tell you the truth," replied Ramesh, "it was myself I was annoyed with, not you."

With a mighty effort he freed himself from the tangle of his thoughts and set about engaging Kamala in conversation. "Come now, Kamala," he said briskly, "tell me what you've been learning at school all this time."

Kamala began readily enough to display her learning. She tried to astonish Ramesh by her knowledge of the fact that the earth is round. Ramesh duly declared himself a sceptic on the subject and asked how such a thing was possible. Kamala opened her eyes: "Why, it's in our book; we learned all about it."

"You don't say so," said Ramesh, affecting surprise. "It's in a book, is it? How big is the book?"

This query brought Kamala up in arms. "It's not so very big, but it's in print, and there are pictures in it too!" This was incontestable proof and Ramesh had to succumb.

When Kamala had finished detailing all that she had learnt she launched forth on an account of the other girls, of the teachers, and of the school routine. Ramesh became absent-minded again, but murmured assent now and then. At times he caught the tail-end of a sentence and threw in half a question. Suddenly Kamala exclaimed, "You're not listening to me at all!" and stood up in vexation.

"Come, come, Kamala," said Ramesh hastily, "don't get angry; I'm not quite myself to-day."

"Aren't you well? What's the matter?" asked Kamala, turning round again.

"I'm not exactly unwell; it's nothing at all really; I feel like this sometimes. Please go on again."

"Would you like to see the picture in my geography primer?" asked Kamala, bent on entertaining him with her newly-acquired learning.

Ramesh demanded its production with apparent alacrity.

Kamala brought her book at once and held it open in front of him. "These two globes that you see," she proceeded," are really one. You know, one can never see both sides of a round thing at the same time."

Ramesh appeared to ponder over this. "It's the same if a thing's flat," he remarked.

"That's why the two hemispheres are shown separately in this picture," went on Kamala; and thus they spent the first evening of the holidays.

Chapter 20

*A*nnada Babu prayed most fervently that Jogendra would bring back good tidings and that the whole misunderstanding would be cleared up. He looked up nervously when Jogendra and Akshay entered the room.

"Well, dad," began his son, "I could never have believed that you would let Ramesh go so far. I shouldn't have introduced him to you if I had foreseen what would happen."

Annada Babu. "You've often told me yourself how pleased you would be if Ramesh married Hemnalini. If you wanted to prevent it, why —?"

Jogendra. "Naturally I never thought of trying to prevent it, still —"

Annada Babu. "I don't see how there can be any 'still' about it! One had either to let it go on or to stop it; there's no middle course."

Jogendra. "Still, to let it go so far —"

Akshay now broke in with a smirk, "there are some things that go forward of their own momentum; one doesn't need to push them. They go on swelling till they're ready to burst. Still, it's no good crying over spilt milk. We had better decide now what to do next."

"Did you see Ramesh?" asked Annada Babu anxiously.

Jogendra. "We did indeed. We saw him in the bosom of his family and actually made his wife's acquaintance."

Annada Babu was thunderstruck. "Made his wife's acquaintance?" he repeated when he found his voice.

Jogendra. "Yes, Ramesh's wife."

Annada Babu. "I don't quite understand. What Ramesh's wife?"

Jogendra. "Our Ramesh's! It was to be married that he went home that time."

Annada Babu. "I thought his father's death had knocked that on the head."

Jogendra. "He was married before his father died."

Annada Babu sat stroking his head, quite dumbfounded. "In that case he can't marry our Hem!" he said after a while.

Jogendra. "And so we want to say——"

Annada Babu. "Say what you like, the fact remains that the preparations for the wedding are almost complete. We wrote to everyone saying that it couldn't take place this Sunday and had been put off to the following Sunday. I suppose we'll have to write now and say that it's off altogether?"

"We needn't put it off again; we need only make one change and our arrangements will hold good in every other respect," said Jogendra.

"What change could you make?" asked Annada Babu in astonishment.

Jogendra. "Surely it's obvious enough. We must substitute another bridegroom for Ramesh and carry through the ceremony next Sunday as planned. Otherwise we shan't be able to show our faces in public," and Jogendra glanced at Akshay.

Akshay's eyes were bent modestly to the ground.

Annada Babu. "How are you going to find a bridegroom so soon?"

Jogendra. "You needn't be anxious on that score."

Annada Babu. "But you'll need to get Hem's consent."

Jogendra. "She's certain to consent when she hears how Ramesh has behaved."

Annada Babu. "Very well, do what you think best, but it is a pity all the same. Ramesh was quite well off and he had good brains and education as well as means. Only yesterday we settled that he should go and practise at Etawah after they were married, and look what has happened since!"

Jogendra. "Well, you needn't trouble about that anymore, dad. Let Ramesh go and practise at Etawah if he likes. I had better call in Hem at once. There isn't much time to lose."

He went out and returned in a minute or two with Hemnalini. Akshay took cover behind a bookcase in the corner.

"Sit down, Hem," said Jogendra, "we have something to say to you."

Hem took a chair without a word and resigned herself to an inquisition.

"Haven't you noticed anything suspicious about Ramesh's behaviour?" began Jogendra by way of breaking the news gently to her.

Hemnalini merely shook her head.

"He had the marriage postponed for a week; what reason could he have had that he could not disclose to us?"

"There must have been some reason," said Hemnalini without raising her eyes.

"You're perfectly right; there was a reason, but isn't that suspicious enough in itself?"

Hemnalini signified by a shake of the head that she did not think so.

The implicit faith in Ramesh displayed by his relatives irritated Jogendra. He made no further attempt to mince matters but broke out harshly: "You remember when Ramesh went home with his father? We did not hear from him for a long time after that and naturally we thought his conduct strange. You know, too, that in the old days he lived next door to us and used to drop in twice a day, while after he returned to Calcutta he burrowed somewhere miles away and never even called. Even then you two continued to believe in him and you invited him back on the old footing. Such a thing could never have happened if I had been here."

Still Hemnalini did not open her mouth.

Jogendra. "Did either of you make any attempt to fathom the meaning of his extraordinary behaviour? Did you never feel the slightest curiosity about it? You seem to have had very strong faith in him."

Still Hemnalini said nothing.

Jogendra. "Very good. One is driven to the conclusion that you have a natural disinclination to suspect anyone. I hope you'll believe what I'm going to tell you now. I went personally to the girls' school and found that Ramesh has a wife who is a boarder there, and he had arranged to leave her there for the holidays. Two or three days ago came a bolt from the blue in the shape of a letter from the headmistress saying that she couldn't keep Kamala — that's Ramesh's wife — there during the vacation. The school broke up to-day, and Kamala was deposited by the school omnibus at their old rooms in Darjjipara. I went there myself and found Kamala peeling and cutting up an apple with a chopper while Ramesh was sitting on the floor in front of her taking the pieces from her and putting them in his mouth. I asked Ramesh for an explanation and he said he would tell us nothing. If he had made the least attempt to deny that Kamala was his wife we should have accepted his word and should have endeavoured to allay our suspicions, but he would neither affirm nor deny it. Can you continue to trust Ramesh after that?"

Jogendra waited for an answer with eyes on his sister's face. She had turned strangely pale and was gripping the arms of the chair with all her strength. Next moment her head fell forward, and she sank unconscious to the ground.

Annada Babu's distress was pitiful. He raised his daughter's head from the floor and laid it on his breast, exclaiming, "What is it, dear, what is it? Don't believe a word they say! It's all a lie."

Jogendra thrust his father aside and at once lifted Hemnalini on to the sofa. A jug of water was handy and he sprinkled drops on her face, while Akshay fanned her vigorously with a hand *punkah*.

Hemnalini soon opened her eyes and started up in consternation. She turned to her father crying, "Daddy, daddy, do tell Akshay Babu to go away."

Akshay promptly put the *punkah* down and went out into the passage.

Annada Babu sat down on the sofa beside Hemnalini and gently stroked her head and neck. He could only sigh and ejaculate "My dear, my dear!"

Suddenly her eyes filled with tears and her bosom began to heave. She leaned her breast against her father's knee in an attempt to repress her uncontrollable grief.

"Never mind, dear, never mind," murmured Annada Babu in broken accents. "I know Ramesh well and he would never deceive us. Jogen must have made a mistake."

Jogendra's patience was at an end. "Don't delude her with false hopes, dad," he exclaimed. "If you try to spare her feelings now it'll only be the worse for her in the end. Give her a chance to think it over."

Hemnalini raised her head from her father's knee, sat up, and looked Jogendra in the face. "I tell you plainly that I'll never believe it till I hear it from his own lips," and she staggered to her feet. Annada Babu sprang up with an exclamation and saved her from falling.

Hemnalini took his arm and he supported her to her own room.

"Please leave me to myself for a little, dad, and I'll go to sleep," she said as she lay down.

"Shall I send up your old nurse to fan you?" asked her father.

"No, thank you, I should prefer to be alone."

Annada Babu retired into the room adjoining hers. His thoughts went back to Hem's mother, who had died when the girl was three years old, and he recalled her devotion, her patience, and her unfailing cheerfulness. His heart was torn with anxiety for the daughter for whom he had endeavoured all these years to take a mother's place and who had grown up to be the image of the lost one. His mind pierced the physical barrier of the partition between them and he found himself mentally addressing the prostrate girl. "Dear, I pray that Heaven may remove all obstacles from your path and that you may be happy all the rest of your life. I pray that before I join your mother I may see you blissful and contented, safely installed by the hearth of a man whom you love!" and he wiped his moist eyes with the fringe of his coat.

Jogendra had always rated women's intelligence low and the day's events only confirmed him in his estimate. How could one cope with a sex that disregarded the clearest evidence? A woman is quite ready to deny that two and two make four if a question of individual happiness is concerned. If reason tells her that black is black and love tells her that black is white, poor reason is soundly rated.

How in spite of woman the world manages to conduct its affairs Jogendra could not imagine!

He hailed Akshay.

Akshay sidled into the room. "You've heard everything. What is to be done now?" asked Jogendra.

"Why do you drag me into it, old man? It's no concern of mine. I've kept quiet all these days. It was hardly fair play to involve me in the mess!"

Jogendra. "All right, your complaint will be attended to later. In the meantime I don't see what can be done unless we can persuade Ramesh to make a full confession to Hemnalini herself."

Akshay. "Are you mad? Can you expect a man to——?"

Jogendra. "It would be still better if we could induce him to write to her. That'll be a job for you. But you'll have to set to work at once."

Akshay. "I'll see what I can do."

Chapter 21

amesh carried Kamala off to Sealdah Station at nine o'clock that night. Under his instructions the driver took a circuitous route by the Kalutola lanes, and Ramesh thrust his head eagerly out of the window as the carriage passed a certain house. He noticed no change in any of its familiar features.

He sighed so deeply that Kamala started out of her doze and asked what was the matter. "Nothing," said Ramesh and subsided into his seat, where he remained till the carriage reached its destination. Kamala lay back in her corner and soon fell asleep again. Ramesh could not resist a momentary impulse of resentment at her very existence.

They arrived at the station in good time and were soon ensconced in the second-class compartment which Ramesh had engaged for the journey. Ramesh made a bed for Kamala on one of the lower bunks, lowered the light, closed the shutters, and remarked, "It's long past your bed-time; you had better go to sleep now."

"Mayn't I sit here and look out till the train starts? I'll go to sleep after that." Ramesh assented, so Kamala drew her veil over her head and seated herself on the edge of the bunk by the window to watch the crowds, while Ramesh himself sat on the centre bunk gazing out absent-mindedly. The train had just begun to move when his eye fell on a belated passenger who was hurrying up the platform and whose features seemed vaguely familiar to him.

Next moment Kamala began to shriek with laughter. Ramesh put his head out and observed the late arrival struggling in the grasp of one of the station officials who tried to hold him back from the moving train. He succeeded, however, in boarding the train, though his shawl remained in the official's hand. As the tardy one leaned forward out of the carriage window and reached for the shawl Ramesh recognised him as — Akshay.

It was some time before Kamala stopped laughing over the scuffle she had watched.

"It's half-past ten and we're off; you had better go to sleep now," said Ramesh.

The girl went obediently to bed, but until she fell asleep she had frequent fits of giggling.

Ramesh, on his part, had failed to perceive the humour of the incident. Akshay, he knew, had no country home; his family had lived in Calcutta for generations. So why had he been in such a desperate hurry to catch that particular train? The only possible explanation was that he and Kamala were being shadowed.

The idea that Akshay would institute inquiries in his native village was most distasteful to Ramesh; his reputation would inevitably become the sport of contending factions there, and the whole business would appear unspeakably sordid.

He could imagine exactly what sort of scandal would be bruited about in the village. In a city like Calcutta one can always find unplumbed depths into which to dive, but the slightest impact sets the shallows of a small country place tossing with excitement. The more he reflected the more he shuddered at the prospect.

When the train stopped at Barrackpore Ramesh put his head out, but he did not see Akshay alight. At Naihati many passengers entered and left the train, but Akshay was not among them. At Bogoola Ramesh looked out again, but once more he was disappointed. It was most unlikely that Akshay would leave the train at any of the other stations.

Fatigued though Ramesh was, it was late before he fell asleep. Early in the morning the train reached Goalundo — the terminus at which passengers embark for Eastern Bengal — and Ramesh caught sight of Akshay hurrying towards the river-steamers, with his head and face muffled in a shawl, carrying a hand-bag. The boat which was bound for Ramesh's village would not start for some hours, but there was another at the landing-place, with steam up, whistling impatiently. "Where does this one go?" asked Ramesh.

"West," was the reply.

"How far?"

"Up to Benares if there's enough water in the river."

Ramesh at once installed Kamala in one of the cabins and hurried ashore to lay in a stock of rice and pulse, milk and plantains, for the journey. Akshay, in the meantime, had embarked on the other steamer ahead of everyone else and had taken up a position from which he could survey the whole crowd. The passengers who intended to embark on this vessel showed no particular haste, as she was not yet due to start; they spent the interim in washing or bathing, and some of them even cooked their food and ate it on the river-bank.

Akshay supposed that Ramesh had taken Kamala to some eating-house in the neighbourhood for breakfast, but as he did not know his way about in Goalundo he thought it safer to remain on board.

At last the whistle blew, but still there was no sign of Ramesh. The passengers began to stream on board across the swaying plank that served for a gangway. As the whistle became more insistent late-comers hurried on board, but still Ramesh was not to be seen either among the new arrivals or among those who had already embarked.

Every one was on board, the gang-plank had been withdrawn, and the skipper had given the order to weigh anchor, when Akshay finally ejaculated, "I want to get off!" but the crew paid no attention to him. The steamer was quite close to the bank and he leaped off on to terra firma.

There was no trace of Ramesh ashore. The morning train to Calcutta had just steamed out and Akshay came to the conclusion that Ramesh had espied him when he struggled to enter the train, and that, supposing him to have some hostile intention, Ramesh had abandoned his journey to his native place and had doubled back to Calcutta by the morning train. It would be exceedingly difficult to unearth any one in a place the size of Calcutta.

Chapter 22

Akshay spent the whole day kicking his heels in Goalundo and in the evening he boarded the mail train for Calcutta. Arriving there early on the following morning, he went first of all to Ramesh's rooms in Darjjipara, but he found the door locked and was informed that no one had been there.

He then proceeded to Kalutola, but the rooms there were also untenanted, so he repaired to Annada Babu's, next door, and announced to Jogendra, "He has bolted! I couldn't catch him."

"What do you mean?" exclaimed Jogendra.

Akshay related his experiences in detail. Jogendra's suspicions of Ramesh turned to absolute certainty when he learned that he had taken to flight with Kamala at the mere sight of Akshay. "But after all," he said, "though we have this evidence it won't serve our purpose. It's not only Hemnalini; dad talks just the same kind of nonsense about never losing faith in Ramesh till he hears the whole story from his own lips. Matters have come to such a pitch that if Ramesh were to come to-day and say, 'I can't tell you anything yet,' I'm sure dad would have no hesitation in allowing him to marry Hemnalini. However is one to deal with people of that kind! Dad can't bear to see Hemnalini distressed about anything. If she went to him to-day and whimpered that she wanted to marry Ramesh even though he has another wife, I believe he would give his consent. We must extract a full confession from Ramesh somehow or other, and the sooner the better. Don't let us give up hope. I would tackle the job myself, but I can't think how to go about it, and I should probably only come to blows with Ramesh! Well, I suppose you want a wash and some tea."

Akshay performed his ablutions and then sat down to drink his tea, with his brain busily employed. His thoughts were interrupted by the entrance of Annada Babu, leading his daughter by the hand. Hemnalini turned on her heel when she saw Akshay and left the room.

"It's too bad of Hem!" exclaimed Jogendra hotly. "Dad, you mustn't encourage her in that sort of rudeness. You ought to compel her to come down," and he shouted, "Hem! Hem!" but Hemnalini was already upstairs.

Akshay now intervened: "I really think you're spoiling my case, Jogen. It would be much better if you said nothing to her about me. Leave time to do its work. If you bully her now you'll only do irretrievable mischief."

Akshay finished his tea and departed. This young man's fund of patience was inexhaustible. When the signals were against him he knew that there was nothing to do but to sit down and wait. His temper was very even. When insulted he neither looked haughty nor turned away in disgust. Snubs and slights left him unmoved, so thick was his hide. His friends might treat him in the most cavalier fashion and he never even winced.

No sooner had he departed than Annada Babu brought Hemnalini back to the tea-table. The colour had left her cheeks, and there were dark rings round her eyes. As she entered the room she did not raise her eyes, for she could not face Jogendra. She knew that he was out of patience with Ramesh and herself and that he had already passed a harsh sentence on them both, hence she shrank from meeting his eye.

Though love had sustained Hemnalini's faith in Ramesh, it could not hush the voice of reason altogether. She had proclaimed her belief in him to Jogendra before she swept out of the room two days before, but in the solitude of the night-watches her faith had weakened.

She could not, to tell the truth, conceive any plausible explanation of Ramesh's extraordinary conduct. She laboured to bar out suspicion from the stronghold of her faith yet doubts rained blows on the postern. Like a mother who endeavours to protect her babe by clasping it to her breast, she clutched her trust in Ramesh to her heart when assailed by the damning evidence against him. But alas! would her strength always be equal to the effort?

Annada Babu had again slept in the room next to Hemnalini's and he knew what a restless night she had passed. Several times he had gone into her room and found her awake. Her answer to his anxious inquiries had been, "Why aren't you asleep yourself, dad? I feel sleepy enough; I'm just dropping off."

She rose early and walked on the roof. Every door and window in Ramesh's lodging was shut and barred. The sun climbed slowly over the eastern escarpment of roofs, but to Hemnalini the new-born day seemed so dull, so listless, so joyless and dreary that she sank down in a corner of the roof, buried her face in her hands, and burst into tears. The day would pass without a visit from her lover. Even at the festive evening hour she would not have his advent to look forward to; and the empty consolation of feeling that he was near her, in the neighbouring house, that, too, was denied her.

She was startled by her father's voice calling, "Hem! Hem!" She hastily wiped away the traces of her grief and responded, "Yes, dad?"

"I got up late this morning," said Annada Babu, as he emerged on to the roof and fell to stroking her shoulder.

Anxiety for his daughter had made his rest a disturbed one, and he had not fallen asleep till dawn was approaching. The sun shining on his face had awakened him again, and after a hasty toilet he had gone in search of his daughter. Her room, however, was empty, and the thought that she still courted solitude caused him a fresh pang.

"Come down and have your tea, dear," he said.

Hemnalini shrank from facing Jogendra across the tea-table, but she knew that any departure from her usual routine would distress her father; moreover, it was her invariable custom to pour out his tea for him herself and she did not wish to omit this slight attention.

As they reached the door she heard Jogendra conversing with some one inside, and her heart fluttered at the sudden thought that Ramesh might be there, for no one else was likely to come in so early. Quaking in every limb she entered the room and beheld — Akshay! It was the last straw, and she turned and fled. When her father brought her back again, she pressed close to his chair and concentrated her whole attention on the preparation of his tea.

Jogendra was seriously offended at her behaviour. That Hem should take Ramesh's defection so much to heart seemed to him insufferable. His digust was intensified when he perceived that Annada Babu shared in her sorrow, and that she was trying to use his affection as a shield between herself and the world. "We are all criminals!" he thought. "When our fondness for her enjoins us to do our duty and to work for her true happiness, not only do we receive no word of thanks but she secretly regards us as wrongdoers. Dad doesn't know how to handle the situation at all; at this stage he ought to use the knife instead of trying to console her. For fear of inflicting pain he is only keeping back the unwelcome truth from her."

"Do you know what has happened, dad?" he said aloud.

"No, what is it?" asked Annada Babu eagerly.

"Ramesh started for home the night before last in the Goalundo mail, taking his wife with him. When he saw Akshay get into the train, he changed his plans and came back to Calcutta."

Hemnalini's hand shook and she spilt the tea which she was pouring out. She subsided hastily into a chair.

Jogendra glanced at her out of the corner of his eye. "I can't conceive what his motive was in running away, seeing that Akshay knew everything already. His former conduct was mean enough in itself, but on the top of that to take fright and run away like a thief! In my opinion it's simply disgusting. I don't know what Hem thinks of it, but I consider his flight sufficient evidence of guilt."

'Trembling in every limb, Hemnalini rose to her feet. "I don't want your evidence, thank you," she said to her brother; "you can condemn him if you like, but I'm not his judge."

Jogendra. "Have we nothing to do with the man who was going to marry you?"

Hemnalini. "I said nothing about marriage. Break the engagement or not just as you think fit; but you needn't try to break my resolution."

A fit of sobbing choked any further utterance; Annada Babu rose and clasped her tear-bedewed face to his breast.

"Come, dear, we'll go upstairs," was all that he said.

Chapter 23

$\mathcal{T}$he steamer in which Ramesh and Kamala had embarked duly left Goalundo. There were no other first or second class passengers and Ramesh annexed a cabin and deposited their belongings in it.

Kamala took a morning draught of milk and then settled down to admire the ever-shifting river-scenery through the open door of the cabin.

"Do you know where we're going, Kamala?" asked Ramesh.

"Home," said Kamala.

Ramesh. "You don't want to go there, so we're not going."

Kamala. "Was it on my account that you gave up the idea?"

Ramesh. "Yes, it was on your account."

"Why did you do that?" said Kamala, pouting. "You needn't have made so much of a chance remark that I dropped. You're very easily offended."

Ramesh smiled. "I wasn't offended at all; I don't want to go home either."

"Where are we going to then?" queried Kamala eagerly.

Ramesh. "We're going to the west-country."

Kamala opened her eyes when she heard this. What a world of meaning that word "West" conjures up to stay-at-home folk! — sacred shrines, invigorating air, new places, new sights, the past splendours of kings and emperors, wonderfully wrought temples, fables of eld, and legends of the heroic age!

"What places are we going to?" asked Kamala in a flutter of delight.

"I haven't decided yet. We pass Monghyr, Patna, Dinapore, Buxar, Ghazipur, and Benares, and we'll get off at one of these places." Some of the names were familiar to Kamala and some were not, but her imagination took fire as he reeled them off.

"What fun it'll be!" and she clapped her hands.

"The fun will come later," said Ramesh, "in the meantime we must see about feeding ourselves. You don't want meals from the crew's galley, I suppose!"

"Heaven help us! I should think not!" cried Kamala with a grimace.

Ramesh. "What'll we do then?"

Kamala. "I'll do the cooking."

Ramesh. "Can you cook?"

Kamala burst into laughter: "I don't know what you take me for? Can I cook? What a little noodle you must think of me! Why, I did all the cooking at my uncle's."

Ramesh became apologetic: "I shouldn't have asked you that. Well, we had better make our preparations now, hadn't we?" and he went off and soon returned with an iron cooking-stove; nor was that all. There was a lad called Umesh on board belonging to the Kayastha or writer caste, inferior only to Brahmans in Bengal; him Ramesh engaged as Kamala's assistant in the kitchen in return for his fare to Benares and a daily wage.

"What are we to have for breakfast, Kamala?" he asked next.

"What can you expect when you bring me only rice and pulse? We'll have kedgeree to-day."

In accordance with Kamala's directions Ramesh procured some spices from the deck-hands. "What do you expect me to do with them now?" she asked, tickled by his ignorance of culinary matters. "I can't pound them without a pestle and a currystone, you know! You really are the limit!"

Ramesh swallowed this rebuke and hurried off in search of the required implements. He could not find exactly what was wanted, but he managed to borrow an iron pestle and a mortar from the crew. These were hardly what Kamala was accustomed to, but she had to make shift with them. Ramesh suggested getting someone else to pound the spices, but she scouted this proposal and fell to work with alacrity. Her struggle with the unfamiliar instruments entertained her hugely, and she only laughed when the spices shot out of the mortar and scattered in all directions; Ramesh found her hilarity infectious and joined in.

When the spice-pounding episode was over, Kamala kilted her skirts and fenced off a corner for her cooking operations. A large earthenware receptacle which they had brought from Calcutta to hold sweetstuff served the purpose of a cooking-pot. Having set this on to boil, Kamala suggested that Ramesh should take his bath at once and by the time he returned his breakfast would be ready. He did accordingly and found on his return that the food had been cooked. The next question was, what to use as a plate?

Ramesh made the halting suggestion that he might borrow a dish from the Mahommendan deck-hands, but

Kamala was horrified at the idea, though he confessed to her in an undertone that it would not be the first time that he had committed this offence against Hindu ceremonial purity.

"You can't undo it now," was her comment, "but you must never do it again. I couldn't bear such a thing," and she took the flat lid of the cooking-pot, cleaned it thoroughly, and laid it down in front of him. "You must use this to-day; we'll get something better when we can."

Ramesh fetched water, washed down a portion of the deck, and sat down to his meal, satisfied that he had complied with his ceremonial obligations.

He had only taken one or two mouthfuls when he exclaimed, "I say, how splendidly you cook!"

"You needn't try to be funny!" protested Kamala in confusion.

"I'm not being funny; you'll see for yourself when your turn comes," and he very soon polished off his plateful and asked for more. Kamala gave him a much larger helping this time.

"What are you doing?" he exclaimed; "have you left enough for yourself?"

"Oh, that's all right! there's plenty left." She was delighted to see Ramesh enjoying his food.

"What are you going to eat off?" he asked next.

"Why, the lid, of course," she replied, serene in her belief that as his wife she might use his plate.

"Oh no, you mustn't do that," cried Ramesh in horror.

"Why not?" asked Kamala surprised.

"It would never do at all."

"Of course it would; I know what I'm about. What are you going to eat off, Ramesh?"

"There's a confectioner selling sweets below decks; I'll get some *sál* leaves from him to use as a plate," said Ramesh.

"If you're going to use that lid," Ramesh went on, "give it to me and I'll wash it thoroughly first."

"What a fuss about nothing!" was her comment on his officiousness.

A few minutes later she exclaimed, 'You never brought me any *pán*, so I can't get any ready for you to chew."

"There's a man selling it below," remarked Ramesh; and so their modest requirements were soon satisfied. Ramesh's reflections, however, were profoundly disturbing. "How on earth am I to get this idea that we're man and wife out of her head?" he asked himself.

Kamala was quite ready to assume the role of housewife without expecting any outside help or instruction, for her life at her uncle's had been a continuous round of cooking, nursing, and housework. Her neatness, dexterity, and the cheerful alacrity with which she went about her duties enchanted Ramesh, but simultaneously he was assailed by tormenting questions: What were their future relations to be? To keep her with him and to turn her away were alike unthinkable. Where was he to draw the line in his daily intercourse with her? If only Hemnalini had been one of the party everything would be simple! But that was impossible, and he could think of no other solution to his present entanglement. He finally decided to have done with concealment; Kamala must know the whole truth.

Chapter 24

$\mathcal{E}$arly in the afternoon the steamer grounded on a shoal. All efforts to set her afloat proved unavailing and evening found her still fast aground. From the high bank, which marked the river's flood-level, a wide stretch of sand covered with footprints of waterfowl shelved gradually to the water's edge.

The village girls, who had flocked down to the river to fill their water-pots for the last time before dark, turned curious eyes on the steamer, the bashful ones from behind their veils, while the bolder spirits dispensed with any such concealment.

A host of urchins danced and shouted on the top of the high bank, mocking at the plight of the leviathan which was wont to steam proudly past them, rose in air.

The sun went down behind the waste of sand. Ramesh was standing by the rail gazing across the river at the western sky lit up by the last rays of sunset when Kamala stepped out of her fenced-off kitchen and, halting at the cabin door, coughed gently to attract Ramesh's attention. As he did not turn his head she took her bunch of keys and rattled it against the door. She had to rattle loudly before he turned round and, seeing her, stepped across the deck to her side.

"So that's your way of calling me, is it?" he remarked.
"I couldn't think of any other way."

"Why, what do you think my parents gave me a name for, if they didn't intend it to be used? Why not call out, 'Ramesh Babu!' when you want me for anything?"

Again that distasteful form of pleasantry. As though a Hindu wife would address her husband by his name! The hue of Kamala's cheeks vied with that of the crimson sunset. "I don't know what you're talking about!" she exclaimed with averted face. "Look here, your supper's ready; you had better eat it at once, as you didn't have a good breakfast to-day."

The river breeze had given Ramesh an appetite, though he had not mentioned this to Kamala, for fear she might overtax herself while her resources were still limited. Nevertheless, the pleasure which he felt when she — without any reminder on his part — announced supper was a complex sensation. True, one element in the feeling was the simple anticipation of satisfying physical hunger; but added to it was the exhilarating reflection that some one had taken thought for him and that a beneficent agency had been at work on his behalf. The existence of this factor he could not conceal from himself, and yet he had to face the unpleasant truth that this solicitude for his comfort was not his due and that, greatly as he valued it, it was based on a delusion. It was with a sigh and a dispirited air that he entered the cabin.

His expression did not escape Kamala's notice. "You don't look as if you wanted your supper," she said in surprise. "I thought you would be hungry. I'm sorry if I dragged you in against your will."

Ramesh at once assumed an air of cheerfulness. "It wasn't you but my own appetite that dragged me in. If you rattle your keys as loudly as that to attract my attention you'll find a harpy swooping down on the feast next time."

"Hallo, I don't see anything to eat," he went on, looking round; "I'm hungry enough but I don't fancy I could digest this sort of thing," and he pointed to the bedding and cabin furniture; "I wasn't brought up on that kind of fare."

Kamala burst into a peal of laughter; when the fit was over she remarked, "Funny that you can't wait a little longer! You didn't seem to be hungry or thirsty when you were gazing at the sunset. Your appetite came on all of a sudden when I called you in, I suppose. All right, wait a minute and I'll bring your supper."

"Well, you had better be quick; you'll only have yourself to blame if I eat up all the bed-clothes while you're fetching it."

The jest seemed to have lost nothing in the repetition and Kamala was again convulsed. Her silvery laughter rang through the cabin as she went to fetch the food. Ramesh's feigned cheerfulness changed to gloom when her back was turned.

Kamala was back soon, carrying a pan covered with *sál* leaves. She put this down on the bedding and wiped the floor clean with the fringe of her dress.

What's that you're doing?" exclaimed Ramesh.

"It's all right: I'm just going to change my clothes in any case," and taking off the leaves she daintily served up a dish of *luchis* (fried cakes) and vegetables.

"Bless my soul!" cried Ramesh, "where did you get the *luchis*?"

Kamala had no intention of letting him into the secret all at once. "Just try to guess," she responded with a mysterious air.

Ramesh fell to, making various wild conjectures about the origin of the *luchis*, much to Kamala's wrath. When

he finally suggested that "Aladdin of the Wonderful
Lamp — the fellow in the *Arabian Nights* — had sent a genie
with them piping hot from Baluchistan," she lost patience
. and turned away in chagrin, declaring that she would not
tell him at all if he were going to be so silly.

"I give it up," pleaded Ramesh, "do tell me. I really
can't guess how you produced *luchis* out in mid-river, but
they're jolly good, anyway," and he gave a practical
demonstration of the extent to which his appetite dominated
his zeal for knowledge.

The truth was this: When the steamer grounded on the
shoal Kamala had despatched Umesh to the nearest village
to replenish her empty larder. She still had a few rupees
left over from the pocket-money which Ramesh had given
her when she went to school and these she spent on flour
and *ghi* (clarified butter for frying). "What will you get for
yourself?" she asked Umesh.

"Please, mother, I noticed some nice curds at a
dairyman's in the village. We've plenty of plantains in the
cabin and if I could get a half-pennyworth of ground-rice
I could make myself a fine pudding."

Kamala sympathised with the lad's sweet tooth. "Have
you any money left, Umesh?" she asked.

"None at all, mother."

This was the crux, for Kamala shrank from proffering
a direct request for money to Ramesh. After a little reflection
she proceeded: "Well, if you can't get your pudding to-
day, there are the *luchis*, so you'll be all right. Come along
now and help me with the dough."

"What about the curds, mother?"

"Look here, Umesh, wait till your master is at supper
. and then tell him you need money for shopping."

Umesh appeared when Ramesh was half-way through
his meal and waited, scratching his head diffidently. When
Ramesh looked up at him, he murmured:

"About that money for marketing, mother."

Ramesh suddenly awoke to the consciousness that if a man will not pay us then can he eat and that he had no Aladdin's lamp at this command.

"Why, of course, you've no money, Kamala!"

Kamala tacitly admitted her fault, and after supper Ramesh handed her a small cash-box with the remark, "you had better keep your money and valuables in this for the present."

Realising that the logic of circumstances had now imposed on Kamala the whole burden of the *ménage*, he went back to the rail and stood there watching the last light fade from the western sky.

Umesh compounded his pudding of ground-rice, curds, and plantains, and ate his fill, while Kamala stood by and drew from him an account of his life.

An unwanted child in a house ruled by a stepmother, he had run away from home and was making for Benares, where one of his own mother's relations lived.

"If you'll let me stay with you, mother, I shan't want to go anywhere else," he concluded.

The maternal instinct deep down in the girl's heart was stirred by his *naiveté* in addressing her as "mother."

"All right, Umesh, you come along with us," she said encouragingly.

Chapter 25

The undergrowth that fringed the river-bank showed like a dark border to the twilight sky's saffron robe. The ducks returned in flights through the gathering dusk from their day-long sojourn on the feeding-grounds to their night-quarters in the lonely pools among the sand-banks. The crows had retired to their roosts and hushed their clamour. All boats had sought the bank except one large craft which was being towed silently upstream, making a black smudge on the dark golden-green of the still water.

Ramesh dragged a cane chair up to the bow and sat there in the faint light of the new moon. In the western sky the shades of night swallowed up the last golden glimmer of twilight, and in the witchery of the moonlight the solid earth seemed to melt into haze. Ramesh murmured to himself, "Hem, Hem"; and the beloved name twined itself round his heart with a contact ineffably sweet. The mere utterance of the name conjured up a vision of his lost mistress's eyes, moist with the dew of supreme tenderness, gazing through a mist, yet pouring forth the sorrow that lay in them. A shudder passed through his frame and tears rose to his eyes.

The whole of his life for the past two years unfolded itself before him. He recalled the occasion of his first meeting with Hemnalini; little had he realised what a fateful day it was for him! Jogendra had brought him home, and the shy youth was in great distress when he saw Hemnalini presiding over the tea-table. Little by little his bashfulness left him and he began to feel at ease in her society. As their intimacy ripened he waxed lyrical, and saw in Hemnalini the subject of all the love-poetry that he had read. He began secretly to take pride in the fact that he was in love, and he pitied those fellow-students of his who had to study love-poems for their examinations, while to him love was a living reality.

As he reflected, he realised that in those days he had stood merely at Love's outer portals. When Kamala suddenly appeared on the scene and made the riddle of his existence an insoluble one, then only, in the swirl of opposing currents, did his love for Hemnalini take true shape and become a living thing.

Ramesh let his head fall on his hands as he pondered. Life stretched before him, a life of heart-hunger that was never to be satisfied, the life of a creature caught in a net and struggling vainly to free itself. Could he not tear the net asunder if he roused himself to a mighty effort?

He threw up his head in the heat of his resolve, and as he did so he caught sight of Kamala standing close by him with her arms resting on the back of another cane chair. His gesture startled her. "You must have been asleep, and now I've wakened you!" she exclaimed, and was turning penitently to leave him when he called her back. "It's all right, Kamala; I wasn't asleep. Come and sit down, and I'll tell you a story."

The prospect of a story gave Kamala a thrill of delight; she pulled her chair close up to his and nestled into it.

Ramesh had decided that she must know the whole truth, but he felt that without some preparation the shock of his avowal would be too much for her; hence his invitation to her to sit down and hear a story.

"Once upon a time," he began, "there was a tribe of Rajputs and they——"

"When was this?" asked Kamala; "was it a long, long time ago?"

"Yes, a long time ago; you weren't born then!"

Kamala. "But you were, of course! You're such a greybeard yourself, aren't you! Well, go on."

Ramesh. "These Rajputs had a peculiar custom. When one of them was going to marry he did not go himself to the bride's house but sent his sword. She went through the wedding ceremony with the sword, then came to the Rajput's house and was married to him properly."

Kamala. "Oh, I say! What an extraordinary way of doing it!"

Ramesh. "I don't fancy it myself, but that can't be helped. It's part of the story. You see these Rajputs thought it beneath them to go in person to the bride's house to be married. The king that the story is about belonged to that tribe. One day he——"

Kamala. "You haven't told me what place he was king of."

Ramesh. "He was king of Madura; one day he——"

"You must tell me his name first," said Kamala, who insisted on having everything cut and dried and would take nothing for granted. Had Ramesh been aware of this he would have come better prepared to the task. He now perceived that eager as she was to hear the story she would not suffer him to omit any details.

"His name was Ranjit Singh," he went on after a moment's hesitation.

"Ranjit Singh, king of Madura," repeated Kamala; "go on now."

Ramesh. "One day the king heard from a wandering minstrel that another king of the same race as himself had a very beautiful daughter."

Kamala. "King of what country?"

Ramesh. "We'll suppose that he was king of Conjeveram."

Kamala. "Why should we suppose it? Wasn't he really king of Conjeveram?"

Ramesh. "Of course he was! Would you like to know his name too? His name was Amar Singh."

Kamala. "You haven't told me the name of the girl—the very beautiful daughter."

Ramesh. "Sorry, I forgot that too. Her name was—her name was—oh yes, her name was Chandra——"

Kamala. "It's extraordinary how you forget things. Why you forgot my name even!"

Ramesh. "Well, when the king of Oudh heard this from the minstrel——"

Kamala. "What's this about the king of Oudh? You said he was king of Madura!"

Ramesh. "You don't surely suppose that he was king of only one country! He was king of Oudh and of Madura too."

Kamala. "They were adjoining kingdoms, I suppose."

Ramesh. "Just next door to each other."

As he proceeded the vigilant Kamala detected other contradictions, but finally he succeeded in reconciling all discrepancies, and launched forth into the following narrative:

"Ranjit Singh, king of Madura, despatched a herald to the king of Conjeveram asking for the princess's hand in marriage. Amar Singh, king of Conjeveram, readily gave his consent to the match.

"Then Indrajit Singh, Ranjit Singh's younger brother, marched his forces into Amar Singh's kingdom with banners flying and a great clamour of drums and trumpets and camped in the royal park. Conjeveram city held high revel in honour of the happy occasion.

"The royal astrologers made their calculations and fixed upon an auspicious day and hour for the wedding. The time chosen was the twelfth night of the dark fortnight, two hours after mid-night. That night all houses were festooned with garlands and the whole city was illuminated to celebrate the marriage of the princess Chandra.

"And yet the princess did not know who her destined husband was. At the time of her birth the sage Paramananda Swami had announced to her father, 'The aspect of one of the planets portends evil to your daughter. When the time comes for her marriage do not divulge to her the name of the man whom she is to wed.'

"At the time appointed the princess went through the marriage ceremony with the sword. Indrajit Singh proffered the customary gifts on the bridegroom's behalf, and did obeisance to his brother's wife. Indrajit was as loyal to his brother Ranjit as Lakshman was to Rama, and he did not raise his eyes to the face of the noble maid blushing behind her well, but kept them fixed on her lovely little feet dyed with lac beneath the jingling anklets.

"On the day after the nuptials Indrajit installed the princess in a bejewelled and canopied litter and set forth for his own country. With dread in his heart, as he remembered the evil planet that threatened mishap to his daughter, the king of Conjeveram laid his right hand on her head and gave her his farewell benediction. The queen could not restrain her tears as she kissed her daughter on the lips. In the temples a thousand priests were repeating incantations to propitiate the evil destiny.

"Conjeveram is far distant from Madura — nearly a month's journey. On the second evening the Rajputs had pitched their tents on the banks of the Vetsha river and were preparing for the night's rest when the blaze of torches was descried in the neighbouring forest. Indrajit sent a man-at-arms to investigate and he brought back the following report: 'Sire, the lights are those of a party like our own returning from a wedding. They are Rajputs of our own race and are escorting a bride to her husband's home with an armed retinue. The road is unsafe, so they crave your Highness's protection and pray that you will convey them a part of the way.'

"The prince answered, 'It is a righteous duty to succour those who seek our protection; let us defend them to the best of our power,' and so the two parties joined forces.

"The third night was the last of the dark fortnight. Ahead lay a range of hills and behind was a thick forest. The weary soldiers were soon deep in repose, lulled to sleep by the chirping of crickets and the sound of falling waters.

"Then in an instant such a din arose as startled them all from their slumbers. In the Madura camp horses were galloping about madly, for some one had cut their picketing ropes. Here and there a tent was blazing and its flames reddened the moonless sky.

"The warriors perceived in a moment that they had been attacked by brigands. A desperate mêlée followed. In the darkness it was difficult to distinguish friend from foe and hopeless confusion was the result. Under cover of the tumult the brigands sacked the camp and disappeared into the mountains with their booty.

"When the fight was over the princess was nowhere to be seen. She had fled in terror from the camp and had joined a party of fugitives in the belief that they were her own people.

"As a matter of fact these fugitives belonged to the other bridal party. In the confusion the brigands had carried off the bride whom they were escorting, but they assumed that the princess Chandra was their charge and marched off with her at top-speed to their own land.

"They belonged to an insignificant tribe of Rajputs living on the Carnatic coast. The princess duly met the chief—his name was Chet Singh—who was the destined husband of the other bride.

"Chet Singh's mother welcomed the girl and escorted her to her chamber, while the assembled kinsfolk murmured, 'Never have we seen such beauty!'

"Chet Singh saw that he had won a prize, and he worshipped her inwardly, infatuated with her loveliness. The princess on her part knew what was incumbent on a virtuous wife. Looking on Chet Singh as her lawful husband she resolved to devote her life to his service.

"In a few days the restraint that these two felt in each other's society wore off; and as they talked Chet Singh discovered that the girl whom he had taken into his house as his bride was no other than the princess Chandra!"

Chapter 26

"And then?" asked Kamala eagerly; she had been following the story with bated breath.

"I only know that much; I don't know any more. Tell me yourself what you think happened in the end."

Kamala. "No, no, that's not fair. You must tell me the rest."

"Honour bright, Kamala, I'm telling you the truth! Only the first volume of the book from which I got that tale has been published so far, and I've no idea when the next volume will be out."

"Well, you're very mean; it was too bad of you!" cried Kamala in vexation.

Ramesh. "It's the author you should be angry with ... I only want to ask you this: What was Chet Singh to do with Chandra?"

Kamala thought for a long time with her eyes on the river.

"I don't know what he could do; I can't think at all," she said at last.

Ramesh paused for a minute, then went on, "Should Chet Singh tell Chandra everything?"

"What funny things you say! If he didn't tell her there would be an awful muddle; it would be simply horrid! Much better to ṭell the truth."

"Much better," repeated Ramesh mechanically; he went on again after a short pause; "Well, Kamala, suppose——"

Kamala. "Suppose what?"

Ramesh. "Supposing I were Chet Singh and you were Chandra."

Kamala. "Please don't say that sort of thing to me! I don't like it!"

Ramesh. "Well, but I must say it. What would be my duty in that case and what would be yours?"

Kamala did not answer this question. Instead, she rose abruptly from her chair and left him. She came upon Umesh sitting at the door of their cabin in silent contemplation of the river.

"Umesh, have you ever seen a ghost?" she asked.

"Yes, mother, I have."

"What kind of a ghost was it? Tell me about it," and she drew up a cane stool and sat down beside him.

Left to himself Ramesh decided not to call Kamala back, for there was no doubt that she was seriously annoyed. The tiny wisp of the new moon disappeared from view behind the bamboo clumps. The lights on the deck had been extinguished and the ship's company had retired below for food and rest. There were no other cabin passengers, and the bulk of the third-class folk had dropped over the steamer's side and waded ashore to cook their supper on the bank. Landward the lights of the village street shone here and there between the thickets. The strong current in mid-stream tugged at the anchor chain, and now and then a throb of the great river's pulse set the whole steamer vibrating.

In this strange environment, under the vast canopy of the night-sky, Ramesh strove hard to solve the knotty problem that his conscience set him. Clearly, he must give up either Kamala or Hemnalini; there was no possible compromise by which he could retain both in his life. Nor was there any doubt which way duty pointed. Hemnalini had alternatives; she could dismiss him from her mind and give her hand to another suitor; but to forsake Kamala would be to cast her naked on the world. And yet—such a selfish being is man—Ramesh found no consolation in the fact that Hemnalini might forget him, that she had other resources, and that her sole salvation did not lie in him. Rather the thought intensified his craving for her. She seemed to hover before his vision, just out of reach, as though he had only to stretch out his hands to grasp her.

He had let his head fall on his hands as he meditated. In the distance a jackal howled and set some of the village dogs barking incontinently. He raised his head at the sound and his eyes fell on Kamala standing near him in the darkness by the rail. He rose from his chair. "Haven't you gone to bed yet, Kamala? It's quite late."

"Aren't you going to bed?"

"I'm just going; I've put my bedding in the starboard cabin. You shouldn't wait up any longer."

Kamala crept silently away to the cabin which had been allotted to her. She could not bring herself to tell Ramesh that she had just been listening to a ghost-story and that she dreaded solitude. The obvious reluctance shown in her dragging gait caused Ramesh a pang.

"Don't be afraid, Kamala," he called to her, "my cabin is next to yours and I'll leave the door open between them."

Kamala tossed her head defiantly. "What is there to be afraid of?"

Ramesh extinguished the light in his cabin and lay down to sleep.

"I can never desert Kamala," he said to himself, "so farewell, Hemnalini! This is my final decision and there must be no more wavering." But as he lay in the darkness he brooded over all that he was losing in renouncing Hemnalini till his thoughts became unbearable, and he sprang up and quitted his cabin. The deep gloom of the over-arching sky forced on him the conviction that, after all, his shame and his heartache were not infinite things encompassing all time and space. Those stars shining overhead were things of eternity, and the pitiful little story of the loves of Ramesh and Hemnalini would never even reach them. On how many such autumn nights would the great river flow on through the starlight by sandy shoal, waving reeds, and tree-girt sleeping village long after Ramesh's mortal frame, burnt to ashes on the pyre, had mingled with the much-enduring earth, and his troubled spirit was forever still!

Chapter 27

$\mathcal{K}$amala awoke while it was still dark and looking round perceived that she was alone; it was a minute or two before she realised where she was. She dragged herself from her couch, opened the door, and looked out. A thin blanket of white mist lay over the still water, a grey pallor overspread the darkness, and there was a glimmer of dawn in the sky behind the trees that lined the eastern bank. As she gazed the white sails of fishing boats began to dot the steely-hued water.

There was a dull ache in Kamala's heart, the source of which she could not divine. Why was the aspect of the misty autumn morning so forbidding? Whence came those sobs that welled up in her breast, choked her utterance, and threatened to bring the tears to her eyes? Why did she brood now over her forlorn condition? Twenty-four hours ago she had been oblivious of the fact that both she and her husband were orphans, that she had no kin or companion of her own. What had happened in the meantime to bring her loneliness home to her? Was not Ramesh alone sufficient prop and stay? Why was she weighed down with a sense of the vastness of the universe and her own insignificance?

As she lingered by the open door, the bosom of the river began to glow like a stream of shimmering gold. The crew resumed their labours and the engines clanked again. The rattle of the hawse-chain and the creaking of the windlass awoke the village urchins betimes and sent them scampering down to the bank.

The din aroused Ramesh too, and brought him to the door of his cabin in search of Kamala. She gave a start of surprise when she saw him, and discreetly veiled though she was already, she essayed to shroud her face still more completely.

"Have you had a wash yet, Kamala?" Ramesh asked.

It seemed an innocent enough question, affording no excuse for loss of temper; and yet she obviously did take offence, for she turned away and merely shook her head.

"People will be about soon," he went on; "you had better get ready now."

Kamala said nothing in reply; she snatched up her day-apparel from the chair on which it lay and marched off past him towards the bathroom.

That Ramesh should rise early in order to superintend her toilet seemed to Kamala not only unnecessary but an impertinence. She was quite aware that in his dealings with her he drew a line, and that he never overstepped it in the direction of familiarity. She had never sat at a mother-in-law's feet and learned the usual lessons in deportment—when and where modesty prescribes the use of the veil. Yet she was unaccountably overcome with shyness in Ramesh's presence that morning.

When Kamala returned to her cabin after bathing, her day's work lay before her. She took out the bunch of keys from the loose end of her garment which was flung over her shoulder and proceeded to open the trunk containing her clothes, but as she did so the little cash-box which

Ramesh had presented to her caught her eye. Yesterday it
had seemed to her a new delight, its possession had given
her a sense of power and independence, and she had locked
it up as carefully as any costly treasure; but to-day the thrill
of pleasure with which she had handled it was absent. The
box after all was Ramesh's property, not her own; she was
not its sole owner and it was not at her unquestioned
disposal; she could only regard it as a responsibility.

"You're very quiet," remarked Ramesh, entering the cabin;
"did you find a ghost in the box when you opened it?"

"This is yours," said Kamala, holding the cash-box out
to him.

"What am I to do with it?" he asked.

"You have only to tell me when you need anything and
I'll have it fetched for you."

"But won't you need anything yourself?"

"I don't want any money," answered Kamala, with a
slight toss of her head.

Ramesh smiled. "It's not many people who can say as
much! However, if you value it so little why not make a
present of it to a stranger? Why give it to me of all people?"

Without a word Kamala laid the cash-box on the floor.

"Now just tell me the truth, Kamala," Ramesh went
on, "are you annoyed because I didn't tell you the end of
that story?"

"I'm not annoyed," replied Kamala, with her eyes on
the ground.

Ramesh. "All right then, stick to that box. If you do that
I'll know you're telling the truth."

Kamala. "I don't see the connection. It's your property,
and you ought to keep it."

Ramesh. "But it isn't mine! People who take back gifts
become ghosts when they die. Do you think I want to be
a ghost?"

The idea of Ramesh as a ghost tickled Kamala and she could not restrain her laugher.

"Certainly not! Do people who take back gifts really become ghosts? I never heard that. Hostilities came to an end with Kamala's involuntary merriment.

"There's only one way to find out the truth," said Ramesh, "and that is to ask a ghost about it yourself next time you meet one."

Kamala's curiosity was aroused. "Seriously, have you ever seen a real ghost?" she asked.

"Not a real one; I've seen lots of imitations; the genuine article is rare!"

Kamala. "Well, Umesh says——"

"Umesh; who is Umesh?"

Kamala. "Why, the boy who's travelling with us. He has see a ghost."

Ramesh. "Well, I must confess he has the advantage of me there!"

Meanwhile after a great struggle the crew had succeeded in getting the vessel afloat. She had not steamed far when the figure of a boy appeared on the bank. He carried a basket on his head and was running at top-speed and waving his arms as a signal to the boat to stop. The skipper took not the slightest notice of his predicament. Catching sight of Ramesh the runner hailed him, "Babu! Babu!"

"Takes me for the ticket-babu," remarked Ramesh, and signed to him that he had no control over the steamer's proceedings.

"Why, it's Umesh!" exclaimed Kamala; "we can't leave him behind. You must have him taken on board."

"They won't stop for me," said Ramesh.

"Oh, you must tell them to stop!" cried Kamala, genuinely distressed. "Do tell them. We're quite close to the bank."

Ramesh accosted the skipper accordingly with a request to stop the steamer.

"It's against the rules, sir," was all the answer he received.

Kamala had followed Ramesh and she now joined her entreaties to his. "You mustn't leave him behind! Do stop for a moment! My poor Umesh!"

Ramesh now resorted to a simple method of overcoming the master's scruples, and for a suitable consideration the man stopped the vessel and took the lad on board. He then proceeded to administer a dressing-down to the culprit. Umesh, however, did not turn a hair; he laid his basket at Kamala's feet and grinned as though nothing had happened.

"It's no laughing matter," said Kamala, who had not quite recovered her equanimity." What would have happened to you if the steamer had not stopped?"

Instead of replying Umesh turned over the basket and emptied out on the deck a bunch of green plantains, an assortment of spinach, and a number of pumpkins and brinjals.

"Where did you get all these?" demanded Kamala.

The account that Umesh gave would not have been classed by the police as "satisfactory." On the day before, when he had gone to the village market to buy curds and other provisions, he had noted where these vegetables were growing in various gardens and on various roofs, and going ashore early that morning while the steamer was still aground he had made his selection without asking anyone's leave.

"What do you mean by stealing things from people's gardens?" thundered Ramesh.

"It wasn't stealing; I only took a little from each garden. No one's any the worse."

"So it isn't theft when you only take a little! You rascal! Get out of my sight, and take these things with you!"

Umesh looked appealingly at Kamala. "Mother, this kind of spinach is what we call *piring* in my part of the country; it makes fine stew; and this we call *beto*, and——"

"Clear out!" cried Ramesh, thoroughly exasperated by this time," you and your spinach, or I'll kick the lot into the river."

Umesh looked to Kamala for guidance and she signed to him to take the stuff away. He gauged from her manner that she still had a soft place in her heart for him, and collecting the vegetables he replaced them in the basket and sauntered off with them.

"It was very wrong of him; you mustn't countenance that sort of thing," was Ramesh's comment as he went off to his cabin to write a letter.

Kamala looked round and espied Umesh sitting at the stern beyond the second-class deck near her improvised kitchen.

There being no second-class passengers Kamala went up to where he was sitting, after first veiling herself in a shawl. "Well, have you thrown the things away?" she asked.

"Oh, no; I put them all in the deck-house here."

"It was very naughty of you, you know," said Kamala, trying to look stern. "You're never to do it again. Think what would have happened if you had been left behind!" She went into the deck-house and called out peremptorily, "Bring me a chopper!"

Umesh obeyed, and Kamala began to slice up the appropriated vegetables.

"Pounded mustard goes very well with that spinach, mother," remarked Umesh.

"All right, get some ready," said Kamala.

She was anxious to avoid the appearance of giving countenance to Umesh's misdeeds, and it was with a very severe expression that she sliced up spinach, pumpkins, and brinjals.

Alas! How could she do other than countenance the helpless waif? She herself regarded the theft of garden-stuff as a trifle compared with the homeless lad's craving for protection. There was a touch of pathos about the affair that appealed to her; it was to please her that the scapegrace had planned and carried out his raid on the gardens, nearly losing the steamer thereby.

"There's some of yesterday's curds left over, Umesh," she said, "and you can have them, but remember never to do such a thing again."

"Didn't you eat the curds yesterday, mother?" he asked penitently.

"I'm not as fond of them as you are. Look here now, we have everything except fish. How are we to get some fish for your master's breakfast?"

"I can get you some fish, mother, but you'll have to pay for it this time."

Kamala had to administer another scolding. "I never saw such a silly boy as you, Umesh," she said, trying to knit her beautiful brows. "As if I ever told you to get things without paying for them!"

The previous day's incident had somehow given Umesh the notion that Kamala found it a difficult undertaking to extract money from Ramesh, and for this and other reasons he had conceived a dislike for his employer. Only the two dependents — himself and Kamala — came within the purview of the schemes that he devised for keeping the wolf from the door. There was no place for Ramesh in them.

The provision of vegetables was a comparatively simple matter, but fish was not so easily procured. A world so constituted that without money one could not obtain even a small quantity of fish and curds for the object of one's adoration appeared to Kamala's youthful worshipper a hard and unsympathetic place.

"If you could only get five annas out of master," he said disconsolately, "I could get you a big carp, mother."

"That won't do," said Kamala reprovingly. "I can't allow you to leave the steamer again. They won't let you on board another time if you're left behind."

"I don't want to go ashore; the crew netted some big fish this morning and they could sell us one or part of one."

Kamala at once fetched a rupee and gave it to him.

"Pay for it out of that and bring back the change."

Umesh duly produced the fish, but there was no change. "They wouldn't take less than a rupee," he announced.

Kamala knew that this was not the literal truth, and she observed, with a smile:

"Next time the steamer stops we'll have to get some rupees changed."

"Yes, indeed," said Umesh, with becoming gravity; "once you show them a whole rupee it's a job to get any of it back."

"My eye! this is good," remarked Ramesh a little later as he fell to his breakfast, "but where did you get it? Why, here's a carp's head," and he held it up with a ceremonious air. "It's neither a dream, nor an optical illusion, nor a figment of the imagination, but the genuine headpiece of Cyprinus Rohita!"

That day's breakfast was a great success. After Ramesh had retired to a long chair on the deck to let his meal digest it was Umesh's turn. His enjoyment of the fish-stew was so great that he went on eating steadily till Kamala from being amused became seriously alarmed. "Don't take any more just now, Umesh," she cried anxiously, "I've put some by for your supper."

Her varied activities and her sense of humour imperceptibly weaned Kamala from her morning fit of depression. The day wore on, and the sun sloping westward worked his way steadily across the deck under the awning. Over the throbbing steamer the air shimmered in the afternoon heat. Down the narrow tracks that threaded the fresh green of the autumn crops flocked rustic matrons, water-pot on hip, bound for their evening ablutions. Kamala was busy all the afternoon preparing *pán*, braiding her hair, washing, and changing her clothes, and the sun had set behind the bamboo clumps that marked the sites of villages before she was ready for the evening.

As on the previous day, the steamer lay up for the night off one of its regular landing-places. Kamala had just decided that the vegetables left over from breakfast would serve for supper, and that there was not much cooking to be done, when Ramesh came and announced that he had eaten such a hearty meal at midday that he did not require any supper.

"Won't you have anything at all?" asked Kamala regretfully, "not even a little fried fish?"

"No, thank you," he replied curtly and went away, whereupon Kamala heaped the whole of the savoury mess on Umesh's plate.

"Haven't you kept any for yourself?" he asked.

"I've had my supper," was her reply, and the labours of her little water-borne *ménage* were over for the day.

The new moon was now spreading its radiance over stream and shore. There was no village close to the steamer-station, and the silent lustrous night seemed to be keeping vigil, like a lady whose lover has not kept tryst, over the soft green expanse of the rice-fields.

On a stool in the tin-roofed office on the bank sat a wizened little clerk, totalling figures by the light of a kerosene lamp. Ramesh could see him through the open door. "Would that Fate," he sighed, "had set me in some groove like that clerk's — narrow but clearly defined! What harm could come to one in such a life — writing up accounts all day, scolded by one's master when one makes mistakes, and going home at night with a day's work behind one?"

By and by the light in the office went out. The clerk wrapped his head in a shawl to keep out the night air and slowly disappeared from view across the deserted fields.

Kamala had been standing for some time behind him by the rail, but Ramesh was unaware of her presence. She had expected a summons from him after the evening meal. Her work was now over but no summons had come, so she had herself emerged quietly on to the deck.

But at sight of Ramesh she came to a sudden halt and her limbs refused to carry her farther. The moon shone on his face and his expression showed that his mind was far away — far away from her; she had no place in his thoughts. Between Ramesh, absorbed in his reverie, and herself she seemed to see the spirit of Night like a gigantic sentinel clad from head to foot in a robe of moonlight, with a finger laid on its lips.

When Ramesh covered his face with his hands and let his head sink upon the table Kamala stole away to her own cabin. She dared not make a sound lest he should hear it and discover that she had come in search of him.

Her cabin loomed dark and forbidding. She shivered as she crossed the threshold, and the full consciousness of her forlorn and solitary state swept over her like a flood. In the darkness the interior of the ramshackle little room seemed to gape at her like the jaws of some strange monster; but what other shelter could she seek? there was no spot in which she could lay her poor little body down and close her eyes with the knowledge that it was hers by right.

She peered in once, then shrank back again. As she recrossed the threshold Ramesh's umbrella fell with a clatter against her tin trunk.

Startled by the noise Ramesh glanced up and rose from his chair. "It's you, Kamala!" he exclaimed, perceiving her standing in the doorway of her cabin. "I thought you had turned in long ago. I'm afraid you're a bit nervous. Look here, I shan't stay outside any longer. I'm going to sleep in the next cabin and I'll leave the door open between us."

"I'm not afraid," said Kamala haughtily. She stepped hastily into her cabin again and closed the door which Ramesh had opened; then she flung herself down on her bed and muffled her face in a shawl. She was acutely conscious of the loneliness of her own personality, utterly bereft of human companionship. Her whole being rose in revolt. If she were neither to have a protector nor to be her own mistress, life would indeed be insupportable!

Time dragged; Ramesh was sound asleep in the neighbouring cabin. Kamala could be still no longer; and she rose slowly, went out and stood by the rail, gazing at the river-bank.

There was no sight or sound of any living creature. The moon was near its setting and the narrow paths through the crops were now invisible, but Kamala strained her eyes towards them. "What numbers of women must have carried water up these paths, each bound to her own home!" she reflected. Home! Her heart leapt at the thought. If only she had a little home somewhere! but where?

The banks of the river seemed to stretch unendingly into space. Overhead the huge vault of the sky extended from pole to pole; earth and sky both alike useless to her in their immensity! To the human atom all this illimitable vastness was hopelessly inadequate, for what she desired was a little home.

Kamala was startled to find someone standing by her. "It's all right, mother, its' only I" — the voice was Umesh's.

"It's very late; why aren't you asleep?"

Then at last the tears streamed into her eyes; there was no damming them and they fell in big drops. Kamala turned away to hide her face from Umesh.

A water-laden cloud glides along till it meets a fellow-wanderer in the shape of a breeze; then it can no longer sustain its load. Thus with Kamala; a word of sympathy from the poor homeless lad and she could not hold back the tears that welled up in her breast. She essayed to speak but sobs choked her utterance.

In his distress Umesh cast about four means to console her. After a long silence he blurted out, "I say, mother, there's seven annas left out of the rupee that you gave me."

The current of Kamala's tears was checked, and she smiled and loved him for his inapposite remark. "Keep the money for the present," she said. "Now be off to bed."

The moon sank behind the trees. This time Kamala's weary eyes closed as soon as she laid her head on the pillow. In the morning the sun's imperious summons to arise found her still buried in slumber.

Chapter 28

Kamala began the next day with a feeling of lassitude; the sunlight seemed to lack lustre, the river flowed languidly, and the trees on the bank drooped like tired wayfarers.

When Umesh came to assist her with her work she said wearily, "Run away, Umesh; you mustn't worry me to-day"; but Umesh was not easily repressed.

"I'm not going to worry you, mother; I've just come to grind the spices."

Later her haggard look attracted Ramesh's notice. "Are you not feeling well, Kamala?" he asked, but he received no reply. Kamala signified by an emphatic shake of her head that she considered his inquiry superfluous and in bad taste, and departed towards the kitchen.

Ramesh realised that every day that passed accentuated the complexity of his problem and that there must be no further delay in finding a solution. He came to the conclusion that if he could only unbosom himself to Hemnalini, it would be easy to decide where his duty lay. After prolonged reflection he sat down to write to Hem.

He had been writing for some time and then erasing what he had written, when he heard a strange voice.

"May I inquire your name, sir?" and he looked up in surprise. He saw before him an elderly gentleman with a grey moustache and hair that thinned over the forehead.

Ramesh's mind had been concentrated on his letter and he could not immediately collect his scattered wits.

"You're a Brahman, aren't you?" the stranger went on. "Good-morning to you. Your name is Ramesh Babu; that much I know already. In our country, you see, asking a man's name is the first step to acquaintance, so it's really an act of courtesy, but nowadays it offends some people. If you're offended you must repay the insult with interest! You've only to ask me and I'll tell you my own name and my father's name too. In fact I shan't mind telling you my grandfather's name!"

Ramesh laughed. "I'm not so deeply offended as all that! If you tell me your own name I'll be quite satisfied."

"My name is Trailakya Chakrabartti, and I'm known to every one up-river as 'Uncle.' You've read your history, I suppose? Bharata was 'King Chakrabartti' — that means 'Emperor' — of Hindustan, and in the same way I'm 'Uncle Chakrabartti' of the whole west-country. You're sure to hear all about me when you go west. By the say, sir, where are you bound for?"

"I haven't decided yet where to leave the steamer."

Trailakya. "You're in no hurry to decide where to disembark. When it's a question of embarking, one had to decide in a hurry!"

"I heard the steamer whistle as I left the train at Goalundo. I realised then that she wouldn't wait till I made up my mind where I was going. So I employed haste where haste was essential."

Trailakya. "I take off my hat to you, sir; you're the sort of man whom I admire. You and I are the exact opposite. I have to make up my mind before I go on board a steamer because I'm an irresolute sort of person. I respect a man who can make up his mind to start though he doesn't know where he's bound for. Is your wife on board, sir?"

Ramesh felt a momentary scruple against answering this question in the affirmative.

Chakrabartti observed his hesitation and went on: "You must forgive me, but I have already learnt from a most reliable source that she is on board. Your good lady happened to be cooking when my own hunger led me in the direction of the kitchen. I said to her, "Madam, you mustn't be shy of me. I'm "Uncle Chakrabartti" of the west-country.' What a perfect little housewife she is! I went on to say, 'I see you're in possession of the kitchen; I've no one to look after me and I hope you won't deny me my share of the good things.' She smiled so sweetly that I knew she would be kind to me and that my troubles were over. You know, I always look out an auspicious day in the almanac before I set off on a journey, but I don't strike such luck as this every time! I see you're busy, so I shan't intrude on you any longer. If you'll allow me I'll go and lend a hand to the little lady. She mustn't soil her pretty hands with the tongs while I'm there. Now don't get up, please. You just go on with your writing. I know how to introduce myself"; and taking leave of Ramesh "Uncle Chakrabartti" strolled off towards the kitchen.

"There's a glorious smell coming from this place," he remarked as he entered. "One can tell it's fish-pilao before one tastes it. I must make you some buttermilk, though. It's only people living in the heat of the north-west that can make a good job of buttermilk. I know what you're thinking—you're wondering what the old man's talking about and how he can make buttermilk without tamarinds! Well, you won't need to bother about tamarinds while I'm here. Just wait a minute while I make my preparations";

and he fetched a small pot wrapped up in paper and containing pickles. "When I've made the buttermilk you take what you want for to-day and keep the rest for four days. Then taste it and you'll see that Uncle Chakrabartti makes no vain boast when he says he can prepare buttermilk. Run away now and wash your hands; it's nearly breakfast-time. I'll finish what cooking there is to be done. Now don't be nervous; I've had plenty of experience. My wife has always been delicate and I've learned how to prepare buttermilk from making it for her to tempt her appetite. You're laughing at the old man, but I'm not joking, it's the honest truth!"

"You'll have to teach me how to make it," said Kamala, smiling.

"Steady on! I can't impart knowledge as readily as all that! The goddess of learning will look askance at me if I impair the dignity of knowledge by communicating it on the first day of our acquaintance. You'll have to flatter the old man for three or four days first. You won't have to puzzle your brains to find out how to satisfy me, I'll explain that to you myself. Rule No. 1 is: I'm very fond of *pán*, but I don't like to take my betel nuts whole. It's not easy to make a conquest of me, but you've accomplished a lot already, my dear, with that sweet face of yours. Hullo you! what's your name?" but Umesh made no response; he was not at all pleased at the old man's advent, for he did not relish the idea of a rival in Kamala's affections.

"A nice boy!" continued the old man, "he doesn't let you know all at once what's going on in his mind, but I'm sure he and I'll get on capitally together. Now we mustn't waste any more time, I must hurry up with my cooking."

The old man's society served to fill up the blank in Kamala's existence, while his appearance on the scene was a relief to Ramesh also. The pronounced contrast between Ramesh's present manner and the unrestrained intimacy which had characterised their relations in the first few months, when he had believed Kamala to be his wedded wife, had inevitably wounded the girl's feelings. Anything that would tend to divert her thoughts from him was welcome and would leave him free to see a cure for his own heartache.

While Ramesh was ruminating Kamala appeared at the door of her own cabin. Her intention was to claim Chakrabartti's company throughout the long-drawn taskless afternoon, but when the old man noticed her he exclaimed at once, "It's not good enough, my dear! No it won't do at all." Kamala could not construe this dark saying; the outburst at once surprised her and awakened her curiosity.

"Why, those shoes of course," the old man went on in answer to her inquiring look. "Ramesh Babu, this is your doing. Say what you like it's a positive impiety. He despises his country who interposes anything between his feet and her sacred soil. If Ram Chandra had made Sita wear 'Dawson's' boots do you think Lakshman would have stuck to them for the fourteen years that they spent in the forests? You may laugh, Ramesh Babu! you're not really convinced and I'm not surprised. Anything is possible with people who jump on board a steamer when they hear the whistle without troubling about her destination!"

"Well, Uncle," said Ramesh, "you had better decide where we are to disembark. Your recommendation will carry more weight than a blast from a steamer's whistle."

"Dear me, you've learned very quickly how to make up your mind. Why, we've only known each other for a few hours. Well, you had better get off at Ghazipur. Will you come to Ghazipur, my dear? They grow fine roses there, and that's where this old admirer of yours lives."

Ramesh looked at Kamala and she at once nodded to show that she approved of the suggestion.

Chakrabartti and Umesh now settled down for the afternoon in Kamala's cabin, somewhat to her embarrassment, leaving Ramesh disconsolate outside. The steamer ploughed on steadily, and in the bright hues of the autumn sunshine the banks slid past like some peaceful but ever-changing vision — a panorama of rice-fields, landing-places, sandy slopes, farm-steadings, and tin-roofed markets, with here and there a little group of travellers waiting under the shade of an ancient banyan tree for the ferry-boat. From time to time the ripple of Kamala's laughter in the neighbouring cabin reached Ramesh's ear through the pleasant stillness of the autumn afternoon. "How beautiful it all is and how remote!" was the refrain that it set up in his heart.

Chapter 29

At Kamala's age doubts, fears, and anxiety find no abiding-place in the heart. Time no longer hung heavy on her hands and she had no inclination to brood over Ramesh's attitude towards her.

The autumn sunshine displayed the countryside in its most varied aspects, with the golden river as a setting to the whole. Kamala delighted in her role of mistress of a little household, and each day, as it went by, was like a fresh page in some book of artless poems.

She faced the day's work every morning with renewed ardour. Umesh did not miss the steamer again, and he always returned from foraging expeditions with a full basket, and its contents never failed to excite wonder among the members of the little party.

"My goodness, look at the gourds! Where on earth did you get the beans? Look, Uncle, he has brought sour beets! I never knew one could get such things in these up-country places." Such were the exclamations that might be heard any morning over the basket.

Only when Ramesh was present was there a jarring note, for he always suspected pilfering. Kamala would exclaim, "Why, I counted the money out to him myself!"

and Ramesh would reply, "That only gives him a twofold opportunity; he can steal both the money and the vegetables!" Then he would summon Umesh and bid him to give an account of his expenditure.

Of course the boy's figures could never be made to agree. If one went by his own statements the amount that he had spent always exceeded the amount that had been given him; but that did not disturb Umesh in the slightest. As he said himself, "If I could keep accounts correctly I shouldn't be here at all, I'd be bailiff of an estate, shouldn't I, grandpapa?"

Then Chakrabartti would put in a word. "Adjourn the case till after breakfast, Ramesh Babu; you'll be able to deliver a sound judgement then. For the moment I can't resist taking the boy's side. Umesh, my lad the art of acquisition is no easy one, and it's not many people that can practise it. Many try, but few succeed. I know how to appraise talent when I find it, Ramesh Babu. This isn't the season for beans and I don't think there are many boys who would manage to get you some so early in the morning in a strange place. Any one is capable of suspecting, sir; it's only one in a thousand who can acquire!"

Ramesh. "Now this isn't right, Uncle; you shouldn't take his side."

Chakrabartti. "He hasn't many talents and if we allow this one to run to waste for lack of encouragement we'll regret it before we leave this steamer. Look here, Umesh, I'll want some *zim* leaves to-morrow—the higher up the tree the better they are. I need something like that, my dear. They call me a physician—well, blow the physic, I'm wasting time! Mind and wash the greens well, Umesh."

The more Ramesh suspected and scolded Umesh the closer was the boy drawn to Kamala. With the adherence of Chakrabartti, Kamala's party became independent of

Ramesh. Ramesh and his scruples were left out in the cold while Chakrabartti, Umesh, and Kamala worked and played together with mutual sympathy as the cement of their alliance. Chakrabartti, since his arrival, had infected Ramesh with some of the fervour of his devotion to Kamala, yet Ramesh could not go the length of enrolling himself among her followers. He was like a vessel of great draught which cannot lie up against the bank, but has to anchor in midstream and contemplate the land from a distance while small boats and skiffs pass easily over the shallows.

The moon was now nearly full. One morning the travellers rose to find the sky overspread with dark clouds while the breeze veered from one point of the compass to another. Showers alternated with spells of sunshine. There was no other craft in midstream. A few boats were to be seen inshore, but their movements betrayed the uneasiness of their crews. Women who descended to the waterside to fill their jars did not linger there long, and now and then the surface of the river seemed to shiver from bank to bank.

The steamer ploughed on as usual and Kamala did not allow the elements to interfere with her culinary operations.

"You may not be able to cook this evening," remarked Chakrabartti, with a glance at the sky, "so you had better get food ready for supper now. If you put the kedgeree on now I'll mix some dough for bread."

It was late before they all finished breakfast. The squalls gradually increased in violence and the river foamed up in billows. The sun disappeared behind banks of clouds long before nightfall and no one marked his setting. The anchor was dropped betimes.

Night fell and the moon gleamed out now and then from among the ragged clouds with a wan delirious smile. The wind rose to a hurricane and the rain came down in sheets.

Kamala had suffered shipwreck once and the force of the gale naturally alarmed her. "There's nothing to be afraid of, Kamala," said Ramesh reassuringly; "we're safe enough on the steamer. Go to sleep and don't worry about it. I'll be in the next cabin and I shan't go to bed just yet."

Chakrabartti came to her door next. "Don't be frightened, dear; I dare this cursed storm to touch you!" Cursed though the storm might be, there was no doubt about its effect on Kamala. She sprang to the door and cried beseechingly, "Come in and sit beside me, please, Uncle!"

Chakrabartti hesitated. "It's time you people were in bed. I had better——" He stepped inside as he spoke and at once noticed that Ramesh was not in the cabin. "Why, where's Ramesh Babu?" he exclaimed in surprise; "he surely hasn't gone off to steal vegetables on a wild night like this!"

"Hallo, is that you, Uncle? I'm in here, next door."

Chakrabartti peeped into the adjoining cabin and saw Ramesh lying propped up in bed reading a book in the lamplight.

"Your good lady's nervous, all by herself," he remarked, "you had better put away your book seeing that you can't frighten the storm away with it! Come along in here."

An uncontrollable instinct deprived Kamala of her self-command. "No, no, Uncle!" she ejaculated in a half-stifled voice, seizing him by the hand. In that howling tempest her voice did not penetrate to Ramesh's ears, but Chakrabartti heard and turned back in dismay.

Ramesh laid down his book and entered the other cabin. "What's the mater, Uncle Chakrabartti?" he asked; "Kamala and you seem to be——"

"No, no!" interjected Kamala, without looking up at Ramesh; 'I just asked him to come in for a chat." What

she was negativing when she exclaimed, 'No, no!" she did
not herself know, but the meaning behind the words was,
"If you think I need someone to allay my fears you're
mistaken; I don't! If you imagine that I require company
you're wrong; I do not!"

"It's getting late, Uncle," she went on, "you had better
go to bed; you might just see if Umesh is all right. I'm afraid
he may be frightened at the storm."

"Nothing frightens me, mother," said a voice in the
darkness outside; Umesh, it appeared, was sitting shivering
outside his mistress's door.

Touched by his devotion Kamala hurried out, crying,
"Umesh, you're just getting soaked with the rain! Run
away, you bad boy, and sleep in Uncle's cabin."

Umesh trotted off obediently with Uncle Chakrabartti.
Affectionate though her tone was, the fact that Kamala
had called him a bad boy impressed the lad.

"Shall I talk to you till you go to sleep?" Ramesh asked
Kamala.

"No, thank you. I'm very sleepy."

Ramesh fully understood the current of Kamala's
thoughts, but he did not attempt to gainsay her. He saw
at a glance the injured pride in her expression and slunk
away to his own cabin.

Kamala was far too agitated to compose herself to
sleep, but she forced herself to lie down. The waves were
now running high as the storm increased in violence. The
deck-hands were astir and at intervals the ting-ting of the
telegraph conveyed some order from the master to the
engine-room. The anchor alone did not suffice to hold the
steamer in the teeth of the gale and the engines were now
working slowly.

Kamala threw off her bedclothes and stepped out on
to the deck. The rain had ceased for the moment, but the

wind roared like a stricken creature as it veered from one quarter to another.

The night was overcast, and a full moon faintly illumined the wild sky in which clouds scurried before the storm like spirits of destruction. The banks were almost blotted out, the surface of the river was barely visible, but sky and earth, the near and the distant, the seen and the unseen, were all blended in one swirling tumult which seemed to take shape as the fabled black buffalo of King Death, a hideous monster tossing its horned head aloft in fury.

Kamala could not define the emotion that stirred in her breast as she gazed upon the wild sky and the turmoil of the night; it may have been fear and it may have been joy.

There was an untamed force, an untrammelled freedom, in the raging of the elements that struck some dormant chord in her soul. The violence of Nature's revolt fascinated her. Against what was Nature rebelling? In the roaring of the tempest Kamala heard no answer to this question. The reply was inarticulate, like the storm in her own breast. Surely it was an effort to tear asunder and cast aside some formless impalpable web of deceit, illusion, and obscurity that shook the earth to its foundations to the accompaniment of the agonised shrieking of the tempest.

It was "No, no!" simply a blank refusal that the whirlwind vociferated as it swept from the uttermost confines of trackless space across the blackness of the night. What, then, was it refusing? There could be no certain answer, but it was emphatically a "No, no, never; no, no, no!"

Chapter 30

*N*ext morning the gale had abated somewhat, but it still blew strongly. The skipper gazed anxiously at the sky undecided whether to weigh anchor or not.

Chakrabartti paid an early visit to Ramesh in the cabin next to Kamala's. He was still in his bunk, but he sat up at once when he saw Chakrabartti. Perceiving that he had spent the night there and remembering the previous evening's incident, the old man put two and two together. "I suppose you slept here last night?" he said inquiringly.

Ramesh evaded the question. "What a wretched morning!" he observed. "How did you sleep, Uncle?"

"Ramesh Babu," retorted Chakrabartti, "you must have been thinking me an old fool and I certainly talk like one, but I haven't come to my time of life without having to tackle many problems. I've been able to solve most of them, but you're the hardest one I've struck yet!"

Ramesh flushed involuntarily, but he quickly regained control of his features and smiled. "It isn't a crime to be insoluble, Uncle. Take a weird language like Telegu, for instance. We'd find it difficult to grasp even the rudiments, but to a Telinga child it comes as easily as winking. You mustn't be in a hurry to condemn what you don't understand. When one encounters strange symbols one shouldn't look despairingly at them and give up hope of ever being able to decipher them."

"Forgive me, Ramesh Babu," said the old man. "It would be presumptuous of me to try and understand a man whose confidence I don't possess; but it so happens now and then that one meets a fellow-creature with whom one becomes intimate at first sight. I cite that fellow with the beard—our skipper—as a witness. He'll have to admit that he looks on your little lady as a dear friend. Just ask him and if he doesn't acknowledge it he's no true Mussulman. When things are like that it's very hard to be brought up suddenly against a puzzle like the Telegu language. When you come to think it over, Ramesh Babu, you won't be offended any longer."

"It's because I have thought it over that I'm not offended. But whether I'm offended or not and whether I've hurt your feelings or not, the Telegu language remains the Telegu language. It's a cruel law of Nature," and Ramesh heaved a sigh.

Ramesh now began to wonder whether after all it was advisable to settle in Ghazipur. His first thought had been that their intimacy with the old man would be useful when it came to setting up house in a new place, but he now felt that there were disadvantages in having local acquaintances. If his relations with Kamala became a subject of discussion and inquiry it would go hard with her eventually. It would be safer to bury themselves in some place where all were strangers and there would be nobody to ask questions.

Accordingly on the day before the steamer was due at Ghazipur he remarked to Chakrabartti, "Uncle, I don't think Ghazipur would suit me professionally, so I intend to go on to Benares."

The note of decision in Ramesh's tone amused the old man. "To be constantly changing one's plans isn't decision at all, it's indecision! However, for the present you've definitely settled on going to Benares?"

"Yes," said Ramesh curtly.

The old man went off without a word and began to pack.

"Have you taken a dislike to me to-day, Uncle?" asked Kamala slyly.

"What can you expect when we quarrel from morning to night?" he replied. "You know I've never got the better of you yet!"

Kamala. "You've been avoiding me all morning."

Chakrabartti. "Do you dare to charge me with avoiding you? Why, it's you who are going to run away from me altogether."

Kamala stared at him, uncomprehending. "Hasn't Ramesh Babu told you?" the old man went on. "It has been decided that you're going to Benares.

Kamala neither admitted nor denied this.

"You'll never be able to do that, Uncle," she remarked after a short pause. "Let me pack your box for you."

Chakrabartti was deeply hurt at Kamala's indifference to the abandonment of the Ghazipur project. "Perhaps it's just as well," he said to himself. "What's the use of forming new ties at my times in life?"

Ramesh now appeared in person to announce to Kamala his change of plan. "I was looking for you," he remarked, whereupon she began to sort and fold Chakrabartti's clothes.

"We're not going to Ghazipur for the present, Kamala," Ramesh continued. "I've decided to start practising in Benares instead. Are you agreed?"

"No, I'm going to Ghazipur," replied Kamala without

lifting her eyes from Chakrabartti's trunk. "I've packed up everything already."

"Are you going there alone, then?" asked Ramesh, taken aback by Kamala's decided refusal.

"Oh no; Uncle will be there ——" this with an affectionate glance at the old man.

Chakrabartti did not altogether relish the situation. "My dear," he observed, "if you show me such partiality you'll make Ramesh Babu jealous"; but Kamala merely repeated, "I'm going to Ghazipur." Her tone showed that she considered herself at liberty to act as she pleased.

"All right, Uncle," said Ramesh, "Ghazipur let it be."

In the evening the sky cleared after the rain and Ramesh sat till late in the moonlight meditating. "We can't go on this way any longer," he said to himself. "The situation will become impossible if Kamala turns rebellious. I don't see how I'm going to live with her and yet keep my distance. I can't keep it up any longer. After all, Kamala really is my wife. I regarded her as my wife from the first, and I need have no scruples because we did not actually recite the regular formulas. Death himself gave her to me and made us one that night on the sandbank; surely he is more potent than any earthly priest!"

Between him and Hemnalini lay a hostile army in full panoply. He must fight his way through obstacles, doubts, and disgrace before he could stand before her with head erect, and he shrank from the contemplation of the battles before him. What hope had he off victory? How could he establish his innocence? Even if he could prove himself guiltless, society would draw up, as it were, her skirts from contact with him, and the result would be so disastrous for Kamala that this course was inconceivable. Away with cowardice and wavering! There was nothing for it but to make Kamala his wife indeed. Hemnalini must now regard him with aversion—an aversion which would have the advantage of inclining her favourably to the address of some other suitor. Ramesh sighed and flung his hopes of Hemnalini to the winds.

Chapter 31

"*H*allo!" cried Ramesh, "where are you off to, Umesh?"

"I'm going with mother."

Ramesh. "But I took a ticket for you as far as Benares and this is only Ghazipur. We're not going to Benares."

Umesh. "Neither am I."

Ramesh had not anticipated that Umesh would be a permanent addition to their household, but he was amazed at the boy's calm assurance.

"Are we going to take Umesh with us then?" he asked Kamala.

"He has nowhere else to go."

Ramesh. "He has some relation or other in Benares."

Kamala. "He wants to come with us instead. Now remember you're in a strange place, Umesh, and keep close to Uncle or we'll lose you in the crowd."

It was evident that Kamala had taken sole command and assumed entire responsibility for the destination and constitution of the party. The phase in which she had meekly accepted Ramesh's dictates had come to an abrupt close. Umesh accompanied them accordingly without further discussion, carrying a little bundle of clothes under his arm.

Uncle lived in a small bungalow between the city and the European quarter. In front of the house was a stone-built well and behind it a mango-orchard. The compound was separated from the road by a low wall, and between the wall and the house was a small kitchen-garden irrigated from the well. Ramesh and Kamala were offered hospitality here till they could find a house of their own.

Uncle's wife, Haribhabhini, though always described by her husband as delicate, betrayed no outward sign of a weak constitution. She was past middle age, but her face was strong and capable, and only at the temples did she show a few grey hairs. Age had, so to speak, obtained a decree against her, but had not yet executed it.

The fact was that soon after Chakrabartti married her she had fallen a victim to malarial fever, for which a change of air was, in her husband's opinion, the only cure, so he had found employment as a schoolmaster in Ghazipur and had migrated there with his family.

Haribhabhini's health had long been re-established, but her husband never relaxed his watchful care over her.

Chakrabartti ushered his guests into an outer room and then proceeded into the inner apartments in search of his wife; he found her in the walled courtyard laying her pots and pans out in the sun and winnowing wheat.

"Here you are!" cried Chakrabartti. "It's rather cold to-day. Shouldn't you be wearing a shawl?"

Haribhabhini. "What can you be thinking of? Cold! Why, the sun's scorching my back."

Chakrabartti. "That'll never do. Surely we can afford a sunshade for you."

Haribhabhini. "All right, I'll get one. Tell me now, why were you away for so long?"

Chakrabartti. "It's a long story. I've brought some guests with me, and we'll have to attend to them before we do anything else," and he briefly described the new arrivals.

It was by no means the first time that Chakrabartti had offered hospitality to strangers, but Haribhabhini was hardly prepared to receive a married couple. "Bless me, we've nowhere to put them!" she exclaimed.

"You had better see them first," said her husband, "then we can decide about accommodation for them. Where's my Saila?"

"She's bathing the child."

Chakrabartti then ushered Kamala into his wife's presence.

Kamala saluted Haribhabhini with the respect due to her years. The old lady in her turn touched Kamala on the chin, then kissed her own finger and remarked to her husband, "Don't you think her very like our Bidhu?" — Bidhu being their elder daughter, who lived with her husband in Allahabad.

Chakrabartti was secretly amused at the comparison. As a matter of fact there was not the slightest resemblance between Bidhu and Kamala, but Haribhabhini would never admit that any other girl was her own daughter's superior in beauty or attainments. Their other daughter Sailaja lived with her parents and was liable to be worsted in a contest of looks, hence the mother kept the flag flying by instituting comparisons with the absent one only.

"We're very pleased to have you," Haribhabhini went on, "but I'm afraid you won't be very comfortable. Our new house is under repair at present and it's all we can do to squeeze in here." True enough, Chakrabartti did own a small house in the bazaar which happened to be undergoing repairs at the moment; but it was not the sort of place which they could ever use as a residence nor had they ever contemplated doing so!

Chakrabartti chuckled over his wife's fib, but he did not give her away. "If you objected to discomfort I should never have brought you here," he marked to Kamala, then turned to his wife: "Well, you had better not stand out here any longer. The autumn sun isn't safe for you," and he departed in search of Ramesh.

Left alone with Kamala, Haribhabhini plied the girl with questions about herself.

"Your husband is a lawyer, isn't he? How long has he been practising? What income does he make out of it? Oh, he hasn't started practising yet? How do you live then? Did your father-in-law leave him well off? You don't know? What a queer girl you are! Don't you know anything about your husband's people? How much does your husband allow you for housekeeping every month? You ought to see to everything yourself when you've no mother-in-law, a girl of your age! My daughter Bidhu's husband hands over all his earnings to her."

With such a running fire of questions and comments the old lady soon demonstrated to Kamala her own incapacity, and the girl saw clearly how unusual and ignominious her ignorance of her husband's worldly position and family history must appear. She realised that she had hitherto never had an opportunity for a heart-to-heart talk with Ramesh about his affairs and that she knew almost nothing about his affairs and that she knew almost nothing about the man who was her husband. For the first time she felt how peculiar her position was, and a sense of her own unworthiness overwhelmed her with confusion.

Let me see your bangles, dear?" Haribhabhini began again; "the gold isn't very good, is it? Didn't your father give you any ornaments when you were married? Oh, you've no father? You should have some things all the same. Hasn't your husband given you any? Bidhu's husband manages to give her some sort of trinket every two months or so."

This cross-examination was interrupted by the entrance of Sailaja, leading her two-year-old daughter Umi by the hand. Sailaja had a dark complexion and small features, but her expression was animated and her forehead broad. She gave promise of possessing sound sense and a placid disposition.

After a brief inspection of Kamala, Sailaja's little daughter hailed her as "auntie" — not that she saw in her any resemblance to Bidhu, but she unhesitatingly classed as an "auntie" any adult female to whom she took a fancy. Kamala lifted the child on to her lap at once.

Haribhabhini introduced Kamala to Sailaja in these words: "This lady's husband is a lawyer; he has come up-country to practise his profession. They met your father on the way and he brought them here."

The eyes of the two girls met and that one look made them fast friends.

Haribhabhini went off to arrange for her guests' comfort, and Sailaja took Kamala by the hand and invited her into her own room.

It was not long before they found themselves talking quite intimately. The disparity in age between the two was hardly noticeable.

In breadth and subtlety of view Kamala was much in advance of her years. It may have been because her individuality had never undergone the chastening effects of a mother-in-law's discipline. Such phrases as "Hold your tongue!" "Do what I tell you!" "Young girls shouldn't say 'No' so often," had never been dinned in her ears. Consequently she faced the world with body erect and head held high, a graceful plant with a tough stem.

The two new-found friends soon became immersed in conversation in spite of the little girl Umi's unceasing efforts to attract all their attention to herself. Kamala could not but be aware of her conversational inferiority to the other. Sailaja had much to say, she herself almost nothing. The sketch that Kamala presented of her wedded life was a mere pencil outline, incomplete in parts and totally uncoloured.

Hitherto she had never found occasion distinctly to note the meagreness of it. She had known instinctively that something was lacking and there had been promptings to revolt, but she had never clearly envisaged what it was that was wanting.

No sooner was the ice broken than Sailaja began to talk of her husband; one had but to touch what was the keynote of her life and it gave forth no uncertain sound; but Kamala knew that she could not play on that string; she had nothing to say about her husband; for such discourse she had neither the material nor the desire.

While Sailaja's craft coursed merrily downstream with its freight of happiness, Kamala's empty bark stuck miserably in the shallows.

Sailaja's husband, Bipin, was employed in the Opium Factory at Ghazipur. Chakrabartti had only two daughters and the elder lived with her husband's people. The old man could not face separation from the younger, hence he had selected as her husband a young man without means who was content to accept the post which Chakrabartti by judicious wire-pulling obtained for him and to live with his wife's parents.

Sailaja suddenly broke off the conversation in the middle with the remark, "Excuse me for a few minutes, dear; I shan't be long." She then proceeded to explain a little self-consciously that her husband had just come in from his bath and that she must give him breakfast before he went to the office.

"How did you know he had come in?" asked Kamala in the innocence of her heart.

"Now don't make fun of me," retorted Sailaja. "How does anyone know that? Don't you know your husband's step when you hear it?"

She laughed, pinched Kamala's cheek, flung over her shoulder the loose end of her dress in which her bunch of keys was tied, snatched up Umi, and left the room.

Kamala had not known before that the language of footsteps was so easy to learn. She gazed out of the window absorbed in thought.

Outside was a guava tree; and about its blossom-laden branches, intent marauders, the bees hummed.

Chapter 32

Ramesh was now in treaty for a house which stood in an isolated position on the bank of the Ganges. To fetch his belongings and to go through the necessary formalities which would enable him to enrol himself at the Ghazipur bar, a journey to Calcutta was necessary; but he shrank from re-visiting the city. The memory of a certain street there was like a weight pressing on his mind. He was still fast in the toils of duplicity and yet matters had come to such a pitch that he could delay no longer to accept his position as Kamala's husband with all that it entailed.

Unable to face the inevitable, he kept on postponing his departure.

As space in the little bungalow was limited, Kamala had quarters in Chakrabartti's *zenana*, while Ramesh was housed in the outer rooms, and he and Kamala hardly ever saw each other. Sailaja confided to Kamala how much she regretted this unavoidable separation.

"Why make such a fuss about it?" asked Kamala. "It's nothing so very dreadful!"

Sailaja laughed, "What a hard-hearted young woman you are! You can't deceive me with that kind of pretence! I know quite well what you're thinking!"

"Now tell me the truth," began Kamala, "supposing Bipin Babu didn't come near you for a couple of days would you ——?"

"Why, he couldn't stay away from me for two days!" vaunted Sailaja, and she proceeded to cite instances of Bipin Babu's uxoriousness. She recounted the artifices to which the youth had resorted after their marriage in order to pass through the lines of their enemies — the old people — and visit his girl-bride; the times when he had been unsuccessful and the times when he had been caught; and how when all meetings had been forbidden they had consoled themselves by exchanging glances in a mirror without their elder's knowledge while Bipin was at his midday meal. Sailaja's face lit up as she recalled the fun they had enjoyed in those bygone days.

A time had come when Bipin had to attend the office all day, and she described at length how they missed each other and how Bipin would occasionally play truant and slink off home.

It had been arranged once that he should be absent in Patna for a few days in connection with his father's business. Sailaja had said to him, "Do you feel that you can go to Patna and stay there?" and he had answered boastfully, "Of course I can." The tone of his reply had hurt Sailaja's pride and she had vowed to herself that she would not show the least sign of regret on the eve of his departure; but her determination had dissolved in a flood of tears, and next day when all was ready for the journey Bipin had developed a headache and some mysterious malady which necessitated his arrangements being cancelled. Then the doctor had come and prescribed for him, and he and Sailaja had secretly poured the medicine down the drain and the patient had marvellously recovered!

To all appearances Sailaja was so absorbed in her reminiscences that she had lost all count of time; yet at a faint sound from the front gate she jumped up at once. It was Bipin Babu back from the office. While apparently immersed in her diverting memories of the past she had been listening eagerly for that distant footfall out on the road by the garden-gate.

It must not be supposed that Kamala regarded Sailaja's attitude to wedded life as mere delusion; she had had glimmerings of the same feeling herself. At times during the first few months with Ramesh a certain chord had been struck which seemed to give her the key to some of the mystery of wedlock. Later, when she had escaped from the bondage of school and returned to Ramesh, there had been moments when her soul seemed to thrill with the strange rhythm of some mystic dance. As she listened to Sailaja's recital she gained some insight into the meaning of these sensations. But there had been nothing deep or lasting in her own experiences and the impression left on her was a fleeting one. There had been nothing between Ramesh and herself to compare with the fervour that characterised the relations of Sailaja and Bipin. Her temporary separation from Ramesh had not caused her any inward pang, and she could not imagine Ramesh sitting outside the zenana trying to devise subterfuges that would afford him a glimpse of her.

When Sunday came round Sailaja found herself in a quandary. She was reluctant to leave her new friend alone for the whole day, while on the other hand she did not feel sufficiently altruistic to sacrifice the only day in the week on which she could enjoy Bipin's society. Yet she could never taste the full savour of the holiday while she knew that, though Ramesh was living under the same roof, communication between him and Kamala was barred. Alas! If she could only succeed in bringing about a meeting!

She did not consult the elders at all about her schemes, but Chakrabartti was not the sort of man who waits to be consulted. He proclaimed his intention of going out of town for the day on some urgent business, and he impressed on Ramesh that no strangers were expected and that he would lock the front door when he sallied forth. He took care that his daughter should hear this, knowing full well that the hint would not be lost on her.

"Come along, dear, and we'll dry your hair," remarked Sailaja to Kamala as they returned from their bath in the river.

"Is there any particular hurry to-day?"

"I'll tell you later; let me do your hair first," replied Sailaja, and she set to work. There seemed to be a great many braids and the resulting coiffure was an elaborate affair. The next item was a heated argument about the dress that Kamala was to wear.

Sailaja insisted on something brightly coloured, while Kamala could not understand the motive underlying her insistence. Finally, however, to humour Sailaja, she yielded the point.

After the midday meal Sailaja whispered something in her husband's ear and was granted a short leave of absence. She then tried to induce Kamala to pay a visit to the men's part of the house.

On previous occasions Kamala had shown no particular constraint about seeking Ramesh's society and she had never been taught that there was anything unconventional in such conduct. Ramesh himself had broken down the barriers of reserve at the outset and she had had no confidante of her own sex to reproach her with impropriety. Yet on this occasion she shrank from yielding to Sailaja's importunity. She knew what it was that gave Sailaja the right of access to her husband. She was not conscious of possessing the same title herself, and she could not approach Ramesh in the guise of a suppliant.

When Sailaja found that her exhortations had no effect on Kamala she came to the conclusion that the girl was too proud to take the initiative; of course pride must be at the bottom of it! The pair had now been living apart for several days and yet Ramesh had never sought a pretext to visit his wife.

The lady of the house was taking a post-prandial nap behind closed doors and Sailaja went to Bipin. "You must give Ramesh Babu a message from Kamala," she said, "inviting him to her room. Dad won't mind and mother won't know anything about it."

Bipin was a quiet, reserved youth, and he did not relish an errand of this sort; however, he did not care to spoil his Sunday peace by demurring at his wife's instructions.

Ramesh was lying on a rug in the outer room, with one knee up and his other foot resting on it, reading the *Pioneer*. He had perused all the news of the day, and for want of something better to do had turned his attention to the advertisement pages when Bipin entered the room. Ramesh rose with alacrity. "Come along in, Bipin Babu, come along!" Though Bipin was not particularly companionable he was a distinct acquisition when it came to whiling away an afternoon in a strange place.

Instead of sitting down, however, Bipin merely stood and scratched his head. "She wants you to come inside," he said.

"Who? Kamala?"

"Yes."

Ramesh was taken aback. He had decided that for the future Kamala must be his wife in fact as well as in name,

but the present enforced separation had been in the nature
of a reprieve and he had gladly relapsed into his old state
of indecision. True, he had rapturous visions of the
happiness that would be his when Kamala became his true
helpmate, but how was he to break the ice? It would be
no simple matter suddenly to throw off the restraint which
had marked his relations with Kamala of late and he could
not decide how to set about it. Consequently he had shown
no particular haste in negotiating for a house.

When he heard Bipin's announcement he assumed that
Kamala merely wished to discuss some matter of business,
and yet, though this was the view taken by his sober senses,
a wave of emotion passed over him when he heard the
summons. As he laid aside the *Pioneer* and followed Bipin
through the languorous stillness of the autumn afternoon,
broken only by the drowsy hum of bees, he experienced
something of the thrill of the lover going in quest of his mate.

Bipin pointed to a door and then left him.

Kamala had come to the conclusion that Sailaja had
abandoned her schemes and had joined her husband, and
she was sitting on the threshold of the outer door gazing
out into the garden. Sailaja had unconsciously attuned
Kamala to love. Just as the warm breeze outside set the
leaves whispering and trembling, so from time to time the
sough of a sigh in Kamala's breast set something quivering
strangely there in inarticulate anguish.

Suddenly Ramesh entered the room and stood behind
her and she started up in consternation at his low-spoken
cry of "Kamala!" The blood coursed through her veins and
she who had never felt abashed in his presence before
hung her head, unable to face him, and blushed crimson.

In her festive attire and her new-awakened self-
consciousness Kamala seemed to Ramesh a new being.
Beholding her suddenly in this guise he was thrown off

his guard and succumbed to her charm. He slowly approached and paused for a moment or two before he addressed her softly. "Did you send for me, Kamala?"

Kamala winced at his words. "Most certainly not! I did nothing of the kind. Why should I send for you?" she answered with unnecessary vehemence.

"Well, if you had sent for me it wouldn't have been a crime, Kamala."

"I never sent for you!" repeated Kamala with redoubled emphasis.

"Very well then, I have come without being invited. You won't surely send me away in disgrace on that account?"

"They'll all know that you've come and they'll be angry. Please go away at once. I didn't send for you."

"All right," said Ramesh, taking her by the hand, "you come to my room instead; there's no one else there."

Trembling in every limb Kamala tore her hand from his grasp, fled into the adjoining room, and shut the door.

Ramesh understood now what had happened; the whole thing had been a scheme concocted by one of the womenfolk. With all his nerves on edge he returned to the outer room. He lay down again, took up the *Pioneer*, and ran his eye up and down the advertisements, but he took nothing in. One perturbing thought after another coursed through his mind like clouds scurrying before the wind.

Sailaja knocked at the door that Kamala had bolted, but there was no response. She thrust her hand through the venetians, pulled back the bolt, and entered the room. To her astonishment she found Kamala prostrate on the floor, her face buried in her hands, weeping. Unable to conceive what had reduced Kamala to this pass Saila plumped down beside her and murmured gently, "What is it, dear? What's the matter? Why are you crying?"

"Oh, why did you send for him? It was very wrong of you!"

Kamala, no more than anyone else, could assign a reason for her sudden and violent outburst of grief. No one knew of the hidden sorrow that she had been cherishing for days past.

She had been building for herself castles in the air and had just put the finishing touches when Ramesh entered. Had he broken in more gently upon her vision all might have been well, but at his supposition that she had sent for him her castles crumbled to earth. His attempt to keep her a prisoner at school during the holidays, his indifference to her on the steamer, these and other memories crowded in upon her. Spontaneous intimacy was one thing, mere obedience to a summons was quite another. It was only since coming to Ghazipur that she had realised the world of difference between the two.

But Saila would never be able to understand. That there could be a real barrier between Ramesh and Kamala was beyond her powers of comprehension.

With an effort she lifted Kamala's head on to her lap, exclaiming, "Tell me, dear, did Ramesh Babu say anything unkind to you? Perhaps he was annoyed because my husband went to fetch him. You should have told him it was all my doing."

"No, no, he said nothing about that! but why did you send for him?"

"It was wrong of me," said Sailaja contritely, "you must forgive me."

Kamala sat up at once and threw her arms round Saila's neck. "Run away now, dear," she said, "Bipin Babu will be getting impatient."

Meanwhile Ramesh had been idly scanning the pages of the *Pioneer* till at last he roused himself and flung the paper from him. "Enough of this," he said to himself; "I'll go to Calcutta to-morrow and get through my business there. The longer I delay to make Kamala my wife the more of a scoundrel I feel!"

Chapter 33

*R*amesh fully intended to despatch his business in
Calcutta with all possible speed, and on no account to set
foot in Kalutola.

He went back to his old quarters in Darjjipara, but his
business occupied very little of his time each day and the
remaining hours of the twenty-four dragged interminably.
He could not face any of his former acquaintances and he
even took precautions to avoid chance encounters in the
street.

He found, however, that the return to his old haunts
had unconsciously worked a change in him. Under wide
horizons, in the unruffled peace of the countryside, the
charm of Kamala's adolescent beauty had cast its spell over
him, but here in the city the glamour had almost faded. In
the Darjjipara house Ramesh tried to conjure up the girl's
image to feast his ravished eyes on, but his imagination did
not respond. Ramesh vowed repeatedly that he would never
again harbour a thought of Hemnalini, yet her memory rose
vividly before him day and night. His rigid determination
to forget her became a potent ally to his memory of her.

Had Ramesh been at all capable of expedition he would
have finished his business and returned long before he

actually did; but with procrastination even the most trifling matters assumed alarming proportions. Even these, however, were disposed of in the end, and a day came when he decided to leave for Allahabad on the morrow and to return thence to Ghazipur. The unbending self-control that he had exercised had gone completely unrewarded. It would do no harm, he reasoned, to pay one secret visit to Kalutola before he left Calcutta.

Having decided on this course he sat down and indited a letter to Hemnalini. He gave her a full and detailed account of all his relations with Kamala, and he went the length of revealing his intention of making that helpless unfortunate his wife in reality when he returned to Ghazipur. It was a message of farewell, in which he unbosomed himself to his old love before his final and complete separation from her.

He enclosed the letter in an envelope, but neither outside nor inside did he inscribe the name of the person addressed. He knew that he would find partisans in Annada Babu's servants, for Ramesh had a soft side for all those who surrounded Hemnalini and he had been lavish with gifts in cash and kind on the slightest excuse. He planned accordingly to visit the neighbourhood as soon as dusk had fallen and to try to obtain a glimpse of Hemnalini from a distance; he would then hand the letter to one of the servants with instructions to convey it unostentatiously to Hemnalini, and this must be the final severance of the old ties between them.

At nightfall he sallied out with his letter and crept with quaking limbs and palpitating heart into that street of ineffaceable memories. He found the door closed, and looking up saw that all the windows were shuttered. The house was untenanted and in darkness.

He knocked at the door. At the third or fourth knock a bearer undid the bolts and opened.

"It's Sukhan, isn't it?" said Ramesh.

"Yes, sir, I'm Sukhan."

Ramesh. "Where has your master gone?"

Bearer. "He has gone up-country with the young mistress for a change of air."

Ramesh. "What place have they gone to?"

Bearer. "I don't know."

Ramesh. "Did any one else go with them?"

Bearer. "Yes, Nalin Babu."

Ramesh. "Who is Nalin Babu?"

Bearer. "I don't know."

Ramesh Babu elicited from Sukhan that this Nalin was a young gentleman who had been a frequent visitor at the house of late. Though Ramesh had renounced all hopes of Hemnalini for himself, he felt distinctly prejudiced against Nalin Babu.

"Was the young lady in good health when she left?" he asked.

"Oh yes, she was quite well" — the answer was intended to be reassuring and to please Ramesh, but Heaven only knows how far out Sukhan was in his calculations!

"I should like to go upstairs for a minute or two," said Ramesh.

The bearer took his smoking kerosene lamp and led the way upstairs.

Ramesh flitted from room to room like a ghost, stopping now and then to seat himself again on some familiar chair or sofa. Furniture, fittings, everything was the same except for this interloper Nalin Babu, who had suddenly appeared from nowhere. Nature abhors a vacuum and will never suffer one long! There was the window-bay in which Ramesh had stood by Hemnalini's side in the glow of the autumn sunset while their two hearts beat as one. Each day as the sun descended its rays must reillumine that room. Must Ramesh have a successor who would try to rearrange the tableau of two heads framed in that window? And would the spirit of the past not take its stand between them and silently drive them apart with an upraised finger of warning? Wounded pride raged in Ramesh's breast.

Next day instead of going to Allahabad he took train for Ghazipur direct.

Chapter 34

$\mathcal{R}$amesh had been absent in Calcutta for nearly a month and to a girl of Kamala's age in the full current of adolescence a month is a long period. Just as the dawn-light is suddenly transformed into the glory of sunrise, so her womanhood had scarcely stirred from sleep before it burst into full consciousness. She might have had to wait long for this awakening had not her close intimacy with Sailaja and the light and warmth of love that Sailaja's personality shed on her accelerated the transformation.

Meanwhile Ramesh's tardiness and Sailaja's insistence had stimulated Uncle to go house-hunting in earnest, and he had rented for the young pair a small bungalow standing outside the town on the bank of the Ganges. He had been assiduously employed in collecting such furniture as was necessary to make the house habitable, and had engaged enough servants to enable them to start housekeeping.

When Ramesh returned to Ghazipur after his long absence Kamala had at last a house of her own, and the young people were no longer dependent on Uncle's hospitality for a roof over their heads.

Ground sufficient for a garden surrounded the bungalow. Between two rows of tall *sisu* trees ran a shaded path. The river was shrunken to its cold-weather dimensions, and between the house and the channel stretched a sandy flat on which patches of young wheat alternated with melon-beds. On the southern edge of the compound towards the river stood a huge *nim* tree, with a pavement around its roots.

The property had been long without a tenant and both house and grounds showed signs of much neglect. The garden was a wilderness, and the rooms were unswept and filthy, but Kamala had no qualms on that account. She was so delighted at attaining the status of a housewife that everything in her eyes was beautiful. She lost no time in deciding to what use each room was to be put and what was to grow in each corner of the garden, and she took measures, in consultation with Uncle, to reclaim the whole of the wilderness. She personally superintended the construction of fireplaces in the kitchen and the necessary alterations in the store-room adjoining it. She spent the whole day cleaning, sweeping, and tidying, and her energy was ever finding some new vent.

Housework displays feminine beauty in its most varied and alluring forms, and Kamala at her work reminded Ramesh of a bird freed from its cage and soaring aloft. Her radiant face and the finished dexterity with which she went about her tasks gave him new sensations of mingled wonder and delight.

It was the first time that he had beheld her in the guise of housewife; she had, as it were, come into her kingdom and something of dignity was added to her beauty.

"What are you doing, Kamala?" he asked; "you'll wear yourself out!"

Kamala stopped for a minute in the middle of her task and looked up at Ramesh with a happy smile. "No fear, I'll be all right," and she resumed her work, gratified to know that Ramesh was taking an interest in her doings.

Ramesh's infatuation soon brought him back on another pretext. "Have you had breakfast yet, Kamala?" he asked.

"Of course I have! Hours ago!" she replied.

Ramesh knew this as well as she did, but he could not forbear asking the question by way of paying her a slight attention; nor was Kamala displeased, futile though the inquiry was.

To keep up the conversation Ramesh continued: "Why are you doing all this by yourself, Kamala? You had better give me a job."

Now good workers have this failing that they tend to mistrust the capacity of others, so Kamala merely smiled and answered, "No, this is not a man's job."

"We're very forbearing, we men," said Ramesh; "we put up meekly with insults to our sex. If I were a woman there would be a scrap! After all, you don't hesitate to employ Uncle. Why do you think me so useless?"

"I don't know, but I should laugh to see you sweeping the soot out of the kitchen! You had better get out of this. I'm raising a fearful dust!"

To keep the ball rolling Ramesh went on: "Dust is no respecter of persons; it treats you and me in exactly the same way."

"I put up with it because I have to," said Kamala; "I don't see why you should when you don't have to."

Ramesh dropped his voice so that the servants should not overhear. "I want to share whatever you have to put up with, whether it's work or anything else."

This brought a faint blush to Kamala's cheek and instead of answering she stepped aside and called to Umesh:

"Umesh, you had better give this place another bucketful of water; just look how thick the dust is. Here, give me the broom," and she began to sweep vigorously.

"What are you doing, Kamala?" exclaimed Ramesh, distressed to see her engaged in so menial a task.

"Why, Ramesh Babu," said a voice behind him, "what's the harm in honest work? You people with an English education prate about equality. If you regard sweeping as degrading work why do you allow a servant to do it? I haven't your education, but if you ask me my opinion it's this: when I see a virtuous woman handling a broom every fibre of it sparkles in my eyes like a sunbeam! (To Kamala) I've nearly finished with your wilderness, dear; you'll have to show me now where the vegetable-beds are to be."

"Just wait a minute please, Uncle; I haven't finished with this room yet," and Kamala resumed her labours.

When the room was swept clean she undid the veil which was fastened round her waist, pulled it over her head, and sallied forth to engage in a serious conversation with Uncle about the best situation for the vegetable-plots.

The day soon passed, but the house was not yet sufficiently clean to satisfy Kamala's exacting standards. The traces of long neglect were not easily removed, and some of the rooms were obviously still uninhabitable without further cleansing and airing, so to Ramesh's great disappointment he and Kamala had perforce to spend another night at Uncle's. He had looked forward all day to the evening hour in their own little home and had pictured Kamala smiling shyly at his side in the lamplight as he unburdened his heart to her. With three or four more day's delay in prospect he could not postpone any longer his enrolment at the provincial bar, and accordingly he departed for Allahabad next day.

Chapter 35

*U*ncle himself left for Allahabad a day or two later on a visit to his eldest daughter Bidhu.

On the morning of his departure Kamala invited Sailaja to a picnic meal with her at the new house, and Saila joined her there after giving Bipin his breakfast and seeing him off to the city.

The two friends set to work and with Umesh's help prepared a meal under the *nim* tree. When breakfast was over they settled down for a day-long talk under the tree. The cool shade, the tempered sunshine, and the view over the river seemed to Kamala a wonderful setting to their conversation, and the purposeless longing that had found place in her heart became as remote as the kites that circle around in the sky above them, looking like specks in the blue.

The afternoon was still young when Saila bestirred herself; her husband would soon he back from the office and she must go.

"Could you not depart for once from your usual custom?" asked Kamala; but Saila merely smiled and shook her head while she fondled Kamala's chin. When leaving she enjoined on Kamala to return before dark.

The sun was still above the horizon when Kamala finished her housework. She wrapped a shawl round her head and shoulders and settled down again under the *nim* tree to watch the sun sinking behind the high bank across the river, where a few fishing-boats were moored with masts silhouetted against the glowing sky.

Umesh now came out with an excuse to engage her in conversation. "You haven't taken any *pán* for a long time, mother," he said. "I got some ready at the other house and brought it along with me," and he handed her some *pán* wrapped in paper.

Kamala awoke to the consciousness that dusk was falling and she sprang to her feet.

"Uncle Chakrabartti has sent a carriage for you," added Umesh.

Kamala entered the bungalow for a last look round before driving home. In the principal room was a fireplace of the English pattern in which a fire could be lighted for warmth in winter, and on the mantelpiece above it a kerosene lamp was burning. Kamala stopped to lay the packet of *pán* on the mantelpiece, and was on the point of resuming her perambulations when her eye caught her own name in Ramesh's handwriting on the paper of the parcel.

"Where did you find that paper?" she asked Umesh.

"It was lying in a corner of master's room. I picked it up when the floor was being swept."

Kamala took it up and began to read. It was the letter in which Ramesh had made a clean breast to Hemnalini and which with his extraordinary carelessness he must have thrown aside.

She read the letter through.

"Why do you stand there and say nothing, mother?" asked Umesh; "it's getting dark."

One might have heard a pin drop in the room and Kamala's expression alarmed Umesh. "Don't you near me, mother." We must be going home; it's late," he pleaded; but she did not stir till one of Uncle's servants came in and announced pointedly that the carriage had been standing for a long time.

Chapter 36

"Aren't you well to-day, dear," asked Sailaja when Kamala returned; "have you a headache?"

"No, I'm all right; why isn't Uncle here?"

"Mother sent him off to Allahabad to see my sister there; she hasn't been well for some time."

"When will he be back?"

"He'll be away for a week at least, they say. You've been overdoing it, working at that bungalow of yours all day. You're looking very tired. Have your supper early and go to bed."

Kamala's only salvation at this stage would have been to take Saila into her confidence, but that, she felt, was impossible. Nothing would induce her to confess to Saila of all people that the man whom she supposed to be her husband was not her husband at all.

Kamala shut herself into her own room and read Ramesh's letter again by the light of her lamp.

Neither the name nor the whereabouts of the person addressed appeared in the letter, but the contents clearly indicated that that person was a woman, that she had been betrothed to Ramesh, and that his connection with Kamala had caused the engagement to be broken off.

Further, Ramesh had not concealed the fact that he loved with all his heart the woman to whom he was writing and that it was for the sake of the hapless Kamala, whose fate had been so curiously linked with his own, that he had severed connection with her.

Kamala recalled bit by bit the whole of her life with Ramesh from that first meeting on the sandbank to their arrival in Ghazipur, and what had been obscure before became clear as daylight. Ramesh had known throughout that she was not his wife, and had been at his wits end wondering how he could dispose of her, while she had calmly assumed him to be her husband and was preparing, unabashed, to settle down with him in life-long companionship.

Shame pierced her heart like a dagger, and as various incidents recurred to her memory she would gladly have sunk into the floor. Disgrace would cling to her all her life; there was no escape from its stigma.

She threw open the door and passed out into the garden behind the house. The dark wintry sky stretched above her in repellent coldness like a vault of black marble. No wisp of cloud, no haze was to be seen, and the stars shone clearly. A plantation of mango saplings in the foreground accentuated the gloom. No avenue of escape from her misery opened before her mental vision. She sank down on the chilly grass and sat there, in statue-like rigidity, without shedding a tear or uttering a sound.

She took no count of the passage of time, but by and by the biting cold pierced her to the heart and she shivered in every limb. When at last the waning moon cleft the darkness behind the motionless palms Kamala slowly rose, retired to her own chamber, and closed the door.

In the morning when she opened her eyes Saila stood by her bed. Kamala sat up at once, ashamed that she had slept so late.

"Don't get up, dear," said Saila, "you had better sleep on for a little; I'm sure you're not well. You look tired and there are dark lines under your eyes. Tell me what the matter is, dear," and Sailaja sat down beside her and put her arm round Kamala's neck.

Kamala's breast heaved and she could restrain her tears no longer. She hid her face on Saila's shoulder and wept freely, while Saila held her in a firm embrace, making no attempt at consoling speeches.

At last Kamala withdrew from Saila's encircling arm, wiped her eyes, and began to laugh boisterously.

"Come, come, that's enough," said Saila; "you're the most secretive girl I ever met; but you needn't think I don't know what it's all about; I'm not so green as that! Shall I tell you what it is? Since Ramesh Babu went to Allahabad he hasn't written you a single letter and you're vexed about it, though you're too proud to say so. But you must remember that he has a lot to do there and he'll be back in a couple of days. You mustn't mind if he doesn't find an opportunity to write when he's only away for that short time. Silly girl! But do you know, dear, though I'm giving you this good advice, had it happened to me I should have done the same! Women do cry over foolish things. Once you have had your cry out and start smiling again you'll forget about it."

She drew Kamala to her breast and went on: "You feel now that you'll never be able to forgive Ramesh Babu, don't you? Tell me the truth now."

"Yes, that's the truth," said Kamala.

Saila tapped her on the cheek. "I thought so; of course it was that! All right, we'll see. Only don't take it to heart."

That very morning Saila despatched a letter to her father in Allahabad. "Kamala is in great distress," she wrote, "because she has not heard from Ramesh Babu.

One can well imagine what it must mean for the poor child when he brings her to a strange place and then goes off whenever he likes, leaving her behind and never writing to her. Can't he get his business in Allahabad over? Plenty of people have business to do and yet find time for writing."

Uncle hunted up Ramesh, read him an extract from his daughter's letter, and then lectured him severely. Now the real truth was not that Kamala had been too little in Ramesh's thoughts but that the more he pondered the deeper his perplexity had grown. It was not indifference but indecision that had caused him to linger in Allahabad. Then on the top of all his bewilderment came this extract from Saila's letter.

The wording of the letter clearly indicated that Kamala missed him sorely, though diffidence forbade her to write herself. Ramesh had come to the parting of the ways and he decided at once what course to take. Not his happiness alone but Kamala's love for him must be the guiding factor. Providence had not only linked their lives but had knit their hearts on that distant sandbank.

So he bestirred himself and composed the following letter to Kamala:

Dearest—You must not regard this form of address as a mere epistolary convention, Kamala. I should never address you as "dearest" were you not actually the person whom I love most in the world. If you have entertained any doubts—if I have ever wounded your feelings, may the fact that in all sincerity I address you as "dearest" dissipate those doubts and assuage the pain of those wounds for ever!

What need to enlarge on this? Much of my behaviour in the past must have pained you. If in your heart you indict me for that, the charge is one that I cannot refute. I can only reiterate that you are my dearest and that there is none for whom I cherish the same affection. This may not be a complete defence for all my shortcomings of behaviour, but it is the only one that I can offer. So, Kamala, in addressing you as "dearest" I draw the sponge over all our doubt-infested past and lay the foundations of our future love. Believe me, I have no thought for any one but you and you are indeed my "dearest". If you are once firmly convinced of this, doubts and questionings may be finally set at rest.

I would ask you next if I have won your love or not, but I dare not ask that. Love prompts the question and I do not for an instant doubt that one day it will be answered. No words will be uttered, but heart will peak to heart; it is my love for you that gives me this assurance. I do not boast myself worthy of you, but I feel that my adoration cannot be in vain.

I fully realise that this letter reads like a laboured composition and for that reason I have an impulse to tear it up; but it is impossible for me yet to write a letter that will truly express my feelings. After all, letters are things that two persons must interchange. In the first letter of a series the writer can hardly give true expression to his sentiments. When our two minds are in full communion then I shall be able to write to you letters that are real letters. Only when the doors on both sides of a room are open can the wind blow through it freely.

Kamala, dearest, when shall I find the door of your heart?

All this will come to fruition slowly and haste would defeat its own purpose. I shall reach Ghazipur on the morning of the day after you receive this. I beg that I may find you in our house on my arrival. We have been long homeless and I can endure this life no longer. Now at last I look forward to crossing our own threshold and beholding in the queen of my heart the mistress of my house. That moment will be our second "auspicious look."

Do you remember our first on that moonlight night by the riverside on the lonely sandbank—under the open sky, without the semblance of a roof over our heads and no parents or relations to preside over the ceremony?

It seems unreal to me, like a dream. And so I ardently anticipate another "auspicious look" in the clear calm light of morning surrounded by four walls and solid reality. Your sweet smiling face framed in our own doorway will for ever remain enshrined in my memory. It is a picture that I long to behold. Dearest, I am a suppliant at the gate of your heart; do not send me empty away! Your devoted.

Ramesh

Chapter 37

"*A*ren't you going to your bungalow?" asked Saila next day in an attempt to rouse Kamala from the dumps.

"No, there's nothing left to do."

Saila. "Are all the rooms ready?"

Kamala. "Yes, I've finished with them."

Saila was soon back. "What will you give me if I give you something?" she asked.

"I've nothing to give you, *didi*" (elder sister), said Kamala.

Saila. "Nothing at all?"

Kamala. "Nothing at all."

Saila flicked her on the cheek. "So that's how it is! You've given all you possess to a certain person to keep, have you? What do you call this?" and she took a letter out of the fold of her dress.

Kamala turned pale when she saw Ramesh's handwriting on the envelope, and she half turned away.

"Now then," said Saila, "you've given a sufficient exhibition of that pride of yours. Drop it now. I know you're itching to snatch this letter from me, but I shan't give it to you at all till you ask for it nicely. We'll see how long you can keep it up."

Just then Umi burst into the room with a shout of "Auntie! Auntie!" dragging a soap-box behind her by a string.

Kamala snatched her up and bore her off, smothering her with kisses. Umi set up a howl of protest at being separated from her toy-cart, but Kamala would not be denied. She carried the child into her own room, soothing her with an unceasing patter of baby-talk.

Saila followed, exclaiming, "I'm beaten; you've won this time! I can't keep it up. Please, Kamala! take it. I'll never be rude to you again!"

She threw the letter down on the bed, rescued Umi from Kamala's clutches, and carried her off.

Kamala turned the envelope over and over, then opened it and began to read, but she had only glanced through the first lines when she flushed angrily and flung the letter from her. Then she mastered her first impulse of profound disgust, picked up the letter again, and read it through.

Whether she understood the whole of it or not is impossible to say, but she felt as though she were handling some filthy thing and once more she threw the letter away. It was a proposal that she should make a home for a man who was not her husband! Fully cognisant of all the facts, Ramesh had bided his time to fling this insult at her. If after their arrival in Ghazipur her heart had warmed towards him, did he imagine it was because he was Ramesh and not because he was — as she believed — her husband? Ramesh had jumped at conclusions, and pity for an unfortunate outcast had prompted him to write this love-letter. How could she now — or ever — dispel the mistaken inference that he had drawn from her behaviour? Shame and disgust were destined to be her portion in life, though never since she came into the world had she sinned against a soul. She pictured "home" now as a dreadful monster ready to swallow her up, and she cast about in vain for a way of escape. Two days ago she could never have conceived that Ramesh would appear such an ogre to her.

She was interrupted in her reflections by a cough from Umesh, who stood at the door. Getting no response from Kamala he called softly, "Mother!"

Kamala went to the door, and, scratching his head, Umesh announced, "Mother, Sidhu Babu's people have brought up a troupe of actors from Calcutta for their daughter's wedding."

"All right, Umesh, you can go and see the performance."

Umesh. "What kind of flowers shall I bring you in the morning?"

Kamala. "Never mind about any flowers."

He was going away when Kamala suddenly called him back. "Wait, Umesh, as you're going to the play here's five rupees for you."

Umesh was taken aback; no charge for admission was made at such entertainments. "Do you want me to buy you something in town, mother?" he asked.

Kamala. "No, I don't want anything. Take the money and it'll come in handy for something."

Umesh was going off in bewilderment when Kamala called him back again. "What will people say if they see you at the performance in those clothes?" she asked.

Umesh had never imagined that people expected much from him in the way of dress, or that a deficiency in that respect would make him the subject of criticism. He was quite indifferent to the absence of elegance in his waist-cloth and his complete lack of any other garment, so Kamala's query only brought a grin to his countenance.

"Here, take these and put them on." Kamala pulled out a couple of her own dresses and threw them to Umesh. Being oblong sheets, these garments served equally well for masculine and for feminine attire according to the method of folding, and they had broad ornamental borders which vastly delighted Umesh. He fell at Kamala's feet in a clumsy obeisance, then picked up the dresses and departed, contorting his face in a fruitless effort to suppress a broad grin.

After his departure Kamala wiped away a tear and took her stand by the window.

"Won't you show me your letter, Kamala dear?" said Saila, entering the room. She herself had no secrets from Kamala, and this emboldened her to make the request.

"There it is, *didi*, read it," said Kamala, pointing to where the letter lay on the floor.

"She hasn't got over her temper yet," thought Saila in surprise, and she picked up the letter and read it through. It was certainly affectionate enough, but what a queer letter for a man to write to his wife! It was an extraordinary composition! "Does your husband write novels, dear?" she asked.

Dazed as she was, Kamala winced at the word "husband." "I don't know," she replied.

"Well, are you going round to the bungalow to-day?"

Kamala merely nodded in reply.

"I could have spent the day with you there, but you know, dear, I have to be present at the reception to the bride at Narsingh Babu's house; so mother had better go with you instead."

"Oh, no, your mother mustn't trouble to go!" cried Kamala; "the servants are there."

Saila smiled. "Well, perhaps after all you needn't be nervous when you have a stout retainer like Umesh."

Umi had picked up a pencil in the meantime, and she was busy making scratches with it on various objects, while she talked a language of her own which she considered to be "reading aloud." When Saila tore her away from her literary pursuits she set up a shrill protest, which only subsided when Kamala interposed: "Come with me and I'll give you something pretty."

Kamala then carried her off to her room, seated her on the bed, and played with her till she had quite forgotten her troubles. When she demanded the promised gift Kamala produced from her box a pair of golden bracelets. They were the finest toys that Umi had ever seen and she was enchanted with them. When "auntie" put them on her wrists she swung her arms aloft to admire the effect, then danced off proudly to show them to her mother.

Saila at once pulled the bracelets off to return them to their owner. "What on earth are you thinking of, Kamal?" she cried. "What made you put them on her?"

"I made a present of them to Umi," said Kamala, coming closer; Umi's shrieks of lamentation at the outrage were piercing the heavens.

"Are you mad?" ejaculated Saila.

"Didi, I dare you to return them to me! You can have them cut up and made into a necklace for her."

"I swear I never saw anyone to beat you!" and Saila put her arm round Kamala's neck.

"I must say good-bye to you to-day, didi," Kamala went on, "I've been very happy here, I never was so happy in my life," and the tears came in a flood.

Saila found it hard to restrain her own. "Don't talk that way, Kamal, as though you were going away altogether. I can't believe that you were really happy here. It's different now that you'll have a house of your own to be really happy in. We'll drop in to see you now and then, and when our backs are turned you'll say, 'Thank Heaven, they've gone at last!'"

When the time came for Kamala to start and she had said her good-byes, Saila remarked: "I'll come and see you to-morrow at midday," but Kamala neither accepted nor declined this offer.

She found Umesh at the bungalow on her arrival. "So, you're here!" she exclaimed. "I thought you were going to the play."

"So I was, but as you were coming here——"

Kamala. "Never mind about me; go off and see the performance. Bishan's here. Hurry up or you'll be late."

Umesh. "It doesn't start for some time yet."

Kamala. "Never mind. There's always lots going on at a wedding; go along and see all the fun."

Umesh did not need much encouragement, and he was on the point of setting out when Kamala called to him: "Look here, if Uncle comes you should——" but having got thus far she could not think how to finish the sentence. Umesh stared at her open-mouthed. After a pause she went on. "Remember, you have a good friend in Uncle. If you happen to want anything go to him and ask for it with my love and he'll give it you. Now mind and don't forget to give him my love."

"All right," said Umesh, and he started off, quite at a loss to understand the significance of this injunction.

"Where are you going, madam?" Bishan had occasion to ask in the course of the afternoon.

"I'm going to bathe in the Ganges."

"Shall I go with you?"

"No, stay and watch the house," and she presented him with a rupee for no apparent reason and sallied forth in the direction of the river.

Chapter 38

One afternoon Annada Babu went upstairs in search of Hemnalini, looking forward to taking tea alone with her. He looked for her in the sitting-room upstairs and in her bedroom, but she was in neither room, and he learned from the bearer that she had not left the house.

Vaguely uneasy about her he ascended to the roof. As far as the eye could see stretched an unbroken succession of housetops, faintly illuminated by the pale winter sunshine. The evening breeze veered fitfully from one quarter to another. Hemnalini sat buried in thought in the shadow of the stair-turret.

Annada Babu emerged on to the roof and stood behind her, but she was oblivious of his presence. When at last he went softly up to her and laid his hand on her shoulder she started in surprise, and then blushed with confusion; he had seated himself beside her before she could rise to her feet. He waited a moment or two, then sighed deeply. "Oh, Hem, if only your mother were alive now! I'm no use to you at all !"

This piteous outcry from the old man roused Hemnalini from the semblance of stupor into which she had fallen and her eyes sought her father's face. Oh, the love, the

sympathy, and the pain that she saw there! A sad change
had come over his expression in the last few days. It was
her old father who had borne the brunt of the storm that
had burst over Hemnalini; he had never relaxed his
endeavours to alleviate his daughter's distress; and when
he had found all his efforts to comfort her unavailing his
thoughts had turned to her mother and he had brought
out this cry of helplessness from the depths of his loving
heart—Hemnalini saw it all in a flash. Conscience dealt
her a buffet and swept her instantly out of her absorption
in her own misery. The world that had seemed to her like
a dream suddenly sprang into reality and in a moment
shame overwhelmed her. By an effort of will she rent
asunder and cast aside the entangling net of memories in
which she had wrapped herself.

"How do you feel to-day, dad?" she asked.

She was inquiring about his health! In the last few days
Annada Babu had entirely forgotten that one's health
could be a subject of conversation.

"How am I? There's nothing wrong with me physically,
dear! I'm only worried to see how ill you're looking these
days. A tough old person like me can stand a lot, but I'm
afraid the shock may be too severe for a young thing like
you," and he patted her gently on the shoulder.

"I say, dad," said Hemnalini," how old was I when
mother died?"

"You were only three then and had just begun to talk.
I remember quite well your asking me, 'Where mother?'
and my saying, 'She has gone to her daddy' — your mother's
father died before you were born and you never knew him.
You didn't understand what I meant and you said nothing
but just stood and looked solemnly at me. Then you took
me by the hand and pulled me into your mother's room.
You thought that though the room was empty I should

find some clue there to tell me where she was. You knew that your father could do a lot, but you didn't realise that when it came to matters of life and death your big daddy was as ignorant and helpless as a baby. You can realise now how helpless I am! God has given your father the capacity to love you but not to help you," and he laid his hand on his daughter's head.

Hemnalini took her father's trembling old hand in her own and stroked it. "I can hardly recall mother at all," she said. "I remember that she used to lie down at midday and read a book; I didn't approve of that and I used to try to snatch the book from her," and they fell to conversing once more on the past. Hem plied her father with questions about her mother's appearance and habits and the family life of those days, and he answered them to the best of his ability. The sun went down while they talked and the sky turned to the hue of dull copper. That hour of quiet communion on the housetop, amid the bustle and tumult of the great city, set the seal on the mutual affection of the father and daughter, the old man and the young woman. They lingered till the daylight faded and the soft dews descended on them like tears.

Suddenly Jogendra's step sounded on the stair. The murmured talk came to a sudden end and both sprang to their feet.

"Hem seems to hold her receptions on the roof nowadays." Jogendra remarked with a searching glance at the two faces.

Jogendra was gravely dissatisfied with the turn affairs had taken. Day and night a pall of depression lay over the house, and he found life at home almost unendurable; and yet he was disinclined to seek others' society, for whenever he visited the houses of friends or acquaintances he had to furnish explanations of the rupture of Hemnalini's engagement.

"Hemnalini is really carrying things too far," he would say on these occasions. "It comes of letting girls read English novels. Hem's idea is that as Ramesh has deserted her she must be broken-hearted; so she has settled down to make a great parade of breaking her heart. It's a unique opportunity for a novel-reading young lady to show how she can endure being crossed in love!"

"I chose this place for a quiet talk with Hem," Annada Babu hastened to explain. His intention was to protect his daughter from Jogendra's unfeeling taunts, but his words were capable of the interpretation that he had dragged Hem up to the roof to engage her in conversation.

"Can't one talk just as well at the tea-table?" cried Jogendra. "You're just encouraging Hem in her foolishness, dad. You'll drive me out of the house altogether at this rate."

"Haven't you had your tea yet, dad?" asked Hemnalini, conscience-stricken.

Jogendra. "Tea isn't like poetic fancy; it won't rain down on one of its own volition from the sunset glow in the evening sky. The cups won't fill themselves and come up to you while you sit in a corner of the roof! I need hardly tell you that!"

To cover Hemnalini's confusion Annada Babu interposed hastily. "I've decided not to have any tea to-day."

Jogendra. "Why, dad, are you going to turn an out-and-out ascetic? What's to happen to me, then? I can't live on air."

Annada. "Oh, no, it's not a question of asceticism. I didn't sleep well last night so I thought of trying the effect of a little abstinence."

Truth to tell, in the course of former conversations with Hemnalini the apparition of a brimming cup of tea had often floated before Annada Babu's mental vision, but this had not been so to-day. Since Hemnalini had at last regained her normal tone, her father and she had been having a really intimate talk in the privacy of the housetop and had sounded depths not hitherto reached. The effort of moving might have had a disastrous effect and have scared away like frightened deer the thoughts that were about to find utterance; so to-day Annada Babu had resisted the call of the teapot.

Hemnalini did not believe that her father seriously meant to cure himself of sleeplessness by abstaining from his usual indulgence. "Come along, dad, you must have your tea," she cried, and, forgetting his dread of insomnia, Annada Babu hurried off with her.

When he entered the room he found to his dismay Akshay already installed there; for the time being Hem was her old self again, but the sight of Akshay would be a set-back; however, it was too late to remedy the situation for Hemnalini had already followed him into the room. Akshay rose at once.

"Well, Jogen, I had better be off now," he said, but to the astonishment of all present Hemnalini only remarked: "What's the matter, Akshay Babu? Are you in such a hurry? Have a cup of tea first."

Akshay resumed his seat. "I had two cups before you came in. I might be able to manage another brace if you pressed me."

Hemnalini smiled. "It's be the first time we've had to do any pressing."

"True," said Akshay, "I have enough sense never to refuse a good thing when I'm offered it."

"By the same token, may a good thing never refuse you when you offer yourself! Could a priest give you a better blessing than that?" said Jogendra.

After a long intermission conversation was again in full swing round Annada Babu's tea-table. Hemnalini's laughter had never been boisterous, but to-day it rose from time to time above the talk. She had a dig at her father. "Akshay Babu has forgotten himself, dad. He's perfectly well though he hasn't taken any of your pills for days. If they're any use at all he would have a headache at least."

Jogendra. "Talk about betraying one's salt. He's a traitor to his pill!"

Annada Babu laughed happily. That his family should again poke fun at him about his pill-box he took as a sign of renewed harmony, and a load was lifted from his mind.

"I see what you're after," he said, "you're trying to undermine his faith. He's the sole survivor of my band of pill-takers and you're out to break his allegiance."

"No fear of that, Annada Babu," said Akshay, "they'll never change Akshay's allegiance."

Jogendra. "Why is Akshay like a bad rupee? Try to change him and you'll get into trouble!" and an outburst of merriment dispelled the cloud that had loomed over Annada Babu's tea-table.

The symposium might have been a protracted one had Hemnalini not excused herself on the grounds that her hair required attention. Then Akshay remembered an engagement and he too departed.

"Dad, we mustn't wait any longer," said Jogendra, when he and his father were left to themselves; "we must get Hem married."

Annada Babu stared at him in consternation.

"There's a lot of gossip going on," Jogendra proceeded, "about her engagement to Ramesh being broken off. I can't go on fighting single-handed like this. If I were in a position to tell the whole truth I shouldn't mind the scapping, but for Hem's sake I can't speak out freely, so I have to fight with my mouth shut. Just the other day, you know, I had to trounce Akhil. I heard he had been speaking too freely. If we can get her married soon the talk will subside, and I shan't have to go round playing the part of sole champion, turning up my sleeves and challenging the world. I strongly advise you not to put it off any longer."

Annada. "But whom is she to marry, Jogen?"

Jogendra. "There's only one man. It would be difficult to find any one else after what has happened and all the talk that's going on. There's only poor old Akshay; he's not easily choked off. Tell him to take a pill and he'll take it. Bid him marry and he'll marry."

Annada. "Are you mad, Jogen? Do you think Hem would ever marry Akshay?"

Jogendra. "I'll manage to get her consent if only you don't interfere."

"No, Jogen, no," exclaimed his father, "I can't have you trying your persuasion on Hem; you'll only frighten her and worry her out of her wits. Leave her alone for a little. Poor girl, she has had a trying experience and she needn't marry all at once."

"I'm not going to put any pressure on her; I'll make every endeavour to be considerate and gentle with her. Do you think I can't speak to her without quarrelling?"

Jogendra was not in the habit of letting the grass grow under his feet. He accosted Hemnalini as soon as she had completed her coiffure and emerged from her room. "Hem, I want to have a talk with you."

Hem's pulse quickened at his words. She followed slowly to the sitting-room and waited for him to begin.

"Have you noticed how ill dad is looking?" he asked her.

Hemnalini said nothing, but her expression betrayed the anxiety that she felt.

Jogendra. "Mark my words, he'll have a serious illness unless we do something."

His tone indicated that he held her responsible for the state of their father's health. Hemnalini looked down and began to pluck the fringe of her dress.

"What's over is over," Jogendra proceeded; "the more regrets you entertain for the past the more disgrace for us. If you want to set dad's mind entirely at rest you must eradicate every vestige of this unfortunate affair," and he waited expectantly for an answer, with his eyes on his sister's face.

"You needn't be afraid that I shall ever trouble dad by talking about it," returned Hemnalini in confusion.

Jogendra. "I know you won't, but that's not enough to shut people's mouths."

"Well, how can I do that?" asked Hemnalini.

Jogendra. "There's only one way of stopping all this talk."

Hemnalini knew what means Jogendra had in his mind and she hastened to reply. "Wouldn't it be a good idea to take dad up-country now for a change? We could stay away three or four months, and by the time we came back the gossip would have died down."

"That wouldn't be a complete cure. You must convince dad that your mind is at rest. Until then his wound will rankle and he'll never be his old self."

Hemnalini eyes incontinently filled with tears, which she wiped away hastily.

"What do you want me to do then?" she asked.

"I know it sounds unpleasant, but if you want to make everyone happy you must get married at once."

Hemnalini was stunned into silence.

Jogendra went on impatiently: "You girls love to make mountains out of molehills. The same thing has happened to lots of others before. There has been some muddle over their marriage, then they quietly marry someone else and there's no more fuss. Otherwise the sort of thing that one reads of in novels would be constantly happening in the family circle, and existence would be unbearable. You may not be ashamed to talk melodrama in public—this sort of thing: 'I shall renounce the world for ever and shall abide on the house-top gazing at the heavens; I shall set up the memory of that worthless deceiver in my heart and worship it as in a shrine'; but the disgrace will be the death of us. Marry some decent fellow and be quit of all this wretched melodrama as soon as you can."

Hemnalini was perfectly aware of the absurdity of being melodramatic in public, so Jogendra's gibes stabbed her like a knife.

"Have I ever said that I renounce the world and shall never marry?"

"If that isn't your intention then get married. Of course if you say that you could never love a man unless he is a sort of demi-god, then you'll have to stick to your vow of celibacy. We seldom find things just to our taste in this world. We have to accommodate ourselves to what we can get, and put up with that as human beings."

"Why do you taunt me like this?" exclaimed Hemnalini, stung to the quick. "Did I say anything to you about love?"

Jogendra. "You haven't said anything, I admit, but I've noticed things. When for frivolous or unfair reasons you have conceived a dislike for well-meaning friends, you haven't hesitated to betray your feelings. But you must admit that among all your friends there is one in particular who has been true to you in prosperity and adversity, through good and bad repute, and whom I respect greatly in consequence. If you want a husband who would give his life to see you happy you know where to look for him. But if you want melodrama——"

Hemnalini rose to her feet. "Please don't speak to me like that. If dad orders me to marry anyone I shall do as he tells me. Wait till I disobey him before you talk about melodrama."

Jogendra's tone softened at once. "Hem, dear, you mustn't be angry with me. You know that when anything annoys me I'm apt to talk wildly and say the first thing that comes into my head. We've known one another since we were children and I'm quite aware how sensitive you are and how fond you are of dad." And he departed in quest of his father.

Annada was sitting in his room. His conscience had been troubling him as he pictured Jogendra bullying his sister, and he had been on the point of rising to interrupt their conversation when Jogendra entered. He waited for his son to begin.

"Dad, Hem has agreed to marry," Jogendra began. "Perhaps you think that I put a good deal of pressure on her to obtain her consent, but I didn't as a matter of fact. She won't object now to marry Akshay if only you tell her distinctly that she must do it."

"Am I to tell her?"

"Yes, you can hardly expect her to come of her own accord and say, "Am I to marry Akshay?' If you hesitate to speak to her yourself you can authorise me to communicate your orders to her."

"Certainly not!" exclaimed Annada Babu at once. "I'll say to her myself what there is to be said; but why are you in such a hurry? I think we should wait for a few days."

"No, dad; if we wait, something is sure to come in the way. We can't go on like this any longer."

None of the family could cope with Jogendra when he was in earnest; he would never take his hand from the plough, and even Annada went in inward fear of him.

"All right, I'll speak to her," he said, with the idea of shelving the question.

"No time like the present, dad," said Jogendra; "she's sitting there waiting for you. Try to get it settled to-day."

"Well, you wait here, Jogen, and I'll see her alone."

"All right, you'll find me here when you come back."

Annada Babu found the sitting-room in darkness. Someone rose hurriedly from a chair, and a moment or two later a tearful voice said, "The lamp went out, dad. Shall I tell the bearer to light it?" but Annada knew full well that the lamp had not been extinguished accidentally.

"Never mind, dear," he said, "we don't need a light"; and he groped his way to a chair beside his daughter's.

"You're not taking enough care of yourself, dad," said Hemnalini.

"And with good reason, dear. My health is all right, so it needs no care. It's you that ought to take care of yourself."

"You all say the same, dad," exclaimed Hemnalini petulantly. "It isn't fair at all. Surely I'm a perfectly amenable person! What makes you say that I'm indifferent to my health? If you prescribe any particular treatment for me you have only to say so. I've never said 'No' to you yet, dad, have I?" and the sobs came back with redoubled force.

"Never, dear, never," exclaimed Annada, anxious above all to console her. "I've never even had to tell you to do a thing. You know what is in my thoughts just as though you were my own mother; and you've always done what I wanted without being told. If a father's whole-hearted blessing is of any avail you will be happy all your days."

"Won't you keep me with you, dad?"

Annada. "Of course I will."

Hem. "May I stay with you as long as Jogen remains

unmarried anyway? Who is going to look after you if I'm not there?"

"Look after me? Never mind that, dear. I'm not worth it."

"The room's very dark, dad; I must fetch a light," and she brought a hand-lamp from the adjoining room. "We've been so upset the last few days that you haven't had the newspaper read to you in the evenings. Shall I read it now?"

Annada got up. "All right, dear; just wait a minute; you'll read to me when I come back," and he returned to Jogendra. What he intended to say was: "I couldn't mention it to-day; we had better wait till to-morrow"; but when Jogendra burst out, "Well, dad, what happened? Did you speak to her about getting married?" he hastened to reply, "Yes, I've spoken to her"; he was afraid that otherwise Jogendra would renew the attack on Hemnalini.

"She consented of course?"

"Yes, in a way."

"Well, I'll go and tell Akshay." cried Jogendra.

"No, no, don't say anything to Akshay yet!" said his father hurriedly. "You know you'll spoil everything, Jogen, if you're so precipitate. You needn't tell any one yet; it'll be better to postpone the final arrangements till we return from up-country."

Jogendra went off without any reply. He threw a shawl round his shoulders and made straight for Akshay's house, where he found his friend immersed in an English work on book-keeping. Jogendra flung the book aside. "Never mind that just now; we have to fix a day for your wedding."

"Good Lord!" exclaimed Akshay.

Chapter 39

*N*ext morning Hemnalini rose betimes to seek her father. She found Annada Babu in his bedroom; he had drawn a deck-chair into the window-bay and was silently meditating.

The room was scantily furnished, containing only a cot and a wardrobe. Hanging on one wall was a faded photograph of Hemnalini's dead mother in an elaborate frame, and on the opposite wall was a piece of her work in wools. The wardrobe contained her trinkets and personal effects and had been left undisturbed at her death.

Hemnalini placed herself behind her father and caressed his head gently on the pretext of plucking out grey hairs.

"Dad," she said, "suppose we have our tea early this morning, then we'll sit in your room and you'll tell me stories about the old days. You can't imagine how I love listening to them."

Annada Babu's understanding of his daughter's moods had become so acute that he instantly divined her motive in wishing to hurry over tea. Akshay would shortly put in an appearance at the tea-table, and Hem intended to avoid him by retiring at the earliest possible moment to the privacy of her father's room.

The state of his daughter's nerves distressed him profoundly: she was as timorous as a frightened deer.

Descending the stairs he found that the water was not yet boiling, and he vented his spleen on the unfortunate servant whom he considered at fault. The man protested in vain that he had not anticipated that tea would be ordered before the usual hour. Annada Babu trumpeted forth his unalterable conviction that present-day servants had ideas above their station, and that his own staff required a special attendant to arouse them from their beauty-sleep.

The boiling water was produced without further delay. Instead, however, of sipping his tea with his usual deliberation while he smacked his lips over the flavour and chatted to his daughter, Annada Babu began to drain his cup with unnecessary haste.

"Are you in a hurry to go out, dad?" asked Hemnalini in surprise.

"Oh no! when the weather is cold I like to drink my tea straight off; the hot tea brings out the sweat and does one good," replied her father; but before the desired perspiration appeared Jogendra entered the room with Akshay at his heels.

Akshay had bestowed special attention on his toilet; he flaunted a silver-mounted walking-stick, and a handsome watch-chain adorned his bosom; in his left hand he carried a book in a brown-paper wrapping. Instead of taking his usual place at the table he drew a chair up beside Hemnalini's and observed with a smirk, "Your clock is fast to-day."

Hemnalini neither looked in his direction nor vouchsafed any reply.

"Hem, dear, let us go upstairs," said Annada Babu, "we must put my winter clothes out in the sun."

"You needn't be in such a hurry, dad," expostulated Jogendra, "the sun won't run away. Hem, won't you pour out a cup of tea for Akshay? I want some too, but visitors first, you know!"

Akshay laughed and turned to Hemnalini. "Did you ever see such self-sacrifice? He's a regular Sir Philip Sidney!"

Without taking the slightest notice of Akshay's facetiousness Hemnalini poured out two cups of tea, handed one to Jogendra, pushed the other towards Akshay, and caught her father's eye.

"If we wait any longer it'll be too hot on the roof," said Annada Babu "Come along, Hem, we have better go upstairs at once."

"Oh, bother the clothes!" exclaimed Jogendra, "Akshay came to——"

Annada Babu's anger blazed up. "You two are just trying to bully us! When a person is suffering mental tortures you have no right to try to browbeat her into compliance with your wishes. I have endured it without protest for days on end, but I can stand it no longer. Hem, dear, in future you and I will have our tea together upstairs."

He essayed to draw Hem out of the room, but she interposed quietly, "Don't go just yet, dad. You haven't finished your tea. Akshay Babu, may I inquire what the contents of that mysterious parcel are?"

"Not only may you ask, but you may solve the mystery for yourself," and Akshay held the package out to her.

Hem removed the wrapper and disclosed a copy of Tennyson bound in morocoo. She started as if struck and turned pale. Once before had she received just such a present. Unknown to others, she treasured in a drawer upstairs a copy of the same edition of Tennyson in this identical binding.

Jogendra smiled. "The mystery has not been entirely solved yet," and he opened the book at the title-page and showed it to his sister; on the page was written: "To Srimati Hemnalini as a token of Akshay's esteem."

Hemnalini dropped the book like a hot potato and averted her eyes from it. "Come, dad," she said, and father and daughter left the room.

Jogendra's eyes blazed. "I can't stay a moment longer under this roof!" he exclaimed. "I'll clear out and earn my living as a school-master somewhere."

"You're taking it too much to heart, old man," said Akshay. "I told you, you know, that in my opinion you were mistaken. I yielded to your insistence, but I'm convinced now that Hemnalini will never care for me. You must put that idea out of your head. If we want to do the right thing, our next task must be to make her forget Ramesh."

"That's true enough; how are we to proceed, though?"

"Well, we needn't assume that I'm the only marriageable young man in the world. Of course if you were your sister things would be different and my ancestors would not be anxiously counting the days till I cease to be a bachelor. But as it is, what we really want is a suitor who will meet her taste—not one on whose appearance she flies off to air the clothes!"

Jogendra. "One can't go into a shop and order a bridegroom."

Akshay. "You're very easily discouraged. Though our real object is to find a husband for Hemnalini still, if you are too precipitate, the whole thing will end in smoke. You mustn't broach the subject of marriage prematurely or you'll scare both parties away. Let their acquaintance ripen gradually and watch your opportunity to make a proposal."

Jogendra. "Sound tactics, I admit, but tell me his name."

Akshay. "You don't know him well, but you've seen him—Doctor Nalinaksha."

Jogendra. "Nalinaksha!"

Akshay. "You seem surprised! There's some scandal about him in the Brahmo Samaj, but never mind that. You wouldn't let so eligible a catch slip out of your hands on that account, I'm sure."

Jogendra. "If I once got anyone so eligible into my hands, I shouldn't worry about the rest! Do you suppose, however, that Nalinaksha would consent?"

Akshay. "I don't say he would if you sprang a proposal on him to-day; but time works marvels! Just listen to me, Jogen. Nalinaksha is to deliver a lecture to-morrow. Take Hemnalini to hear him. The fellow's a real orator. There's nothing like eloquence to attract women. Poor creatures, they don't realise that a husband who can listen is infinitely preferable to one who can talk!"

Jogendra. "but look here, you must tell me Nalinaksha's history; I want to know more about him."

Akshay. "All right, Jogen, I'll tell you his history, but if you discover a flaw somewhere you mustn't let that worry you. A slight flaw is an advantage in my opinion; it brings within one's means an article that would otherwise be too expensive."

Nalinaksha's story, as told by Akshay, may be summarised as follows:

His father Rajballabh was a petty landholder in the neighbourhood of Faridpur. At the age of thirty Rajballabh joined the Brahmo Samaj sect. His wife, however, refused to embrace her husband's new faith, and she resolutely went her own way, taking every precaution to maintain her ceremonial purity. Naturally Rajballabh found his wife's attitude extremely unpalatable. Their son Nalinaksha's missionary zeal and remarkable eloquence procured his admission into the fold of the Brahmo Samaj at an early age. He entered the provincial medical service and lived the usual nomadic life of the government servant in Bengal.

Wherever he went he left behind him a reputation for upright conduct, professional skill, and fervid piety.

Then came a bolt from the blue. In his old age Rajballabh formed a sudden resolve to marry a certain widow of his acquaintance, and nothing would alter his determination. His invariable answer to protests was: "My present wife is not my true consort, for she does not share my faith; it would be positively wrong to abstain from marrying a woman who, in conduct and religion, in heart and mind, will be one with me."

In spite of a general chorus of disapproval Rajballabh insisted on marrying the widow according to Hindu rites.

Nalinaksha's mother prepared to leave her husband and migrate to Benares. Nalinaksha was then in private practice at Rangpur. He at once threw up his practice and announced to his mother his intention of accompanying her to the holy city.

"My son," said the old lady with tears in her eyes, "our ideas are at variance. Why should you put yourself to unnecessary discomfort?"

"There will be no variance," replied Nalinaksha, who felt keenly the stigma cast on his mother by his father's betrayal and had determined to make her happiness his prime object. He accompanied her to Benares accordingly. At an early opportunity she inquired if he did not intend to marry.

Nalinaksha was in a quandary: "Why should I, mother?" he asked. "I'm very well as I am."

The mother's intuition divined the cause of his hesitation. In cutting himself off from his former circle he had renounced much, but he was not prepared to go to the length of marrying outside the Brahmo connection.

Anxious not to stand in his way, she replied, "My dear boy, you can't take a vow of celibacy on my account.

Marry whomsoever you please; you need not fear any opposition from me."

Nalinaksha thought the matter over for a day or two, then announced his decision.

"Mother," he said, "I'm going to present you with a daughter-in-law after your own heart, a dutiful little girl with whom you will never find yourself out of harmony and whose conduct will never cause you a pang"; and he departed for Bengal in search of a bride.

As to what happened after that, accounts were divergent. One story was that he made a secret expedition to some country place and married an orphan girl who died immediately afterwards; but other chroniclers cast doubts on this version. Personally, Akshay believed that he had been on the point of marrying, but had changed his mind at the eleventh hour.

However that might be, Akshay was of opinion that Nalinaksha's mother would raise no objections to the proposed match, in fact she would be delighted if he married the girl of his heart, and so charming a bride as Hemnalini would be far to seek. Moreover Hem's lovable disposition would inevitably impel her to treat her mother-in-law with the respect that was her due and to avoid carefully any cause of offence. A very short acquaintance with Hem would convince Nalinaksha that she possessed the necessary qualifications.

Akshay's advice accordingly was to introduce the young people to each other as early as possible.

Chapter 40

*A*s soon as Akshay had left the house Jogendra went upstairs. He found Annada Babu and Hemnalini in the sitting-room engaged in conversation. Annada looked a trifle ashamed of himself when he saw his son. He regretted his outburst at the tea-table and the temporary loss of his usual composure; and he greeted Jogendra accordingly with more than his customary heartiness.

"Come along, Jogendra, come and sit down, lad!"

"Look here, dad," began Jogendra, "you and Hemnalini never seem to stir out of the house nowadays. Staying indoors all day can't be good for you."

"Well, well," replied Annada, "we've always been stay-at-home folk. Besides, one has to cudgel one's brains for an excuse to take Hem out."

"Come now, dad," put in Hemnalini, "you mustn't put the blame on me. You know I'm quite ready to go anywhere with you."

Uncongenial though the effort was, the girl was anxious to convince them that she did not intend her secret sorrow to keep her a prisoner within four walls. She would have them believe that she took a lively interest in all that happened outside.

"Well, dad," said Jogendra, "there's to be a meeting to-morrow; you had better take Hem to it."

Annada was aware of Hemnalini's constitutional distaste for crowded public assemblies, and instead of answering he looked across at his daughter for guidance.

"A meeting!" she cried, with forced animation. "Who is the speaker to be?"

Jogendra. "Doctor Nalinaksha."

Annada. "Nalinaksha!"

Jogendra. "He's a remarkably fine speaker, and what's more he has a most extraordinary history. Such self-denial! Such constancy! He's a man in a million," and yet two hours before Jogendra had known nothing of Nalinaksha save one vague rumour!

"Well, dad," said Hemnalini, with a display of alacrity, "we must certainly go and hear this paragon."

Annada was by no means convinced by Hemnalini's show of eagerness; still he was sensible of a certain relief. Let Hemnalini, even though it cost her a struggle, only continue to go out into the world and mingle with her kind and she would soon regain her normal tone. The society of one's fellow-men is the surest remedy for mental disorders.

"All right," he said to Jogendra, "you take us to the meeting to-morrow and see that we're there in good time; but tell me what you know about Nalinaksha. One hears so many different stories about him."

Jogendra commenced with a tirade against scandal-mongers in general.

"The ultra-religious," he began, "believe that Heaven entrusted them at birth with a licence to slander and abuse their fellow-men indiscriminately. There's no one more uncharitable and malevolent than these piety-merchants!" and Jogendra's indignation boiled over.

"I'm with you; I'm with you," repeated Annada soothingly. "To be always discussing his neighbours' failings makes a man sour, narrow-minded, and suspicious."

"Hallo, dad!" exclaimed Jogendra, "are you having a dig at me? I'm not like these pious folk, you know; I can praise as well as blame. I'm quite prepared to tell a man my opinion of him to his face and back it up with my fists if necessary!"

"Don't be foolish, Jogen," Annada hastened to reply; "of course, I wasn't thinking of you. Surely I know you by this time!"

Jogendra now launched forth into the story of Nalinaksha, lavishing on his subject all the eulogy at his command.

"It was to make his mother happy," he concluded, "that Nalinaksha subdued his natural instincts and went to live in Benares; and all these friends of yours, dad, have seized the opportunity to invent scandalous stories about him. Personally, I admire his conduct. What do you say, Hem?"

"I'm of your opinion," said Hemnalini.

"I knew that Hem would approve of his action," resumed Jogendra. "I haven't the least doubt that if the occasion arose she would exercise equal self-denial to make her father happy."

Annada cast an affectionate glance at his daughter. Hem's face turned crimson, and she dropped her eyes in confusion.

Chapter 41

*A*nnada Babu and Hemnalini returned from the meeting late in the afternoon.

"Well, that was indeed a treat," remarked the old gentleman as he seated himself at the tea-table.

He made no further comment, but his mind was so busy that when Hemnalini slipped upstairs after tea he failed to notice her departure.

The lecturer — this Nalinaksha — had looked astonishingly young and boyish on the platform. Although he had attained maturity his countenance retained the freshness of youth. Withal he had an air of mystic gravity that seemed to emanate from his inner consciousness.

The subject of his address was "Loss," and its burden was that without loss there can be no genuine gain. What we obtain without effort is not true gain; only what is acquired through sacrifice becomes our own in the true and inner sense. He who sees his tangible possessions glide out of his grasp is unfortunate indeed; but in truth the human soul, in the very act of losing, retains the power to win back with interest that which is lost.

If when we suffer loss we can bow our heads, clasp our hands, and pronounce the words, "It is a gift — a gift of renunciation, a gift of sorrow, a gift of my tears," then the merest trifle acquires significance, the transient becomes the eternal, and what was a mere instrument of our daily use becomes an appurtenance of our worship, stored up everlastingly in the treasure-house of the temple of our heart.

His words had made a deep impression on Hemnalini. As she sat in a silent reverie on the house-top under the star-studded heavens, her heart was full and earth and sky seemed to her no longer an empty void.

As they were returning from the lecture Jogendra had remarked to Akshay:

"Well, you've hit on a most eligible man and no mistake! But what a mystic he is! Half of what he said was Greek to me."

"One has to diagnose the case before one can prescribe the medicine that the patient needs," returned Akshay. "Hemnalini is suffering from a delusion about Ramesh and it requires a mystic to arouse her from it. Simple folk like you and me couldn't do it. Did you look at her face while the fellow was spouting?"

Jogendra. "I did indeed. It was quite clear that she appreciated the stuff; but it doesn't follow that because she appreciated the lecture, she'll be prepared to bestow her hand on the lecturer."

Akshay. "She wouldn't have been enraptured with the lecture if you or I had delivered it. Asceticism has a great attraction for women, you know. Kalidas describes in his poem how Uma mortified the flesh for the sake of an ascetic. I tell you, Jogen, if you produce anyone else Hemnalini will contrast him with Ramesh and he won't come well out of the comparison. Now Nalinaksha is not like an ordinary person—it would never occur to one to compare him with anyone else. If you presented any other young man to her she would guess your motive and her whole mind would rise in revolt. But if you can invent some pretext for bringing Nalinaksha here and introducing him to her she'll suspect nothing. Then from respectful admiration to an engagement the transition will be gradual and easy."

Jogendra. "I'm no use at finesse; I prefer speaking out; and I must confess I'm not greatly impressed by the fellow."

Akshay. "Now, Jogen, if you bring in your own prejudices the whole thing will end in smoke. You mustn't expect to have everything exactly to your taste. We'll never succeed unless we can induce Hemnalini to forget Ramesh altogether. Don't imagine for a moment that you can accomplish that by brute force. You must follow my advice to the letter if you want to produce the desired result.

Jogendra. "The fact of the matter is, I find Nalinaksha a trifle mysterious. I'm nervous of dealing with that kind of person. It may be a case of 'out of the frying-pan into the fire.' "

Akshay. "Well, old man, if you get burnt it'll be your own fault. You tremble at a shadow these days. Where Ramesh was concerned you people were blind from the start. You thought the world of Ramesh — he was incapable of deceit, the greatest philosopher since Sankaracharyya, the most gifted writer of the century, and so on. Personally, I never took to Ramesh; I've seen lots like him in my time, people with the loftiest ideals. But I never dared open my mouth; you wouldn't have believed that a worthless incompetent like myself could have any motive but jealousy in criticising such a genius. I daresay you realise by this time that these supermen are best worshipped from afar; it's hardly safe to betroth one's sister to them. However, to return to the main issue. Remember the Sanskrit proverb, 'One thorn drives out another.' What I propose is the only course open to us at present, and you mustn't cavil at it."

Jogendra. "Look here, Akshay, you'll never make me believe that you were the first of us to see through Ramesh, not if you repeat it a thousand times. The truth was, you were so prejudiced against him that nothing he could do was right in your eyes, so you needn't try to impress me with your superior wisdom. Now remember, if there's to be any scheming and plotting you'll have to do it all yourself; you needn't expect any help from me. I don't care for Nalinaksha, and there's an end of it."

As Jogendra and Akshay entered Annada's room together Hemnalini slipped out by the other door.

"She must have looked out of the window and seen us coming up the street," thought Akshay. He smiled and seated himself beside Annada, remarking as he helped himself to a cup of tea, "Nalinaksha's words go to the heart, and the reason is that he speaks from the heart."

"He certainly has ability," said Annada Babu.

"Ability!" cried Akshay; "something more than that! Why, he's the saintliest character that walks the earth!"

Although Jogendra was a fellow-conspirator he could not help exclaiming, "For goodness' sake don't talk of saintly characters! Heaven preserve us from your saints!" And yet it was Jogendra who only the day before had lauded to the skies Nalinaksha's nobility of character, and had inveighed against his traducers as malevolent backbiters!

"Come, Jogendra," said his father, "you mustn't say things like that. Personally, I prefer to assume that people who are virtuous to outward appearance are virtuous at heart also. I may be mistaken in my judgement, but surely that's better then to be constantly suspecting saintly people, in the hope of preserving any reputation for sagacity that I may have.

"Nalinaksha didn't get his subject-matter at second-hand. He derived his material from his own spiritual experience, and I found his message a fresh and inspiring one. A hypocrite can't produce a genuine article. You couldn't tinker up an address like Nalinaksha's from borrowed materials, any more than a chemist can make synthetic gold. I felt inclined to go and thank him in person."

"My only fear is that his health may not stand the strain," groaned Akshay.

"Why, is his constitution not good?" exclaimed Annada Babu.

"He doesn't give it a fair chance. He spends the whole day praying and studying the scriptures, and pays no attention to his health."

"Well, that's very wrong of him," said Annada; "we have no right to neglect our bodies; we didn't create them ourselves. If I only had the opportunity I'd soon be able to restore him to health. To preserve one's health it is only necessary to follow a few simple rules; the first of them is —"

At this point Jogendra's patience gave out. "All this is beside the point, dad! Nalinaksha Babu is perfectly well. When I saw him this afternoon it struck me that the saintly life must conduce to bodily fitness. I've a good mind to try it myself!"

"I don't know, Jogendra," resumed Annada; "what Akshay says may be quite correct. Most of our greatest men die young. They do a dis-service to their country in neglecting their own health. It's not right that this should be so. You know, Jogendra, I think you're mistaken in your estimate of Nalinaksha Babu. He has the right stuff in him. He ought to be advised to take care of himself."

"Look here," said Akshay, "I'll bring him along and introduce him to you; I think it would be a good thing if you had a serious talk with him. That reminds me, there's that vegetable-juice that you prescribed for me when the examinations were on, it's a magnificent tonic. It's the finest stimulant imaginable for a brain-worker. You just take Nalinaksha Babu in hand and——"

Jogendra leapt to his feet. "Askahy, you'll drive me mad! You're talking the most utter nonsense. I can't stand this any longer," and he flung out of the room.

Chapter 42

*B*efore the crisis in Hemnalini's affairs Annada Babu had always enjoyed perfect health, nevertheless he had been in the habit of constantly swallowing nostrums prescribed by physicians of both the western and the indigenous schools of medicine. Now, however, he had lost all inclination for drugs. When his physical disorders existed only in his imagination he had found them an absorbing topic of conversation; but now that his health was really affected he never made any allusion to his bodily ailments.

He had fallen asleep in his chair from utter weariness when Hemnalini, hearing Jogendra's step on the stair, laid down her needlework and hurried to the door to warn her brother not to disturb the sleeper. To her dismay she found that he had brought Nalinaksha home with him! She was on the point of taking refuge in another room when Jogendra interposed.

"Hem!" he called to her, "I've brought Nalinaksha Babu. Let me introduce him to you."

Hem stood still in confusion while Nalinaksha approached and bowed without raising his eyes to her face.

Meanwhile Annada Babu had awakened and called
for his daughter. Hem re-entered the room and announced
in a whisper that "Nalinaksha Babu" was there.

Jogendra ushered in his guest and Annada Babu bustled
forward to greet him.

"We are indeed fortunate!" he exclaimed, "in having
a visit from you. Hem, dear, don't run away; sit down
here. Nalinaksha Babu, this is my daughter Hem. She and
I went to hear your address the other day and enjoyed it
greatly. There was one thing you said—about never losing
what we have once gained and incomplete gain being
really a loss—that struck me as a very profound truth.
Don't you agree, Hem? The real test comes when a thing
passes out of our possession. Then we know whether it
was truly our own or not. I have a request to make of you,
Nalin Babu. If you could drop in now and then for a talk
we should consider it a great favour. We don't go out
much. You may be certain of finding my daughter and
myself in this room at whatever hour you call."

Nalinaksha threw one glance at Hemnalini's self-
conscious face before he replied:

"You mustn't imagine me a solemn prig because I used
a lot of long words on the lecture-platform. It was only
because the students insisted that I consented to lecture at
all—I never could withstand importunate people—but I
think I have successfully deterred them from asking for a
repetition of the dose! The lads make no secret of the fact
that three-quarters of my address was incomprehensible
to them. You were there too, Jogen Babu, and you mustn't
suppose that your appealing glances at your watch left me
unmoved!"

"You mustn't mind me," said Jogendra; "if I couldn't
follow it all, my own intelligence must be at fault."

Annada. "After all, Jogen, there are certain things that
only people of a certain age can understand."

Nalinaksha. "Yes, and at certain ages one does not need to understand everything."

Annada. "By the way, Nalin Babu, there is one subject which I feel I must mention to you. The Creator sent men of your stamp into the world to perform certain tasks, hence you ought not to despise your body. People who have something to bestow have to be reminded that they ought not to squander their capital, otherwise they lose the power of giving."

Nalinaksha. "I think you will find when we become further acquainted that I despise nothing on earth. When I came into the world I was utterly dependent on the charity of others. It cost much labour and the fostering care of many individuals to bring my mind and body gradually to maturity. It would be unbecoming arrogance on my part to despise anything. What one cannot construct one has no title to destroy."

Annada. "Very true, very true. You said something to the same effect in your address."

Jogendra. "Well, I must be off; I have an engagement, but please don't let me disturb you.

Nalinaksha. "I must have your forgiveness before you go, Jogen Babu. I assure you I'm not in the habit of puzzling people. I had better be off too; we can go part of the way together."

Jogendra. "No, please, don't go. You mustn't mind me. I'm incapable of sitting still for long in one place."

Annada. "Never mind Jogen, please, Nalinaksha Babu. He comes and goes as he pleases and it's not easy to pin him down."

After Jogendra's departure Annada Babu asked Nalinaksha where he was residing. Nalinaksha laughed.

"I can't say that I'm living in any particular place at the moment. I have a great many acquaintances and they drag me about with them. I like it well enough, but one requires a little peace and quiet now and then, so Jogen Babu has taken rooms for me in the house next to this. This lane of yours is certainly a restful place."

Annada Babu was hugely gratified at this announcement, but if he had happened to glance at his daughter he would have noticed a momentary spasm of pain pass over her countenance. The next-door house was the one in which Ramesh had lived.

Tea was announced at this point and an adjournment was made to the ground floor.

"Hem, dear, give Nalin Babu a cup of tea," was Annada Babu's next remark.

The guest, however, politely declined the proffered refreshment.

Annada. "What's this, Nalin Babu? Won't you really have some tea? A cake, at least?"

Nalinaksha. "I must really ask you to excuse me."

Annada. "You're a doctor, so I can't lay down the law to you. But, personally, I look on tea as a pretext for drinking a modicum of hot water three or four hours after the midday meal, and I find it of benefit to my digestion. If you're not in the habit of drinking tea we can make it specially weak for you."

Nalinaksha glanced diffidently at Hemnalini and read in her expression that she was exercised over his reluctance and that she had been guessing at the cause of it. With his eyes on her face he proceeded: "I fear I have given you a wrong impression. Don't suppose for a moment that I have any prejudices against your customs. I used to take tea regularly at one time, I still enjoy its aroma, and I sympathise with your liking for it. You probably do not know, however, that my mother's view on ceremonial purity are very strict; and she is practically alone in the world but for me. I have to avoid any act that would impair the intimacy of our relations, and that is why I abstain from tea nowadays. In so far as you derive pleasure from drinking tea I can share in that pleasure, and my scruples do not debar me in the least from enjoying your hospitality."

Nalinaksha's first utterances had been in the nature of a shock to Hemnalini. It was patent to her that he had not revealed his true self to his auditors, but had merely been trying to conceal his real personality in a flood of talk. What she did not realise was that he was constitutionally incapable of talking to strangers without constraint, and that at his first meeting with anyone his shyness led him to assume an air of assurance foreign to his real nature. Even when he essayed to speak out his true thoughts, a jarring note was audible of which he was not unconscious himself. It was for this reason that when the restless Jogendra rose to go Nalinaksha's conscience had reproached him with insincerity, and he had attempted to escape also. When, however, Nalinaksha alluded to his mother, Hemnalini could not forbear gazing at him in reverent admiration, and her heart went out to him when she observed the expression of grave and earnest devotion that lit up his face the moment he mentioned her. She was conscious of an impulse to question him about his mother, but diffidence forbade.

"You're perfectly right," Annada Babu replied at once to Nalinaksha's last speech. "Had I known this I should never have invited you to take tea. Please forgive me."

"Why should I be denied your kind invitation merely because I don't drink tea?" was Nalinaksha's smiling rejoinder.

After the guest had departed Hemnalini took her father upstairs and began to read the articles in a Bengal review to him till he dropped off to sleep. Such surrenders to fatigue had become habitual with the old gentleman of late.

Chapter 43

Nalinaksha's acquaintance with Annada Babu and his daughter soon ripened into intimacy. Before she knew him Hemnalini had supposed that Nalinaksha's discourse would be confined to spiritual matters and she had never imagined that one could converse as freely with him on every-day topics as one could with ordinary people. She soon found that he was quite capable of light conversation, and yet in the midst of the most animated talk he retained an air of aloofness.

On one occasion while Annada Babu and Hemnalini were conversing with Nalinaksha Jogendra burst in and addressed himself to his father. "I say, dad," he exclaimed, "people in the Samaj have begun to call us Nalinaksha Babu's 'disciples,' and I've just had a serious quarrel with Paresh about it!"

"I don't consider it anything to take offence at," said Annada Babu, smiling; "I should be ashamed to belong to a society in which all were teachers and none disciples. You'd have everybody lecturing at the top of his voice and there would be no chance to learn anything."

Nalinaksha. "I'll enrol myself under your banner, Annada Babu. Let us all be disciples. We'll start on a round tour, halting at any place where we're likely to learn something."

Jogendra, however, was not to be appeased.

That's all very well," he said, "but it's a serious matter. Why, Nalin Babu, your own friends and relations won't be allowed to visit you without being dubbed your 'disciples.' One can't laugh away an insult like that. You really should give up these practices of yours."

Nalinaksha. "What practices?"

Jogendra. "I've been told that you breathe through your nostrils like a Yogi, and gaze at the rising sun, and that you can't eat or drink without all sorts of ceremonial. The result is that you're out of place—' out of the scabbard,' as we say—in ordinary society."

Hemnalini dropped her eyes in disgust at Jogendra's unmannerly outburst, but Nalinaksha only smiled.

"Well, Jogen Babu," he replied, "I admit that the man who is out of place in ordinary society must be at fault, but surely no human being, and more than a sword, should always remain in the scabbard? The part of a sword which the scabbard conceals is the essential part of the weapon, common to all swords. It is on the hilt that the artificer displays his individual craftsmanship in whatever design suits his taste. Similarly a human being finds scope for exhibiting his own peculiar pattern outside society's scabbard and you surely would not wish to deprive him of that liberty! But what astonishes me is how people can see and find opportunity to discuss what I do out of the public eye in the privacy of my own room."

Jogendra. "You are perhaps unaware that those who have imposed on themselves the task of regenerating the world consider it their bounden duty to discover what is going on in their neighbours' houses. Even when knowledge is lacking they call in another faculty to supply the deficiency. It must be so, otherwise the process of remodelling the world would be arrested. Besides, Nalin Babu, it is when one does unconventional things, even in supposed privacy, that people take notice. Observe the ordinary conventions and no one will waste a glance on you. Why, Hem here has noticed your proceedings on the roof of your house and she told dad about them, though she hasn't assumed the task of regenerating you!"

Hemnalini's expression clearly showed the indignation that she felt. She was about to speak when Nalinaksha turned to her.

"There is nothing to be ashamed of! If you happened to be taking the air on the roof at the time of my morning or evening worship you did nothing wrong. You needn't be ashamed of possessing a pair of eyes; that's a crime of which we are all guilty!"

Annada. "What's more, Hem never told me that she disapproved of your daily worship. She simply, and in all reverence, questioned me about your devotional practices."

Jogendra. "Well the fact is I don't understand your point of view. I find no discomfort in the ordinary course of human life and conduct and I can't see the advantage of carrying on strange practices in secret. That sort of thing tends to upset the mind's balance and make a man one-sided. You mustn't take offence because I say so. I'm a very commonplace person. I occupy one of the lowest seats in the world's theatre and have no means of reaching those who sit in the high places except by throwing bricks at them. There are innumerable people like myself, so if you leave them behind and climb into an unreal world of your own you become the target of innumerable bricks."

Nalinaksha. "Well, there are bricks and bricks. Some only graze, others leave a mark. Call a man mad or childish and no harm is done, but call him a religious maniac, accuse him of setting himself up as a prophet and trying to gather disciples round him, and all the laughter in the world is insufficient to laugh the charge out of court!"

Jogendra. "I must beg you again not to take offence, Nalin Babu. Do what you please on your own roof, I have no right to object. My only comment is that so long as one keeps oneself within the limits of convention no occasion for remark arises. Personally, I'm quite content to tread the same oath as other people. Once you overstep the boundaries a crowd collects. Whether it scoffs or prays is immaterial. Life in the middle of a crowd would be insupportable!"

Nalinaksha. "Hallo, where are you off to, Jogen Babu? You have just hurled me down from the house-top to the prosaic level of the ground floor and you want to rush away. This will never do!"

Jogendra. "I've had enough for to-day. I'm going out for a walk."

After her brother's exit Hemnalini sat with downcast eyes nervously fingering the fringe of the table-cloth. Close inspection would have revealed tear-drops trembling on her eyelashes. Daily contact with Nalinaksha had laid bare to her her own failings of character and she strove passionately to follow in the track that he had indicated. In her hour of trial, when she cast about in vain for some external or internal support, Nalinaksha had shown her the world in a new aspect, and now as time went on she became more and more enamoured of the idea of subjecting herself, after the fashion of a devotee, to a stern self-discipline which in itself would serve as a support.

Moreover sorrow is an emotion which is not content to exist merely as a certain frame of the mind. It seeks to find an outlet in the performance of some difficult task. Hitherto Hemnalini had not been able to nerve herself to any such effort and in her shrinking from publicity she had cherished her grief in the most secret chambers of her heart. Great was the relief when she formed the resolution to follow in Nalinaksha's footsteps and subject herself to an austere ordinance and a fleshless diet. In pursuance of her decision she stripped her room bare. Carpet and rugs were lifted and stored away, and her bed was hidden behind a screen. Everyday she sprinkled water on the floor with her own hands and swept it clean. A flower-bowl was the only ornament that she retained. After bathing she would dress in spotless white and seat herself on the floor, while the sunshine poured unobstructed through the open windows and flooded the room, and she steeped her whole being in the light and the winds of heaven.

Annada Babu could not rise to the same height of religious ecstasy as his daughter, but the old man rejoiced at the radiance that her self-imposed discipline imparted to Hemnalini's face. When Nalinaksha visited the house it was on the floor of Hemnalini's room that the trio sat and held converse.

Jogendra voiced his disapproval loudly. "I don't know what has come over you all," he snarled. "Between the three of you you've made nearly the whole house holy ground; there's hardly a sport where a fellow like me can set foot."

There was a time when Hemnalini would have been deeply offended by her brother's taunts, but now, though Annada Babu's temper occasionally gave way under the lash of Jogendra's sarcasm, Hemnalini followed Nalinaksha's lead and merely smiled sweetly. She had at last found a sure, unfailing, and complete support, and to be ashamed would have been contemptible weakness. That her acquaintances derided her austerity as mere eccentricity she knew full well, but her trust in Nalinaksha and her

admiration for his ideals armed her against all mankind
and she faced the world unabashed.

One morning she had bathed and finished her devotions
and was sitting in the solitude of her chamber before the
open window, absorbed in meditation, when Annada Babu
ushered in Nalinaksha. Hemnalini's heart was full to
overflowing. With a gesture of reverence, due only to an
honoured parent or a venerated preceptor she prostrated
herself before each in turn and touched the dust of their
feet, much to Nalinaksha's confusion.

Annada Babu, however, reassured him. "Don't be
embarrassed, Nalinaksha Babu," he said, "she is only doing
what is right."

Nalinaksha had never visited them so early in the
morning and Hemnalini glanced up expectantly at his
face. He explained that he had just heard from Benares
that his mother was ill; he would have to leave Calcutta
by the night train, and as the whole day would be taken
up with preparations for the journey he had come thus
early to bid them farewell.

"I'm greatly distressed to hear of your mother's illness,"
said Annada Babu. "May Heaven soon restore her to
health. I shall never be able to repay you for all the help
you have given us during the past weeks."

"It is I who am in your debt, I assure you," Nalinaksha
replied. "You showed true neighbourly feeling in the trouble
that you took to make me comfortable next door. Moreover
your earnestness has given a new meaning to the profound
problems on which I have been meditating for some time
past. Your manner of life has been an inspiration to me
in my speculations and my devotions and has made them
appear doubly efficacious. The benefit to be derived from
communion with fellow-creatures who share the same
aspirations has been brought home to me."

"The strange thing," resumed Annada Babu, "is that before we knew you, we stood in sore need of something that we could not define. At this juncture you suddenly appeared on the scene and I realised that your help was indispensable. We are stay-at-home folk who do not go much into society and we never shared the craze for attending meetings and listening to speeches; even if I went myself it was very difficult to persuade Hem to stir. What happened then was in the nature of a miracle. As soon as we heard from Jogen that you were to lecture we went straight off to hear you without the slightest demur — quite an unprecedented thing, I assure you, Nalin Babu! Such a thing could never have happened had you not been marked out by Providence to assist us. We are eternally in your debt."

Nalinaksha. "Let me tell you something in my turn. I have never disclosed the intimate facts of my life to anyone but yourselves. To reach the highest pitch of truthfulness one must lay bare all secrets and it is your help that has enabled me to comply with this insistent requirement. I must impress on you accordingly how indispensable you have been to me."

Hemnalini took no part in the conversation but sat in silent contemplation of the sunshine, that glowed through the windows and lit up the floor around her, till Nalinaksha was about to take leave. Then she simply said, "Be sure to let us know how your mother is," and as he rose to depart she prostrated herself before him once more.

Chapter 44

*A*kshay had given the house a wide berth of late, but, after Nalinaksha's departure for Benares, Jogendra brought him in to tea again. Akshay hoped to gauge from Hemnalini's behaviour to what extent the memory of Ramesh still obsessed her thoughts, but as a matter of fact she appeared perfectly at ease.

"We've seen very little of you lately," she remarked with unaffected friendliness.

"Do you think I'm worth seeing everyday?" he retorted.

"Well," laughed Hemnalini, "if you really think one shouldn't pay calls unless one is worth seeing, many of us would have to spend our days in solitude!"

Jogendra. "Akshay thought he would take a prize for humility, but Hem goes one better and tries to excel all mankind in that quality. However, I have something to say on that point. Ordinary people like myself are suitable company everyday, but there are exceptional persons whom one can only endure now and then; to meet them often would be unbearable. That's why they go wandering about among forests and mountains and caverns. If they settled down permanently in people's houses humble individuals like Jogendra and Akshay would have to take to the woods."

There was a sting in Jogendra's words and Hemnalini was conscious of it, but instead of retorting she merely poured out a cup of tea for each of the three men.

"Aren't you going to have any tea?" asked her brother.

Hemnalini knew that she must expect a scolding from Jogendra, but she answered with perfect composure, "No, I've given up tea."

Jogendra. "So you've turned ascetic in right earnest. Tea-leaves don't contain enough of the true spiritual essence, I suppose? That's reserved for the myrobalans that ascetics use. This really is the limit! For Heaven's sake drop it, Hem! Never mind if drinking a cup of tea does interrupt your penance. The most lasting things don't endure for long, so why make a fuss about trifles"; and he poured out another cup and placed it before Hemnalini.

Leaving it untouched, she exclaimed, "Why, dad, you've taken nothing with your tea! Won't you eat anything?"

Annada Babu's voice and hands trembled as he replied: "Believe me, dear, if I tried to eat anything now it would choke me. I've been trying for a long time to submit in silence to Jogen's rudeness and I'm reduced to such a state that, if I spoke, I should say something in the heat of the moment for which I should be sorry afterwards."

Hemnalini rose and went over to her father's chair.

"Don't be angry, dad," she murmured. "It was kind of Jogen to offer me a cup of tea and I'm not offended in the least. Come now, you must take something. I know tea doesn't agree with you unless you eat something with it," and she brought a plate of cakes and laid it before him.

Annada began to eat very slowly.

Hemnalini returned to her own seat and was on the point of drinking out of the cup that Jogendra had poured out for her when Akshay jumped up and exclaimed—

"Excuse me, let me have that cup! I've finished mine."

Jogendra rose and took the cup from Hemnalini, then, turning to his father, he said, "I am sorry, please forgive me."

Annada could not command his voice sufficiently to reply and tears gathered in his eyes. Jogendra and Akshay slipped quietly out of the room. After a few mouthfuls Ammada Babu also rose, took his daughter's arm, and tottered upstairs.

That night he had an attack of acute pain. The doctor was called in and announced that the patient was suffering from internal inflammation; a stay of a year, or six months at least, in some bracing locality up-country might restore his health completely.

"Hem, dear," said the old man when the pain was easier and the doctor had departed, "let us go to Benares and stay there for a while."

The same idea had simultaneously occurred to Hemnalini.

Since Nalinaksha's departure she had become conscious of a certain weakening in her devotions. So long as he was at hand she had found her austerities an unfailing solace, and the glow of steadfast piety and tranquil kindness that illuminated his face had served, as it were, to confirm her faith.

In his absence it seemed as though her zeal had suffered an eclipse, albeit on the day after his departure she had striven hard against her own inclinations and had attempted to follow his precepts with redoubled keenness. Lassitude had however, inevitably set in and generated such despair that she could restrain her tears no longer.

At the tea-table she had nerved herself to the exercise of hospitality, but a weight had been pressing on her heart and the pain of the old memories reasserted itself in a still more formidable guise. The consciousness that she was without prospect and the impulse to cast herself adrift in desperation returned. Her father's proposal was accordingly most opportune and she embraced it eagerly.

"Yes, let us go there, dad!" she exclaimed.

Noticing the bustle of preparation next day Jogendra asked what was up, and his father informed him that he and Hemnalini were going up-country.

"Where to?" inquired Jogendra.

"We'll tour abut a little before we settle down," replied Annada, who shrank from admitting to his son that their destination was Benares.

"Sorry I can't come with you," said Jogendra, "I have sent in my application for that head-mastership and I'm waiting for an answer."

Chapter 45

*R*amesh returned to Ghazipur from Allahabad at an early hour in the morning. The streets were almost empty and in the piercing cold the trees bordering the road seemed to huddle for warmth into their leafy coverings. A fleecy mist lay over each hamlet, like a mother-swan brooding over her eggs. As he drove along the deserted thoroughfare to his bungalow, wrapped in a huge overcoat, Ramesh was conscious of nothing but the pulsations of his eager heart.

He stopped his carriage at the gate and alighted; Kamala must have heard the sound of the wheels and would be awaiting him on the verandah. He had brought with him from Allahabad a costly necklace which he intended to throw over her neck himself, and he now took the box containing this ornament out of the capacious pocket of his overcoat. As he approached the bungalow, however, he found all the doors closed and the bearer Bishan slumbering peacefully on the verandah. He paused for a moment in chagrin, then shouted to Bishan by name, in the hope that the sound would penetrate indoors and awaken another sleeper. This was a cold welcome for one whom excitement had kept awake half the night!

Repeated shouts failed to awaken Bishan and finally Ramesh had to shake him. The bearer sat up and gazed round for a second or two in bewilderment.

"Is your mistress at home?" asked Ramesh.

For a moment Bishan looked puzzled, then the purport of the question suddenly dawned on him.

"Yes, she's at home," he murmured drowsily, and falling back composed himself to sleep again.

The door opened at a push. Ramesh entered and glanced into one room after another, but all were untenanted.

He shouted "Kamala!" but there was no response.

He made the round of the garden, going as far as the *nim*-tree, and searched the kitchen, the servants' quarters, and the stables, but Kamala was nowhere to be found.

In the meantime the sun had risen, the crows had begun to caw, and two or three village girls had appeared, carrying jars on their heads, in quest of water from the well of the compound.

In a walled courtyard across the road peasant women had set to work grinding wheat, singing the while in shrill discordant notes.

Returning to the bungalow, Ramesh found that Bishan was once more buried in slumber. Bending down and shaking the sleeper vigorously Ramesh noticed that his breath smelt strongly of toddy. The rough handling partially restored Bishan to his senses and he scrambled to his feet.

"Where's your mistress?" inquired Ramesh.

"Why, surely she's in the house."

Ramesh. "Nonsense, she's not there."

Bishan. "She certainly came here yesterday."

Ramesh. "Where did she go after that?"

Bishan merely gaped, and at that moment Umesh appeared, gorgeously attired in Kamala's finery, with eyes bloodshot from want of sleep.

"Where's mother, Umesh?" inquired his master.

"She has been here since yesterday."

"Where have you been?"

"Mother sent me to see the play at Sidhu Babu's."

"What about my fare, sir?" interjected the driver at this point.

Ramesh leaped into the carriage and drove straight to Uncle's house. Everything there was in confusion, and his first thought was that Kamala had been taken ill, but he was mistaken. Late in the evening Umi had suddenly commenced to scream, her face had turned blue, and her hands and feet had become cold as ice, to the great alarm of all the elders. The whole household had been kept busy attending to her and no one had had a wink of sleep. Ramesh jumped to the conclusion that Kamala had been called in to assist in nursing the sick child and he remarked to Bipin accordingly: "Kamala must be greatly worried about poor little Umi." Bipin did not know for certain whether Kamala had come over during the night or not, so he simply nodded and answered, "Yes, she was very fond of the child and she must certainly be anxious. However, the doctor says there is no cause for alarm."

Reassuring as this might be, Ramesh's lively hopes had received a check; he felt correspondingly depressed and it seemed to him that some malevolent agency was working against his union with Kamala.

Umesh now arrived from the bungalow. The boy had free access to the *zenana* and Sailaja was very fond of him.

Seeing him enter the house and approach her room, she had hastened to the door to warn him against wakening the child, when to her astonishment he asked where Kamala was.

"Why, dear me, you went off with her to your house yesterday!" said Sailaja. "I thought of sending Lachminia to her last night, but Umi's sickness prevented that."

"And she's not here now?" groaned Umesh.

"What do you mean?" snapped out Saila. "Where were you all night?"

Umesh. "Mother wouldn't let me stay with her. When we got to the bungalow she packed me off to Siddhu Babu's to see the play."

Saila. "You're a fine fellow! Where was Bishan?"

Umesh. "Bishan knows nothing at all. He drank too much toddy last night."

Saila. "Call my husband then, and be quick about it."

"I say!" she exclaimed when Bipin appeared, "a terrible thing has happened!"

Bipin turned pale. "Why, what is it?" he exclaimed anxiously.

Saila. "Kamala went to her bungalow yesterday, but they can't find her there now!"

Bipin. "Didn't she come here last night?"

Saila. "Of course not! I thought of sending for her when Umi was taken ill, but I couldn't spare anyone to fetch her. Has Ramesh Babu come here?"

Bipin. "I suppose when he couldn't find her there he assumed she had come here. Yes, he's in the house."

Saila. "Go off with him at once and look for her! Umi's asleep, she's all right now."

Bipin and Ramesh drove straight to the bugalow in Ramesh's carriage and tackled Bishan again. By their united efforts they succeeded at last in eliciting from him the following meagre details:

Late in the afternoon Kamala had started off alone towards the river. Bishan had offered to accompany her, but she had declined his escort and had given him a rupee. He had then taken his post at the gate to guard the bungalow and while he was there a toddy-tapper had come along carrying a pot of fresh-drawn toddy, frothing and bubbling over. As to what happened after that Bishan had no clear recollection!

He pointed out the path which Kamala had taken on her way towards the Ganges.

Along that path through the dewy crops Ramesh, Bipin, and Umesh set forth in search of Kamala, Umesh darting frenzied glances from side to side like a tigress robbed of her young.

Reaching the river-bank all three halted; they had here an uninterrupted view of the whole waste of sand shimmering in the morning sun, but not a soul was in sight.

Umesh called aloud, "O mother, where are you?" but there was no response except from the echo which flung back the words from the high bank across the wide river.

Prowling around Umesh espied a white object in the distance, and darting towards it, found a bunch of keys wrapped in a handkerchief lying at the water's edge.

"Hallo, what's that?" called Ramesh, arriving simultaneously.

It was indeed Kamala's bunch of keys. Close to where the keys lay the stream had left a small deposit of alluvium and in the soft mud they described the deep prints of two little feet leading towards the water. A glistening object in the shallow water caught Umesh's roving eye. He drew it out and it proved to be a small enamel brooch mounted in gold, Ramesh's gift to Kamala.

Realising that all the indications pointed clearly towards the Ganges, Umesh broke down completely.

He leapt into the shallow water shrieking, "Mother, O mother!" and plunged again and again below the surface like a mad creature, groping with his hands at the bottom till the water was turbid.

Ramesh was too dazed to utter a word and it was Bipin who called to Umesh:

"What are you doing? Come out of that!"

"I won't come out," sputtered Umesh. "Oh, mother, how could you go and leave me like that?"

Bipin had really no cause to be nervous, for the boy could swim like a fish and could hardly have drowned himself if he had tried. He wearied at last of floundering in the water, and emerging from the river, wallowed on the sand, weeping bitterly.

Bipin laid his hand on Ramesh's shoulder to arouse him from his stupor.

"Come, Ramesh Babu," he said, "we're only wasting time here. We'll send word to the police and they'll make all possible inquiries."

No one in Sailaja's entourage had any food or sleep that day and the house resounded with cries of grief.

Fishermen were engaged to drag the river thoroughly and the police scoured the whole countryside. Special inquiries were made at the railway station, but no Bengali girl answering to Kamala's description had been seen entering the night train.

Uncle arrived that afternoon, and when he heard a detailed account of the occurrence and of Kamala's strange beheaviour prior to her disappearance, he became convinced that she had committed suicide by drowning.

"I know now," remarked Lachminia, "why Umi cried so and took such a turn last night. We'll need to exorcise her bad luck pretty thoroughly!"

So utterly stupefied was Ramesh by the catastrophe that he could not shed a single tear.

"To think," he mused, "that Kamala should come to me out of the Ganges and that she should be swallowed up again in the self-same river like some innocent flower that a worshipper throws into the stream!"

He returned to the river after sunset, and standing on the spot where the keys had been found, gazed once more at the little footprints. Then he removed his shoes, girt up his waist-cloth, and wading out into the river, took from its box the necklace that he had brought from Allahabad and flung it into midstream.

He remained no longer in Ghazipur, but the inmates of Uncle's house were so prostrated by the sad event that at the time no one missed him.

Chapter 46

*R*amesh's future was now a blank. He had nothing to look forward to, no regular work, no settled habitation. It must not be supposed that he had completely forgotten Hemnalini. Rather, he had cast the thought of her aside.

"The cruel blow that Fate has dealt me has made me permanently unfit for this world's affairs," he said to himself. "A blasted tree is out of place in a green-wood."

He sought relief in travel and flitted restlessly from place to place. He surveyed the pageant of the Benares ghats from a boat on the Ganges. He proceeded to Delhi and ascended the Kutub Minar; thence to Agra, where he visited the Taj Mahal in the moonlight. From Amritsar, with its Golden Temple, he journeyed to Rajputana and made pilgrimage to the shrines on Mount Abu. Neither body nor mind had any rest while the roaming spirit possessed him.

But at last nostalgia set in and his thoughts turned to home — the peaceful home of his childhood, now almost forgotten, and the ideal home of his whilom imagination. When the call became too insistent, the wanderings by which he had hoped to assuage his misery came to a sudden end. He secured a seat in the next Calcutta-bound express and with a prodigious sigh took his place in the train.

Ramesh had been some days in Calcutta before he nerved himself to set foot in Kalutola. One day he went as far as the entrance to the lane in which he had lived, and on the following evening he summoned up courage and marched up to the front door of Annada Babu's house. All the doors and windows were shut and barred, and there were no signs of human occupancy. It occurred to him that the bearer Sukhan might have been left behind to guard the empty house, and he knocked at the door several times and called to the bearer, but there was no response. A neighbour, Chandra Mohan, who was sitting in his porch smoking a *hookah*, now hailed him: "Hallo, Ramesh Babu, is that really you? How are you? None of Annada Babu's people are at home."

"Do you happen to know where they've gone, sir?" asked Ramesh.

Chandra Mohan. "I can't say. They're gone somewhere up-country, that's all I know."

Ramesh. "Which of them went there?"

Chandra. "Annada Babu and his daughter."

Ramesh. "Do you know for certain that no one else went with them?"

Chandra. "Yes, I'm quite sure of that; I saw them start."

Ramesh could contain himself no longer.

"Some one told me," he proceeded, "that a gentleman called Nalin Babu accompanied them."

Chandra. "Your informant was wrong. Nalin Babu stayed for some time in your old lodgings there, but he started for Benares several days before Annada Babu left Calcutta."

Ramesh then proceeded to draw out Chandra Mohan on the subject of this Nalin Babu, and was informed that his full name was Nalinaksha Chattopadhyay; he was supposed to have had a practice in Rangpur, but was now living with his mother in Benares.

After a short pause Ramesh asked if Chandra Mohan knew where Jogen was at the moment. He was told that Jogendra had gone to a place called Bisaipur, in Mymensingh, where he was headmaster of a high school established by a landowner of the place.

Chandra Mohan now began to question Ramesh in turn.

"I haven't seen you for a long time, Ramesh Babu," he remarked. "Where have you been all these days?"

Ramesh saw no reason for further concealment.

"I went to practise in Ghazipur," he answered.

"Are you going to make your home there?"

"No, I don't mean to settle down there after all. I haven't decided where to go next."

Ramesh was not long gone when Akshay arrived. When Jogendra left Calcutta he had requested Akshay to visit the house occasionally during the family's absence.

Akshay never neglected a duty that he had undertaken, and he made a practice of dropping in at odd times to see that one or other of the two bearers was duly guarding the premises.

Chandra Mohan greeted him with the remark, "Ramesh Babu was here a few minutes ago; he has just left."

Akshay. "Really? What did he want here?"

Chandra. "I don't know; I gave him all the information I could about the family. He looked so ill that I couldn't recognise him at first. It was only when he called for the bearer and I heard his voice that I spotted who it was."

Akshay. "Did you find out where he's staying now?"

Chandra. "He has been at Ghazipur all this time. He has left the place now and hasn't decided where he's going to live."

"Oh," said Akshay, and turned his attention to his own business.

Ramesh returned to his lodgings, musing as he went: "Fate continues to make terrible game of me! My relations with Kamala on the one hand and Nalinaksha's with Hemnalini on the other would make a plot for a novel—and a crude one at that! Such a mix-up is worthy of an author like Fate, who will stick at nothing! It is in real life that the most extraordinary things happen—things that are the most hardened novelist would never dare to spring on the public as his own invention!" Nevertheless, he now felt himself free from the worst of his entanglement. When it came to composing a finale to the last chapter of his intricate life's history Fate would surely not be too hard on him!

Jogendra lived in a one-storied house near the landowner's residence. He was reading the newspaper there one Sunday morning when a man from the bazaar brought him a note. He rubbed his eyes when he saw the handwriting on the envelope. Opening it, he found that Ramesh had written to say that he was waiting in a shop at Bisaipur and had something important to communicate.

Jogendra leapt up from his chair. He had parted from Ramesh in anger after a stormy scene, but that was long ago, and when the friend of his boyhood suddenly appeared in these wilds he could not send him abruptly to the right-about. Jogendra was actually pleased at the thought of meeting Ramesh, nor was his mind free from curiosity. It would do no harm to see him, especially as Hemnalini was far away.

Taking the bearer of the note with him, Jogendra set off himself in quest of Ramesh. He found him sitting alone on an upturned kerosene tin in a grocer's shop. The grocer had offered him tobacco in the hookah reserved for

Brahmans, but when he learned the spectacled gentleman was no smoker, the worthy tradesman had classed him as some unaccountable product of city life and had made no further attempt to discover his identity or to engage him in conversation.

Jogendra went forward at once, grasped Ramesh by the hand and drew him to his feet.

"I really can't cope with you!" he cried, "you're as diffident as ever. Why couldn't you come straight to my quarters instead of sticking in a grocer's shop half-way? One would think you enjoyed the aroma of treacle and the perfume of fried rice!"

Taken aback by this greeting, Ramesh merely smiled. Jogendra hurried him off, keeping up an incessant flow of talk.

"The theologians may preach what they like," he said, "but to me the workings of Providence are inscrutable. Look at me now! I was brought up in a city to be a thorough townsman, and now I'm cast into this howling wilderness to starve my soul among the clods!"

"It's not a bad place at all," remarked Ramesh, looking round.

Jogendra. "Meaning——?"

Ramesh. "Meaning that there's solitude——"

Jogendra. "And consequently I'm trying hard to intensify the solitude by driving away the only companionable soul in the place!"

Ramesh. "All the same, if it's peace of mind——"

Jogendra. "Don't tell me that! For a time I was absolutely stiffed with excessive peace of mind here. It wasn't long before I took to my favourite pastime of breaking the peace. At present I'm at daggers drawn with the secretary of the school committee, and after the sample of my temper that I've given the landlord he won't be in a hurry to attack

me again. He wanted to employ me as his trumpeter in
the English newspapers, but I made it quite plain to him
that I am my own master. It isn't my virtues that keep me
on here. The Joint Magistrate thinks a lot of me, so the
landlord is afraid to turn me out. Some day I'll see in the
Gazette that the Joint Magistrate has been transferred to
some other district. Then I'll know that my sun has set and
that the days of my headmastership at Bisaipur are
numbered. Now I've only one person left to talk to—my
dog Punch. The looks that other people cast at me aren't
what one calls auspicious!"

They reached Jogendra's quarters, where Ramesh at
once subsided into a chair.

"Don't sit down yet," said Jogendra. "I haven't
forgotten your prejudice in favour of a morning bath. Go
and have your tub now. Meanwhile I'll put the kettle on
again and make your arrival an excuse to indulge in a
second brew of tea."

The whole day passed in eating, talking, and resting,
and Jogendra never gave Ramesh a chance to mention the
important business which had brought him to Bisaipur.

After supper, however, they drew their chairs into the
lamplight, and while jackals howled outside and the
darkness vibrated to the trilling of the crickets, Ramesh
had at last an opportunity to explain his errand.

"Well, Jogen," he began, "your intuition must tell you
what has brought me here. You once asked me a question
which at the time I was unable to answer. There is no
longer anything to prevent my answering it."

Ramesh relapsed into silence. After a few moments he
proceeded slowly to relate the whole story of his connection
with Kamala from beginning to end. At times he choked
and his voice trembled, and at certain points he stopped
altogether. Jogendra heard him out in silence.

When he had finished Jogendra sighed.

"Had you told it all to me that day I couldn't have believed it!"

"It's just as incredible to-day as it was then. I want you to come with me to the village where I was married; then I'll take you on to Kamala's uncle's house."

"I refuse to stir a step. I'm ready to believe every word you say without moving from this chair. I had always been in the habit of trusting you implicitly and you must forgive me for my one departure from a life long custom."

Jogendra rose from his chair and the two old friends embraced.

When Ramesh found his voice he went on: "Fate involved me in such an inextricable web of falsehood that I could see no remedy except to draw everything into its meshes. Now that I am clear of it and have nothing more to conceal I can breathe freely again. I don't know to this day, and am never likely to know, what induced Kamala to commit suicide, but this much is certain, it was the only possible solution for her. The pair of us were in such a tangle that I shudder to think of the difficulties with which we should ultimately have been faced had she not cut the Gordian knot in this way. She was snatched suddenly and unexpectedly out of the jaws of death, and as suddenly and unexpectedly she disappeared into them again!"

"You needn't take it for granted that Kamala committed suicide. However, the way is clear for you, so far as that is concerned. There's only the question of Nalinaksha now," and Jogendra proceeded to discourse on Nalinaksha. "I don't understand that type of person," he said, "and what I don't understand I don't like; but a lot of people are the other way about—what they don't understand appeals to them most. That's why I'm afraid for Hem. Things began to look bad when she gave up tea and wouldn't eat meat or fish. Then her eyes lost their old sparkle and even when one said something cutting she only smiled sweetly. However, if I have your help, we'll rescue her in no time, you may be sure of that. So gird on your armour and the two of us will join battle against the ascetic."

Ramesh laughed.

"I haven't much reputation as a fighting-man, but I'm ready."

Jogendra. "Just wait till the Christmas holidays."

Ramesh. "They don't begin for some days yet. Hadn't I better go ahead by myself."

Jogendra. "No, no, that would never do. It was I who broke off your engagement and I must renew it again by my own efforts. I can't let you go on with the advance-guard and rob me of so congenial a task."

Ramesh. "Then in the meantime I had better——"

Jogendra. "Certainly not! You are my guest for the next ten days. I've polished off all the people there are to quarrel with here and I need a friend's society to enable me to change my tune. I've had nothing to occupy me in the evenings so far except to listen to the jackals howling, and I'm in such a parlous state that your voice sounds to me like the sweetest of music!"

Chapter 47

The information which he had received from Chandra Mohan afforded Akshay much food for thought.

"What can be at the bottom of it," he asked himself. "So Ramesh has been practising at Ghazipur, has he? He succeeded in covering his tracks pretty well! What can have induced him to throw up his practice and to have the effrontery to show his face again in this street? He's bound to discover sooner or later that Annada Babu and Hemnalini are in Benares; then he'll make a bee-line for the place."

Akshay resolved to visit Ghazipur in the meantime and to collect all possible information there; after that he would proceed to Benares and seek an interview with Annada Babu.

It thus happened that on a December afternoon shortly afterwards Akshay might have been seen alighting at Ghazipur, bag in hand.

He commenced operations by tackling the shopkeepers in the market and asking if anyone knew the address of a Bengali pleader named Ramesh Babu; but exhaustive inquiries convinced him that no lawyer of that name was known to the local tradesmen.

He next tried the courts, which had just closed for the day. A beturbaned Bengali pleader was on the point of stepping into his carriage when Akshay accosted him with the remark, "Excuse me, sir. I'm looking for one Ramesh Chandra Chaudhuri, a Bengali pleader who came here recently; do you happen to know where he lives?"

He was informed that Ramesh had lived for some time in Uncle's house, but whether he was still there or not the pleader did not know; his wife was missing and it was believed that she had been drowned.

Akshay now directed his steps to Uncle's house.

"I see Ramesh's game now," he mused as he went along, "his wife is dead and he will now proceed to demonstrate to Hemnalini's satisfaction that he never had a wife. In her present frame of mind Hemnalini will believe anything that she hears from Ramesh. These over-righteous folk are really terrible fellows when one penetrates their secrets!' and Akshay mentally congratulated himself on his own integrity.

Questioned by Akshay regarding Ramesh and Kamala, Uncle was unable to control his emotion and tears flowed from his eyes.

"As you are a special friend of Ramesh Babu," he said, "you must have known that dear girl Kamala intimately; so you will not be surprised to hear that I had only known her for a day or two when I completely forgot that she was not one of my own daughters. How could I have foreseen that the dear girl would inflict such a terrible blow on one whom she had so thoroughly captivated in so short a time?"

"The whole thing seems to me inexplicable," replied Akshay in feigned sympathy. "It's obvious that Ramesh can't have treated her well."

"Ramesh is a friend of yours and you mustn't take offence at what I say; but to tell the truth, I've never been able to understand him. He's a pleasant enough fellow to talk to, but it's impossible to know what's going on in his mind. He must be abnormal, otherwise one can't explain how he could neglect such a charming little wife as Kamala. She was so true to him that though she and my daughter were as intimate as two sisters she never breathed a word against her husband. My daughter could tell very well at times that Kamala was brooding over something, but to the end she never got a word out of the child. It breaks my heart, as you may well imagine, to think what a girl like her must have suffered before she took the final plunge. The cruellest feature is that I happened to be away in Allahabad at the time. Had I been on the spot I do not believe she would have had the heart to desert me."

Next morning Uncle conducted Akshay to Ramesh's bungalow and together they visited the scene of Kamala's disappearance.

Akshay made no comment till their return to Chakrabartti's house, when he remarked to the old gentleman, "Do you know, sir, I can't feel as certain as you that Kamala actually committed suicide by drowning herself in the Ganges."

Uncle. "What's your opinion then?"

Akshay. "I'm inclined to believe that she ran away from home. We ought to have a thorough search made for her."

Uncle leapt up from his chair in his excitement.

"You may be right!" he exclaimed, "it's by no means improbable."

Akshay, "Benares is not far from here. A family with whom both Ramesh and myself were very intimate is living there. It's possible that Kamala took shelter with them."

Why, Ramesh Babu never told me that!" cried Uncle, his natural buoyancy reasserting itself. "Had I known, I should certainly have made inquiries from these people."

Akshay. "Well, suppose now we both go to Benares. You know this part of the country very well, so you'll be able to make the fullest possible investigation."

Uncle readily agreed to this proposal. That Hemnalini would believe his unsupported word Akshay could hardly expect, but with Uncle's testimony to corroborate his, he hoped to convince her of Ramesh's double-dealing. So it was as a witness for the prosecution that the unsuspecting old gentleman was carried off to Benares.

Chapter 48

$\mathcal{A}$ nnada Babu had rented a bungalow in a secluded part of the cantonment outside the city.

On his arrival in Benares he had learned that the simple fever and cough from which Nalinaksha's mother, Kshemankari, had been suffering had developed into pneumonia. The fever had been aggravated by the chilly weather and by her refusal to give up her customary morning bath in the Ganges, and her condition had become really critical. As a result of Hemnalini's unremitting care the crisis was now over, but her illness had left the old lady deplorably weak. In one respect Hemnalini could offer her no assistance. Kshemankari's views on ceremonial purity were rigid, and she could not take from the hands of the Bramho girl such potions and nourishment as were prescribed for her. She had been accustomed to cook her own food, and now Nalinaksha himself prepared the invalid's diet and served up all her meals, greatly to his mother's distress.

"It's time I were out of the way," she lamented. "Why did the Lord keep me alive only to be a burden to you?"

Austere as she was in respect of her own comfort and personal adornment, Kshemankari had a keen eye for

order and beauty in her surroundings; this Hemnalini had
learned from Nalinaksha. The girl accordingly made it her
special care to keep the whole house in apple-pie order,
and she bestowed particular attention on her dress before
she visited the old lady. Annada Babu supplied her with
flowers from a garden which he had leased in the
cantonment, and Hemnalini used to arrange these tastefully
round the sick-bed.

Nalinaksha made periodical attempts to induce his
mother to allow a maid to wait on her, but she would
never consent to accept services from a menial. The
household included, of course, various servants — men and
women — employed on the rough work of the
establishment, but the old lady could not bear to have any
of the more intimate personal offices performed for her by
a hireling. Since the death of her old nurse she had never
suffered a woman-servant to fan her or to massage her
even when she was prostrate with sickness.

She had a weakness for pretty children of both sexes.
As she returned from her morning immersion in the
Ganges, sedulously sprinkling blossoms and holy water on
each emblem of Siva that she passed, she would pick up
some handsome peasant-lad, or a fair-skinned little
Brahman maid, and bring the child home with her.
Attracted by their looks, she had won the hearts of several
of the neighbours' children with gifts of toys, coppers, and
sweets.

At times a detachment of these youngsters would
descend upon her house and scamper all over the premises,
to the old lady's unfeigned delight. She had yet another
weakness. She could never resist purchasing any dainty
trifle that caught her eye, not that she collected such
objects herself, but because she took special pleasure in
bestowing them on such recipients as she knew would

really appreciate the gifts. Even at the houses of distant relations and casual acquaintances mysterious parcel would be delivered from time to time to the great surprise of the inmates. She possessed a large ebony chest, in which she had stored a number of pretty trinkets and silken garments. These were intended for the bride whom Nalinaksha was one day to bring home. She pictured her daughter-in-law as a young girl of great beauty, who would brighten the drab house with her vivacity and winning ways, and whom it would be a delight to deck in her treasured finery. Such anticipations provided the old lady with material for many a pleasant day-dream.

Kshemankari's own habits were those of an ascetic, but though she spent nearly the whole day in prayer and ceremonial observances, taking but one meal of milk and fruit, she strongly disapproved of Nalinaksha's austere mode of life. Undue insistence on ritual she considered unbecoming in a man. She regarded men as mere overgrown children, and displayed a large-hearted and affectionate tolerance towards such of them as showed lack of restraint or discrimination in matters of eating and drinking.

"Why should a man be severe on himself?" she would ask indulgently. Actual impiety should not be condoned, but she had a settled conviction that rules were not intended for men-folk. She would have been quite satisfied had Nalinaksha exhibited in a modified degree the thoughtlessness and selfishness of the normal male, had he merely refrained from disturbing her at her prayers and carefully avoided contact with her at times when his touch was ceremonially defiling.

When Kshemankari rose from her sick-bed she was vastly tickled to find not only that Hemnalini had become an enthusiastic convert to Nalinaksha's teaching, but that the grey-haired Annada Babu also sat at his feet and hearkened to his dicta with the reverence due to the inspired utterances of a prophet.

She took Hemnalini aside one day and laughingly remarked: "My dear, I am afraid you people are encouraging Nalinaksha in his foolishness. Why do you pay any attention to the nonsense he talks? At your age you should be enjoying life thoroughly; you should be thinking of clothes and amusements instead of religion. You may ask why I don't practise myself what I preach. Well, there is some excuse for it in my case. My parents were very strict and all of us, boys and girls, were brought up in an atmosphere of piety. We shouldn't know where we were if we altered our habits now. But your upbringing has been different. I know exactly the sort of atmosphere in which you were reared, and it goes against the grain with you to adopt a different mode of life. It's no good forcing your inclinations, my dear. What I say is, let everyone follow his natural bent in these matters. It won't do, dear; you should give it up. Fasting and prayer aren't in your line. This idea that Nalin is an inspired teacher is something quite new; he really knows nothing about such things. Up till a short time ago he followed his own inclinations and pulled a long face if he heard a text quoted. It was only to please me that he launched out in this way, and I'm afraid he'll turn into a full-blown anchorite one of these days. 'Stick to the faith of your childhood,' I keep on telling him. 'I have no fault to find with it, in fact nothing would please me better,' but he only laughs; it's a way he has. He never opens his mouth whatever you say to him. Scold him even and he won't answer back!"

This conversation took place in the late afternoon while the old lady was dressing Hemnalini's hair. She did not approve of the girl's simple style of coiffure.

"You think I'm very old-fashioned, dear," she would say, "and know nothing about the latest modes. Well, I think I may safely boast that I know more styles of hair dressing than you do. I once knew a very nice English lady. She used to come here and give me sewing-lessons, and she taught me a lot about hair-dressing too. Of course, I had to bathe and change my clothes after each of her visits! It may or may not be right to be so scrupulous, but I'm built that way. You mustn't mind my being squeamish with you too, dear; you know it isn't aversion, only my regular custom. It was a terrible blow to me when my husband's people ceased to be orthodox Hindus, but I made no protest. All I said was: 'Obey your own conscience; I'm only an ignorant woman and can't give up the ways to which I have been accustomed," and Kshemankari brushed aside a tear.

The old lady thoroughly enjoyed loosening Hemnalini's long tresses and braiding them afresh in some ever-novel fashion. She even went to the length of unlocking her ebony chest and tricking the girl out in the bright-coloured garments that she loved. Dressing-up was a game in which she took heart felt delight. Hemnalini brought over her needlework almost everyday and spent the evening in learning new methods.

Kshemankari was also very fond of reading Bengali novels and Hemnalini brought her all the books and periodicals that she possessed. Hem marvelled at the shrewdness of the old lady's comments on the stories and essays; she had always imagined that such discrimination could only be the product of an English education. The wittiness of her discourse and the piety of her mode of life made Nalinaksha's mother appear a very wonderful woman in Hemnalini's eyes. There was nothing commonplace or conventional about her, and Hemnalini's intercourse with her was a series of delightful surprises to the girl.

Chapter 49

Kshemankari soon succumbed to another attack of fever, but this bout did not last so long as the last. One morning during her convalescence, when Nalinaksha came in and saluted her like a dutiful son by touching her feet, he took the opportunity to urge her to allow herself to be treated as an invalid. Her usual austerities, he observed, were not suited to a person in her condition.

"So I'm to renounce my old habits while you proceed to renounce the world altogether?" cried the old lady. "My dear Nalin, you can't keep up this farce any longer. Kindly do as your mother tells you and get married!"

Nalinaksha was silent and Kshemankari proceeded: "You see, my dear, this old body of mine won't last much longer. I shan't die happy unless I see you mated first. There was a time when I looked forward to your marrying a slip of a girl whom I could train myself. I had visions of dressing her up to suit my own ideas. But during this last spell of sickness my eyes were opened. There's no saying how long I shall live, and I can't take for granted that my remaining lease of life will be a long one. It would not be fair to leave you with an unformed girl on your hands. Much better marry someone whose age is nearer your own. I lay awake every night, while I had fever, thinking this out. I feel very strongly that this is the last duty that I owe to you, and I must live to perform it, otherwise my mind will never be at rest."

"But where am I to find a girl who would settle down contentedly with me?" asked Nalinaksha.

"Don't trouble your head about that. I'll arrange matters for you and you'll know the result in good time."

Kshemankari had never personally encountered Annada Babu, for she had always remained in her customary seclusion when he visited her house. That day, however, when the old gentleman looked in during his evening constitutional, she intimated that she wished to see him; and no sooner was he ushered into her presence than she went straight to the point.

"Your daughter," she began, "is a very charming girl, and I am exceedingly fond of her. You both know my son Nalin. His character is irreproachable and his professional reputation is high. Do you not agree with me that you might have difficulty in finding a better husband for your daughter?"

"You really mean this?" exclaimed Annada Babu. "Why, I never dared to hope for such a thing. I should certainly consider myself very lucky to have Nalinaksha for a son-in-law. But what does he——?"

"Oh, Nalin will be quite agreeable. Unlike most young men of the present day he does what his mother tells him. After all, he should not require much persuasion! No one could help falling in love with that dear girl. I should like, however, to have them definitely engaged as soon as possible, for I may not have much longer to live."

Annada Babu went home elated, and he lost no time in sending for Hem.

"My dear," he commenced, "I'm an old man and my health is far from good, but unless I see you settled first

I cannot end my days in peace. You must allow me to be quite frank with you, Hem. You have no mother and I feel entirely responsible for you."

Hemnalini stared at her father, wondering what was coming.

"I'm so delighted at the prospect of this match, dear," he went on, "that I can't contain myself any longer. My one fear is that something may happen to prevent it. It's this, dear: Nalinaksha mother has this evening made a proposal of marriage to you on her son's behalf."

Hemnalini blushed and faltered, "Why, really, dad! "It's quite impossible."

She was overcome with confusion when her father sprang this proposal on her, for she had never thought of Nalinaksha as a possible husband.

"Why is it impossible?" asked Annada Babu.

"Nalinaksha!" exclaimed Hemnalini, "how could it be possible?"

It was hardly a logical answer, but it was infinitely more conclusive than any logic. Hemnalini took refuge in the verandah from a situation that was becoming strained.

Annada Babu's hopes were dashed; this opposition was a thing that he had not anticipated. He had confidently assumed that his daughter would be delighted at the prospect of marrying Nalinaksha. Stunned by his disappointment the old man stared ruefully at the flickering oil-lamp while he mused over the insoluble riddle of the feminine temperament, and not for the first time lamented that Hemnalini had no mother.

Meanwhile Hem herself sat in the unlighted verandah while the hours slipped by. At last she happened to glance into the room, and at the sight of her father's disconsolate face her conscience smote her. She hurried indoors and posted herself behind his chair, murmuring, as she stroked his head, "Come, father, your supper was ready long ago; it must be cold by now."

Annada Babu rose mechanically and made for the supper-room, but he had little appetite for food. In the belief that the clouds that darkened Hemnalini's life had lifted he had entertained high hopes for the future, and her rejection of the proposal had been a bitter disappointment to him. "So Hem has not been able to forget Ramesh after all,," he sighed to himself.

It was his custom to retire to bed immediately after supper, but this evening he lingered on. Instead of retiring he subsided into a deck-chair on the verandah and stared out across the garden at the deserted cantonment road, deep in thought.

Finding him there Hemnalini took him playfully to task. "Now go to bed, please, dad; it's too cold for you out here."

"You had better go to bed yourself, dear. I shall be turning in soon."

But Hemnalini was not to be dismissed so easily. After a short pause she proceeded, "You're catching cold here, dad. Come into the sitting-room anyway."

Annada Babu rose from his chair and departed silently to bed.

Hemnalini had sternly resolved to exclude all thought of Ramesh from her mind lest she should be tempted to swerve from her duty, and this self-denying ordinance had cost her many a hard mental struggle. It only needed an external shock to cause the old wound to smart afresh. She had never been able definitely to map out her future course of conduct. Hence she had cast about her for means to sustain her in her resolve.

When she finally determined to regard Nalinaksha as her spiritual preceptor and to order her life according to his teaching, she supposed that her object was attained. But when this marriage was proposed and she essayed to root out the old love from its lurking-place in the innermost recesses of her heart she realised how ineradicable it really was. A threat to sever the old attachment was enough to make Hemnalini cling to it in her despair more resolutely than ever.

Chapter 50

Kshemankari had in the meantime sent for Nalinaksha and informed him that she had made a proposal on his behalf and that it had been accepted.

Nalinaksha smiled. "Have you arranged it definitely already?" he asked; "you've been very quick about it!"

Kshemankari. "Of course I have. I shan't live forever, you know. You see, I've taken a great fancy to Hemnalini. She's quite an exceptional girl. Of course, as far as looks go—her complexion is not very good, but——"

Nalinaksha. "Spare me, mother! I wasn't thinking of her complexion but of the impossibility of my marrying Hemnalini. I really can't do it."

Kshemankari. "Don't talk nonsense! I see no reason against it."

It was not easy for Nalinaksha to formulate his objections, but his unspoken thought was this: Here was Hemnalini, a girl towards whom he had definitely assumed the role of father-confessor; to turn round suddenly and propose marriage to her seemed almost an outrage.

Taking Nalinaksha's silence for acquiescence, his mother resumed: "I won't listen to any objections this time. You seem determined to renounce the world and become a regular Benares hermit for my sake. It's absurd at your age and I decline to put up with it any longer. Now mind and don't let this opportunity slip. The first auspicious day that comes along you must bring it off."

It was some time before Nalinaksha could command his voice.

"There's one thing that I must tell you, mother," he began at last, "but let me first beseech you not to distress yourself about it. The incident that I am about to relate to you happened nine or ten months ago and it is useless to grieve over it now. Still I know that it is a characteristic of yours, mother, to shudder at the horror of a calamity even when all is over and irremediable. It is for that reason that I have never told you this story, though I have been constantly on the point of doing so. Take what measures you like to propitiate my evil destiny but do not distress yourself with vain regrets."

Kshemankari was profoundly disturbed.

"I don't know what you're going to tell me, lad," she said, "but your preface only makes me dread the worst. Never, so long as I live, shall I be able to repress my emotions. It is useless trying to keep aloof from worldly affairs. You do not have to go in search of misfortune; it swoops down on you uninvited. Tell me your story at once and never mind whether the news is good or bad."

"Last February," began Nalinaksha accordingly, "I sold up all my property in Rangpur, found a tenant for my garden-house, and started for Calcutta. When I reached the river-crossing at Sara I took a whim to abandon the railway and to proceed the rest of the way by water; so I hired a large country-boat at Sara and set off. When we had been on the water for two days we tied up at a sand-bank, and I had gone ashore to bathe when I suddenly encountered our old friend Bhupen carrying a gun. He gave a jump when he saw me and called out, "Here's a fine bird for the bag!' It appeared that he was a Deputy Magistrate in these parts and had come out into his district on a tour of inspection. It was many years since we had met, and he refused to let me go, insisting on my accompanying him on his rounds. We camped one day at a village called Dhobapukur, and in the evening we went for a stroll round the place; it is quite a small village. In the course of our walk Bhupen suddenly led me into the walled courtyard of a thatched house standing on the edge of a stretch of plough-land. The owner of the house brought out cane stools and made us sit down. The verandah was being used as a schoolroom at the time. The village dominie sat on a wooden-bottomed chair, with his feet propped against one of the pillars, while the children squatted on the ground before him, slate in hand, chanting their lessons in chorus. The owner of the house was one Tarini Chaturjye. He cross-questioned Bhupen till he had my history by heart. As we were returning to camp Bhupen remarked; 'You're in luck to-day; you're about to receive a proposal of marriage.' I asked what he meant, and he went on to say: 'That fellow Tarini Chaturjye is a money-lender and a bigger miser doesn't exist. When a new magistrate comes along he makes a great parade of his public spirit in allowing school to be held in his house. Actually he does nothing for the schoolmaster except to provide his meals, and in return the poor wretch has to work till ten o'clock at night writing up Tarini's accounts; his salary is paid out of the school fees and the Government grant. Tarini had a sister who was left penniless at her husband's death and to whom he had to give shelter in consequence. She was pregnant at the time and died in giving birth to a daughter. Her death was entirely due to want of proper medical attendance. He had another widowed sister who did all the

housework and so saved him a servant's wages. This poor
creature took charge of the orphan, but she too died a few
years later. The girl has been leading a dog's life ever since,
slaving for her uncle and aunt and getting nothing but
scolding in return. She has nearly passed the marrying age,
but it's not easy task to find a husband for a friendless
orphan like her, especially as no one in the village knew
her parents. She was a posthumous child too, and the
village gossips whisper scandal about her origin. Tarini
Chaturjye is notoriously rolling in wealth, so they depreciate
the girl in the hope of squeezing a big dowry out of him
before he can get her married. For the last four years he
has been describing her as ten years old, so by that calculation
she must be at least fourteen now. And yet, you know,
she's the loveliest girl that ever I saw. She's called Kamala,
after the goddess Lakshmi, and she's the perfect image of
her namesake in every respect. Whenever a young Brahman
stranger comes here Tarini goes down on his knees and
implores him to marry his niece, but even when the lad is
willing the villagers scare him away and the engagement
is broken off. It's your turn now, you may be certain.' Do
you know, mother, I was in such a dare-devil mood that
I said at once, without a moment's reflection, 'All right, I'll
marry the girl.' I had always intended to give you a surprise
by bringing you home an orthodox little Hindu daughter-
in-law—I knew quite well that if I married a grown-up
Brahmo lady none of us would be happy. Bhupen was
flabbergasted. 'You don't mean it!' he exclaimed. 'Indeed
I do,' said I; 'my mind is made up.' 'Are you serious?' asked
Bhupen. I assured him that I was. Tarini Chaturjye called
at our camp that very evening and made his supplication,
clasping his hands over his Brahmanical thread. 'I implore
you to come to my rescue,' he said. 'See the girl for yourself—
then, of course, if you don't fancy her that's an end to the

matter, but on no account listen to the misrepresentations of my enemies.' 'I don't require to see her,' I replied; 'you can fix a day for the wedding.' The day after to-morrow will do,' said Tarini; 'let us have it then.' Of course, one could see the motive underlying his piteous appeal and his indecent haste; he wanted to avoid a heavy outlay on the wedding festivities. However, the marriage duly took place."

"The marriage took place!" exclaimed Kshemankari in consternation; "are you serious, Nalin?"

Nalinaksha. "Perfectly serious, mother. I re-embarked on the boat with my bride. We set off in the afternoon— it was only March, mind you, when one has every reason to expect fine weather—and that same evening, only a couple of hours later, an intensely hot blast of wind descended on us and in some inexplicable way overturned the boat and left no trace of it."

"Gracious heavens!" ejaculated Kshemankari with a thrill of horror.

Nalinaksha. "When I regained consciousness a little later I found myself struggling in deep water and there was no sign of the boat or of any of its occupants. I informed the police and a thorough search was made, but without result."

Kshemankari's face had turned grey.

"Amen," she said; "we cannot help the past, but never mention this to me again. I shudder to think of it."

Nalinaksha. "I should never have told you, mother, had you not been so insistent about my marriage."

Kshemankari. "Why, is this calamity to prevent you marrying at all?"

Nalinaksha. "The girl may have survived after all; that is why I have scruples about marrying."

Kshemankari. "Are you mad? You would certainly have heard of her had she been alive."

Nalinaksha. "She knows nothing about me. I was as complete a stranger to her as anyone could be. I don't suppose she has ever seen my face. When I arrived in Benares I wrote to Tarini Caturjye giving him my address, but apparently my letter never reached him for it came back to me through the dead-letter office."

Kshemankari. "Well?"

Nalinaksha. "I have decided to let a whole year elapse before I take her death for granted."

Kshemankari. "You always were over-scrupulous! Why make it a whole year?"

Nalinaksha. "It'll soon be over, mother. This is December; next month's unlucky for weddings. That only leaves February and the year is up in March."

Kshemankari. "Very well. Still you must consider yourself definitely engaged. I made a formal proposal to Hemnalini's father."

Nalinaksha. "Man may propose; but there is Another who disposes, and I leave the matter in His hands."

Kshemankari. "So be it; but, dear, what an awful thing it was that you told me! I'm still trembling at the thought of it."

Nalinaksha. "I was afraid of that, mother, and I fear it will be a long time before you are your normal self again. Once anything disturbs your composure you do not regain it easily. You understand now my reluctance to tell you this story."

Kshemankari. "You did well, my son. I don't know what has come over me nowadays but when I hear any evil tidings the horror of it grips me. I shrink from opening a letter for fear it may contain bad news. As you know, I have even requested you to keep news back from me. I fear that I have lived too long, else why these repeated shocks?"

Chapter 51

*W*hen Kamala reached the bank of the Ganges the short-lived December sun had already sunk to the verge of the pallid sky. Facing the oncoming dusk Kamala saluted the departing deity. She sprinkled drops of the sacred water on her head, then stepping into the stream and raising a handful of water in her joined palms, she bestowed a libation on the holy river and threw flowers into the current.

She bowed herself in adoration of all the heavenly powers. As she raised her head from the ground she remembered one more being to whom she owed worship. She had never aspired to look upon his face. On that one night which she had spent by his side her eyes had never rested even on his feet. In the bridal chamber he had spoken a word or two to her girl-companions, but his accents had scarcely penetrated the barriers of the veil and of her own reserve. Now she stood at the river's brink she strove intensely but unsuccessfully to recall the sound of his voice.

The night had been far spent before the wedding ceremonies were over. So utterly wearied had she been that sleep descended suddenly on her, when and where she could not tell. She awoke to find a young married neighbour shaking her out of her drowsiness with shrieks of laughter. She was alone on the couch. In this last moment of her existence her mind could grasp nothing tangible to remind her of the lord of that existence. His personality was a closed book to her. Face, voice, visible token, there was nothing that she could recall. Even the thread of red silk with which the bridegroom's upper garment had been knotted during the ceremony—unknown to Kamala, it was the cheapest that Tarini Chaturjye could procure— she had never troubled to preserve.

The letter that Ramesh had written to Hemnalini was still fastened into the corner of her dress. She drew it out and, sitting on the sand, re-read one of the sheets in the twilight. It was the portion of the letter which mentioned her husband—there were no details, only the fact that his name was Nalinaksha Chattopadhyay, that he had been a doctor at Rangpur, and that Ramesh could find no trace of him there. She searched for the remaining sheets but they were missing.

Nalinaksha! the name was balm to the wound in her soul. It seemed to fill her heart to over-flowing, to take to itself an impalpable body and pervade her whole being. Tears flowed freely, melting the crust of her resolution and lightening the intolerable burden of her sorrow. A voice within her spoke: "The void is filled, the darkness has lifted; now I know that I too am part of the living world"; and she cried fervently, "If I would be a true wife to him I must live to prostrate myself at his feet. Nothing will rob me of this guerdon. While life endures he is not lost to me. The Lord has preserved me from death that I may serve him!"

She took the bunch of keys from the kerchief in which they were wrapped and flung them from her. Then she recollected that she wore as a fastening a brooch that

Ramesh had given her, and this too she hastily undid and cast into the stream. Then, turning westward, she set forth. Whither she was bound and how she would set about her quest she had no clear conception. She only knew that she must go forward, that she could not tarry a moment longer where she was.

The last glimmer of the wintry twilight soon faded from the sky. The sandy margin of the river gleamed faintly in the darkness, as though some painter had smudged out the figures on his brightly-hued landscape and left only the colourless canvas. The moonless sky studded with unwinking stars breathed gently down on the deserted river-bank.

Kamala could descry nothing before her but a seemingly endless, unpeopled void, but she knew that she must go forward and she never paused to consider what lay at the end of her march. She decided, however, to follow the bank of the river. This would relieve her of the necessity of asking her way, and if danger threatened she could at once find asylum in the bosom of Mother Ganges.

There was not a particle of vapour in the air, and the darkness enveloped Kamala but did not blind her. As the night wore on jackals emerged from the shelter of the wheat-fields and howled discordantly. Kamala had been walking for some hours when the flats gave place to a high bank and the sand to cultivable soil. A village barred the way, but as she approached it with beating heart it became apparent that all the inhabitants were sound asleep. Strength began to fail her as she skirted timidly round the village, and when at last she reached the top of an apparently sheer declivity she sank down at the foot of a banyan tree and slept the sleep of utter exhaustion.

When she awoke towards dawn, the waning moon had risen and cast some light on the darkness. Beside her stood an elderly woman who was plying her with questions in her own tongue. "Who are you, there? What are you doing, sleeping under a tree on a cold night like this?"

Kamala started up in alarm. Looking round she espied near at hand a landing-place at which two barges were moored. The old lady was on a journey and had risen early to bathe before other people were stirring.

"You look like a Bengali, you do," she went on.

"I am a Bengali," said Kamala.

"What are you doing lying here?"

"I started off for Benares. Late at night I felt sleepy so I lay down here."

"Did you ever hear the like? Going to Benares on foot! Well, you had better get on board that barge. I'll be along as soon as I've had my bath."

The old lady bathed, and then joining Kamala launched forth into an account of herself and her errand. She was related to the Siddhu Babu in Ghazipur, one of the members of whose family had just been married with great pomp and circumstance. Her own name was Nabinkali and her husband's name was Mukundalal Datta; they were Kayasthas by caste, natives of Bengal, but they had been residing for some time in Benares. They had not been invited to their kins-folk's house for the wedding but had taken boat to Ghazipur in the hope that Siddhu Babu might after all find quarters for them. The mistress of the house had, however, regretted her inability to offer them hospitality. "You know, my dear," she had said to Nabinkali, "my husband is very delicate; ever since he was a child he has had to live on special diet. We keep a cow in the house and churn its milk into butter; out of the butter we make *ghi*, and with the *ghi* we prepare *luchis* for him. A cow like that can't be fed on any fodder that comes along——" and so forth and so on.

"What's your name?" she asked after this recital.

"Kamala."

Nabinkali. "I see you're wearing iron bangles; your husband is alive then?"

"He disappeared the day after our wedding."

Nabinkali. "Well I never! You look quite young too! Why, you can't be more than fifteen," she went on, after scanning Kamala from head to foot.

"I'm not certain about my age, but I must be about fifteen."

Nabinkali. "You're a Brahman, aren't you?"

"Yes."

"Where do your folk live?"

Kamala. "I've never been to my husband's native place; my father came from Bisukali" (though she had never been there Kamala knew that Bisukali was the name of her father's birthplace).

Nabinkali. "Then your parents——?"

Kamala. "Both my father and my mother are dead."

Nabinkali. "Bless my soul! What are you going to do?"

Kamala. "I only want a roof over my head and two meals a day. If I can find some decent people in Benares who will give me these I'll work for my keep. I know how to cook."

Nabinkali was secretly delighted at the prospect of obtaining the services of a Brahman lady-cook gratis. She took care, however, to dissemble her joy.

"We don't need you ourselves," she said," we brought our own Brahman servants up-country with us. Moreover, we can't employ anyone who has no qualification save that of being a Brahman. My husband mustn't have his meals served up anyhow. One can't get a good man under fourteen rupees a month, and he wants his food and clothes besides. Still, here you are, a Brahman girl and in a difficulty; so perhaps you had better come along with us after all. We've such a number of mouths to feed and such a lot of stuff is thrown away, one more won't make any difference. You won't find the work too heavy for you. There's only my husband and myself at home now. I've got all my daughters off my hands now and they've married well too. We've only one son and he's a magistrate stationed at Serajganj jut now. We had a letter from the Governor appointing him two months back. I said to my husband, 'Our Noto—that's his name—isn't hard up, why should he be treated like this? I know it's not many people who have the luck to get such a good position, but it's too bad that the poor lad should have to live so far from home. Why should he? What's the necessity?' But my husband only said, 'Good Lord! That isn't the point. You women don't understand these things. Do you think it was for a living that I got Noto made a magistrate? We aren't so badly off as all that! He must have a profession, you know, a young fellow like him, otherwise he'll be up to some mischief or other."

The boats sped upstream before the wind and Benares was reached in a few hours. The whole party repaired to a two-storied house standing in a small garden on the outskirts of the city. There was no sign there of the fourteen-rupee Brahman cook. One of the servants was a Brahman, it is true, but he hailed from Orissa, and Uriya labour is notoriously the cheapest in north-eastern India. Moreover, a few days after Kamala's arrival Nabinkali dismissed him without paying his wages, in a sudden explosion of wrath. The difficulty of finding another cook on fourteen rupees a month proving insurmountable, Kamala had to assume entire charge of the kitchen.

Nabinkali was not sparing of good advice.

"You know, my dear," she would admonish Kamala, "Benares city is a bad place for young girls like you. You must never set foot outside the compound alone. When I go to bathe in the Ganges or to worship the Bisweswar image I'll take you along with me."

She took careful precautions lest Kamala should escape from her clutches. The girl had practically no opportunity of meeting companions of her own sex and race. Household duties took up her whole day, and in the evening Nabinkali would discourse on the wealth of ornaments and jewellery, the gold and silver plate, and the rich brocades which fear of thieves had deterred her from bringing to Benares.

"My husband has never been accustomed to eat off brass, and he grumbled no end at first. He would say, 'What does it matter if a few of the things are stolen? We can replace them in no time,' but I could never reconcile myself to such a waste of money. I much prefer putting up with hardships for the time being. At home, you know, we have a huge house and a host of servants, more than I can count, but we can't lug two or three dozen people about with us. My husband suggested renting an extra house near this one, but I said 'No,' I couldn't stand that. It's a good opportunity to have a little peace here. I should have no rest day or night if we had more servants and rooms to look after," and so on *ad nauseam*.

Chapter 52

*K*amala's life in Nabinkali's house resembled that of a fish imprisoned in a shallow and muddy pond. Her only salvation lay in escape, but escape was out of the question so long as she had no obvious goal for flight. Her recent escapade had taught her how forbidding the outside world appears by night, and she shrank from once more entrusting herself to the unknown.

In her own peculiar way Nabinkali was fond of Kamala, but her affection took distasteful forms. She had come to the girl's rescue in the hour of need, but she made it hard for Kamala to feel correspondingly grateful, and Kamala infinitely preferred her menial duties to the boredom of the leisure hours which she was forced to spend in Nabinkali's society.

One morning the old lady summoned her to listen to the following tirade: "Look here, young lady, my husband is not very well to-day and he must have *luchis* instead of his usual food. All the same, you needn't use such a colossal quantity of *ghi*. You're a good cook, I admit, but I fail to understand what you do with all the *ghi*. That Uriya Brahman was your superior there. He used *ghi*, of course, but the taste of it was hardly noticeable in his cooking."

Kamala never answered back; after a scolding she would go on quietly with her work as though she had heard nothing. On this particular morning, however, the thrust went home and Kamala continued to brood over the slight as she chopped up the vegetables. She had just arrived at the conclusion that the world is a joyless place and life a burden when her ear caught something which arrested her attention. Nabinkali had summoned the bearer to her room and was issuing instructions to him, and this is what Kamala overhead:

"Hi, you, Tulsi, run off to the city and fetch Dr. Nalinaksha at once; tell him your master's not at all well."

Dr. Nalinaksha! The sunbeams danced before Kamala's eyes like golden lute-strings struck by invisible fingers. She flung down her vegetables and posted herself at the kitchen door to waylay Tulsi as he descended. No sooner had he appeared than she inquired where he was bound for.

"I'm off to fetch Dr. Nalinaksha," said Tulsi.

"Who may he be?"

"Why, he's by way of being the best doctor in the place."

"Where does he live?" asked Kamala.

"In the city, about a mile away."

Kamala made a habit of dividing among the servants such small quantities of food as were left over when their superiors' wants had been satisfied. Frequent scoldings had failed to deter her from this practice, her resolution being fortified by the fact that under Nabinkali's harsh rule the underlings never had enough to eat. Moreover, the master and mistress were seldom punctual at their meals and the servants had to wait their turn. Hence Kamala was beset every day with plaintive appeals for a snack to stave off hunger, which she had not the heart to refuse. Kindly acts of this nature soon made all the servants her willing slaves.

"What are you plotting there at the kitchen-door, you, Tulsi?" shrilled a voice upstairs. "You think I haven't got my eye on you? You can't go to the city without consulting the cook first? No wonder so many things are missing! Look here, young lady, please remember that I picked you off the road and gave you shelter here. That's nice way to repay my kindness!"

Nabinkali was firmly convinced that the entire household was engaged in a conspiracy to rob her. She believed that if you drew a bow at a venture at least fifty percent of the arrows would find targets, and that the servants must be made to understand that she was always wide-awake and not easily deceived.

On this occasion, however, her outburst fell on deaf ears so far as Kamala was concerned. The girl proceeded with her task like an automation, her mind in the clouds.

She waited again at the kitchen door for Tulsi's return, and he appeared in due course, but alone.

"Has the doctor come, Tulsi?" asked Kamala.

Tulsi. "No, he couldn't come."

Kamala. "Why not?"

Tulsi. "His mother is ill."

Kamala. "His mother? Hasn't he anyone to look after her?"

Tulsi. "No, he's not married."

Kamala. "How do you know that?"

Tulsi. "I heard from the servants that he has no wife."

Kamala. "Perhaps his wife is dead."

Tulsi. "Maybe; but his servant Braja said that when he was practising at Rangpur he had no wife there either."

"Tulsi!" shrieked his mistress from the stairhead.

Kamala fled back into her kitchen and Tulsi hastened to obey the summons.

Nalinaksha—a practice at Rangpur—Kamala's doubts were completely set at rest. On Tulsi's next appearance she put a further question to him.

"I say, Tulsi, I have a relation of the same name as the doctor—he's Brahman, isn't he?"

Tulsi. "Oh, yes, he's a Brahman, a Chaturjye."

Tulsi was afraid that his mistress might detect him if he lingered to converse with Kamala, so at this point he left her abruptly.

Kamala went straight to Nabinkali and informed her that she had finished her work and wished to go and bathe at the Dasaswamedh Ghat.

Nabinkali. "That would be most inconvenient. My husband is ill and one can't foresee what he may require. What do you want to go off there to-day in particular?"

"I have just heard that a relation of mine whom I want very much to meet is in Benares."

Nabinkali. "No, thank you! I'm not so green as all that! Who was your informant? Tulsi, I suppose? We must get rid of that boy. Now you must understand, young lady, so long as you're in my house you're not to go off alone to bathe or to hunt up relatives in the city. It can't be done and I won't allow it."

The porter was directed to send Tulsi about his business without a moment's notice, and never to allow him to show his face in the house again, while the other servants received strict orders against holding any communication with Kamala.

Kamala had exercised patience so long as she had no positive information about Nalinaksha, but her spirit now began to chafe. She could not bear to remain another moment under a stranger's roof while her husband lived in the same city. Her capacity for work progressively declined and Nabinkali did not fail to comment on her shortcomings.

"Look here, young lady," she said, "I don't like the way you're behaving. Have you taken the sulks? You're at liberty to fast yourself if you like, but you needn't try to starve us to death. The stuff you cook nowadays isn't fit to eat."

"I can't work for you any longer," replied Kamala. "I can't stand it. Please let me go."

"Oh, indeed?" snarled Nabinkali. "That comes of doing people a good turn these days! To think that, just to make room for you, I turned away that good old Brahman who had worked for us so long, and now he has gone, goodness knows where. You call yourself a true Brahman! Think you've only to come along and say, 'Please let me go!' Wait till you try to run away and see if the police don't hear about it. My son's a magistrate and many a man has gone to the gallows at a word from him. You needn't try any of your games with me. Perhaps you've heard about Gada? He cheeked his master and we taught him a lesson; he's in jail to this day! You can't play fast and loose with us!"

The story about the servant Gada was perfectly true. The poor wretch had been sentenced to imprisonment for the alleged theft of a watch.

Kamala had come to the end of her resources. When it seemed as though life-long happiness lay within her grasp her hands were fettered. Fate had played her a cruel practical joke. Her life of drudgery as a prisoner within four walls became intolerable. She took to donning a wrapper and sallying forth into the cold night air of the garden as soon as her evening's toil was ended. There, she would stand by the compound wall and gaze out upon the road leading to the city. Her passionate zeal for devoted service impelled her, in imagination, along that dark lonely road in search of a house that she had never seen. Thus she would stand immovable for hours on end. At last she would bow herself to the ground in a deep obeisance and retire to her chamber.

But soon even this poor consolation, this small degree of liberty, was denied her. One evening Nabinkali chose to send for her after her labours were over for the day. The bearer, however, returned with the announcement that the Brahman lady was nowhere to be found.

"Do you men to tell me she has bolted?" exclaimed Nabinkali, and snatching up a lamp she personally searched the house from top to bottom, but found no trace of Kamala.

She sought out her husband, Mukunda Babu — he was pulling at a hookah with his eyes half-closed — and informed him that to all appearances Kamala had run away. Mukunda Babu took the news quite calmly. "I told her not to," he murmured drowsily; "she's an inattentive creature. Has she taken anything with her?"

"The wrapper that I gave her to keep her warm in this weather — it's not in her room now. I haven't noticed if anything else is missing."

"Send word to the police," said her husband in a matter-of-fact tone. One of the servants was accordingly despatched with a lantern on this errand. Kamala had in the meantime retired indoors, where she came upon Nabinkali turning the whole contents of the room upside down in the endeavour to ascertain if anything had been stolen.

"Well, what mischief have you been up to? Where did you go?" she cried, as soon as she caught sight of Kamala.

"I went for a walk in the garden after I had finished my work."

Nabinkali opened the vials of her wrath. She did not pick her words, and the servants all gathered round the door to listen.

Storm as Nabinkali might, Kamala had never allowed her to see her in tears, and this occasion was no exception;

the girl never flinched but stood like a statue under the torrent of vituperation. When it showed signs of slackening she interjected: "I am afraid you are dissatisfied with me; you had better let me go."

"I certainly will. If you think I'm going to feed and clothe such an ungrateful creature any longer you're mistaken, but I'll teach you whom you have to deal with before I dismiss you."

Kamala did not venture out of doors again. She shut herself into her room, comforting herself with the reflection that her sufferings had reached their climax and that Heaven must needs grant her relief now.

On the following evening Mukunda Babu went out for a drive, taking two of his servants with him, and the front door was bolted from inside after his departure. Dusk had fallen when a voice was heard outside inquiring if the master was at home.

Nabinkali jumped up at once.

"Goodness me, that's Doctor Nalinaksha! Budhiya! Budhiya!" But there was no sign of Budhiya, so she turned to Kamala:

"Just run down and open the door, will you? Tell the doctor that my husband has gone out for a drive and will be back very soon. Ask him to wait for a few minutes."

Kamala took a lantern and went downstairs. Her limbs trembled, her heart fluttered, and her hands had turned cold and clammy. She dreaded lest her perturbation should blind her vision.

She slid back the bolt, veiled her face, opened the door, and stood on the threshold confronting Nalinaksha.

"Is Mukunda Babu at home?" he asked.

"No; please come in," replied Kamala.

Nalinaksha entered the sitting-room and had just settled into a chair when Budhiya appeared and delivered the message that had been entrusted to Kamala.

Kamala's lungs seemed to be on the point of bursting; she tottered to a position on the verandah which offered her a clear view of Nalinaksha and sank down there to allow the tumult in her bosom to subside. Her throbbing heart combined with the piercing cold to set her quivering from head to foot.

Nalinaksha sat musing in the circle of light cast by the solitary oil-lamp, while the shivering Kamala gazed intently at him from the darkness of the verandah. Tears welled up incessantly, clouding her vision, but she hastily wiped them away. She threw her whole soul into her gaze till it seemed that its magnetic attraction must draw Nalinaksha into the focus of her being. The light shone on his lofty brow and composed features. Every lineament stamped and impressed itself on Kamala's heart till her entire frame grew benumbed and appeared to melt into encircling space. There was nothing before her save his face in the circle of light. All else was unreal, everything around it seemed to fade away and resolve itself into that one countenance.

Kamala fell into a half-trance from which she awoke suddenly to find that Nalinaksha had risen to his feet and was conversing with Mukunda Babu. At any moment the two men might move into the verandah and catch her eaves-dropping, so she hurried away and took refuge in her kitchen. The kitchen opened on to a small courtyard through which anyone leaving the house must pass.

Kamala waited with body and brain on fire. How could such a man be husband to a miserable wretch like herself! There was something god-like in the unruffled serenity and gracious beauty of his countenance. Conscious that her sufferings had not been in vain she bowed herself again and again in thankfulness to Heaven.

Steps were heard descending the stairs and Kamala hurried across to the unlighted doorway. Budhiya passed carrying a lamp with Nalinaksha following her across the courtyard. Kamala found herself apostrophising him in the language of the poets.

"My lord, thy handmaiden is a slave under a stranger's roof; thou passes her by and wettest not of it."

She watched Mukunda Babu leave the sitting-room in quest of supper and she crept into the room that he had vacated. She prostrated herself before Nalinaksha's chair, touched the ground with her forehead, and kissed the dust. Alas! That she was debarred from serving him! Her heart was sick with the consciousness of devotion thwarted.

Next day Kamala learned that the doctor had prescribed for Mukunda Babu a prolonged stay at some health resort hundreds of miles west of Benares; preparations for the journey had already been set on foot.

Kamala went straight to her mistress.

"I'm afraid I cannot leave Benares," she announced.

"We can; why can't you? You've become very devout all of a sudden!" said Nabinkali, who supposed that Kamala made religion a cloak for her reluctance to leave the holy city.

Kamala. "You may say what you like, but I intend to remain here."

Nabinkali. "Very well, we'll see."

Kamala. "I implore you not to take me away."

Nabinkali. "You really are a terror! We have everything ready to start when you get some bee in your bonnet. How on earth are we to find another cook at such short notice? We can't possibly dispense with you."

Kamala's entreaties were of no avail; she shut herself into her room and wept and prayed alternately.

Chapter 53

On the night following his conversation with his daughter Annada Babu had a recurrence of the severe pain which had attacked him in Calcutta. He spent the night in agony, but the morning brought relief, and he had his chair taken into the garden and sat there in view of the road, basking in the mild December sunshine while Hemnalini prepared his tea. His face was pale and wrung with the torture he had suffered, there were dark rings round his eyes, and he seemed to have aged several years in the night.

Every time Hemnalini's eyes fell on her father's worn countenance she felt a stab of remorse. She attributed his relapse to disappointment at her rejection of the proposed marriage, and her conscience was troubled by the reflection that mental worry had aggravated the old man's bodily weakness. The problem of finding some means of alleviating his distress dominated all others in her thoughts, but she was totally unable to solve it.

The sudden appearance of Akshay and Uncle took her by surprise, and she was about to hasten away when Akshay interposed:

"Please don't go. This gentleman is our worthy fellow-countryman Chakrabartti of Ghazipur, whose name is well-known throughout these provinces. He has something very important to tell you."

The new arrivals seated themselves on a stone parapet near which Annada Babu's chair had been placed, and Uncle proceeded to explain their errand.

"I am informed," he began, "that you are old friends of Ramesh Babu, so I have come to ask you if you can give me any tidings of his wife."

Surprise at this opening deprived Annada Babu of breath. "Ramesh's wife!" he exclaimed when he found his voice.

Hemnalini dropped her eyes, and Chakrabartti resumed: "You must think me very old-fashioned and ill-mannered, but if you will have patience and hear me out I think you will be convinced that I haven't come all the way from Ghazipur simply to discuss other people's affairs with you! It was during the Puja holidays that I met Ramesh Babu; I made his acquaintance on the steamer in which he was travelling up-country with his wife. You know yourselves that no one can meet Kamala without succumbing to her charm. I am an old man and sorrow and affliction have toughened my fibre, but I can never forget that dear little woman. On the steamer Ramesh Babu was still undecided about a destination, but when we had known each other only a couple of days Kamala became so attached to my old self that she persuaded her husband to disembark at Ghazipur and put up with us. My second daughter Saila loved her more than her own sister. I can't bear to speak of what happened after that. Why the dear girl should suddenly disappear, leaving us heart-broken, I have never yet been able to conceive. Saila's eyes have never been dry since we lost her"; and Uncle completely broke down at the recollection.

"What happened to her, where did she go?" asked Annada Babu in great concern.

"Akshay Babu," said Uncle, "you have heard every-thing; you tell him. It breaks my heart to think of it."

Akshay recounted the whole story in detail. Without adding any comment of his own he succeeded in depicting Ramesh's behaviour in the blackest colours.

At the conclusion of the recital Annada Babu said emphatically, "This is all new to us, I assure you. From the day that Ramesh left Calcutta we have not had a single line from him."

"Yes," chimed in Akshay, "we were so far in the dark that we didn't even know for certain that he had married Kamala. Let me ask you one question, sir. Are you certain that Kamala is his wife? She couldn't be his sister or some such relation?"

"What on earth do you mean, Akshay Babu?" exclaimed Uncle. "Certainly she was his wife, and the best wife that man ever had."

"It is a curious thing," commented Akshay, "that the more virtuous a wife, is, the worse treatment she receives. Heaven reserves the hardest trials for the most deserving!" and he heaved a portentous sigh.

"It is certainly a most tragic story," said Annada Babu, running his fingers through his scanty locks, "but nothing can be done now, so why waste tears over it?"

"Well, the fact is," returned Akshay, "that I was by no means fully convinced that Kamala had committed suicide. It seemed to me possible that she had merely run away from home and consequently this gentleman and I have come to Benares to prosecute a thorough search. It is quite evident that you can throw no light on the subject. However, we shall spend a few days making inquiries here."

"Where is Ramesh now?" asked Annada Babu.

"He left us without giving any address," replied Uncle; while Akshay said in turn, "I haven't seen him, but I am

informed that he has returned to Calcutta and I presume
he will rejoin the Alipore bar. A man can't go on mourning
indefinitely, especially at Ramesh's age. (To Chakrabartti)
Come along, sir, we'll go and make thorough inquiries in
the city."

"Will you stay with us, Akshay?" asked Annada Babu.

"I'm afraid I can't give you a definite answer," said
Akshay; "I've taken this affair so much to heart, Annada
Babu. I'll have to devote all my time in Benares to this
search. Think of the position of this delicately-nurtured
girl; we assume that she found life at home unbearable and
was forced to leave it! Consider what she may be suffering
now. Ramesh may be indifferent to her fate, but I'm not
built that way."

Akshay and Uncle departed, leaving Annada Babu
anxiously scanning his daughter's face. Hemnalini on her
part had a tremendous struggle to retain her composure,
knowing, as she did, her father's fears on her behalf.

"Dad," she said at length, "I think you should get a doctor to examine you thoroughly to-day. So little upsets your
health nowadays that you obviously need special treatment."

Annada Babu felt considerably relieved. To find that,
after Ramesh's conduct had been so fully canvassed,
Hemnalini was still capable of solicitude about his health
lifted a weight off his mind. In ordinary circumstances he
would have endeavoured to dismiss the subject summarily,
but as it was he replied: "That's a good idea. It would be
just as well if I did have myself examined. I had better send
for Dr. Nalinaksha at once, don't you think so?"

Hemnalini was conscious of a light shrinking at the
mention of Nalinaksha. It would require a considerable
effort to meet him on the old footing in her father's presence.
However, she answered cheerfully, "That will be best. I'll
send some one to fetch him."

Annada Babu now took courage from Hemnalini's apparent insensibility and broached the thorny subject.

"By the way, Hem," he began, "about this affair of Ramesh——" but Hemnalini cut him short.

"The sun's too hot for you now, dad; you must come inside immediately"; and without allowing him a chance to protest she took his arm and drew him into the house. There she installed him in an armchair, wrapped hot flannels round his body, gave him the newspaper, herself took his spectacles out of the case and put them on his nose, and left him with the parting injunction, "Now read your paper, I must leave you for a little."

Like a docile child Annada Babu strove to comply with Hemnalini's dictates, but anxiety for his daughter prevented him from concentrating his thoughts on the newspaper, and at last he laid it aside and went in search of her. Early though it was, he found the door of her chamber closed and he retired silently to the verandah, where he paced up and down till in desperation he made another attempt. Her door was, however, still fast. Again he retreated to the verandah and collapsed wearily into his chair, where he sat nervously rumpling his thin hair till Nalinaksha arrived.

After examining Annada Babu and prescribing a course of treatment for him the doctor turned to Hem and asked if the patient had been worrying over anything.

Hem answered this question with a qualified affirmative.

"If possible," said Nalinaksha, "he should be kept free from all anxiety. I find the same difficulty with my own mother. She takes trifling matters so much to heart that it is not easy to keep her in good health. Some petty worry — presumably something that happened yesterday — kept her awake the whole of last night. Of course I try to shield her from anything that might excite her, but the world being what it is, it is hardly possible to do so altogether."

"You're not looking very fit yourself to-day," remarked Hemnalini.

Nalinaksha. "Oh, I'm perfectly well! I'm practically never out of sorts. I sat up for part of the night and that probably explains why I am not looking my best."

Hemnalini. "It would be better if your mother had a woman in constant attendance on her. You can't nurse her properly by yourself and you have your work to do besides."

Hemnalini had spoken without any thought of herself and there was no gainsaying the appositeness of her remark, but no sooner had she uttered the words than she blushed crimson with shame; for it suddenly struck her that Nalinaksha might draw some inference from what she had said. He, too, when he noticed her confusion, was irresistibly reminded of his mother's proposal.

Hemnalini hastened to cover her indiscretion by adding, "Shouldn't she have a maid-servant to wait on her?"

"I've often tried to persuade her to engage a woman," said Nalinaksha, "but so far without success. She is very scrupulous about ceremonial purity and she could not trust a paid servant to be as particular as she is herself. Moreover, she has an instinctive dislike to accepting any service that is not entirely voluntary."

Hemnalini did not pursue the subject further, and after a short pause she went on: "When I endeavour to act according to your teaching I find myself continually brought up against obstacles and I allow them to turn me aside from my quest. They terrify me and reduce me to despair. Do you think I shall never achieve stability of purpose? Shall I always be liable to waver under external shocks?"

Hemnalini's pathetic appeal caused Nalinaksha to reflect.

"You must understand," he replied, after a brief pause, "that it is in order to nerve us to effort that difficulties are placed in our way. You must not be discouraged."

"Will you be able to visit us to-morrow morning?" said Hemnalini. "To know that I have your help gives me added strength."

Hemnalini found in the calm strength of Nalinaksha's tone and expression the tranquilising influence that she needed. Even after he had gone her heart was still conscious of his healing touch. Standing in the verandah outside her room she gazed upon the sun-bathed landscape. In the splendour of the perfect noonday she beheld the whole created world at once toiling and at rest, powerful and yet serene, alike forceful and patient, and she consigned her troubled spirit to the embrace of this vast macrocosm. In that propitious moment the sunlight and the dazzling blue of the heavens showered creations eternal blessing on her soul.

Hemnalini's thoughts now turned to Nalinaksha's mother. The cause of the old lady's agitation and sleepless night was patent to her. The first shock of the announcement of the proposed marriage had passed away and Hemnalini no longer shrank instinctively from the idea. More than ever she felt dependent on Nalinaksha and devoted to him, only the restless pangs that betoken love were totally wanting. In his passionless altruism he was independent of woman's love, but to him, no less than to others, service was due. His mother was old and ill, and he had no one to care for him. In a world like ours Nalinaksha's life was no negligible asset. To serve a man like him was a work of piety.

The chapter in Ramesh's history that had been related to her that morning had been such a crushing blow that she had to summon up all her forces to shield herself from its cruel impact. In her present mood she considered it unseemly to entertain any regret for Ramesh. She had no desire to sit in judgement and pass sentence on him. Our planet continues to revolve on its course while its myriad denizens are engaged in multitudinous activities, good and evil, and Hemnalini did not feel called on to play the censor's part. Her instinct was to banish from her mind all thoughts of Ramesh. When at times she envisaged Kamala's fate a shudder passed over her, but after all, she asked herself, what link had she with the luckless suicide? Then shame, loathing, and pity reasserted themselves, and clasping her hands she prayed: "O Lord, why do these thoughts vex me when I have committed no fault? Release me, I pray Thee, from these earthly ties. Let them be severed once for all. I desire nothing more, only that I may live at peace in this Thy world!"

Though Annada Babu longed to know what impression the story of Ramesh and Kamala had made on Hemnalini he could not pluck up courage to mention the subject openly. He approached her as she sat sewing and musing on the verandah, but one look at her far-away expression drove him away again. It was only in the evening when she sat beside him while he drank a glass of milk, in which the powder prescribed for him by the doctor had been mixed, that he found an opportunity to speak. He first requested Hemnalini to shut out the glare, and when the room was darkened to his satisfaction he remarked tentatively, "He seemed a good sort, that old fellow who came to see us this morning." Hemnalini, however, offered no comment, and unable to think of another opening he went straight to the point:

"I was really surprised at Ramesh's conduct. One had heard a good deal of gossip about him, but I never believed it till to-day. Still——"

"Don't let's talk about it, dad," implored Hemnalini.

"I don't want to discuss it, dear," said Annada Babu, "but by the working of Providence our happiness and misery are inextricably bound up with one person and another and we cannot afford to ignore their conduct."

"No, no!" protested Hemnalini. "We cannot allow our happiness and misery to depend on any individual at all. I'm all right, dad. If you distress yourself unnecessarily about me, you only make me ashamed."

"Hem, dear, I'm an old man and I shan't be happy till I see you settled. How can I die and leave you unmarried!"

Hemnalini did not reply, and her father continued: "You see, dear, the fact that we have had a grievous disappointment should not lead us to spurn other valuable things that life has to offer. It may be that in your sorrow you do not see for the moment how you can make your life happy and useful, but remember I have no motive except desire for your well-being. I know where your happiness and welfare lie, so I ask you not to reject the proposal that I communicated to you."

Hemnalini's eyelids fluttered as she exclaimed: "Please don't say that! I should never reject any proposal that came from you. Whatever order you give me I shall obey. All that I ask for is an opportunity to purge my heart of doubts and to prepare myself first."

Annada Babu reached out through the darkness, felt his daughter's cheek wet with tears, and laid his hand lightly on her head. He said nothing more to her.

Next morning the father and daughter were seated at their tea in the shade when Akshay appeared.

"No trace of her yet," he said, in answer to the unspoken query in Annada Babu's eye; then, accepting a cup of tea, he took his place at the table.

"Some things belonging to Ramesh Babu and Kamala," he went on, "are still lying at Chakrabartti's and he has been wondering where he ought to send them. If Ramesh Babu discovers your present whereabouts he is sure to come straight here, so perhaps you ——"

"I thought you had more sense, Akshay!" broke in Annada Babu angrily. "Why should Ramesh come here and why should I take charge of his belongings?"

"Well, whatever faults Ramesh Babu has committed and whatever mistakes he has made, he must be sincerely penitent now, and surely it is the duty of his old friends to offer him their sympathy. Do you think one ought to cut him altogether?"

"You're only trying to annoy us by constantly referring to this matter, Akshay. I request you on no account ever to mention the subject to me again."

"You mustn't be angry, dad," put in Hemnalini soothingly, "you'll only make yourself ill. Let Akshay Babu say what he likes, he's doing nothing wrong."

"Never again!" said Akshay. "I ask your forgiveness; I didn't understand."

Chapter 54

$\mathcal{T}$he eve of Mukunda Babu's departure for Meerut had arrived. The whole household was to accompany him and everything was packed and ready. Kamala longed for some accident which would prevent the journey and she prayed fervently that Dr. Nalinaksha might pay at least one final visit to his patient, but both hopes were doomed to disappointment.

Nabinkali feared lest in the bustle of preparation for the journey her lady-cook might find an opportunity to give her the slip, and for some days accordingly she had never let Kamala out of her sight and had kept her busily employed packing boxes.

Kamala was reduced to the despairing hope that she might be attacked suddenly with so severe an illness that Nabinkali would be forced to leave her behind. She did not ignore the possibility that a certain doctor might be called in to attend to her. The illness might conceivably have a fatal termination, but she closed her eyes and pictured herself dying contentedly after reverently prostrating herself before her physician.

Nabinkali made Kamala sleep with her that night and took her to the station in her own carriage next morning.

Mukunda Babu was to travel second class, while Nabinkali and Kamala were installed in an intermediate-class ladies' compartment.

The train duly left Benares. Its roar was like the bellowing of a mad elephant bent on destruction, and Kamala seemed to feel the frenzied animal's tusks rending her soul. She stared out of the window with hungry eyes till Nabinkali interrupted her reverie with an inquiry about the betel-box.

Kamala produced the box, but no sooner had Nabinkali opened it than her anger broke loose.

"Well! Just as I expected! You've left the lime behind! What do you expect me to do now? Everything goes wrong unless I see it done myself. You did it intentionally, simply to annoy me! You're just trying to provoke me! One day there's no salt in the vegetables, another day the milk tastes of earth! Do you think I'm not up to your tricks? All right, wait till we get to Meerut and I'll show you who's who!"

When the train rolled on to the bridge, Kamala leaned out of the carriage window for a last glimpse of the holy city stretching along the bank of the Ganges.

She had no idea in what quarter Nalinaksha lived, but as the train sped along and the panorama of *ghâts*, dwelling-houses, and pinnacled temples passed before her eyes, each and all seemed to her hallowed by his presence.

"Dear me, what are you craning your neck for like that?" exclaimed Nabinkali. "Do you think you're a bird and can spread your wings and fly away?"

Benares was hidden from view. Kamala subsided into her place and gazed mutely into the void.

Moghalserai was reached at last, but all the hubbub of the junction and the thronging crowds seemed unreal to Kamala, like a dream. She stepped like an automation from one train to the other.

The Meerut train was on the point of starting when, to Kamala's astonishment, she heard a well-known voice exclaim, "Mother!" She turned her head towards the platform and beheld Umesh! Her face lit up with joy.

"It's you, Umesh!" she cried.

Umesh opened the door of the carriage and in an instant Kamala was beside him on the platform. He prostrated himself before her with a gesture of the utmost reverence—touching the dust of her feet and placing it on his head. He was grinning from ear to ear with delight.

Next moment the guard slammed the door.

"What are you doing?" shrieked Nabinkali to Kamala. "The train is off! Get in! Get in!" But Kamala was deaf to her outcry.

The engine whistled and the train puffed slowly out of the station.

"Where have you come from, Umesh?" asked Kamala.

"From Ghazipur."

"Are they all well there? What's the news of Uncle?"

"He's quite well."

"How is my sister Sailaja?"

"She's crying her eyes out for you, mother."

Kamala's eyes incontinently filled with tears."

"How is Umi?" she asked next. "Does she still remember her auntie?"

Umesh. "They can never get her to take her milk unless she is wearing those bracelets that you gave her before you left. When she puts them on she flings her arms about and cries, 'Auntie's gone away ta-ta!' and it makes her mother weep to hear her."

Kamala. "What did you come here for?"

Umesh. "I got tired of Ghazipur, so I came away."

Kamala. "Where are you going to?"

Umesh. "I'm going with you, mother."

Kamala. "But I haven't a farthing in the world."

Umesh. "That doesn't matter. I have money."

Kamala. "Where did you get it?"

Umesh. "I never spent those five rupees that you gave me," and he produced the coins in corroboration.

Kamala. "Come along then, Umesh, we'll go to Benares; what do you say? Can you get tickets for us both?"

"Of course I can," and he was back in no time with the tickets.

The train was standing in the station. He saw Kamala into her place and informed her that he would travel in the next compartment.

"Where are we going to?" asked Kamala when they left the train at Benares.

"Don't you worry, mother! I'll take you to the right place."

"The right place, indeed!" exclaimed Kamala. "What do you know of Benares?'

"I know all about it. Just see where I take you."

He escorted Kamala to a hackney-carriage and himself mounted the box. In front of a certain house the carriage stopped, and Umesh announced, "You must get down here, mother."

Kamala alighted and followed Umesh into the house, where he hailed some unseen personage: "Hallo, grandpa, are you in?"

From a side room came the answer, "Is that you, Umesh? Where have you turned up from?"

Next moment Uncle Chakrabartti appeared in person carrying a hookah, and Umesh's countenance became one huge smile.

Utterly amazed, Kamala made Chakrabartti a profound reverence. It was a moment or two before he found his voice, and then he had no consciousness of what he said or where he laid his hookah.

At last he took her by the chin and raised her shrinking face, saying, "My little girl has come back to me. Come upstairs at once, dear"; and he called, "Saila! Saila! Come and see who's here!"

Sailaja rushed out of her room on to the upper verandah and stood at the head of the stairs, while Kamala prostrated herself before her, touching her feet. Sailaja hastened to clasp the truant to her heart and kissed her on the forehead.

The tears coursed down her cheeks as she ejaculated, "My dear! My dear! To go and leave us like that! Didn't you know we'd be heartbroken?"

"Never mind about that, Saila," said Uncle: "you had better see about some breakfast for her."

At that moment Umi dashed out, waving her arms and shrieking in delight:

"Auntie! Auntie!

Kamala snatched her up in her arms, hugged her to her breast, and smothered her in kisses. The sight of Kamala's dishevelled locks and mean attire distressed Sailaja, and she drew her away to attend to her toilet, giving her a bath and her own best clothes to wear.

"I don't suppose you slept well last night," she remarked. "Look how sunken your eyes are. You had better go to bed while I get ready your breakfast."

"No thank you, *didi*. I'd rather go to the kitchen with you myself," and the two friends went off together to their cooking-pots.

When Uncle had resolved to follow Akshay's advice and prepared to start for Benares, Sailaja had insisted that she must accompany him.

"But Bipin hasn't got his holidays yet," protested Uncle.

"That doesn't matter; I'll go without him. Mother's here, and she'll make him quite comfortable" — it was the first time that Sailaja had voluntarily undergone separation from her husband.

Uncle had been forced to consent and his daughter accompanied him on the journey. Alighting at Benares they espied Umesh also descending from the train and both asked him what he meant by coming too. It appeared that his motive was the same as their own, but Umesh was now an indispensable adjunct to the Ghazipur household and the lady of the house would be seriously annoyed at his disappearance. Father and daughter accordingly united their efforts to prevail on him to return and at last succeeded in doing so. The reader already knows the sequel. Finding life at Ghazipur intolerable without Kamala, Umesh had seized his opportunity one morning when he had been sent to make purchases in the market. He had made off with the money entrusted to him and crossed the Ganges to the railway station. Uncle had been furious when he heard of this escapade, but, as events showed, the culprit hardly deserved his strictures.

Chapter 55

Akshay called on Chakrabartti in the course of the day, but nothing was said to him about Kamala's return, for Uncle knew by this time that Ramesh had no particular love for Akshay.

None of the household asked why Kamala had taken to flight or where she had gone, and in fact everyone behaved as though she had accompanied the family on its visit to Benares. Only Umi's nurse, Lachmania, was on the point of administering a gentle scolding when Uncle drew her aside and warned her not to mention the subject.

Sailaja made Kamala sleep with her that night. She put one arm round Kamala's neck, drew her to her breast, and stroked her softly with the other hand. The caressing touch was a mute invitation to Kamala to relate her sorrowful secret.

"What did you all think, *didi*?" asked Kamala; "weren't you angry with me?"

"We were not so foolish as to be angry with you," retorted Saila. "We knew that you would never do such a dreadful thing so long as any other course was open to you. It was only the thought of the awful trouble Heaven had brought upon you that made us sad. To think that the punishment should fall on one who could never conceivably have been the sinner!"

"Would you like to hear the whole story, *didi*?" asked Kamala.

"Of course I should, dear," said Saila tenderly.

I don't know why I couldn't tell it you before; I had no time then to think things out. It came as such a sudden shock that I felt I could never look any of you in the face again. I have no mother or sister, *didi*, but you are both mother and sister to me and that's why I'm ready to tell you the story; otherwise I should never tell it to a soul."

Kamala sat up, feeling that she could lie down no longer. Sailaja too rose and sat facing her; and in this posture they remained while Kamala related the whole tale of her life from her marriage onward.

When she mentioned that neither before her marriage nor on her wedding-night had she set eyes on the bridegroom, Saila interrupted:

"Such a silly girl as you I've never seen! I was younger than you when I was married. You needn't think I was too shy to look at my husband at all!"

"It wasn't shyness, *didi*," Kamala went on. "You see, I was almost past the marrying age, then all of a sudden a marriage was arranged for me and the other girls teased me dreadfully. So just to show that I didn't consider myself extraordinarily lucky in getting a husband at my age I never even glanced at him. I actually went to the length of thinking it immodest and unbecoming to take the least interest in him, even in my thoughts. I'm paying the penalty for that now."

Kamala was silent for a few minutes, then she continued: "I've told you before how we were saved when the boats were swamped after the wedding; but at the time when I told you I didn't know that the man who had rescued me, the man into whose hands I had fallen supposing him to be my husband, was not my husband at all!"

Sailaja started up in amazement; she went to Kamala's side at once and put her arm round her neck. "Oh, you poor thing—to think of it! Now I understand it all. What an awful thing to happen!"

"Yes, *didi*," said Kamala, "it was dreadful! And to think that I might have been drowned and escaped it all!"

"Didn't Ramesh Babu find out the truth either?" asked Sailaja.

"One day, some time after the marriage," Kamala went on, "he called me 'Susila,' and I said to him, 'Why do you call me Susila when my name is Kamala?' I know now that he must have realised his mistake then; but I can't look anyone in the face when I even think of those days, *didi*"; and Kamala again relapsed into silence.

Bit by bit Sailaja extracted the whole story from her.

When she had heard it all she said to Kamala, "It's terrible for you, dear but I can't help thinking that you were fortunate in falling into Ramesh Babu's hands and no one else's. Say what you like, I'm sorry for that poor Ramesh Babu!

Now it's very late, Kamala, you must go to sleep. You've been lying awake and crying so many nights that you look quite ill. Tomorrow we'll decide what is to be done."

Kamala had with her the letter that Ramesh had written to Hemnalini. Next morning Sailaja had a private interview with her father and handed him the letter.

Uncle put his spectacles on and read it through very slowly; then he replaced it in the envelope; took off his spectacles, and said to his daughter, "Well, what's to be done now?"

"Umi has had a cold and a cough for some days now, dad," said Saila; "I should like to call in Dr. Nalinaksha. One hears so much about him and his mother in Benares, but one never sees him."

The doctor came to see the patient, and Saila showed great keenness to see the doctor.

"Come along, Kamala," she cried. But Kamala, who in Nabinkali's house had hardly been able to control her eagerness to see Nalinaksha, was now too shy even to rise to her feet.

"Kamala, you villain," cried Saila, "I can't waste any more time over you; there's nothing much wrong with Umi and the doctor won't be here long. I shan't see him at all if I stay here any longer trying to persuade you to come"; and she fairly dragged Kamala as far as the door.

Nalinaksha sounded Umi's lungs thoroughly front and back, wrote out a prescription, and departed.

"You're in luck now, Kamala," said Saila, "in spite of all your misfortunes. You'll just have to wait patiently for a day or two now, dear. We're arranging things for you. Meanwhile, we'll be constantly requiring the doctor for Umi, so you won't be done out of him altogether!"

One day Uncle went himself for the doctor, carefully choosing a time when Nalinaksha was not at home. A servant announced that his master was out. "Well," said Uncle, "your mistress is in. Tell her that I'm here, will you? Just say that an old Brahman would like to see her."

He was duly ushered into Kshemankari's presence and introduced himself as follows:

"One hears a great deal about you in Benares, mother, so I've come to acquire merit by seeing you. I have no other reason for intruding on you. A little granddaughter of mine is sick and I came for your son, but he is out. I felt that I couldn't but pay my respects to you before I go."

"Nalin will be back soon," said Kshemankari; "won't you sit down and wait a little? It's getting late; let me offer you something to eat."

"I might have known," said Uncle, "that you couldn't send me away empty. Folks recognise me at sight as one who is fond of good eating, and they humour my little weakness."

Kshemankari was delighted to regale Uncle. "You must come and take your midday meal here to-morrow," she said. "I wasn't expecting you to-day, so I haven't much for you."

"Well, you mustn't forget the old man when the time comes," said Uncle. "I live quite near. Say the word and I'll take your servant with me and point out my house to him."

After a few visits of this description Uncle became a *persona grata* at Nalinaksha's house.

One day Kshemankari sent for her son and said to him, "Nalin, you're not to charge any fees to our friend Chakrabartti!"

Uncle laughed. "He obeys his mother's order before he receives it. He hasn't charged me anything at all. The generous recognise a poor man when they see him."

The father and daughter went on maturing their plans for a few more days, then one morning Uncle said to Kamala, "Come on, lass, we must go and bathe; it's the Dasaswamedh festival."

"You'll have to come too, *didi*," said Kamala to Saila.

"Can't come, dear," said Saila, "Umi's not very well.

Uncle brought Kamala back from the bathing *ghât* by a different route from the one which they had taken on the outward journey.

On the way they overtook an old lady returning from her bath dressed in silk and carrying a jar of Ganges water.

Uncle placed Kamala in her path and announced, "This is the doctor babu's mother, dear; make your bow to her." Kamala was startled at his words, but she at once prostrated herself before Kshemankari and reverently touched the dust of her feet.

"Dear me, who's this?" cried Kshemankari, "What a beauty! a perfect little Lakshmi," and she drew aside Kamala's veil and scanned her downcast face. "What is your name, dear?" she asked.

Before Kamala could reply Uncle interrupted: "Her name is Haridasi and she is the daughter of a cousin of mine. She has no parents and is dependent on me."

"Come along, sir!" said Kshemankari, "you had better both come home with me."

Kshemankari took them to her house and called for Nalinaksha, but as it happened he was out. Uncle ensconced himself in a chair and Kamala took a less exalted seat.

Uncle opened the conversation. "I must tell you that this niece of mine has been very unfortunate. The day after her marriage her husband turned ascetic and took to the road, and she has never seen him since. She wants to lead a religious life in some holy place; religion is her only comfort now. But I don't live here and I cannot throw up my post at Ghazipur. I need it to support my family, so I couldn't settle down here with her. That's why I'm asking a favour of you. It would take a load off my mind if she could stay here and be a daughter to you. If at any time you feel disinclined to keep her, then send her to me at Ghazipur; but I assure you that by the time she had been a couple of days with you, you will realise what a treasure she is, and you won't want to part with her for a moment."

"Well, that's a good proposal," said Kshemankari; "it'll be very nice to have a girl like her with me. Many's the time I've been glad to take strange girls off the road and bring them in here to give them something to eat and something to wear, but I can't make them stay with me. Now you've given Haridasi to me and you need have no anxiety about her. You must have heard people talk about my son Nalinaksha—he's a very good lad; there's no one living here except us two."

"Everyone has heard of Nalinaksha," said Uncle, "and I'm heartily glad to know that he's living with you. I've heard that his wife was drowned soon after they were married and that since then he has become a sort of ascetic."

"It was God's will," said Kshemankari, "but please don't talk of it. The thought of it makes me shiver."

"If you'll allow me," said Uncle, "I'll leave Haridasi with you now, but I'll come and see her now and then. There's her big sister too; she will also come and pay her respects to you."

As soon as Uncle had left them Kshemankari drew Kamala to her, saying, "Come here, dear, and let me look at you. You're quite a child. What a clod to go and leave you! Think of there being such people in the world! My prayer for you is that he may come back. Fate never intended such beauty as yours to run to waste," and she pressed a finger caressingly on Kamala's chin. "You'll have no companions here of your own age," she went on; "will you mind living alone with me?"

"No, mother," said Kamala, with a look of perfect submission in her big beautiful eyes.

"I'm worried to think what you're going to do all day."

"I'll work for you."

"You little villain! You're like that too! There's that son of mine—he's a sort of ascetic—if he would only say now and then, 'Mother, I want so and so,' or 'I should like this and that to eat,' or 'I'm fond of what d'ye call it,' how delighted I should be, but he never says anything of the sort.

He makes quite a lot of money, but he doesn't keep a farthing of it, and he never lets anyone know what he spends on good objects. Look here, dear, if you're going to spend all the hours of the twenty-four with me I had better warn you beforehand you'll be quite sick of hearing me sing my son's praises, but you'll have to put up with it."

Kamala's expression was demure, but her heart was athrill with delight.

"I'm wondering what work I'll give you to do," Kshemankari went on. "Can you sew?"

"Not well," said Kamala.

"Well, I'll give you some lessons. Can you read?"

"Yes, I can read," said Kamala.

"I'm glad of that," said Kshemankari. "I can't see now without glasses and you'll be able to read to me."

"I've learnt cooking and housework," Kamala volunteered.

"Well," said Kshemankari, "if you can't cook, your looks belie you altogether. So far, I've always cooked for Nalin myself, and when I'm ill he prefers cooking for himself to eating anything prepared by another person. From now on, thanks to you, I shan't let him cook his own food, and if I can't manage for myself I'll be very glad to have you cook simple things for me. Come along, dear, I'll show you my store-room and kitchen" and she took Kamala behind the scenes of her little home.

Kamala thought this a good opportunity to express her heart's desire, and she whispered, "Please let me cook to-day, mother."

Kshemankari smiled. "The store-room and the kitchen are the housewife's kingdom. I've had to give up a great deal in this world, but these things are bound up with my daily life. Very well, you do the cooking to-day, dear, and for two or three days more if you like; I've no doubt that in course of time you'll find yourself doing the whole of the work. Then I'll have time for my devotions. It's a never-ending responsibility and I'll be glad to be free of it for a few days. The housewife's throne is not embowered in roses!"

When Kamala's initiation into the mysteries of the culinary department was complete Kshemankari went off to her prayer-room, leaving the girl to give a practical demonstration of her abilities as a housewife.

Kamala made all preparations for cooking with her accustomed thoroughness. She tied the slack of her garment round her waist, fastened her hair into a knot, and set to work.

When Nalinaksha came in he always made a point of seeing his mother before he did anything else, for her health was a matter of constant anxiety to him. As soon as he entered the house on this particular morning his ears and nostrils informed him that cooking was in progress. Assuming that his mother was in the kitchen he went there and halted in the doorway.

Startled by the sound of footsteps, Kamala turned round and found herself staring straight into Nalinaksha's face. She dropped her ladle and made an unsuccessful attempt to pull her veil into position, forgetting that it was tied round her waist. Before she could disentangle it and raise it to her face, Nalinaksha, who was no less surprised than she, had turned and gone.

Kamala's hand trembled as she took up the ladle again.

It was still early when Kshemankari finished her devotions and repaired to the kitchen, only to find that cooking was over. Kamala had washed the room out and cleaned it thoroughly; there were no fragments of charred wood or vegetable peelings lying about and everything was as tidy as it could be.

"Well, dear, you're a true Brahman girl and no mistake!" exclaimed Kshemankari in delight.

When Nalinaksha sat down to breakfast, his mother took her place opposite him and a certain very nervous little person stood listening outside the door. She could not summon up courage to peep in and she was frightened almost out of her wits at the thought that her cooking might be a failure.

"What's the cooking like to-day, Nalin?" asked Kshemankari.

Nalinaksha was no gourmet and consequently his mother was not in the habit of questioning him about his food, but this time there was a real note of eagerness in her voice. She did not know that Nalinaksha was already aware of the installation of a mysterious stranger in the kitchen. As his mother's strength declined with age he had done his best to persuade her to engage a cook, but he had never been able to win her consent. He had accordingly been delighted to see a new face in the kitchen, and though he had taken no particular note of the quality of the viands he answered enthusiastically, "It's splendid, mother!"

Unable to sustain the role of eavesdropper after hearing this compliment to her cooking, Kamala fled into another room and clasped her arms over her heaving breast.

After breakfast Nalinaksha retired in a brown study for his usual spell of quiet reading. In the afternoon Kshemankari took Kamala in hand, dressed her hair for her and put vermilion on the parting; then she turned her head this way and that to study the effect.

Kamala was too bashful to look up at all during these operations.

"Ah!" sighed Kshemankari to herself, "if only I had a daughter-in-law like her!"

That night the old lady had another attack of fever, greatly to Nalinaksha's distress.

"Mother," he said, you had better come away with me for a few days' change. Benares doesn't suit you."

"No, my son," said Kshemankari, "I couldn't think of leaving Benares even if it means living a few days longer; I don't want to end my days in a strange place." (To Kamala) "Run away, dear. Don't stand there outside the door. Go to bed. You mustn't lose your sleep. You'll have to do all the housekeeping these few days while I'm laid up, and I can't have you sitting up all night. Go away now, Nalin; be off to your room."

Nalinaksha having retired into the next room, Kamala seated herself at the bedside and began to massage Kshemankari's feet.

"You must have been my mother in some former existence, dear!" said the old lady, "otherwise what have I done to deserve you? You know I'm so constituted that I cannot bear to be waited on by a stranger, but your touch seems to give me strength. It's an extraordinary thing, but I feel as if I had known you for years; I can't look on you as a stranger at all. Now do what I tell you, dear, and go straight off to bed. Nalin is in the next room—he'll never allow anyone else to nurse his mother. I've forbidden him a thousand times and done all I can, but one can't cope with him! One of his virtues is that he can sit up all night and undergo all sorts of discomfort and never show any sign of what he has been through. It's because he always takes things calmly. I'm just the opposite. There, I'm sure you're laughing in your sleeve at me, dear. You're thinking that I've started talking about Nalin and that I'll never stop. It's because he's my only son, dear, and not many mothers have a son like Nalin. Do you know, I find myself imagining that he is my father and that when he's old I'll be able to do for him all that he has done for me! There I'm talking about him again; that's enough, though, for the present! Be off to bed now, dear. No, it can't be done; you really must go. I'll never go to sleep so long as you're here. Old folk can't help talking when there's anyone there."

Next day Kamala took entire charge of the housework. Nalinaksha had made a sitting-room for himself by walling off a small portion of the eastern verandah and paving it with marble, and he used to spend the afternoon sitting there and reading. When he entered this room in the morning he found it swept clean and in perfect order; the brass censer in which he burned incense shone like gold; the books and pamphlets on the shelf had all been dusted and neatly arranged. The rays of the morning sun shining through the open door showed up the spotless cleanliness of the little room; and Nalinaksha, just returned from his morning bath, was pleasantly surprised to find everything so spick and span.

Kamala was early at Kshemankari's bedside with a jar of Ganges water. When the old lady saw her fresh-washed face, she exclaimed, "Well, dear, did you go to the *ghât* all alone? I've been wondering since I woke up who would take you there while I'm laid up. You're young and going alone like that——"

"Mother," said Kamala, "one of my uncle's servants couldn't resist coming here last night to see me. I took him with me to the river."

"Ah," said Kshemankari, "I suppose your aunt was worried about you and that's why she sent him; that's all right, let him stay here; he'll help you with your work. Where is he? Just call him in for a minute."

Kamala fetched in Umesh, who made a low bow to Kshemankari.

"Well, what do they call you?" asked the old lady.

Umesh's face broadened into a quite uncalled-for grin as he gave his name.

"Who gave you such a lovely waistcloth, Umesh?" inquired Kshemankari, laughing.

" 'Mother' gave it to me," said Umesh, indicating Kamala.

Kshemankari looked at Kamala and smiled as she remarked, "It's my belief that Umesh got it as a present from his mother-in-law!"

So Umesh found favour with Kshemankari and became a member of the household.

With his assistance Kamala soon finished the day's work. She swept out Nalinaksha's bedroom herself, laid his bedding out in the sun, and put the room in order. Nalinaksha's soiled clothes had been thrown in a corner; Kamala washed them, dried them, folded them, and hung them on a clothes-horse. Even articles that showed not a speck of dust had to be taken out of their places (in case they required attention) and solemnly put back. There was a wardrobe standing against the wall at the head of the bed. She opened this and found it was empty but for a pair of Nalinaksha's wooden sandals on the bottom shelf. Kamala snatched them up and pressed them against her head; she fondled them like a baby and dusted them with the loose end of her garment.

In the afternoon Kamala was sitting at Kshemankari's bedside massaging the old lady's feet when Hemnalini came into the room with a bunch of flowers and prostrated herself before Kshemankari.

"Come in, Hem," said the old lady, sitting up, "come and sit down. Is Annada Babu quite well?"

"He wasn't very well yesterday; that's why he couldn't come here. He's better to-day."

Kshemankari now proceeded to introduce Kamala. "Do you know, dear," she said, "my mother died when I was a child. She has come to life again after all these years and I met her suddenly on the road yesterday. My mother's name was Haribhagini and now she has taken the name of Haridasi. Did you ever see such a little beauty, though, Hem! Just tell me now!"

Kamala hung her head in shame and it was some time before she felt at ease in Hemnalini's presence.

Hemnalini asked Kshemankari how she was.

"When a person comes to my age," said the old lady, "it doesn't do to make inquiries about her health. I ought to be quite satisfied with being alive at all, but I shan't be able to cheat old Time for ever. However, I'm glad that you raised the subject. I've been intending to speak to you for some time, but haven't had an opportunity. When my fever came on again last night I decided not to put it off any longer. You know, dear, when I was a young girl I nearly died to shame if anyone talked to me about marriage, but you girls have been brought up differently. You're educated and no longer a child and one can talk to you freely about such things. That's why I want to talk about this now and you're not to be shy with me. Now just tell me this, dear. Did your father mention to you the proposal that I made to him the other day?"

"Yes, he mentioned it," said Hemnalini, with downcast eyes.

"But apparently you didn't agree to it, dear," Kshemankari went on, "if you had, Annada Babu would have come straight to me and told me. You took Nalin for an ascetic sort of person who spends the whole day and night in religious observances and you felt you would never be able to marry him. I must face that question though he is my son. Looking at him from the outside one would imagine him incapable of love, but that's where you people go wrong. I've known him all his life and you must take my word for it. He's capable of such strong affection that it frightens him and he keeps his feelings under strict control. Whoever breaks through that crust of asceticism and finds the way to his heart will discover that it's a very warm one, that I can assure you. Hem, dear, you're not a child; you're educated and you've gone to Nalin for advice. I should die perfectly satisfied if I could see you installed in his house. I want to see you married because I know very well that he'll never marry after I die. It's terrible to contemplate! He'll just drift about helplessly. You respect Nalin, I know; tell me, dear, what is it that you object to in him?"

"There is nothing that I object to if you consider me a suitable wife for him, mother," replied Hemnalini, with downcast eyes.

When Kshemankari heard this she drew Hemnalini to her and imprinted a kiss on her forehead. They did not discuss the subject further.

"Haridasi, just take these flowers and——" The old lady looked round and saw that "Haridasi" was not there; she had slipped away quietly while they were talking.

After the conversation that has just been related Hemnalini withdrew into her shell, while Kshemankari on her part showed signs of exhaustion. So Hemnalini cut short her visit, saying as she rose, "I must be off early to-day, mother. Dad's not well."

"Good-bye, dear, good-bye," said Kshemankari, laying her hand on the girl's head.

After Hemnalini's departure Kshemankari sent for Nalinaksha and greeted him on his appearance with the exclamation, "Nalin, I can't wait any longer!"

"What for?" asked Nalinaksha.

"I talked it over with Hem just now," said his mother, "and she has given her consent, so I'm not going to listen to any objections from you. You see how it is with me. I'll never be content till you two are definitely engaged. I lay awake half the night thinking about it."

"Very well, mother," said Nalinaksha, "don't worry about it any longer, but sleep soundly. I'll do as you wish."

As soon as he had left her Kshemankari called for "Haridasi," and Kamala appeared from one of the adjoining rooms; the afternoon light was waning and the room was almost dark. "Put these flowers in water, dear," said Kshemankari, "and arrange them in the rooms." She picked out one rose and pushed the rest of the bunch across to Kamala.

Kamala put some of the flowers in a bowl and set it on Nalinaksha's desk. Others she put in a mug and placed them on a table in his bedroom. Then she opened the wardrobe which stood against the wall, laid the rest of the flowers on his sandals, and bending her head, prostrated herself before them. Tears came to her eyes as she did so at the thought that these were all that she had in the world and that soon she would no longer be able even to worship his feet.

Suddenly Kamala was startled by the sound of footsteps approaching the door. She hurriedly shut the door of the wardrobe and turned round to see — Nalinaksha! Flight was out of the question, and in her dismay she wished she could have melted into the shades of the oncoming night. When Nalinaksha perceived Kamala he left the room abruptly.

Kamala at once seized the opportunity to make her own exit and Nalinaksha returned. Curious to know what the girl had been doing there and why she, on his appearance, had so hurriedly shut the door of the wardrobe, he opened it and saw his sandals, covered with freshly plucked flowers. He closed the door again and crossed to the window. As he gazed out at the sky, darkness fell and swallowed up the last rays of the dying sun.

Chapter 56

*N*ow that Hemnalini had consented to marry Nalinaksha she endeavoured to persuade herself that she was very fortunate; she kept repeating over and over again; "I am no longer bound by my old engagement; the storm clouds that brooded over my horizon have passed away. I am now perfectly free and no longer subject to eternal regrets for the past." And with the constant repetition she began to experience the joy of complete renunciation. When the funeral pyre has ceased to smoke, the huge complexity of worldly concern loses weight for a time, and the mourner feels relieved — almost like a child when, school over, the door opens; so was it with Hemnalini. She savoured the peace that follows on the final close of one chapter in a human life.

When she reached home that evening she said to herself, "If only mother were alive how delighted she would be with the announcement that I have to make! I don't know how I'm going to tell the news to dad."

Annada Babu went early to bed that night on the plea of exhaustion; and Hemnalini retired to her room, took out her diary and sat up late recording her impressions. "I had severed all human ties, and was dead to the world," she wrote; "I could never have believed that God would deliver me and endow me with fresh life. I now prostrate myself before His feet and prepare myself to enter no new paths of duty. Fortune has granted me a boon far above my deserts. May Heaven lend me strength to cleave to it all my days. I am assured that he with whose life my unworthy life is to be linked will make my existence a full and rich one. My only prayer is that I in turn may bring the same measure of fullness and richness into his life."

She closed the book and retired to the garden, where she strolled meditatively up and down the gravelled paths under the star-studded velvetty darkness of the winter night till a late hour, while the boundless sky whispered a message of peace to her troubled soul.

On the following afternoon Annada Babu and Hemnalini were preparing to start for Nalinaksha's house when a carriage drove up and one of Nalinaksha's servants, descending from the box, announced that his mistress had arrived. Annada Babu hastened to meet Kshemankari as she alighted from the carriage and greeted her with the words, "We are indeed fortunate."

"I came to give your daughter my blessing," said the old lady as she entered. Annada Babu ushered her into the sitting-room, and leading her to a sofa, requested her to wait while he called Hemnalini.

Hemnalini was putting the finishing touches to her preparations, but as soon as she heard of Kshemankari's arrival she hastened to make obeisance to her.

"May your days be happy and long!" said Kshemankari. "Just hold out your hands, dear," and she fastened a pair of massive golden bracelets on Hemnalini's wrists; the great bangles hung loosely on the girl's wasted arms.

Hemnalini again prostrated herself before Kshemankari, who took her face between her two hands and kissed her on the forehead. The blessing and the affection with which it was bestowed filled Hemnalini's cup of happiness to the brim.

"Now, sir," said Kshemankari to Annada Babu, addressing him by the title given to the father of a son's wife, "you must both come to breakfast with me to-morrow."

Next morning the father and daughter took tea in the garden, as was their custom in Benares. Delight at Hemnalini's engagement had restored its pristine freshness to Annada Babu's worn countenance, and glancing from time to time at Hemnalini's serene face he fancied that the blessed spirit of his dead wife had descended on his daughter and calmed the exuberance of her joy with a faint suggestion of tears.

Annada Babu was obsessed with the idea that it was already time to prepare for the promised visit to Kshemankari's house and that to delay any longer would make them late. Hemnalini kept assuring him that there was plenty of time — in fact it was barely eight o'clock — but he insisted that preparations took time and that it was better to be early than late.

In the meantime a carriage with luggage on the roof drove up to the front gate and stopped there. "There's Jogen!" exclaimed Hemnalini, and hurried towards the gate. It was indeed Jogendra who stepped out; he wore a very cheerful expression and greeted his sister with the utmost cordiality.

"Have you brought someone with you?" asked Hemnalini.

"I have indeed," laughed Jogendra; "I've brought a Christmas present for dad."

Ramesh now emerged from the carriage, but as soon as she set eyes on him Hemnalini turned on her heel and beat a hurried retreat.

"Don't go, Hem; I've something to tell you," called Jogendra after her. She took no notice, but hastened on as though she were flying for her life from some dreadful apparition.

Ramesh halted for a minute or two in consternation, uncertain whether to follow her or to turn back.

"Come on, Ramesh," called Jogendra, "dad is sitting out here"; and he took Ramesh by the arm and led him up to Annada Babu.

The latter had seen Ramesh arrive and could hardly believe his eyes; he was reduced to rubbing his head and murmuring, "Here's another obstacle to this match!"

Ramesh made a low bow to him.

Annada Babu motioned him into a chair and addressed himself to Jogendra. "Well, Jogen, you've come just in time. I thought of telegraphing to you."

"What about?" asked Jogendra.

"We've arranged a marriage between Hemnalini and Nalinaksha. His mother came to see her yesterday and gave her her blessing."

Jogendra. "Do you mean to say it's a definite engagement, dad? Shouldn't I have been consulted?"

Annada Babu. "One never knows what you'll say, Jogendra. You know you were keen to bring this marriage about before I ever knew Nalinaksha."

Jogendra. "I admit I was, but let that pass; it's not too late yet. I have a lot to tell you. You must hear me first, then you can do whatever you think right."

Annada Babu. "I'll hear you some day when I'm at leisure; I've no time to-day. I have to go out now."

Jogendra. "Where are you off to?"

Annada Babu. "Nalinaksha's mother has invited Hem and me to breakfast at her place. You two had better have breakfast here, then——"

Jogendra. "No, no, don't trouble about us. Ramesh and I can go and feed at one of the hotels here. You'll be back by the evening, I suppose. We'll come along then."

Annada Babu could not bring himself to meet Ramesh's eye, much less to address any word of welcome to him.

Ramesh on his part did not offer any remark, but sat in silence till it was time to take leave, when he bowed to Annada Babu and departed.

Chapter 57

On the day before, Kshemankari had said to Kamala, "I've asked Hemnalini and her father to come to breakfast here to-morrow, dear. What are we going to give them? We ought to feed Annada Babu so well that he'll never be afraid of his daughter not getting enough to eat here; don't you think so, dear? However, you're such a good cook that I know you'll do me credit. I've never known my son make any comment on the food before, but yesterday he couldn't find words to express his appreciation of your cooking! You're not looking very cheerful to-day, dear; are you quite well?"

"I'm all right, thank you, mother," said Kamala, with a forced smile.

Kshemankari shook her head. "I'm afraid you're worrying about something. It's natural enough and you needn't be frightened to tell me. Don't treat me as a stranger, dear; I look on you as my own daughter. You must really tell me if there's anything in the life here that doesn't suit you or if you want to see any of your own folk."

"I don't want anything except to work for you, mother!" exclaimed Kamala eagerly.

Kshemankari went on without noticing this interruption, "Perhaps you had better go to your uncle's and stay there for a few days, then you can come back here when you feel inclined."

"Mother!" cried Kamala in dismay, "so long as I can stay with you I shan't want to see anybody else in the world. If I do anything wrong, please punish me as you think fit, but don't send me away even for one day!"

Kshemankari stroked the girl's cheek as she replied, "That's one of the things that make me think you were my mother in some former life, dear. Otherwise how is it that we took to each other so at first sight? Now be off and go to bed early. You haven't known what it is to rest all day."

Kamala went to her bedroom, locked the door, extinguished the light, and sat down on the floor in the darkness to think. After a long spell of musing her thoughts shaped themselves into this form: "I cannot continue to watch over him when Heaven has deprived me of any right to do so. I must prepare myself to give him up altogether. Nothing is left but the small opportunities I have to serve him from time to time, and these I shall do everything in my power to retain. God, grant me strength to perform these duties with a smiling face, and never even to aspire to anything more! It cost me dear to achieve even this much. If I cannot do cheerfully what there is to do, if I go about my work looking dismal, then I must give up everything."

Having thus reviewed her present situation she schooled herself to the following resolution: "From to-morrow I shall entertain no more regrets; I shall never look unhappy, I shall never allow myself to sigh for the unattainable. I shall be content to serve all the days of my life. I shall never, never, never ask for anything more."

She retired to bed, and after turning over from one side to the other for some time she fell asleep. She awoke twice or thrice in the course of the night and each time she repeated to herself as though it were a sacred text, "I shall never, never, never ask for anything more"; and in the morning when she rose she folded her hands and concentrated all her will-power on the resolution, "I shall serve you till death and shall never, never, never ask for anything more."

She hurriedly washed and dressed and then betook herself to Nalinaksha's study. She dusted every corner of the room with the fringe of her garment, spread all the mats in their places, and hastened off to bathe in the Ganges.

After repeated remonstrances from Nalinaksha, Kshemankari had given up the practice of bathing before sunrise; so it was Umesh who accompanied Kamala to the river in the bitter cold of dawn.

On her return she made her morning salutation of Kshemankari with a smiling face.

The old lady was on the point of starting for the river. "Why did you go off so early?" she asked Kamala; "you should have waited and come with me."

"I couldn't wait to-day, mother," said Kamala, "there's too much to do. I have to slice the vegetables that we got in yesterday evening, and I must send Umesh off early to the market to fetch the things that we still need."

"You've considered everything, dear. Our guest will find his breakfast ready as soon as he arrives."

Nalinaksha came out at this point and Kamala at once pulled her veil over her wet locks and went indoors.

"Going to start bathing again already, mother?" said Nalinaksha. "It would have been better to wait till you were a little stronger."

"*Do* forget that you're a doctor, Nalin," retorted Kshemankari. "There's only one recipe for immortality

and that is to bathe in the Ganges every morning. You're
going out now, are you? Don't be late to-day."

"Why, mother?"

Kshemankari. "I forgot to tell you yesterday: Annada
Babu is coming to-day to give you his blessing."

Nalinaksha. "To give me his blessing? Why has he
become so gracious all of a sudden? I see him everyday."

Kshemankari. "I went round yesterday, presented
Hemnalini with a pair of bangles, and gave her my blessing;
now it's Annada Babu's turn to give you his. Well, don't
be late. They're coming here for breakfast"; and the old
lady went off to her bath.

Nalinaksha strolled away with his head bent,
meditating.

Chapter 58

*W*hen she fled from Ramesh's presence Hemnalini, closing the door of her own room, sat down to compose herself. After the first excitement had subsided, shame obtruded. "Why was I unable to meet Ramesh Babu without losing my self-possession?" she pondered. "Why, when the unexpected happened, did I make such a sorry exhibition of myself? It takes away all confidence in my power to control emotion. I must never make such a display of instability again"; and pulling herself together, she rose, opened the door, and set out for another encounter with Ramesh Babu, saying to herself, "I will not run away this time; I will control my feelings."

Then suddenly recollecting something, she returned to her room. She took from her box the pair of bangles that Kshemankari had given her and slipped them on; thus armed, she nerved herself for the fray, and marched out into the garden with her head erect.

The first person whom she met was her father. "Where are you off to, Hem?" he asked.

"What, isn't Ramesh Babu here? Isn't Jogen here?" she inquired.

"No, they've both gone."

Hemnalini was relieved to find that her powers of self-control were not to be put to the test.

"Well now——" Annada Babu went on.

"Yes, dad; I'll come with you," said Hemnalini. "I shan't be long over my bath. You can send for a carriage now."

Hemnalini's sudden change of front and her unnatural eagerness to hurry off to Kshemankari's were not lost on Annada Babu, and they served to increase his uneasiness.

Hemnalini hurriedly bathed and dressed, then came and inquired if the carriage had arrived.

"Not yet," her father informed her, so she walked about in the garden while Annada Babu sat on the verandah rubbing his head.

It was only half-past ten when they reached Nalinaksha's house and the doctor had not returned from his rounds, so it fell to Kshemankari to entertain the guests. She entered upon a long conversation with Annada Babu about his health and his family, throwing an occasional side-glance in Hemnalini's direction. She was surprised not to see the girl looking more cheerful. With so happy an event in prospect her face should have been lit up like the rosy glow that heralds the sunrise; actually it seemed darkened by clouds of care.

Kshemankari had a sensitive nature and Hemnalini's cheerless expression damped her spirits. "Most girls," she thought, "would consider themselves very lucky to get Nalin, but apparently over-education has turned this one's head and she thinks herself too good for him; I can't explain her anxious abstracted air in any other way. The fault was mine; I am an old woman and impatient; I couldn't bear waiting to see my wishes fulfilled. I arranged for Nalin to marry a girl who is no longer a child and I made no attempt to discover her real character. The pity of it is that I had so little time to make her acquaintance;

but alas! the call has already sounded for me to wind up my worldly affairs." These reflections distracted Kshemankari as she talked to Annada Babu, and she found increasing difficulty in carrying on the conversation. At last what was in her mind found utterance. "After all," she said, "there is no need to hurry on the wedding. They're both of age and can exercise their own judgement; it wouldn't do for us to press them. Of course I don't know how Hem feels about it, but I can speak for Nalin, and he hasn't quite accustomed himself to the idea yet." Her words were directed chiefly at Hemnalini; the girl appeared to be in two minds, and Kshemankari did not desire her guests to carry away the impression that her son was overjoyed at the prospect of the match.

Hemnalini had set out that morning in a mood of forced gaiety and the result was the opposite of what she had intended. Her short-lived hilarity turned to complete lassitude. Suddenly, as she entered Kshemankari's house, a feeling of terror had assailed her and the new path on which she was to tread in life stretched out before her mental vision, rocky, steep, and unending. As the elders continued to exchange courtesies Hemnalini became a prey to doubts of her own constancy; and the result was that two different emotions contended within her when Kshemankari showed signs of cooling from the marriage project. On the one hand, a speedy consummation of the marriage would give her the early release that she desired from her present state of distraction and vacillation, and for that reason she longed to see a definite compact made about her engagement; and yet the hint of an abandonment of the scheme was a momentary relief to her.

After making her momentous pronouncement Kshemankari had glanced at Hemnalini's face and noted the effect of her words. It seemed to her that at last the girl's expression was calmer, and in that instant her heart hardened against Hemnalini. "I was prepared to sell my Nalin very cheaply," she thought, and she rejoiced that he was late in putting in an appearance.

"This is so like Nalinaksha!" she went on, talking at Hemnalini. "He knew quite well that you two people were coming to-day and yet there's no sign of him. He might have cut his work short to-day at any rate. Whenever I'm at all out of sorts he neglects his practice and stays at home—in spite of what he loses by it!"

She then excused herself on the score of ascertaining how far advanced the preparations for the meal were. Her intention was to hand over Hemnalini to Kamala so that she herself might have a private talk with the old gentleman.

She found the food ready cooked and simmering on a slow fire, while Kamala sat in a corner of the kitchen so deep in meditation that Kshemankari's sudden entrance startled her and she sprang to her feet with an embarrassed smile.

"Well, dear, you seem very intent on your cooking," said the old lady.

"Everything is ready, mother," replied Kamala.

"Well, why are you sitting here so quietly, dear? Annada Babu is an old man and you needn't be shy of him. Hem is here and I think you might take her off to your room for a chat. I don't like to bore her by making her talk to an old person like me."

Hemnalini's apparent coldness had only served to intensify Kshemankari's affection for Kamala.

"But I shan't be able to talk to her," pleaded Kamala; "she has learnt such a lot and I know nothing at all."

"What do you mean?" said Kshemankari; "you're as good as anyone. However much people may pride themselves on their learning there are very few as attractive as you. Anyone can learn things from books, but it isn't given to many to be such a sweet little woman as you are. Come along now, dear. You'll have to dress first, though. I'll give you something nice to wear to-day."

Kshemankari was resolved to contrast Hemnalini's faded beauty with the fresh charm of this unlettered girl; she wanted to lower the former's pride in every respect.

Kamala was given no chance to object. Kshemankari decked her out with a cunning hand. She made her don a cream-coloured silk robe and she dressed her hair in the latest mode. She kept turning Kamala's face this way and that to study the effect. Finally she kissed her on the cheek and exclaimed in delight, "You're beautiful enough for a king's palace."

Kamala interjected from time to time: "Mother, they're sitting all by themselves; it's getting late."

"Never mind if it's late," was Kshemankari's rejoinder. "I shan't go till I've finished with you."

When Kamala's toilet was complete Kshemankari said, "Come with me now, dear; you mustn't be shy. When that college-trained beauty sees you she'll be put to shame. You can hold up your head with any of them," and she dragged Kamala with her to the room in which she had left her guests; Nalinaksha had arrived by this time and was chatting with them.

Seeing him, Kamala swung round and attempted to fly, but Kshemankari held her fast.

"There's nothing to be shy of, dear," she said, "we're all friends here."

Kshemankari prided herself on the girl's beauty and on the distinction with which she wore her borrowed feathers, and she wished to give the others a surprise. The mother in her had been aroused by Hemnalini's supposed indifference to her Nalinaksha, and she plumed herself on the idea that he would draw comparisons unfavourable to his betrothed.

Kamala's appearance was indeed a surprise to the rest of the party. When Hemnalini met her at Kshemankari's bedside Kamala was wearing no finery; she had crouched in the background, looking shy and insignificant, and had vanished before Hemnalini could take note of her appearance. Now after a moment of bewilderment she took the shrinking Kamala by the hand and seated her beside herself.

Kshemankari felt that victory was with her; no one could see her charge without admitting in his heart of hearts that such beauty was a rare gift of the gods. She said to Kamala, "Take Hem to your room now, dear, and you can have a talk there. I'll attend to the breakfast-room."

Kamala wondered what Hemnalini would think of her, and it was a trying moment. At no distant date Hemnalini would enter this house as Nalinakshi's bride and she would rise to the position of its mistress, so Kamala could not be indifferent to her good opinion. She refused to entertain the thought that she herself was lady of the house by right. She would never allow herself to harbour the slightest suspicion of jealousy and she would claim no rights whatever.

Her limbs trembled as she left the room.

"I have heard all about you from mother," said Hemnalini gently. "You must look on me as a sister, dear. Have you any sisters of your own?"

"None of my own, only a cousin—daughter of my father's brother," answered Kamala, taking courage from the friendliness of Hemnalini's tone.

"I have no sister either, dear," said the other, "and my mother died when I was a child. Many a time I've thought,

'I've no mother; if only I had a sister to confide in!' I have that longing both when I'm very happy and when I'm very sad. Ever since I was quite small I've had to keep all my thoughts bottled up, and now it has become so habitual with me that I can't unburden myself to anyone. People consider me very conceited, but I hope you won't think that, dear. It's just that I can't speak from the heart."

Kamala's reserve was now entirely broken down. "Is it possible that you could like me, *didi?*" she asked. "I'm so stupid.

Hemnalini smiled. "When you come to know me well you'll find that I'm very stupid too. I don't know anything except a few things I've learned from books; and so if I come to live in this house I want you always to stay with me. I'm terrified at the idea of managing a household by myself."

"Leave it all to me," said Kamala, simply as a child. "I've been doing that sort of work ever since I was quite small. I'm not afraid of anything like that. You and I will do the housekeeping together like two sisters. You'll make him happy and I'll look after you both."

"Tell me, dear," said Hemnalini next: "you can never have seen your husband properly; can you recall what he was like?"

Kamala did not give a direct answer to this question. "I didn't know I should have to remember him, *didi.* When I came to live in my uncle's house my cousin Saila *didi* and I became close friends. I saw myself how she devoted herself to her husband and it opened my eyes. I never saw my husband at all, so to speak, but somehow or other I came to worship him with all my heart. God gave me a reward for my devotion, for I have now a clear picture of my husband in my mind. He never really found a wife in me, but it seems to me now that I have found my husband."

This tale of Kamala's devotion found a response in Hemnalini heart. "I understand exactly what you mean," she said, after a short silence. "To get a thing in that way is real getting. Any other kind is merely physical and do not last."

Whether Kamala fully understood this or not it is impossible to say. She gazed at Hemnalini for a minute or two, then she said, "It must be true when you say it, *didi*. I don't let myself grieve over it; I'm perfectly happy. What I have got is my reward."

Hemnalini took Kamala's hand in her own. "My master says that when loss and gain are alike to one that is real gain. Really and truly, dear, if I get as much out of absolute self-devotion as you do I'll be lucky indeed.

Kamala opened her eyes at this. "What do you mean, *didi*? You'll have everything; surely you won't want for anything?"

"I can be quite content," said Hemnalini, "with getting what I ought to get. To get more than that spells weariness and sorrow. You must be surprised to hear me say this sort of thing, but I feel that God is inspiring me. Do you know, dear, I had a load on my heart to-day, but since I met you it has gone and I feel that I have gained strength. That's why I'm talking such a lot. I've never been able to talk before. How did you manage to draw me out so, dear?"

Chapter 59

*W*hen Hemnalini returned from Kshemankari's she found a large thick envelope addressed to her on the sitting-room table. She knew by the handwriting that it was from Ramesh. Her heart beat fast as she took it to her bedroom, shut the door, and read the contents.

Ramesh had given her the whole story of his connection with Kamala, keeping nothing back. In conclusion he had written: "Circumstances have severed the tie with which Heaven linked your life and mine. You have now given your heart to another. For that I do not blame you at all, but neither must you blame me. Although Kamala and I never lived for a single day together as man and wife, still I ought to confess to you that as time went on I became more and more drawn to her. Precisely what the state of my feelings is now I do not myself know. If you had not cast me off my heart would have found its sure haven in your love. It was with that hope that in my distracted state I hastened to you. But when you so obviously avoided me because you no longer cared for me, and when I heard that you had consented to marry another, then all my doubts and distraction returned.

"I found that I could not forget Kamala altogether. But whether I forget or not, no one in the world except myself will suffer for it. Why, indeed, should I suffer either? I can never forget the only two women who have ever found a place in my heart, and to cherish their memory all my life will be an inestimable boon to me.

"The momentary glimpse that I had of you this morning so affected me that I returned to my quarters commiserating myself as an unfortunate wretch; but I shall never do that again. It is with a composed and indeed a cheerful mind that I bid you farewell; and I take my leave of you with a full heart. Thanks to you both and thanks to Providence I feel no misery at this hour of parting. I will you all happiness and prosperity. Do not think harshly of me, for I have given you no cause to do so."

Annada was disturbed at his reading by Hemnalini's sudden entrance.

"Are you quite well, Hem?" he asked.

"Yes, dad, I'm quite well; I have had a letter from Ramesh Babu. Please take it and read it, then let me have it back"; and handing him the letter she left the room.

Annada Babu put on his spectacles and read the letter through twice. Then he returned it to Hemnalini through a servant and sat down to think. His final comment was: "Not a bad thing in a way! Nalinaksha is a much better match than Ramesh. It's just as well that Ramesh has left the field clear."

Next minute Nalinaksha was shown in. Annada Babu was a little surprised to see him and wondered what business had brought him, inasmuch as they had parted only a few hours before, after a long conversation. He decided that Nalinaksha must be really in love with Hemnalini, and smiled inwardly at the thought.

He was just planning to bring the young people together

and then to retire on some pretext or other when Nalinaksha came straight to the point.

"Annada Babu, there is a proposal that I should marry your daughter. Before we go any further I want to tell you something which you ought to know."

"Very well; in that case you ought to tell it."

"You did not know that I am married already!"

"Yes, I knew, but——"

Nalinaksha. "I'm surprised to hear that you knew it already. Anyhow the point is that you suppose my first wife to be dead; but there's no certainty about that. In fact I believe myself that she is alive."

"I pray Heaven that may be true. Hem! Hem!"

"Yes, dad?" and Hemnalini entered the room.

Annada Babu. "There's something in that letter that Ramesh wrote to you——"

Hemnalini handed the letter to Nalinaksha. "He ought to know the whole of it," she said, and left the room again.

Nalinaksha read the letter through. Amazement deprived him of the power of speech and he could offer no comment.

"It's one of the saddest stories one could imagine," Annada Babu went on. "You must have found the letter painful reading; but it would not have been right for us to keep it back from you."

After a few moments' silence Nalinaksha rose and took leave of Annada Babu. As he went out he noticed Hemnalini standing in the northern verandah a short distance off. The sight of her caused him a distinct shock. He wondered how she could stand there immovable, with her face so set and calm, when a storm must be raging in her breast. Her expression did not betray the workings of her mind in the slightest degree. He could not bring himself to ask her if she had any need of his and he knew that it would not be easy to obtain an answer from her. "Can I give her any consolation or not?" he asked his troubled heart. "No, the barriers set up between one human soul and another are impenetrable. What a fearfully lonely thing the soul is!"

Nalinaksha decided to go out of his way so as to pass close to her before gaining his carriage, in case she had any communication to make; but as he passed her verandah she disappeared indoors. "It is not easy for soul to meet soul," he thought; "the tie between one human being and another is a complex thing"; and he made for his carriage with a heavy heart.

Nalinaksha had not been long gone when Jogendra appeared.

"All alone, Jogen!" remarked his father.

"Whom were you expecting, then?" asked Jogendra.

"Why, Ramesh," said Annada Babu.

Jogendra. "One reception of the kind that you gave him is enough where gentlemen are concerned! I don't know what he has done unless he has gained everlasting bliss by throwing himself into the Ganges at Benares. I haven't seen him again, but he left a slip of paper with 'I'm off, Yours, Ramesh' written on it. I never could fathom this kind of melodrama. I'll have to be off too; my present job suits me very well. A headmaster's work is all clear and straight-forward; none of these half-lights in it!"

"But about Hem? We'll have to decide——" began Annada Babu.

Jogendra. "What more can I do? I should only go on making decisions and you two would continue to upset them. I don't care for that game any longer. Please don't mix me up in it any more. Things I can't understand don't agree with me. Hem's extraordinary faculty for suddenly turning incomprehensible makes me feel powerless. I'll be leaving by the morning train to-morrow; I'll have to stop at Bankipore on the way," and he left the room abruptly.

There was nothing for Annada Babu to do but to stroke his head and ruminate; his world was again full of riddles that he could not solve.

Chapter 60

A day or two later Sailaja and her father were at Nalinaksha's house on a visit. Saila and Kamala sat in a side room talking in whispers while Chakrabartti conversed with Kshemankari.

Chakrabartti. "My leave is up. I have to go back to Ghazipur to-morrow. If Haridasi annoys you in any way or if you——"

Kshemankari. "There you go again! My dear sir, what can you be thinking of? Is this a plot to get your niece back again?"

Chakrabartti. "No, I'm not that sort; I don't take back a gift; but if it's at all inconvenient to you——"

Kshemankari. "You're not being straight-forward with me at all. Nothing could be more convenient than to have a perfect little house-wife like Haridasi with one; you know that as well as I do, so——"

Chakrabartti. "Well, well, we'll say no more about it. You've seen through me. It was only a little dodge of mine to hear you singing Haridasi's praises. There's only one thing that I'm concerned about and that is that Nalinaksha Babu may consider her an incubus. She's proud, that lass of ours; and if Nalinaksha drops the least hint that he is annoyed with her she'll take it very much to heart."

Kshemankari. "My word! Nalin annoyed! He's incapable of it."

Chakrabartti. "You're right there! but you see I love Haridasi very dearly, so I'm not easily satisfied where she is concerned. It's all very well to say that Nalin would never be annoyed with her and that he would take no notice of her at all; but that doesn't seem to me enough. I shall never be happy about her unless I know that while she is living in his house she feels as though he and she were members of the same family. She's not an article of furniture; she's a human being. If he neither resents her presence nor cares for her, and that is to be all the bond between them, then——"

Kshemankari. "Don't worry any more about it, my dear sir. It wouldn't go against the grain for my Nalin to regard her as one of the family. One doesn't notice anything outwardly, but I'm quite sure that Nalin has thought about her position here and has studied her happiness and comfort. It's likely enough that he has been doing things for her and we know nothing about it."

Chakrabartti. "I'm very glad to hear you say so. Still I should like to have a special talk with Nalinaksha Babu before I go. Not many men in the world would make themselves entirely responsible for a woman's happiness. If Heaven has endowed Nalinaksha Babu with that kind of true manliness, then I want to convey to him that he should not proceed by keeping Haridasi at a distance through false modesty; he should accept her and regard her without constraint as real member of the family."

Chakrabartti's faith in her son caused Kshemankari's heart to glow with maternal pride.

"I was afraid that you might not approve," she said, "so I have been keeping Haridasi in the background when Nalinaksha is about, but I know my son and can trust him implicitly."

Chakrabartti. "Then I can tell you frankly what is in my mind. I've heard that Nalinaksha Babu is going to be married, and that his bride is of age and has more education than is usual among our people. So I thought perhaps Haridasi——"

Kshemankari. "I see that, of course. You might certainly have cause for anxiety in that case. But that marriage will never take place."

Chakrabartti. "Has the engagement been broken off?"

Kshemankari. "There was never one to break off. Nalin didn't want it at all; it was only I who urged him to marry, but I've given up pressing him. It's no good trying to force people against their inclination. It may be that I'll die without seeing him married at all. We can't foresee God's purposes."

Chakrabarti. "You mustn't talk like that. What are your friends for? A matchmaker is entitled to a dinner and a present, and the bait tempts me, for one!"

Kshemankari. "Bless your good heart! You see, Nalin is getting on in years and I was greatly distressed to think that it was my fault that he has not entered the holy state. So I went off in too great a hurry and made proposals on his behalf without taking a good look round first. I've had to give up hope of bringing off this particular match, so now you people had better see what you can do; but don't waste time over it, for I haven't much longer to live."

Chakrabartti. "I can't have you saying that. You'll see your son provided with a helpmate yet. I know just the kind of daughter-in-law that will suit you—not too young, but one who'll be attentive and submissive to you; we shan't select one who doesn't answer to that description. Well, you mustn't worry yourself about it any more. God willing, it's as good as settled. Now, if you'll allow me, I'll just give Haridasi a little good advice about her behaviour here, and I'll send Saila in to you; she has been talking about you ever since she first met you."

"You three had better have a talk together," said Kshemankari; "I have some work to do."

Chakrabarti laughed. "It's lucky for people like me that there are people like you in the world!" he said. "We'll know when the time comes what the 'work' is. I hope you're going to start making sweets for the fortunate Brahman who finds a bride for Nalinaksha Babu!"

Chakrabartti sought out Sailaja and Kamala, and found that tears were sparkling in Kamala's eyes. He said nothing, but sat down beside his daughter after one glance at Kamala.

Saila began, "Dad, I've just been saying to Kamala that the time has come to tell Nalinaksha Babu the whole story and this foolish Haridasi of yours is quarrelling with me about it."

"No, *didi*," exclaimed Kamala, "I implore you not to mention such a thing. It's quite impossible."

"How silly you are!" said Saila. "You would sit still and say nothing while Nalinaksha Babu married Hemnalini. Ever since your wedding-day you've been through the most terrible experiences; they've nearly been the death of you, and now you want to endure another ordeal."

"My story mustn't be told to anyone, *didi*," said Kamala." I can bear anything but the shame of it. I'm all right as I am. I'm quite happy now, but if you let out the whole story I shouldn't be able to hold up my head in this house another minute; I should never be able to survive the disgrace."

Saila could not counter this, but it still seemed to her intolerable to sit still and let Nalinaksha marry Hemnalini.

"Is the marriage that you mention really to take place?" asked Chakrabartti.

Saila. "Of course, dad! Nalinaksha Babu's mother has given the bride her blessing."

Chakrabartti. "Well, bless the Lord, that blessing won't operate. Kamala dear, you have nothing to fear. The right has conquered."

Kamala was not sure what he meant and she stared at Uncle with wide-open eyes.

"The engagement has been broken off," he explained. "Not only did Nalinaksha not agree to it, but his mother has come to her senses."

Sailaja was enraptured. "We're saved, dad!" she cried. "I couldn't sleep last night after hearing of the engagement. But anyhow, is Kamal to go on living like a stranger in the house that is hers by right? When are we to straighten out this tangle?"

Chakrabartti. "Don't be in a hurry, Saila. Everything will come right in good time."

Kamala. "But things are all right as they are! I don't want anything changed. I'm perfectly happy and you'll only make me worse off if you try to make me happier. Uncle dear, I beg you not to tell anyone. Just leave me in a corner of this house and forget about me. I'm as happy as I could be," and tears began to flow from her eyes.

Chakrabartti was all solicitude for her. "What's this, dear? Don't cry! I quite understand what you mean. Of course we're not going to disturb your peace. Fate is working on her own lines and she is taking her time; we should be foolish to interfere and upset everything. Don't be afraid! I'm old enough to know when to leave things alone."

At this point Umesh entered the room, grinning as usual from ear to ear.

"Well, what is it, Umesh?" asked Uncle.

"Ramesh Babu is downstairs inquiring for the Doctor Babu," said Umesh.

The colour fled from Kamala's face. Uncle jumped up exclaiming. "Don't be alarmed, dear. I'll see to it." He went downstairs and grasped Ramesh by the hand.

"Come for a walk with me, Ramesh Babu," he said. "I want a few words with you."

"Where did you turn up from, Uncle?" asked Ramesh in surprise.

"It's on your account that I'm here," said Uncle, "and I'm very glad I met you. Come on, we haven't much time; we must get this matter settled," and he drew Ramesh out on to the road. "What brought you to this house, Ramesh Babu?" he asked as soon as they were well on their way.

"I came to look for Nalinaksha Babu," answered Ramesh. "I've decided to tell him all about Kamala. I keep thinking that she may be alive after all."

"Well, suppose she is alive and Nalinaksha should happen to meet her, do you think it would be a good thing for him to hear the story from your lips? He has an old mother and it might go hard with Kamala if she were to hear the truth."

"I don't know how it would affect their position in society," said Ramesh, "but I want Nalinaksha to know that not a shadow of blame attaches to Kamala. If she is really dead, my avowal will enable him to revere her memory."

"I can't understand you modern people's line of thought," said Uncle. "If Kamala is really dead, I don't see the point of bothering him with her memory; after all he was only her husband for one night. Do you see that house there? That's where I live. If you'll come there to-morrow morning I'll tell you everything. Till then I ask you not to see Nalinaksha Babu."

Ramesh assented, and Uncle returned and said to Kamala, "I want you to come to our house to-morrow morning dear. I've decided that you must explain the position to Ramesh Babu yourself."

Kamala made no reply, but dropped her eyes.

"I'm convinced that it's the only thing to do," Uncle went on. "These up-to-date young men don't go by the old standards. Don't shrink from it, dear. You mustn't let anyone else usurp your rights; this is your duty and no one else's. Nothing that any of us could do would have the same effect."

Still Kamala did not raise her eyes.

"We've cleared the ground fairly thoroughly," he continued; "you mustn't hesitate to sweep away the few obstacles that remain."

At that moment Kamala heard a step and looked up. Nalinaksha stood at the door and his eyes met hers; but this time he did not, as on former occasions, immediately avert his eyes and hasten away. It was only for a moment that he gazed at Kamala, but even that momentary glance seemed to take in something of Kamala's face instead of, as before, dismissing it as a thing only to be looked at furtively, without right or title.

Next instant he noticed Sailaja, and he was on the point of retiring when Uncle intervened. "Don't run away, Nalinaksha Babu; we look on you as one of ourselves. This is my daughter Saila, whose little girl you treated when she was sick."

Sailaja bowed to Nalinaksha.

"How is the little girl?" he asked, returning her salutation.

"She's quite well now," said Saila.

"You never give me a chance to get my fill of your society," Chakrabartti went on. "Now that you have come in you had better stay."

Uncle made him sit down, then looked round to find that Kamala had slipped out. Her surprise and joy at the look in Nalinaksha's eyes had been too much for her and she had retired to compose herself.

Kshemankari now entered the room. "I must trouble you to get up now," she said to Chakrabartti.

"My mouth has been watering for a little 'trouble' of that sort ever since you went off to your work," replied Uncle.

He returned to the sitting-room after duly regaling himself. "Just wait here a minute," he announced to Nalinaksha and his mother. "I'm coming back."

He went out again and came back in a minute or two, leading Kamala by the hand, Sailaja bringing up the rear.

"Nalinaksha Babu," began Chakrabartti, "you mustn't treat our Haridasi as a stranger. I'm leaving the poor girl in your house and I want you and your mother to regard her in every respect as one of yourselves. All she will require of you will be full opportunities to serve you both. She'll never knowingly commit any fault, that I can assure you."

"My good sir," said Kshemankari, "you have no cause to worry. We've already made Haridasi a daughter of the house. We've never to this day had to make the least effort to find occupation for her. I'm nobody at all now in the kitchen and the store-room where I've held sway all these years. The servants no longer look on me as their mistress. Somehow or other I've been gradually pushed into the background. I used to keep the keys myself, but Haridasi has contrived to filch them away too. Just tell me what more you want for this robber-girl of yours. Are you threatening to take her away with you? It would be the worst robbery of all if you did that!"

"She wouldn't stir even if I told her, so you can set your mind at rest," retorted Chakrabartti. "You people have cast such a spell over her that she has forgotten the existence of everyone else. Poor girl, she has had a hard time and

she has found peace with you at last. May Heaven keep
her in that peace and may she always find favour in your
eyes; that's my parting blessing to her!" and his eyes
moistened.

Nalinaksha had been listening in fascinated silence.

When the company broke up he went off slowly to his
own room. As the December sun went down it filled the
room with a flood of crimson light like a bride's blush. The
blood-red glow seemed to penetrate his pores and suffuse
his whole being.

One of his Hindustani friends had sent him a basket
of roses that morning and Kshemankari had given them
to Kamala to arrange. She had taken them in a vase to
Nalinaksha's room and their fragrance now greeted his
nostrils. In the stillness the crimson sunset combined with
the scent of the roses to trouble his senses. For years past
his world had been one of abstinence and passionless
austerity; it now seemed to him that his ears were assailed
by the strains of a many-stringed instrument and that the
whole universe resounded with the stamp and the jingling
castanets of invisible dancers.

Nalinaksha turned away from the window and his eye
fell on the roses which were arranged in a recess at the
head of his bed. They were like so many eyes turned on
him, and they seemed to be presenting some silent petition
at the portals of his heart.

He took up one of the roses, a mere bud with petals
yet unfolded, the colour of unpolished gold, but shedding
fragrance without stint. As he fondled it, the touch of a
human finger seemed to answer his and the thrill went
through his whole frame. He pressed the tender bud against
his lips and against his eyelids.

The last rays of the setting sun were now lighting up
the evening sky. As Nalinaksha was about to leave the

room he crossed over to the bed and bent down to raise the cover-lid and lay the rose-bud on his pillow. In raising his head he caught sight of a shrinking form crouched on the far side of the cot. It was Kamala, with her face shrouded in her veil, ready to sink into the floor with shame. Alas! The time for shame was past.

She had been on the point of leaving the room, after arranging the roses in the recess and making Nalinaksha's bed, when she heard his step and had hastened to conceal herself. Flight and concealment were alike out of the question now that, to her utter confusion, she had been detected in her strange hiding place.

Anxious to relieve her embarrassment, Nalinaksha made for the door, but when he reached the threshold a thought struck him and he stood for a moment undecided. Then he slowly returned and said, looking down at Kamala, "Please get up. You must not be shy with me!"

Chapter 61

$\mathcal{N}$ext morning Kamala presented herself at Uncle's house. She took Sailaja aside as soon as she found an opportunity and clung to her in a fond embrace.

"What makes you look so happy to-day, dear?" asked Saila, caressing her.

"I don't know, *didi*; I feel somehow as if all my troubles were over."

Saila. "Come now, you must tell me all about it. We were together yesterday till evening, what happened after that?"

Kamala. "Nothing to speak of, really, but I feel that he is now mine indeed. Heaven has taken pity on me."

Saila. "That's good, dear; you mustn't conceal anything from me, though."

Kamala. "I've nothing to conceal, *didi*; it's only that I can't find words to express myself. When I rose this morning life seemed to have acquired a meaning for me. I felt happier and my work seemed lighter than I can describe. I want nothing more than that. My only fear is that I may lose what I have gained. I cannot believe that Providence will be so kind as to make all my life equally happy."

Saila. "I think myself that your luck has turned and that you won't be cheated out of it. You'll get with interest all the happiness that is due to you."

Kamala. "No, you mustn't say that, *didi.* I've got all the interest already. I've no fault to find with my luck. There's nothing more that I want."

Uncle came in at this point.

"You must come out now for a minute, dear," he said to Kamala; "Ramesh Babu's here."

Uncle had been having a preliminary discussion with Ramesh himself.

"I know the real facts of your relations with Kamala," he had said, "and my advice to you is to start life afresh and to leave her out of the question altogether. If there is any problem still to be solved arising out of your association with her leave it to Providence to settle; don't attempt it yourself."

Ramesh had replied, "Before I finally put Kamala out of my life, I must relate to Nalinaksha the whole story; otherwise I can never start again with a clear conscience. It may or it may not be necessary to discuss Kamala's affairs again in this life. Even if it should prove unnecessary I can never clear my conscience till I tell all that there is to be told."

"Very well," said Uncle, "just wait here. I'll be back in a minute."

Ramesh turned to the window and gazed at the passers-by with an expression of apathy till he heard a step, and looking round beheld a girl in the act of making a deep obeisance to him. When she raised her head he sprang up in amazement, crying, "Kamala!"

It was indeed Kamala who stood before him, silent and motionless.

"Thank Heaven, Ramesh Babu," said Uncle, who had come in with her, "Kamala's misfortunes are at an end and there is clear sky before her. You saved her when she was in great peril and in so doing brought wretchedness on yourself. Now that the time has come for you to part company she cannot pass over in silence all that she owes to you. She has come to-day to bid you farewell and to receive your blessing."

After a short struggle Ramesh found his voice.

"God bless you, Kamala," he said. "Forgive me for any wrongs that I have done you, knowingly or in ignorance."

Kamala supported herself against the wall unable to utter a word in reply.

After a short pause Ramesh went on, "If there is any message that you would like me to convey to anyone, or if there is any misunderstanding that I can clear up, please command me."

Kamala clasped her hands.

"I beg you not to say a word to anyone."

"For a long time I never told anyone about you," said Ramesh. "I kept silent even when silence spelt misery for myself. It was only a few days ago, when I believed you to be out of harm's reach, that I told your story, and even then it was only to the members of one family. That will not, I think, damage your cause; in fact, it should assist it. Uncle apparently knows all. Then there's Annada Babu, whose daughter——"

"You mean Hemnalini, of course," broke in Uncle. "Have they heard the story?"

"Yes," said Ramesh, "and if there's anything else that you would like me to tell them I shall do so. For myself I desire nothing more; I have lost a large slice out of my life and a good deal else besides. Now all that I desire is to be free; I wish to pay off all my outstanding debts and obtain my release.

Uncle grasped him affectionately by the hand.

"No, Ramesh Babu, there's nothing else required of you. You have had much suffering to endure and I pray that from now on your life may be free, happy, and untroubled."

"I shall leave you now," said Ramesh, turning to Kamala. She did not open her mouth, but again made him a low obeisance.

Ramesh walked out on to the road like one in a dream, saying to himself, "I'm glad I met Kamala; this encounter makes a good close to the episode. Though I cannot tell for certain what led her to leave the bungalow at Ghazipur, this much is clear now — that I'm quite superfluous. No one needs me now except myself; I'll go out into the world and lead my own life. There's no necessity to turn and look back."

Chapter 62

*W*hen Kamala reached home she found Annada Babu and Hemnalini sitting with Kshemankari.

"Here's Haridasi!" said Kshemankari, as soon as she saw her. "Will you take your friend to your own room, dear? I'm giving Annada Babu tea here."

No sooner had Hemnalini entered Kamala's room than she clasped her round the neck and cried, "Kamala!"

"How did you know that was my name?" asked Kamala, without showing much surprise.

"Someone told me the whole of your history. I can't explain how it was, but as soon as I heard it I was sure that you were Kamala."

"I don't want anyone to know my name," said Kamala; "my real name has become a reproach to me."

"Yes, but it will enable you to establish your rights."

Kamala shook her head.

"I don't look at it that way. I've no rights to establish and I don't want to establish any."

"But what reason have you for keeping your husband in the dark? Why not submit yourself entirely to him, for better or worse? You oughtn't to hide anything from him."

All at once the colour left Kamala's face. She gazed helplessly at Hemnalini, searching for an answer and finding none; then she subsided on to the bed.

"Heaven only knows why I feel so ashamed when I have done nothing wrong! Why should I be punished when I am quite innocent? How can I tell him my whole story?"

Hemnalini took her by the hand.

"It's not a question of punishment but of absolution. You're in bondage now to deceit and will never be free while you keep anything concealed from your husband. Trust in Providence and burst your bonds."

"It's the fear of losing all that takes the strength out of me, but I understand what you mean. I must not fear what the future may hold for me but must tell him all. He must not be kept in the dark any longer," and she clasped her hands firmly together.

"What do you wish, then?" asked Hemnalini soothingly. "Would you have someone else tell him?"

Kamala shook her head emphatically. "No, no, he must not hear it from anyone else. I'll tell him about it myself; you mustn't suppose that I'm unable."

"That will be best," said Hemnalini. "I don't know whether we shall meet again; I came here to tell you that we are going away."

"Where are you going?"

"To Calcutta. Now I mustn't keep you any longer; you have your morning's work before you. I had better be off, dear. Don't forget your sister."

"You'll write to me, won't you?" said Kamala, seizing her hand.

Hemnalini promised to do so.

"You must write and advise me what to do, I know your letters will give me courage."

Hemnalini smiled.

"Oh, that's all right. You'll have a better counsellor than I could be."

Though she did not show it, Kamala's mind was by no means at ease about Hemnalini. Outwardly tranquil, the other's expression betrayed a degree of inward sorrow that excited Kamala's compassion; and yet there was something unapproachable about Hemnalini which made one reluctant to speak to her and debarred one from asking questions.

Though Kamala had unbosomed herself to her without restraint that morning, Hemnalini went off wrapped in her own close reserve. She wore an air of supreme melancholy and resignation that was like a permanent twilight on her features.

All day long, whenever she had any respite from her household duties, Hemnalini's words and her sweet placid eyes haunted Kamala. She knew nothing of Hemnalini's history except the one fact that her engagement to Nalinaksha has been broken off.

Hemnalini had brought a basket of flowers from her garden that morning, and in the afternoon, after bathing, Kamala sat down to weave garlands. Kshemankari kept her company while he was engaged on this task.

"Oh, my dear," she said to Kamala, "I don't describe how I felt to-day when Hemnalini bade me good-bye. Whatever anyone says she's really sweet girl; I keep thinking how happy I should be to have her as a daughter-in-law. It very nearly came off, but I really can't fathom my son. No one but himself knows what induced him to change his mind."

Kshemankari would not admit to herself that bitterly she had opposed the match.

Hearing a step outside, she called out, "That you, Nalin?"

Kamala hurriedly wrapped the flowers and the garlands in the slack of her dress and veiled herself.

Nalinaksha entered the room and his mother remarked to him, "Hem and her father have just left; did you see them?"

"Yes, I gave them a lift home."

"Say what you like, lad," his mother continued, "there are not many girls like Hem." She spoke as though Nalinaksha were in the habit of contradicting this proposition; but he merely smiled and said nothing.

"Smiling, are you?" his mother went on. I had you engaged to Hem and went to the length of giving her my blessing; then you got some bee in your bonnet and upset the whole arrangement. Aren't you at all sorry about it?"

Nalinaksha seemed to start, and he threw a glance at Kamala and perceived that she was gazing earnestly at him. As their eyes met Kamala desired to be reduced to nothingness and her eyes sought the floor.

"Why, mother," said Nalinaksha, "should you think your son such an eligible match that it must be quite a simple matter to arrange? People don't fall in love easily with a solemn stick like me!"

At this remark Kamala raised her eyes again; as she did so, Nalinaksha threw her another glance full of merriment and she felt that instant flight was the only course open to her.

"Run away and stop talking," said Kshemankari to her son. "You make me angry."

Left to herself Kamala wove all Hemnalini's flowers into one large wreath; this she laid on the basket, then she sprinkled water on it and placed it in Nalinaksha's sitting-room. Her eyes moistened at the thought that this huge garland was Hemnalini's farewell offering.

Returning to her own room, Kamala indulged in a long spell of meditation; she wondered what Nalinaksha's glances at her had conveyed and what his opinion of her was. His eyes had seemed to lay bare all her secret thoughts. There was something to be said for the old days when she remained in seclusion when he was about. Now she was constantly finding herself in embarrassing situations; it was a sort of punishment for concealing her identity.

She said to herself, "Nalinaksha must be thinking, 'Where can mother have brought this girl Haridasi from? I never saw anyone so immodest.' I can't bear to think that he could conceive such an opinion of me for one moment."

She went to bed that night determined that she would seize the first opportunity to disclose her secret next day and that she would accept the consequences.

She rose early in the morning and bathed; she brought back with her a small jar of Ganges water, intending as usual to wash and sweep out Nalinaksha's sitting-room before taking up any other work; but this morning she found him already occupying the room, contrary to his invariable custom.

Full of regret at her inability to discharge her usual task, Kamala turned and started slowly to retrace her steps; then thought struck her and she halted and stood fast.

Slowly she returned and stopped once more outside the door of his room. What it was that possessed her she could not tell; the whole world swam before her in a mist and she had no consciousness of the passage of time.

Suddenly she became aware that Nalinaksha had emerged from the room and was standing before her. In an instant Kamala sprang up, knelt before him, and bowed her head till it touched his feet; her loose hair, wet from bath fell all about and covered them to the instep. Then she rose again and stood before him like a statue; she forgot altogether that her veil had fallen nor did she perceive that Nalinaksha was gazing steadfastly and intently at her face. She was quite unconscious of external things when suddenly a flash of inspiration darted through her brain, and without a tremor in her voice she said, "I am Kamala."

No sooner had she spoken than the sound of her own voice seemed to break the spell and her concentrated purpose dissolved. She trembled in every limb and her head fell forward; she could not stir a step and yet flight seemed her only salvation. She had expended her whole strength and staked her all on the utterance of those three words, "I am Kamala," and on her prostration before Nalinaksha. Nothing was left with which she could cover her shame. She had thrown herself on Nalinaksha's mercy.

Slowly he raised her hands to his lips and murmured, "I know it! You are my Kamala! Come with me."

He drew her into the room and threw about her neck the garland that she had woven.

"Come, let us bow before Him"; and as the twain side by side touched their foreheads to the snowy whiteness of the marble floor the morning sun pouring through the window fell on their bowed heads.

Rising to her feet, Kamala once more prostrated herself before Nalinaksha in profound reverence. When she rose again her painful shyness no longer troubled her. There was no exuberance in her joy, but the settled calm of a great release flooded her whole being as with clear morning light; a sense of absolute devotion filled every corner of her soul and all creation seemed to smoke in the incense of her worship.

Incontinently water from some hidden source welled up in her eyes and great drops rolled down her cheeks unhindered—they were tears of joy that washed away the clouds of sorrow that had brooded over her widowed life.

Nalinaksha did not address her again. With one gesture he swept the damp hair back from her brow, then passed out of the room.

Kamala had not yet expended all her devotion; it still swelled up in her heart and she longed to pour it forth once and for all. She proceeded to Nalinaksha's bedroom and garlanded the old sandals with the wreath from her own neck, pressed them against her forehead, and reverently replaced them.

Then she went about her daily round as though she were ministering to a god; each task as she accomplished it was like a prayer ascending to Heaven on wings of joy.

"What are you doing, dear?" exclaimed Kshemankari. "From the way you're washing and sweeping and cleaning one would think you wanted to renovate the whole house in one day."

When the housework was finished, Kamala left her sewing untouched, and shut herself into her own room; Nalinaksha found her there when he came in with a basketful of arum lilies.

"Kamala," he said, "just put these in water and keep them fresh. In the evening we'll both go and ask for mother's blessing."

"But you haven't heard my whole story yet," said Kamala, with downcast eyes.

"There's nothing for you to tell me; I know all," said Nalinaksha.

Kamala drw her veil across her face.

"But mother——" she began, and could not finish the sentence.

Nalinaksha pulled her veil aside. "In the course of her life mother has forgiven many sins. Surely she can forgive you for what was not a sin at all!"